Also by Paige Toon

Lucy in the Sky

Johnny Be Good

Chasing Daisy

Pictures of Lily

Paige Toon

POCKET
BOOKS

LONDON • SYDNEY • NEW YORK • TORONTO

First published in Great Britain by Pocket Books UK, 2010
An imprint of Simon & Schuster UK Ltd
A CBS COMPANY

1 3 5 7 9 10 8 6 4 2

Simon & Schuster UK Ltd
1st Floor
222 Gray's Inn Road
London WC1X 8HB

Simon & Schuster Australia
Sydney

www.simonandschuster.co.uk

A CIP catalogue record for this book is available from
the British Library

ISBN 978-1-84739-391-3

Typeset in Goudy by M Rules
Printed by CPI Cox & Wyman, Reading, Berkshire RG1 8EX

For my mum
My rock of Uluru proportions
I couldn't have done it without you

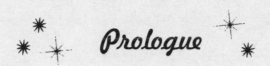 *Prologue*

'Will you marry me?'

I think of you, then. I think of you every day. But usually in the quietest part of the morning, or the darkest part of the night. Not when my boyfriend of two years has just proposed.

I look up at Richard with his hopeful eyes. 'Lily?' he prompts.

It's been ten years, but it feels like only yesterday that you left. How can I say yes to Richard with all my heart when most of it has always belonged to you?

I take a deep breath and will myself to speak . . .

Ten Years Ago

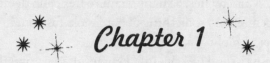# Chapter 1

'Okay, enough! I've had it with your complaining! We're here now and we're here to stay, so get used to it, Lily!'

My mother has finally snapped. I can't say I blame her. I've been bitching about the idea of moving to Australia ever since she first hooked up with Michael on the internet.

'Is the grass ever green here?' I add, bored. If she thinks I'm going to quit complaining now, she has another think coming.

My mum says nothing; she just sighs and checks her rearview mirror before moving into the fast lane.

It's late November – Australian summertime – and we're driving up into the hills from Adelaide airport. To my left the yellow hills slope upwards, and to my right they fall away into deep, tree-covered gullies. The road is ridiculously windy so I'm gripping the armrest and having to squint in the bright sunlight because I forgot to unpack my sunglasses from my suitcase. Needless to say, I'm not in a good mood.

'Don't you think he could at least have come to collect us from the airport?' I grumble.

'We had to pick up the rental car, anyway. And as I've already told you, he had to work.'

'Couldn't the wallabies do without him for a morning?'

The new love of my mum's life looks after the animals at a local wildlife park. All he has to do all day is feed kangaroos and hold koalas for soppy tourists.

'Perhaps,' Mum replies, a slight strain to her calm demeanour, 'but his voicemail said something about a sick Tasmanian Devil.'

'Whatever,' I reply.

'That doesn't sound like the Lily I know,' she says narkily. 'The Lily I know would be concerned about a sick animal. The Lily I know didn't even want to go on holiday one year because her hamster was ill. The Lily I know used to care for her pets as if they were children.'

'Yeah, and now they're all dead,' I interject.

Silence.

'What the hell is a Tasmanian Devil anyway?' I add.

'Oh, shut up, would you.'

I smirk to myself and stare out of the window, pleased with my small victory. Then I remember that we're in another country. On the other side of the world. And I remember that I haven't won at all. I've lost. Big time.

'Crafers – there it is.' Mum flicks on her indicator and starts to move left onto the slip road.

'What if you don't like him?' I ask. 'Does that mean we can go home again?'

'I will like him,' she says determinedly. 'And this is home, now.'

'This will never be home,' I reply darkly.

England is my home. And as soon as I'm eighteen, I'm going back there. But that's over two years away – and that feels like a whole lifetime. I am so pissed off at my mum for doing this to me, I can't even tell you.

Only she could meet a man on the internet. It's almost the year 2000 – who does that sort of thing? I blame that stupid movie *You've Got Mail*. I swear it gave my mum ideas when she saw it last year. It's all very well for Meg Idiot Ryan and Tom Pratty Hanks to email each other till their hearts are content, but who pays the consequences? Me, that's who. Here I am in goddamn Kangaroo Land going to live with a man I've never even met because my mum has fallen in love. Again.

We exit the tiny town that was Crafers and continue to drive up and down the perpetually winding road. We pass a paddock filled with brown and cream-coloured goats.

'So this is Piccadilly,' Mum says.

'Piccadilly?' I scoff. 'Are you taking the piss?'

She glances in my direction. 'That's the name of the town.'

'You're calling *this* a town?' I look pointedly at the occasional house and farm dotting the side of the road. Old cars, trucks and tractors sit unused on the ever-dry grass. 'The Piccadilly I'm used to is Piccadilly bloody Circus in London, and that is a far cry from *this!*'

My mum frowns with irritation as the road takes us through a modest vineyard. 'It's not far from here, according to his directions.'

We pass a few more houses before Mum begins to slow down.

'Roses, that's what he said.' She points ahead at the multitude of pink and red rosebushes on the side of the road, then turns left into the driveway of a red-brick house with a brown-tiled roof, and a veranda overhanging with shady vines.

My mum turns to me. 'Be nice, okay?'

I'm about to ask, 'Why should I?' but she interrupts.

'*Please?*'

7

And at that moment, a tall, dark-haired young guy comes out of the wooden front door and I'm distracted from the look of fear in my mum's eyes because he's, well, unexpectedly hot.

'Who's that?' I ask suspiciously as Mum forcibly relaxes her features and undoes her seatbelt.

'That must be Josh.'

'My new big bro?' My voice is laced with sarcasm, but I'm secretly wishing I'd thought to brush out the knots that have accumulated in my long dark hair courtesy of a twenty-four-hour flight. Mum gives me one last pleading look with tired blue eyes before climbing out of the car. I grudgingly follow her.

'Hi!' she beams as she storms along the gravel footpath, leaving small puffs of cream-coloured dust in her wake. 'I'm Cindy.'

'G'day. I'm Josh.' Josh holds out his hand and Mum shakes it before turning back to me.

'This is my daughter, Lily.'

The enormous smile on my mum's face keeps wavering, but Josh is too busy looking me up and down to notice. I fold my arms across my bust and glare at his chiselled face, waiting indignantly for his dark-brown eyes to meet my light-brown ones.

'G'day.'

'Do they seriously say that over here?' I respond, ignoring his outstretched hand.

'What?' He hooks his thumbs into his jeans pockets and looks amused. His attractiveness has obviously given him far too much confidence and that annoys me.

'G'day. I thought that was just on *Neighbours*.'

'Oh, right.' The corners of his mouth turn down and he glances at Mum. 'Do you need some help with your bags?'

*

'Dad'll be home soon,' Josh says, when we've unloaded our suitcases and relocated to the kitchen. I could really do with some peace and quiet to unpack my bags, but my craving for tea and biscuits is outweighing my desire to be antisocial.

'How far away is the safari park?' Mum asks.

'It's a conservation park,' Josh replies. 'The boundaries extend to right outside our house, but it's a five-minute drive to get to the main bit.'

'Conservation park, that's right,' Mum quietly chides herself as Josh opens up a packet of biscuits and tears back the cellophane. I furtively watch him as he fills up the kettle and puts it on the stove before fetching three mismatched mugs from a painted yellow cupboard. His dark hair is messy, dishevelled. It looks like he's slept on it, and as he rubs at the sleep in his eyes, I realise he probably has. It's only nine o'clock in the morning and he must be, what – eighteen? Nineteen? He doesn't look like an early riser.

Josh turns around and I quickly avert my gaze as he asks, 'Do you want milk or sugar?'

'Yes, please. Milk and one sugar each,' Mum answers for both of us.

Josh dumps a carton of milk and a tea-stained sugar pot on the table. 'Help yourselves,' he says, as the old-fashioned kettle starts to whistle.

I reach for the biscuits. YoYos, they're called.

'So Josh,' Mum says, 'what do you do?'

'I work at a garage in Mount Barker,' he replies.

'Doing what?' she prompts.

'Fixing up cars.'

'How far away is Mount Barker?'

'About twenty Ks further down the Princes Highway.'

'That's right, it's kilometres here, isn't it? We're used to miles.' I yawn. Loudly.

Josh glances at me then his head shoots in the direction of the door.

'Dad's back.' He gets up and goes off down the corridor.

Mum immediately starts chewing on a painted-pink thumb-nail. 'Do you think I should go to the door to meet him?' she whispers across at me. She looks nervous.

'No. Wait here,' I tell her. 'And stop biting your nails.'

She snatches her hand away from her mouth and smooths down her medium-length dyed-blonde hair. A wave of compassion momentarily floods me and dies away again. Listening, I hear the door open and close, the murmur of male voices and then Josh reappears in the kitchen, closely followed by his dad. Mum leaps to her feet and almost topples her chair over. Reaching back to grab it, she knocks the table, spilling tea over the green plastic tablecloth.

'Sorry, I'm so clumsy,' she apologises, flustered.

'Don't worry about it,' Michael booms. 'Josh, whack a tea-towel over that, mate.' Then Michael turns back to my mum. 'Cindy,' he says warmly, shaking his head. 'At last.'

'Hello, Michael,' she says shyly. They step towards each other and awkwardly embrace, not quite managing a proper hug.

Josh looks at me and rolls his eyes. I smirk back at him.

Mum breaks away and turns to me. 'This is Lily.'

Michael comes over and places his hand on my shoulder. 'Don't get up, don't get up,' he insists, even though I was planning on doing no such thing. 'Good to meet you, Lily.'

Michael is in his early forties and older than Mum by about eight years. She was only nineteen when she had me. Mum's five foot eight, but Michael doesn't tower above her at about five foot ten, and he's chunky compared to her slim physique. He has browny-grey hair, a weathered face and kind chocolate-brown eyes. His Australian accent is strong and his voice is loud, but he's not overpowering. Despite all my intentions, I instantly like him. I wonder if he knows what he's let himself in for?

'Chuck the kettle on, son,' he tells Josh. 'I haven't had a cuppa all morning.' Josh complies and Michael lifts out a chair so it doesn't scrape on the floor and sits down next to me. 'How was your flight?' He glances from Mum to me.

'Fine, fine,' Mum replies.

'Long,' I interject. 'And the food was crap.'

'Oh dear,' Michael empathises. 'I thought we'd have a barbie for lunch. If you're still awake by then.'

'Want another tea?' Josh begrudgingly asks Mum and me.

My mum glances into her mug. 'Only if it's not too much trouble.'

'Of course it's no trouble!' Michael practically shouts. 'Lily?'

'No, thanks.'

Josh gets on with the job.

'Has my boy been looking after you?' Michael asks.

'Yes, very well,' Mum replies.

'Good.'

'Pay up, then,' Josh says to his dad, standing over the table with his hand held out.

'Later, son, later.' Michael bats him away.

'Did your dad bribe you to be nice to us?' I ask Josh, amused.

'Twenty bucks,' Josh confirms with a grin.

'I reckon you were ripped off,' I tell Josh.

'I can see these two are going to be trouble,' Michael says to Mum rather wearily.

'Mmm,' she replies.

That evening, Michael takes my mum out for dinner. She came into my bedroom to talk to me about it this afternoon, soon after my alarm clock had hammered its way into my exhausted consciousness. My eyes felt as if someone had taken a nail file to them, but I didn't want to stay in bed too long because I want to be able to sleep tonight.

'Lily,' she said. 'Michael has asked me out to dinner.'

'And?'

'And I was wondering if it's okay if I go.'

'Why are you asking me? You don't normally ask my permission to do things.'

'No, it's just that, well, I feel bad for deserting you on our first night in a new country . . .'

'Oh, a guilt trip. Don't worry about me, Mum, I'm used to looking after myself.' She immediately looked crestfallen. 'Seriously,' I added, feeling bad, 'go out and enjoy yourself. Get to know the guy. He seems nice.'

Her face broke into a huge smile. 'He does, doesn't he?'

'Yeah, so don't dick him around like you did all the others.' Sorry, but my generosity has its bounds.

Josh is in the living room watching telly when I finally emerge from my bedroom. Mum and Michael went out half an hour ago.

'I thought you were asleep,' he says.

'I was,' I reply. 'It's a weird and wonderful phenomenon, but people tend to wake up again.'

'I was about to order a pizza.' He doesn't acknowledge my witty sarcasm. 'Have a look and see what you want.' He hands me a takeaway menu and I flop down on the three-seater sofa. He's sitting on a worn-out armchair in the same faded blue velvetine fabric, with his feet up on the pinewood coffee table. 'Dad left us some money,' he adds.

'Ooh,' I say. 'Whoopdeedoo.' He frowns at me and I struggle to keep a straight face as I study the menu. Spotting what I want immediately, I hand the menu back to him. 'Can I have a crisp?' I nod at the packet of cheese-flavoured Doritos on the coffee table.

'Don't you mean, "chip"?'

'They're called crisps where I come from.'

'They're called chips where you are now.'

'I won't be here for very long so I'm not going to change the way I speak.'

'Is that right? Where are you going, then?'

'Back to England, if you must know.'

'And is your mum going with you?'

'Why, don't you want her here?'

'If she makes my dad happy, she can stick around.'

'I wouldn't bet on that.'

'Do you have to be such a pain in the arse?' he snaps.

'I don't have to be, no.'

'Good.'

'I just choose to be.' He glares at me. 'So can I have a crisp, or what?' He doesn't immediately answer so I reach over and grab the packet.

'Help yourself,' he says gruffly when I'm already chowing down on a Dorito. He reaches for the phone on a side-table. 'Have you decided what you want?'

'Ham and pineapple,' I reply.

'Same as me.'

'Shall we get one between us, then?'

'No, I want a whole one.'

'Don't you like sharing?'

'I'm sharing my house with you, aren't I?'

I tense up inside, but try not to let it show. 'It's big enough,' I mumble. He ignores me, dialling the number.

My new 'home' has four bedrooms, two of which have been allocated to Mum and me, although it's only a matter of time before she moves in with Michael. There's a reasonable-sized kitchen and a fairly large living room. Michael has an ensuite, but there's only one other bathroom – which means I have to share with Josh. Great. I don't care how good-looking he is, if he leaves wet towels on the floor I swear I'll relocate them to his bed.

Josh puts down the phone and turns up the sound on the television. We sit there in silence until the doorbell rings half an hour later to announce the arrival of dinner. It's enough time to give me food for thought. I'm not usually a bitch, I just . . . Oh, I don't know. I suddenly feel deflated.

Josh returns with the pizza boxes and dumps them on the coffee table.

'Are you at work tomorrow?' I ask, as I struggle to detach the strings of mozzarella hanging on for dear life to a piece of pizza. Josh is clearly not a cutlery and crockery type.

'Tomorrow's Sunday, so no,' he replies bluntly.

'I'm forgetting what day it is,' I say quietly. 'That tends to happen when your whole life is uprooted in such a short time.'

Josh glances at me and his face softens. 'This is so unlike my dad,' he comments.

'This is exactly like my mum,' I reply, my tone hardening as I pull the cardboard pizza box onto my lap. 'Another advert break! How many ads do you have on here?'

Josh mutters something to himself and takes an enormous bite out of his pizza. He eats the rest of his meal in silence.

'So when are you going back to England?' he asks eventually.

I sweep my dark hair to one side. 'As soon as I turn eighteen.'

He gives me a curious look. 'How old are you now?'

'Fifteen, nearly sixteen. You?'

'Eighteen.' Pause. 'I thought you were older.'

'Damn, you've rumbled me. I'm actually thirty-five.'

'Is that right?' He raises one eyebrow.

'Yeah. Stuck in a fifteen-year-old's body.' I discard my half-eaten pizza and put my bare feet up on the coffee table, wishing I'd had the foresight to give myself a pedicure before I came away. Josh's eyes skim over my legs and up to my breasts where they pause for a few seconds.

'Lucky thirty-five-year-old,' he murmurs.

'Are you taking the piss?' I immediately bite back. He snorts with derision as I take my feet down, cross them underneath myself on the sofa and fold my arms. He lazily gets to his feet.

'I'm going out in Stirling tonight with some mates,' he says, reaching backwards to scratch one of his shoulderblades. I catch a glimpse of his tanned, fit stomach.

'Have fun.' I look away and pray he doesn't see me blushing.

'Come if you want,' he says casually.

'No, thanks.'

'Why not?'

'I'm knackered.'

'Lightweight.'

'Do you know what time it is in England right now?' I ask hotly, my mind racing as I try to calculate the time difference in my head.

'Suit yourself,' is his reply as he saunters from the room.

It takes me about fifteen seconds to work out that it's nine-thirty in the morning in the UK and, minus my little nap earlier, I've effectively stayed up all night. I'm on the verge of shouting this fact down the corridor to Josh, but realise in time that I'll only sound like a tit. Getting to my feet, I pick up the takeaway boxes, switch off the television and go to the kitchen to get a glass of water. A car horn toots outside. Josh appears in the doorway as I'm filling my glass from the tap.

'I wouldn't drink that,' he says. 'There's rainwater in the fridge.'

I glance down at my glass. 'Oh, okay.'

'That's my ride,' he says as the horn sounds again.

'Who is it? Bruce? Sheila?' Josh doesn't look amused. Well, *I* thought it was funny.

'See you later.'

'Not if I see you first!' I call after him, idiotically. The front door slams.

I pour the tapwater down the sink and sigh as I realise I'm alone in the house. Helping myself to water from the jug in the fridge, I pad barefoot down the corridor to my bedroom. I screw up my nose at the sight of the green and brown curtains and matching bedspread. Maybe I will do something about my bedroom, after all. I decided earlier that I'd leave it as it was because there's no point customising it when this will never feel like my home. But on second thoughts, I don't think I can live like this, even for a short time. Perhaps I'll get a few posters or something, change the bedspread if I can find something cheap and cheerful.

I go to the window and look out. The view looks up into the hills. I notice for the first time what looks like a castle at the top. Weird. I pull the curtains closed.

My suitcase is still sitting on the floor by the window. It didn't take long to unpack; I was only allowed to bring one case, which is something Mum and I fought tooth and nail over before we came away. I go to the bathroom and brush my teeth and then I return to the bedroom and change into my PJs before pushing the suitcase under the bed so it's out of the way.

'AAAARGH!'

I let out a bloodcurdling scream and leap onto the bed as a freakishly huge spider shoots out from under it and scurries at breakneck speed in the direction of the door. As I wobble on top of the mattress, fear clutching my stomach, the horrible realisation sinks in that if I don't get rid of it, I'll have to sleep in the same room as it. Tensely I crane my head in the direction that it fled.

They're more scared of us than we are of them, they're more scared of us than we are of them, they're more scared of us than we are of them . . . It's a mantra that worked well enough back home, but here the spiders can kill you.

I tentatively step down from the bed and snatch up a nearby trainer to use as a weapon. Feeling hopelessly vulnerable in my bare feet, I tread carefully towards the door as I keep my eyes peeled for dark spidery legs pressed up against the skirting board.

Nothing. Nada. Zilch. I don't know if it went out of the door or if it's still lurking somewhere in the bedroom with me. The only thing I do know for certain, I think to myself as I climb uneasily into bed, is that I won't be sleeping well tonight.

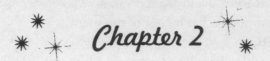

Chapter 2

Five a.m. That's not too bad, all things considered. I did wake up at three, vaguely needing to go to the toilet, but I've managed to hang on because there was no way in hell I was going to go traipsing down the corridor in the dark when there are life-sucking arachnids lurking about. Now I climb out of bed and put on my trainers before making my way to the bathroom. Mum's bedroom door is ajar. I wonder if she's awake too? I push open the door and peer inside. The bed is empty, still neatly made in all its murky-orange and mustard-yellow bedspready glory.

So she slept with Michael on the first night. Am I surprised? I know I shouldn't be, but I still take a deep breath and let out a loud sigh as I leave the room, pulling the door closed behind me.

After a trip to the bathroom, I head into the kitchen, standing there aimlessly as I wonder what to do to pass the time until everyone else wakes up. I didn't even hear them all come back last night, so I must have been out cold, despite my spider trauma.

Maybe Mum didn't come back at all? Maybe something happened to her? If she were dead, they'd *have* to make room for me at Dad's place . . .

A nasty sensation spikes at my head as I realise that my first thought wasn't for my mum's welfare, but before the dark side of my imagination can present an evil scenario explaining her empty bed, I hear a door open down the corridor. Moments later, Michael appears in the kitchen.

'Ah, Lily,' he says warmly. 'I wondered if it was you I could hear.'

'Is Mum in your bedroom?' I ask outright.

'Er, yes,' he replies, looking awkward. I exhale loudly and he gives me a funny look before clapping his hands together once with forced enthusiasm. 'Righto, think I'll put the kettle on. Want a cuppa? Huh . . .' He glances down at my feet, safely encased in my trainers, before his eyes lift to take in my pyjamas. 'Were you planning on going outside?' he asks, baffled.

'No, but I saw a spider in my room last night.' I'm suddenly desperate to tell someone – anyone – about it.

His eyes widen. 'You haven't slept in your sneakers, have you?'

'Sneakers? You mean trainers?'

'Is that what you call 'em?'

'Yeah. Anyway, no, I put them on to go to the bathroom.'

He nods. 'I see. Spider give you a bit of a fright, did he?'

'Yes, it was enormous. Brown and hairy.' I shudder involuntarily.

He casually waves his hand. 'Sounds like a huntsman. Don't worry, darl, they're not deadly. Saying that,' he adds thoughtfully, 'and I don't know if this is fact or one of those urban legends you hear about, but apparently huntsmans cause more deaths than any other spider.'

I give him a quizzical look and immediately regret it because he continues, aided by animated sign-language, 'Imagine you're driving your car down the road, minding your own business, when you pop down your sun visor and a huge spider lands on your lap. BAM!' he shouts, making me jump. 'You crash your car and that's the end of you!'

I can't drive yet, but I'm making a mental note to avoid sun visors when I learn.

'Whoopsie, I've scared you again. All I'm saying is that huntsmans don't tend to bite. And if they do, they won't kill you. You want to see some really venomous spiders, you should come to work with me one day.' I smile feebly and he chuckles. 'Or maybe cuddly koalas are more your scene.'

My mum appears at the kitchen door. 'Good morning,' she chirps, beaming at me. 'Hey, there,' she says huskily to Michael, stretching up to plant a kiss on his cheek. He glances my way and looks embarrassed.

'Blast. I forgot the tea.' He bounds over to the other side of the kitchen. 'I got distracted telling Lily about spiders.'

'I saw a massive one last night,' I interject.

'Ew,' Mum says dismissively as he grabs the kettle and fills it with water.

'Yeah, I said she should come to work with me one day and check 'em out,' Michael goes on. 'I think she'd rather see the koalas though.'

Mum nudges me. 'You'd like to do that, wouldn't you?'

I shrug. 'Maybe.'

In fact, I'd secretly love to. The truth is, I'm dying to get up close to some real Australian wildlife. I adore animals. I once toyed with the idea of becoming a vet, but my grades were never good enough. And Mum wasn't exaggerating when she said I didn't want to go on holiday one year because my hamster was ill. I was twelve and I'd had Billy for two years, but the day before we were due to fly to Tenerife he started shivering and shaking. I was beside myself. I stayed up half the night watching over him and told Mum there was no way I was going on holiday and leaving him with our next-door neighbours if he wasn't better by the morning. I couldn't keep my eyes open after two a.m. though, and when I woke up at six, bleary-eyed and hopeful, little Billy was dead.

As Mum excuses herself to go to the bathroom, Michael puts three mugs of tea on the table and pushes one in my direction. I stir in a teaspoon of sugar and look across at him.

'My mum said yesterday that one of the animals at the conservation park was ill. A Tasmanian Devil or something?'

'Yeah, yeah, poor old Henry was looking a bit dodgy there for a while, but he's going to be fine.'

'Oh, good. What is a Tasmanian Devil, by the way?'

'It's a carnivorous marsupial which is only found in the wild in Tasmania. You know Tasmania, that island that hangs off the bottom of the mainland.'

'Yes, of course.' Yep, I know Tasmania, but what the hell does a carnivorous marsupial look like?

Mum re-enters the room before I can ask. Michael eyes me thoughtfully.

'What did you and Josh get up to last night?' Mum asks, pulling up a chair next to me and reaching for her tea.

'Nothing,' I mumble. 'He went out with some mates.'

'Have you got any plans for today?'

'I don't know, Mum.' I can't help but sound snappy. What does she think I've been doing all night while she's been getting her rocks off? Going from door to door making friends with the neighbours? I get up, huffily. 'I'm going to have a shower.'

'What about your tea?'

'I'll take it with me.' I pick up the steaming mug and try to block out the look of hurt on her face as I leave the room.

An hour and a half later I'm in my bedroom, aimlessly flicking through the pages of a magazine, when there's a knock at the door. I close my eyes resignedly. I can't be bothered to talk to Mum right now.

'Come in,' I call.

I'm surprised when Michael pokes his head around the door, saying, 'I'm leaving for work in forty minutes. Do you fancy coming with me?'

'Oh.' I sit up, surprised.

'No worries if not, there'll be plenty of other opportunities.'

'No, no, I'd . . . Well . . . is my mum coming too?'

'Nah, she said she'd be happy unpacking and settling in at home.'

'Okay, then. If you're sure.'

'Sure I'm sure.'

He turns to leave, but I call him back.

'What should I wear?'

'Anything you like. But it's going to be hot today so bring a hat and a bottle of sunscreen.'

I climb off the bed and open the wardrobe. My only two skirts stare out at me, daring me to choose them over the jeans I'm already wearing, but I leave them where they are and even go one further by pulling on a hooded grey sweatshirt over my black T-shirt. I'll regret my full-body cover-up decision if the temperature rises to the 35 degrees predicted on last night's news, but I'm not yet ready to expose my pale white limbs to the world. I go to close the wardrobe doors and hesitate. Bending down, I drag a small black camera bag out. Do I want this today? Will I use it?

My dad gave me a Nikon F60 as an early birthday/leaving present before I left, making me promise to take lots of photos so he wouldn't miss me too much. A stab of pain shoots through my heart and I carefully push the bag back into the wardrobe.

Josh is still in bed by the time we set off at seven forty-five. Michael drives a white pick-up truck, three seats wide at the front. He reverses down the gravel driveway and out onto the road. We turn left and drive in the opposite direction to the way Mum and I came in yesterday. Through the window I see white nets hanging loose over a multitude of trees in the neighbouring gardens, making me think of children dressed up as low-budget ghosts for Halloween.

'Are they fruit trees?' I ask Michael.

'Yep. Cherries, nectarines, peaches . . . The nets keep the birds off. We've got an apricot tree in the back garden. Help yourself because the fruit always ends up rotting on the ground when no one eats it.' He tuts. 'Such a waste.'

He takes a left onto a dirt track and the road starts to climb steeply into the hills. My ears begin to pop and I have to keep swallowing. Michael winds down his window and I do the same. A fragrant scent, coupled with the aroma of early morning sunshine burning off the dew on the fern-covered banks immediately assaults my senses.

'What's that smell?' I ask.

'Eucalyptus,' Michael replies, pointing out of the window. 'From all the gum trees.'

I breathe in deeply and feel an unexpected burst of happiness. It takes me by surprise.

'Do you usually work on Sundays?' I ask Michael.

'Sometimes,' he replies. 'We all have to work weekends occasionally.'

'What do you do exactly?'

'I'm a senior keeper. I look after the devils and the dingoes, among other things.'

'Cool. Will anyone mind me tagging along today?'

'Course not, sweetheart! Josh used to come all the time before his mum died.'

I wonder what it was about Josh's mum dying that made him stop going to the conservation park. I wonder how his mum died at all. I want to ask, but it doesn't feel right.

We take a left at the top, back onto the main road, and after a while turn right through some rusted wrought-iron gates into the conservation park. I can just make out a hazy view of the city beyond what I now recognise as eucalyptus trees. Eventually the road opens up into a large car park. Michael turns into the staff parking area and switches off the ignition. We both climb out of the truck and I nervously follow him through the gates. I'm starting to regret my impulsive decision to accompany him today when I could be back at the house with my bedroom door closed and not have to speak to anyone.

'Morning, Jim,' Michael calls, as a man dressed in identical clothes to him – beige shorts and a matching long-sleeved shirt – approaches us.

'Morning, Mike. Who's this?'

'Lily!' Michael booms, then in a quieter aside, 'Cindy's daughter.'

'Oh, okay!' the man called Jim exclaims. 'You arrived yesterday, right?'

'Yes.'

'How was your flight?'

'Long,' I reply as an annoying blowfly buzzes around my face.

'I thought Lily might like to get out of the house,' Michael explains.

'Great stuff. And what's your mum up to?'

I shrug. 'She's at, er, the house.' I can't quite bring myself to say 'home'.

'Well, we've all been dying to meet her. And you, of course. Better get on. Got to go see Trudy about my timesheet. Have a good one!' he calls over his shoulder as he heads in the direction of the office off to our right.

'Come on.' Michael beckons.

'Where are we going?' I look around and can just make out stone-walled enclosures through the tree trunks.

'First things first,' he says, winking. 'Let's go and have a cuppa.'

This man drinks a *lot* of tea.

The staffroom has a basic kitchen, a couple of greeny-grey threadbare sofas and a table surrounded by six brown school-style chairs. There are a few people milling about and Michael introduces everyone individually. They're all very welcoming and consequently my nerves start to fade.

'Now, it's up to you,' Michael says to me after ten minutes of general chitchat and tea drinking. 'I've got to muck out the wombats in a minute and you're welcome to watch me shift the sh— *poo*, but I thought you might prefer to go for a wander instead. We open the doors to the general public at nine-thirty, but we don't start feeding time until eleven, and that's with the devils, so you've got a bit of time to kill. Maybe go see the roos. Hey, Janine, have you got a map handy?'

A plain woman with mousy hair tied back into a low ponytail rummages around in a rucksack and hands over a map. Michael unfolds it and pinpoints where the staffroom is.

'This is where you are now. If you want to see those deadly spiders I told you about, you have to go to this building here.'

I grimace my reply.

'No, maybe not. Right then,' he continues. 'The devils are here, the koalas are over here, and the dingoes a bit further round to your right. We feed the dingoes after lunch so it's worth coming to hear my little lecture.' He nudges me. 'And this large paddock here is where you'll find the roos and the emus. Wallabies are here . . .'

'Thanks,' I interrupt, holding out my hand for the map. I'm keen to get going.

'Oh, right, yes – here you go, darl.' He hands it over. 'Getting a bit carried away, but of course you're old enough to read.'

'I hope so.' I smile. 'Will you be at the Tasmanian Devils at eleven?'

'Yep, I'm doing the talk so I'll see you there.'

Map in hand, I walk out of the staffroom feeling full of anticipation as I head in the direction of the kangaroos. There's a slight breeze in the air and I can hear the rustle of the leaves in the nearby trees as I amble along the path towards the boundary fence. Pushing through the gate, I find myself in a large paddock. Off in the distance there's a group of kangaroos. The asphalt path circles the perimeter, but if I want to get close to the wildlife, I have to go cross-country. I pluck up the courage and leave the footpath, dead eucalyptus leaves crunching and crackling under my feet as I go.

The kangaroos regard me with mild interest as I excitedly

venture towards their gathering. There are well over a dozen of them, lying in the shade of an enormous tree, a couple propped up on one elbow in an almost-human fashion. They have a reddish tinge to their fur and their ears twitch to ward off the flies. They're much prettier than I imagined they would be from all the photos and wildlife documentaries I've seen. I keep my distance, not wanting to bother them, but they don't seem phased by my presence so after a while I relax and turn my face up to the sun. The clear blue sky stretches out overhead and I soon feel the bite of the heat.

Stepping into the shade of the tree, I take off my sweatshirt and tie it around my waist before liberally applying some Factor 30 suncream. There isn't another person in sight and a pleasant feeling washes over me because I like being alone like this. I have a sudden desire to sit down on the grass and stay there for hours, but a scuffling noise brings me back to reality with a bump. A large roo has risen to his feet and is sitting on his haunches, facing me. My heart starts to quicken as he slowly advances. If he wants a boxing match, I'm a goner. It fleetingly occurs to me that *that* would teach my parents . . . but when he reaches me, he simply sniffs at my hand.

'You want some food?' I ask, irrationally disappointed that he's not going to pick a fight. He gazes up at me with dark eyes. 'I'm sorry, I don't have any.'

He's almost as tall as me, but I'm no longer frightened. I tentatively reach out and stroke his soft, furry neck and he puts one dark paw on my arm. I giggle to myself, delighted.

'What's your name, hey?' I remember Michael telling me about the Tasmanian Devil called Henry. 'I think I'll call you Roy,' I decide out loud. 'Roy the roo. And I'll recognise you from this little chunk missing from your ear.'

At that moment, Roy's ears prick up and his head whips round in the direction of the gate. I follow his gaze to see a large group of Japanese tourists bustling into the paddock. They animatedly point in our direction, cameras at the ready.

'So much for chilling out on the grass with you,' I say sadly to Roy. He turns and lazily hops away.

I wander aimlessly for a while, pausing to marvel at pelicans half my height and hurrying past scarily enormous emus with long, bendy necks. I eventually consult the map and realise I'm only around the corner from the koalas. I don't want to be a typical tourist, but . . . what the hell. I'll have to keep it from Mum though, otherwise she'll think I've gone soft.

There are only a few people waiting in front of me in the queue to get up close and personal with Australia's most famous animal, and I sit on the long wooden bench and watch as a sandy-haired man in beige shorts and a dark-green polo shirt feeds eucalyptus leaves to a koala while chatting to a couple in their twenties. There's a family waiting in front of me and the two young sisters are bickering about who's going to touch the koala first.

'You can pat him at the same time,' the mother says eventually, rolling her eyes at me. I smile at her as her daughters impatiently push through the gate to take their places next to the koala and its keeper. The oldest girl has hair exactly the same shade of blonde as Kay. Hot tears prick my eyes. I quickly brush them away.

I'm not an only child. My dad has two other daughters: Kay, who's four, and Olivia, who's not yet one. Olivia's first birthday is in two weeks' time, a few days after my own. I'm going to miss her party. I'm going to miss Kay's in March. I'm going to miss so much . . . They'll probably forget all about their big half-sister on the other side of the world. And the new baby won't even know I exist.

Lorraine, my dad's wife, is three months' pregnant, a fact she only revealed to me recently when I raised the possibility of moving into their spare bedroom. It was my last-ditch attempt to avoid leaving England, and it failed.

'Hello?'

I look up to see the sandy-haired keeper waving at me. The family have long gone.

'Sorry.' I jump to my feet, embarrassed.

'Lost in your thoughts?' he asks kindly as I approach him.

'Just a bit.'

'Are you English?'

'Yeah. Did my deathly-white limbs give it away?'

'Accent,' he corrects, smiling. 'Here on holiday?'

I shake my head. 'For good.' *Supposedly.*

'So,' he turns his attention to the koala. 'This is Cindy.'

I snort.

'What?'

'Sorry, it's not that funny. It's just that Cindy is my mother's name,' I explain.

'Oh!' Recognition lights up his face. 'Are you . . .?'

'Lily Neverley. I'm with Michael.'

'Ah, right, gotcha! Welcome to Australia.'

'Thanks. And before you ask, it was long.'

'Long? Oh, the flight.' He grins. 'Been asked that a lot today, have you?'

'By everyone in the staffroom earlier.'

'Well, I'm Ben.'

I reach out and shake his proffered hand. He's probably in his late

29

twenties, early thirties. He has short sandy hair and is tall, lean and as tanned as you'd expect from an Australian who works outside in the sun every day. Just as with Michael, I like him immediately.

I nod at the koala. 'And this is Cindy?'

'Yep. You can pat her on her back if you like.'

'She's really soft,' I murmur. 'Hello,' I say to the koala. 'Are you enjoying those nice green leaves?' I turn to Ben. 'I met a kanga-roo earlier. He was disappointed I didn't bring him any food.'

'They like the pellets you can buy at the entrance.'

'Thanks for the tip. I might get some later. I'll be steering clear of those emus though. I didn't trust the way they looked, with their beady little eyes.'

He laughs and I remember the queue of people waiting, and say, 'I'd better move on.'

'You're alright, our replacements are here.'

The woman I recognise as Janine the Map Bearer comes through the gates on the other side of the small enclosure. She's carrying another koala.

'Hello, there,' Janine says to me and I step aside as Ben lifts Cindy off her perch. 'How's the jetlag?'

'Not bad, thanks.' I remember hearing the word 'jetlag' from my dad when he went to America once.

'Do you want to come with me to put Cindy back?' Ben asks me, positioning the koala over his shoulder like a baby.

'Um,' I reply hesitantly. I don't want to get in his way, but I still have some time to kill before Tasmanian Devil feeding time at eleven. 'Yes please, if that's okay?'

'Of course it is.'

I follow him out of the gates as Cindy looks back at me, lan-guidly chewing on a leaf.

'How many koalas do you have?' I ask.

'About fifty,' he calls back to me. 'The ones who get photographed with the tourists are only allowed twenty minutes per day of handling so we need a fair few, especially if one or more of them are under the weather.'

He walks to the nearest of two koala houses, or 'lofts' as I later discover they're called. Several koalas can be seen snuggled into the branches of a gum tree. Ben climbs over the wall and gently places Cindy on a branch where she carefully ascends into the darkness of the loft's wooden eaves. There's a sign that says *Shhh . . . Please be quiet. Koalas have very sensitive hearing*, so when Ben's walkie-talkie starts to crackle, he leaps over the wall and hurries away, indicating that I should follow him.

'Yep?' he says.

'Ben, it's Michael,' I hear over the buzzing noise of the walkie-talkie. 'Got a problem with one of the wombats. Can you do the devil talk?'

'Sure. I've got Lily here with me, actually.'

'How's she getting on?'

'She's just met Cindy.'

I hear a low-throated chuckle and Ben purses his lips, trying to keep a straight face.

'Can you bring her back to the staffroom for lunch?'

'Will do.'

'Thanks, mate.'

One last crackle and the line goes dead.

'You don't have to look after me,' I say quickly.

'Come on,' he replies, his blue eyes crinkling at the corners.

'Where are we going?'

'To get the devil food.' I start to follow him along a path lined with low dense shrubs and grasses. 'And you're going to tell me how your mum and Michael's date went last night,' he adds.

'Ha! Well, they seemed happy enough this morning.'

'Sleep in the same room?'

'That's a bit nosy, isn't it?'

He laughs. 'That's a yes, then.'

I tut at him before saying, 'Come on then, your turn: who came first, the koala or my mum?'

'What makes you think their names aren't a coincidence?'

'I don't believe in coincidences.'

'Alright then, Michael hooked up with her the week before Cindy was brought in.'

'So you named the koala after my mum? I reckon she'd be flattered. Feel a bit sorry for the koala though. What happened to her? The koala, I mean.'

'Her mother was hit by a car. Cindy got thrown off her back and the driver brought her in.'

The smile drops from my face. 'The mother died?'

'I'm afraid so.'

'That's terrible!'

He gives a little shrug. 'It happens.'

We arrive at a small single-storey brick building with a green corrugated-iron roof. Ben unlocks the door and goes through, holding it back for me and simultaneously switching on the lights. A long row of fluorescents flicker into life, revealing a large room filled with bags of what I assume is animal feed. The air smells musty, but not unpleasant. Ben walks determinedly towards a fridge and pulls it open. He hands me a silver bowl from a nearby shelf.

'Hold this, would you?'

'What's it for?'

'Devil food.' He pulls some furry yellow objects out of the fridge and puts them in the bowl. It takes a moment for it to register that the objects are dead chicks.

'Argh!' I shriek, dropping the bowl with a clatter and clutching my hand to my chest as the birds take one final flight. Ben almost jumps out of his skin.

'Sorry,' I apologise. 'I didn't realise what they were.' I quickly bend down and pick up the bowl, but can't bring myself to touch the dead animals.

'You're alright, don't worry.' Ben chuckles as he takes the bowl from me and retrieves the chicks.

'Sorry,' I say again as my face heats up. 'That was a major overreaction. And to think I used to want to be a vet.'

He puts the bowl filled with chicks on the counter. 'Used to? he says. 'Why not any more?'

'My grades weren't good enough,' I reply, embarrassed, as I watch him go over to the bags of feed and start rummaging around inside one.

'Grades? Are you at uni?'

'No,' I scoff. 'I'm still at school.'

'School?' He stops what he's doing and looks at me with amazement. 'How old are you?'

'Fifteen, almost sixteen.'

His eyes widen. 'I thought you were a lot older than that.'

'You're the second person to say that to me in twenty-four hours.'

'Really? Who was the other person?'

'Josh. Michael's—'

'I know Josh,' he interrupts, shaking his head wryly. 'Watch out for that one.'

A thrill goes through me as I remember glimpsing Josh's sexy stomach last night. 'What makes you say that?' I try to keep my voice sounding light and airy.

'Half of the girls in the area would be able to tell you.'

My heart dips at this revelation. Oblivious, Ben comes over and hands me a small brown paper bag.

'What's this?'

'Pellets. Roo food.'

'Thanks.' I'm touched. He then picks up the bowl from the countertop.

'Anyway, don't worry about Josh,' I say. 'I can look after myself.'

'I'd keep your bedroom door locked at night in any case,' he says, as we leave the building. When I look back at him he appears shamefaced. 'Sorry, that was inappropriate,' he says.

'Why?' I'm confused.

'You're only fifteen.'

I laugh and pat his arm condescendingly, because I hate being treated like a child. 'I'm a big girl, don't worry.'

He scratches his head and tells me, 'Look, I've got to do the devil talk now. If you want to watch, it's just over there. Michael asked me to bring you to the staffroom for lunch afterwards.'

'It's fine, I know where the staffroom is.'

'Okay, whatever you like.' He checks his watch and gives me an awkward smile before nodding at the nearby stone-walled enclosure.

'You go on,' I urge. 'I'll come and watch.' It's about time I discovered what this carnivorous marsupial thingie looks like.

Children are hanging over the edges of the stone walls surrounding the Tasmanian Devil enclosure, seemingly in complete disregard for the sign that says *Danger! These animals bite!*. I gently ease my way through the crowd so I can see what they're looking at, trying to avoid the tiny ants scurrying along the jagged stone edge. A blacky-brown creature is doing a circuit of the enclosure. It looks almost like a cross between a cat and a dog, with a white patch on its belly and its ears glowing red from the sun. Climbing onto a log, it sniffs the air in anticipation of a snack. Just then, Ben appears with his silver bowl and starts to speak. I'm riveted as I watch the Tasmanian Devil crush the chicks with its super-strong jaw and I have a misplaced sense of pride that I know this keeper to whom everyone is listening. When feeding time is over, Ben calls across at me.

'Lunch?'

I smile back at him and nod, relieved that he's not holding my earlier snub against me.

At about three o'clock in the afternoon, my whole body is hit by an overwhelming tiredness and I spend the last couple of hours of the day perusing the gift shop for stuffed koalas for Kay and Olivia and chilling out at a table inside the air-conditioned café. Michael turns up shortly after five.

'You alright, love? Sorry, that was a bit of a long day for you.'

'No, no, it wasn't,' I hurriedly assure him as I get to my feet. 'I think I might be a bit jetlagged, but I absolutely love it here.'

'Ah, that's good. You're welcome to join me anytime.'

'Thanks. I really would like to come back again.'

'I mean it,' he says, as we walk through the exit gates to the truck. 'Just let me know. You've got, what – two months before school starts?'

'Something like that.' My mood does a nosedive.

'Hey, what's with the face?' he calls over the back of the

truck. I shake my head and climb in. The heat inside the cabin is stifling. 'Don't worry, it'll be fine,' Michael says, starting up the engine, and putting the air-conditioning on full blast. 'I know it can't be easy for you, but I hope you come to like Australia.'

'It's fine,' I mutter sheepishly.

'Ah, no,' he says gruffly. 'To be honest, if I were you I'd be scared shitless. Oops. Excuse my French.'

I giggle and he pulls out of the car park.

Cooking smells waft down the hall as we walk through the front door of the house, making me groan inwardly. I don't think Josh is a budding Jamie Oliver, which can only mean one thing: my mum is in the kitchen.

'Wow, that smells good!' Michael enthuses as he bounds away from me. My feet drag after him. The sound of the television emanates from behind the closed door of the living room and I'm guessing Josh is inside. What I wouldn't give to join him and avoid my mother altogether. As if reading my mind, my mum emerges from the kitchen, wiping her hands with a tea-towel.

'Hello,' she calls, her smile practically leaping from her face. 'Welcome home.'

Home? Glad to see someone's settled in.

'Hey there,' Michael says warmly, going in for a kiss. I flinch as the impact lasts slightly longer than necessary.

'Hello, Lily.' Still beaming, Mum beckons me towards her, gets my head in a headlock and kisses my temple. I firmly extract myself. 'Did you have a nice day?'

'Yep.'

'Sit down and tell me all about it!'

'No,' I moan, reverting to the moody teenager she's so familiar with. 'I'm shattered.'

'She is, poor thing,' Michael says. 'It's been a long day.' He
musses my hair and it takes everything in me not to bat him
away.

'I've made Shepherd's Pie,' Mum says proudly.

'In this heat?' I can't help but respond.

'Oh, you,' she says affectionately, reaching out for a killer hug.
I quickly step away.

'I might see what's on the telly.'

'Dinner will be ready in half an hour,' she calls after me.

'You beauty, Cindy,' I hear Michael say as I leave the room. 'It's
so great coming home to you today.'

My mum only ever cooks for the men in her life. Not for me.
Never for me. Oh, sure, she's made me beans on toast, but even
I'm capable of rustling that one up. And I have done. Often.

'Hey,' Josh says when I appear in the living room. He's wearing dark-blue and white Bermuda shorts and a light-blue
T-shirt. His tanned legs are projecting halfway across the coffee
table.

'Alright?' I respond, slumping down on the sofa and staring at
the television. 'What are you watching?'

'The footie.'

My day is steadily going downhill.

'Did you have a good time last night?' I try to make conversation.
He shrugs. 'It was okay.'

'Where did you go?'

'Stirling.'

'Where's Stirling?'

'Five Ks that way.' He points towards the front door, but doesn't take his eyes off the telly, so I give up. He hasn't bothered to ask me how my day went and I don't want to talk about it to him, my mum or anyone, so as soon as I've eaten dinner, I make my excuses and go to bed.

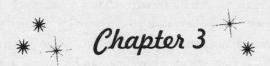

Chapter 3

I'm showered and dressed and have my camera bag at the ready when Michael appears for breakfast. The question bursts out of my mouth before his bum even hits his seat.

'Could I come with you again today?'

'Well, of course,' he replies, surprise written all over his face. 'I didn't think you'd want to so soon, but—'

'Are you sure it's okay?' I chip in, desperate for him to say yes.

'Absolutely, darl, but have you checked with your mum?'

'She won't care.'

'She might want to spend some time with you.'

'She won't. Honest,' I plead.

'It's fine by me if it's fine by her.'

'Wicked!' I jump up.

My mum knows better than to pour water over my protected-species-rare enthusiasm, so she's practically pushing me out of the door an hour later. I join Michael in the staffroom for the requisite cuppa, then head off in the direction of the kangaroos. I never got a chance to feed them the pellets Ben gave to me yesterday.

I find Roy lying in the shade of the same tree.

'Hey you,' I say softly as I approach him. 'I brought some food for you today.'

At the sound of the rustling paper bag, he lazily gets to his feet. The tiny whiskers around his mouth tickle my outstretched palm as he gently eats the pellets one by one until they're all gone. I wipe my hands on my jeans and, on a whim, settle down on the crisp, dry grass. Now towering above me, but not menacingly, Roy puts one paw on my forearm so I open up the bag and feed him another handful from my sitting position. After a while he loses interest, but doesn't hop away. I put my arm around his soft, furry back and pat him, contentment washing over me. This is nice. I could stay here all day in the shade of this tree.

I glance up. Those hefty branches could hold a good-sized tree-house. I could stay here for weeks, in fact. I wouldn't mind this, living here with the roos. Just then, I see something move out of the corner of my eye and spy two emus stalking the boundary fence. I couldn't live with them though. Roy turns to me and sniffs at my nose before looking away again. I giggle. I hear the grass rustling behind me and warily turn around, praying it isn't the feathered fiends. I sigh with relief as I see Ben approaching.

'You look pretty cosy there,' he calls as he gets nearer. Roy slowly hops towards him. Traitor. 'Hello, Freddie,' Ben says affectionately, rubbing the kangaroo's neck.

'Freddie?' I say. 'I thought he was called Roy.'

'Roy?' Ben looks confused as he reaches me. 'Who told you that?'

'I kind of named him that myself,' I admit.

He chuckles and sits down on the grass next to me. 'Roy suits him better.'

'Who was Freddie? That is, assuming he was named after someone.'

'Yep, you're right. Freddie was a German exchange student doing work experience here a few years ago. Before my time.'

'Oh, right. How long have you worked here?'

'Two years in January.'

'And before that?'

'Sydney Zoo.'

'You lived in Sydney?'

'No, I commuted from Adelaide. It's only a two-and-a-half-hour flight.'

I stare at him in confusion.

'I'm joking.' He playfully punches my arm. 'Yes, I used to live in Sydney.'

I tut. 'Okay, so that was a stupid question. What's Sydney like?'

'It's great.'

'Better than Adelaide?'

'Just different. It's got a good vibe, but Adelaide's home.'

'Is this where you grew up?'

'Yep. Mount Barker Primary School followed by Mount Barker High, then Adelaide University. I'm a local boy through and through.'

'Why did you move to Sydney?' I continue my interrogation.

'Felt like a change after uni.'

'Then why did you come back?' I persist.

'My nan fell ill. My mum lives in Perth. She doesn't get along with her mum anyway so I got a job here and came back to keep Nan company.'

'That was nice of you.'

He shrugs. 'I liked my nan. A whole lot more than I like my mum, in any case.'

'Why don't you like your mum?'

'She's a very selfish woman. Always has been. She didn't want kids. I was a mistake and she made sure I knew it.'

'That's awful.' His tone is flippant, but I still feel on edge. 'What about your dad?' I ask hopefully.

'Who knows?' He laughs a brittle laugh. 'Never knew him. I sometimes wonder if my mum even knows who he is.'

I stare at him, shocked. And I thought *I* had it bad. He gives me a wry smile.

'Is your nan still around?' I ask quietly.

'Nope.' He gets to his feet. 'She passed away in the winter.'

'I'm sorry.' It sounds weak, but no other words come to mind.

'Thanks,' he replies. Then: 'I have to check over the roos. Want to help me?'

'I'd love to.' I quickly stand and dust myself off. 'What do I have to do?'

'Check them over for any swellings, lameness, drooling, weepy eyes . . . We're mostly monitoring for lumpy jaw.'

'What's lumpy jaw?'

'A condition that causes abscesses on or near the jaw. It's caused by an infection.'

'Is it serious?'

'Usually we can remove an infected tooth and give them antibiotics. It's very important not to feed them any soft fruit. No bananas or pears. They need crunchy carrots and sweet potatoes, that sort of thing.'

'Interesting,' I comment and he smiles at me.

'You can help me with the headcount,' he says.

One, two, three . . . I silently count them in my head. 'Twenty-five,' I determine as Ben gets on with checking over the roos.

'There should be twenty-six,' he says.

'Twenty-six?' My eyes scan the paddock.

'Closer,' Ben says. He's staring pointedly at a kangaroo sprawled out on the ground about ten metres away. I watch inquisitively as he slowly ventures towards it. 'You're alright, old girl,' he says soothingly as the kangaroo visibly tenses. I spy two legs poking out of her front pouch and my eyes widen as I belatedly realise that the twenty-sixth kangaroo is a baby – or 'joey', as I remember hearing them called on a wildlife documentary. The mother gets to her feet, her pouch bulging as the legs disappear and a tiny face appears in their place. I hold my breath as Ben quickly and efficiently checks over both kangaroos before the mother hops away. He looks across at me.

'What are you waiting for? You can start with Freddie. Or Roy, if you prefer.' He winks.

It vaguely occurs to me as I work that it should feel strange that Ben opened up to me about his life like that. But it doesn't feel strange at all.

'Why are you doing the kangaroos today?' I ask Ben as we walk back across the paddock.

'Colleague called in sick.'

'Are you heading over to the koalas now?'

'Yep. Want to come with me?'

'Yes, please. Is there anything I can do to help?'

'You can help me weigh them, if you like?'

'Cool.'

And just like that, I make my first friend in Australia. A friend called Ben. I reckon Michael Jackson would have approved.

My first few days fly by. I barely see Josh. He's never up when his dad and I leave in the mornings, as the garage where he works in Mount Barker doesn't open until nine, and he's either tied to the television or out with his mates by the time we get home. Mum seems happy enough to let me do my own thing, and she spends her days cooking up a storm in the kitchen or doing God knows what around the house. We came home yesterday to find her making apricot jam using the fruit in the garden. I think Michael fell more in love with her than ever at that point. Last night he took her for dinner in the city and Josh went out with his mates. I've spent every evening this week around the house, practising with my new camera, watching telly and gradually getting over my jetlag, so I was well up for a night out, but an invitation never came. For the first time since we arrived, it bothered me.

Now it's Saturday morning and I've been sitting in the kitchen for half an hour with no sign of anyone. I check my watch again, wondering if I should wake Michael. At this rate we're going to be late. I drum my fingers on the tabletop and decide to give it a few more minutes.

Yesterday, Ben let me put Cindy back into her loft. He had to hold onto her while I clambered over the wall because I'm only five foot six and couldn't quite manage it with a koala in my arms, but I carried her all the way there after her Meet the Tourists session and put her back on her perch. She clutched hold of my arm and held on tight around my neck, just like a small child would. She reminded me of Olivia, and that thought made me smile instead of cry.

Ben told me afterwards that some idiots have been known to climb over the wall and try to pick up a koala, but they don't know how to handle them properly and usually get bitten. I'm glad he waited until after I put her on her perch, otherwise I would have been nervous. I can't wait to see the animals again today.

Right, that's it, I'm waking him.

I stand up and stride purposefully out of the kitchen and down the corridor. I reach Michael's bedroom door and stop in my tracks when I hear voices inside. I quickly retreat to the kitchen and sit back down at the table.

'Good morning!' Michael booms when he appears a moment later. 'You're up bright and early.'

'It's seven-thirty,' I say cautiously. 'Shouldn't we be setting off soon?'

'Oh.' He claps a hand to his head. 'Sorry, darl, I thought I told you – I'm not working today.'

My stomach falls flat. 'You're not working today?'

'No. So you've got the day off.'

But I don't want the day off. I want to go to the conservation park. Maybe I could go with Ben?

'Is Ben at work today?' I ask hopefully as Michael sets about making tea.

'No, he's off today too, I'm afraid. You sure do like it there, don't you?'

I'm so disappointed I can barely speak so I nod my reply.

'We'll have to start paying you at this rate,' Michael continues. 'Ben said you've really been pulling your weight.'

It's true. I've been helping him a lot. At first I thought he was just being nice to me, keeping me company because Michael always seems to be in demand by everyone else, but I think I've been useful. I'm glad he said so to Michael.

'Hmm,' Michael muses. 'I might have to speak to Trudy about that.'

'Trudy in the front office? About what?' I ask.

'If we can get you a little summer job.'

My heart soars. 'Really?'

'I don't see why not. I'll see what I can do.'

'That would be amazing,' I enthuse. That would mean I could go there every day. Well, almost every day. 'Are you back at work tomorrow?' I ask brightly.

'No, Monday.' He chuckles when he sees my face. I try to perk up because I don't want to seem ungrateful. 'Why don't you take a trip into the city today?' he suggests. 'Go shopping, see the sights. I'm sure your mum would let you borrow her car. Or you could even use the truck, for that matter.'

'What, and drive myself?'

He claps his hand over his forehead for the second time this morning, saying, 'I forgot, you can't drive.'

I shake my head, wryly.

'When's your birthday? This coming week, isn't it?'

'Wednesday.'

'Won't be long, then.'

'I'll only be sixteen,' I remind him.

'That's right,' he replies cheerfully.

'But you have to be seventeen to drive.'

'Not in Australia.'

'Seriously?' Why didn't somebody tell me this? I've been wanting my independence behind the wheel for donkey's years! *This* would have made the move Down Under far more palatable.

'You'll have to do your paper test first, but after that you can climb into the driver's seat.'

'No way!'

'As for today,' Michael continues, delighted at my reaction, 'there's a bus service which leaves from Crafers that takes you direct into the city. I'll give you a lift to the bus stop, if you like.'

'Okay!'

He scratches his head in bemusement. 'You have got the prettiest face when you smile.'

And instead of scowling like I usually would at hearing a comment like that, I actually find myself laughing.

Adelaide is a sprawling city, its suburbs reaching far and wide, but the centre is not that big – certainly not by London standards. I hop off the bus and walk in the direction of East Terrace. Michael explained earlier that the main part of the city is surrounded by four roads: North, East, West and South Terrace, with the streets within laid out as a simple grid system, so it's easy to find my way around.

It's only nine o'clock in the morning and the shops don't open until nine-thirty, but Michael told me the Botanic Gardens would be the perfect setting to practise my photography. I still have half a roll of film to finish off before I can get my first photographs developed, and apparently there's a one-hour place in the mall. I'm quietly excited about seeing the results of my efforts.

The main entrance to the Botanic Gardens is on the corner of East and North Terrace. I pass through the gates and after a little while, turn right along a path lined with trees and shrubs. A short way off there's a medium-sized pond covered in its entirety by large, lime-green leaves. A dark-grey statue of a cherub clutching onto a swan sits in the middle. I walk across neatly-mown grass towards the pond and take in the sight of a multitude of tall pink flowers bursting upwards away from the foliage. Lilies. Eagerly I unzip the bag and pull out my camera, stepping away from the pond to survey the scene. Then I zoom in and focus on one bright pink flower, clicking off a single shot. I walk around the pond and dither for a moment before fiddling with the settings on the camera and attempting another shot. I don't have the confidence yet to take lots of photos in one go. Nor do I have the money to waste on film or developing either, for that matter. But I might do if Michael comes good on his promise.

It's another hot day, and the morning sun is bright. Not the best light for taking photographs, I muse. Get me, thinking like a photographer already . . . Perhaps I'll come back later.

I wander in leisurely fashion through the lush green gardens, over tiny bridges and underneath the tallest of trees with the widest of trunks, until eventually I decide to leave the Botanic Gardens and check out the shops.

The pavements are crowded with tables spilling out of dozens of cafés and restaurants, and the chink of cappuccino cups against saucers greets my ears as countless people enjoy lazy breakfasts in the sun. I suddenly wish I was sitting at a table gossiping with a girlfriend, and at that thought, I feel a sharp pang. I don't have any friends. And I certainly don't have any here. Not yet, anyway, and for a brief moment the thought of starting at a new school in a few weeks doesn't seem quite so bad.

Later that day I walk back along the same street, pausing at an Italian café to buy two scoops of lemon and chocolate gelati, then returning to the Botanic Gardens as quickly as possible before the hot sun melts the ice-cream away. After a few mouthfuls, I dig around in one of my shopping bags and check out my purchases.

I have bought a new film for my camera, a couple of cushion covers and a purple throw for my bed, plus a poster of my favourite band, Fence. I fancy their lead singer Johnny Jefferson like mad, so if anything can improve the state of my new bedroom, I reckon his gorgeous face can. I also bought my mum a nice candle and some perfume for Christmas. I suppose I need to get something for Michael and Josh, too, but I have no idea what, yet. Finally I take out the photos that I've had developed. I couldn't resist having a quick look when I got them back, but now I want to scrutinise them in more detail.

The first photograph I pull out is of Roy the kangaroo, propped up on one elbow and looking straight into the camera. There's something quite funny about it. I think my dad would find it amusing. Oh. I can just see the tail of another kangaroo in the background. Bugger, I should have framed it better. I sigh and put the photo to the back of the pile before turning my attention to the next shot. Cindy! She instantly makes me smile. Hmm. I think I might quite like the way I've used the focus in this one, with the leaves blurring behind the koala. Not bad. Right, next!

I go through the whole set like this, peering at each shot with a super-critical eye until I'm either kicking myself or feeling mildly pleased. Once I'm done, I install the new film and then I start to go through the set again until I remember my gelati and turn to see that it's melted away into a syrupy mess.

'Hey!'

The sound of a male voice makes me jump. I look up to see a man stepping off the path onto the grass. It's Ben. I almost didn't recognise him out of his khaki shorts and shirt combo.

'Hello,' I call, pleased to see someone I know.

'I thought it was you.' He grins as he approaches. 'Is there a fly in your cup?'

'Sorry?'

He peers into my ice-cream cup. 'Ah, it's melted,' he says. 'The look on your face was a picture.'

'Ohh . . .' I laugh, realising that my surprise must have looked a bit comical. 'What are you doing here?'

'Had a few errands to run and thought I'd pop by my favourite place in the city before I head home.' He collapses down on the grass and cracks open a can of 7-Up. He's wearing faded black shorts and a turquoise T-shirt with flip flops – or 'thongs' as Josh annoyingly corrected me earlier this week.

'Favourite place?' I prompt.

He indicates the lily pond in front of us. 'I love it at this time of year. Hey, nice camera. Do you mind?' I nod so he reaches for it and fiddles around for a bit before putting his eye to the viewfinder and pointing it at the pond. Then he turns the lens on me.

'Don't!' I cry.

He pulls the camera away from his face, grinning. 'Why not?'

'I hate having my photo taken.'

'Go on, just the one.' He puts the viewfinder back up to his eye.

'No. Please,' I beg, covering my face with my hands.

'Lily!' he snaps. 'Give me a smile.'

I reluctantly drop my hands and tilt my head to one side, shyly. He clicks off a shot.

'There. That wasn't so bad, was it?'

'It was pretty awful.'

He grins and hands the camera back to me, before spying the

pile of photographs with the kangaroo at the top. 'Freddie!' he exclaims. 'Can I see?'

I don't want to make a big deal out of it by saying no, so I manage a slight nod and then sit there nervously while he flicks through the pack, chuckling occasionally and giving me positive feedback. My nerves soon die away and I find myself enjoying his commentary.

'I absolutely love this one,' he says eventually, going back to the photo of Freddie.

'I'm a bit annoyed about the other kangaroo's tail in the background,' I admit.

'Where? Oh, there. You can barely see it.'

'It still annoys me.'

'You're critical, aren't you?'

I shrug.

'Is this what you want to do? Photography?' he asks.

'I don't know. I hadn't really thought about it.'

'Well, I think these are great,' he reiterates, putting the photos back down on the shopping bag. 'I'd love to see your next set.'

And in a funny kind of way, I'm already looking forward to showing him.

'What are you up to after this?' he asks.

'I'll probably head back to Michael's.'

'Still finding it hard to call it home?' He pauses. 'You've been calling it "Michael's" ever since you got here.'

'It *is* Michael's home,' I reply defensively.

'It's yours now, too. Hopefully it won't be long before it feels like it.'

'Mmm.'

'So when did you get your camera?'

'My dad gave it to me as a leaving present.'

'Oh, right. That was nice of him.'

'My dad's a nice man.'

'I bet you miss him.'

'Yes.' I look away.

'When did you find out you were leaving the UK?'

'My mum only told me a couple of months ago,' I mumble.

'Blimey, that all happened very quickly.'

'You're telling me.'

'Bet you wish you could have brought a few mates with you.'

I want to skip over that question for reasons I don't care to explain, so instead I divert attention towards Kay and Olivia. 'I wish I could have brought my sisters.'

'I didn't know you had sisters.'

'Young half-sisters. And my stepmother is pregnant with a third. I'm going to miss the birth of the baby.'

He gives me a sympathetic look. 'That sucks.'

We fall silent for a bit until finally he speaks. 'I should probably set off.'

'Where are you going?'

'Home. Do you want a lift?'

The bus was fine, but you can't beat a lift straight to the front door.

'Er, could I?'

'Sure.' He gets to his feet and I do the same.

'Actually,' I hesitate, remembering my reason for being back in the Botanic Gardens, 'I wanted to take a few more photos. Of the lily pond in this light,' I add self-consciously. 'You go on. I don't want to hold you up.'

'Don't be silly, I can wait.'

'No, really.'

But he sits back down on the grass. I waver for a moment then tell myself, What's the big fuss? You're only taking a bloody photograph. I force myself to chill out and walk away from the pond.

'Am I in the way?' Ben asks.

'Yes, actually,' I reply cheekily.

'Sorry, sorry.' He gets to his feet and goes to sit on a nearby bench. A short while later I join him. 'Are you done?' he asks with surprise.

'Yep.'

'That was quick!'

'I only took a few shots. Don't want to waste film,' I explain, awkwardly.

'You should have got one of those new digital cameras,' he says as we set off towards the gates.

'My dad mentioned them, but I don't like the way they come out when you print the pictures. Too grainy or something.'

'Yep, the resolution's not great. The technology will improve though. It always does. Maybe by the time you upgrade.'

We cross busy North Terrace and head towards Rundle Street. 'I'm in the multi-storey.' He points up the road.

'Are you at work tomorrow?' I ask.

'Nope. Back on Monday. You coming in then?'

'I'd like to. Michael said he might be able to get me a summer job.'

'That would be great,' Ben says sincerely.

We're walking past a pub when I hear my name being shouted.

'Oi! Lily!'

I whip around to see Josh sitting at one of the crowded tables out on the pavement. Damn, he's good-looking. Shame he knows it.

'What are you doing here?' he asks.

He's with a group of five other guys and girls, all of whom regard me with curiosity.

I hold up the bags in my hands. 'Shopping. I just bumped into Ben.'

'Sit down. Have a beer.'

I glance at Ben waiting on the pavement a few feet away.

'Hey, Ben,' Josh calls half-heartedly.

'Alright?' Ben responds in an equally lacklustre fashion.

I look back at Josh. 'Ben was about to give me a lift home.'

'I'll give you a lift home,' he says. There's a half-empty glass of beer on the table in front of him. I don't know how long he's been here, how long he's planning to stay, or if he intends to keep on drinking, but after another night in on my own yesterday, I don't want to turn down what might be my last invitation.

'Do you mind if I stay?' I ask Ben.

'Of course not,' he replies, taking a step backwards. 'See you on Monday?'

'Cool,' I reply.

'Bye, Ben.' Josh waves slightly too enthusiastically.

'See ya.'

My heart dips slightly as I watch Ben walking away. I feel bad about ditching my only friend for a better offer. But oh, he won't care. And as Josh flashes me a sexy grin and beckons me to the table, all thoughts of Ben fly right out of my mind.

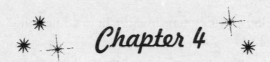

Chapter 4

One of Josh's mates stands up and goes off in search of another chair. Josh indicates the now-free one next to him. I squeeze past the drinkers at another table to get to it and realise I'm nervous.

'There might be one inside,' the guy still searching for a chair says.

'Can you get Lily a drink while you're at it?' Josh calls after him. Then, to me: 'What do you want?'

'Oh, um, may I have a cider, please?' I wonder how hot they are on underage drinking over here. 'Thanks!' I call.

'No worries,' comes the good-natured reply.

'Guys, this is Lily,' Josh says to the people around the table. 'My new – what are you? Stepsister? Half-sister?'

One of the girls sniggers.

'Housemate,' I reply.

'That'll do.'

'Lou, Alex, Tiff, Brian.' He points to each of his friends. 'And the bloke who's gone to get you a drink is Shane,' he adds.

'Aren't you hot in those jeans?' the first girl, Lou, asks me.

'No,' I reply bluntly. She has long, dead-straight blonde hair

55

and is wearing a lime-green vest which brings out the deep tan on her slender arms. I'm guessing she's wearing a very short skirt, but the table is blocking my vision.

'When did you get to Australia?' the other girl, Tiff, asks.

'Saturday.'

'Isn't it, like, a twenty-four-hour flight or something?'

'That's right.'

'I couldn't cope with that,' Lou chips in. 'Flying's supposed to really dry out your skin.' On that note, her eyes flit over my face. I decide then and there that I really don't like her very much.

Shane returns with my drink and another chair. I thank him and peer into the glass. It's full of ice.

'What's wrong?' Josh asks.

I can't help but smirk. 'You serve cider with ice?'

'*Yeah*,' Lou says, pulling a 'dur' face. 'How do you Pommies drink it?'

'We don't drink it with ice.'

'That's right, it's all about warm beer over there, isn't it?' one of the blokes chips in, sniggering. I feel my cheeks reddening.

'You'll be in trouble if you slag off the Pommies, mate,' Josh says.

'Aw, are you missing home?' Tiff asks me, pouting like a little girl.

Shane pulls a face. 'Why?'

'That's what I keep asking.' Josh slaps him on the arm.

I wonder if I can catch Ben up?

'Bloody hell!' Lou squawks, leaping suddenly to her feet.

'Shit, sorry,' one of the blokes says, brushing liquid off her (yep, very short) skirt.

'Get off me, Alex,' she squeals, batting him away. 'Stop sloshing your bloody beer around!'

I take a small gulp of air, relieved that the attention has been diverted from me.

The cider, it turns out, is actually very nice served over ice. Not that I could ever see myself asking for it back home. But it's a hot late afternoon and if the truth be known, I've been sweltering in my jeans all week. I still haven't dared to unveil my pasty white legs. I don't know when I'll do that, if ever. I wonder if I can get through the next couple of years wearing trousers?

Hang on, are they going to make me wear khaki shorts if I work at the conservation park?

Noooooo!

'I know what you're getting for a birthday present.' Josh's singsong voice distracts me.

I twist around to look at him. 'Hey?' He pretends to zip his lips. 'Come on, who's been talking about my birthday?' I persist. He steadfastly shakes his head. 'You can't say stuff like that,' I moan.

'What's this?' Lou interrupts.

'Lily's birthday is on Wednesday.'

'Oh, cool. Are you having a party?' Tiff asks.

'No,' I resolutely reply.

'How old?' Lou asks.

'Sixteen.'

'You're only sixteen!' Alex exclaims, as all eyes fall on me.

'I will be on Wednesday,' I mutter.

'I know, it's mad, isn't it,' Josh addresses them, ignoring me. 'She looks at least as old as us.'

'Aw,' Lou says patronisingly. 'Sweet little sixteen. What are you getting for your birthday?'

'That's what I'm trying to find out.' I stare at Josh expectantly.

'Do you know?' Tiff asks him.

'Yep.'

'Tell us,' she urges.

'Nup.'

'Tell *me*,' Lou insists, leaning towards him, ear at the ready. To my annoyance, Josh complies. I see her hand resting on his thigh and my stomach prickles with jealousy.

'Really?' she says, looking at me.

'What? Tell me!' Tiff pleads.

Lou leans across Alex and whispers into her ear.

'Aw, that will be so cool!'

'This is really bloody annoying,' I say loudly. The next bloke – Brian? – chuckles and pulls Tiff close.

'Come on, let's do Chinese Whispers,' Shane suggests, from beside Brian. A moment later, Shane exclaims, 'What type of car?'

'Mate!' Josh bursts out.

'Am I getting a car?' I turn to him, wide-eyed, as he glares at Shane.

'Oops,' Shane says sheepishly.

'Am I getting a car?' I ask Josh again, my head starting to buzz with excitement.

'Don't tell Dad I told you,' Josh warns me.

'I won't, I promise. What sort?'

Josh sighs and takes a swig of his beer. 'It's only a second-hand one I've been tinkering with at work, so don't get your hopes up. My dad asked me about it today.'

'A car's a car,' Lou says.

'I couldn't agree with you more,' I respond, beaming from ear to ear.

*

We sit there drinking and eating bar snacks until the late-afternoon sun dies away and the street lamps come on outside the pub. Talk turns to going to a nightclub.

'Planet?' Alex suggests.

'Yeah, cool,' Lou affirms.

'I don't have any more money on me,' I murmur to Josh.

'I'll lend you some.' He downs his pint and stands up. Everyone else does the same so I quickly knock back the last of my cider and get to my feet.

Whoa. That was my fourth drink and I am feeling more than a little bit pissed. I stumble out past the tables to the pavement. Tiff skips on ahead, dragging two of the boys with her, while Lou turns around and starts to beg Josh for a piggyback.

'Go on, then,' he concedes eventually as we all head down a side street away from the busy part of town. She climbs onto his back, giggling annoyingly. I watch as her long, tanned legs wrap around him.

I wish I had legs like that.

No, Lily, no, you don't.

Yes, you do.

You're fine as you are.

Could do with a tan though.

Oh, whatever.

'She's been trying to get into his pants for weeks,' Shane says from beside me. He nods ahead at Lou and Josh.

Here we go again with the jealousy. You'd think alcohol would dull your senses, but if anything it makes it worse. 'What's the hold-up?' I manage to ask.

'She just split up with her ex. Big, beefy, Army bloke. Josh is scared shitless of him.' He starts to laugh.

'What are you laughing at?' Josh shouts back at us.

'Nothing,' Shane replies, still sniggering, then to me, 'It's only a matter of time.'

Great. Now I hate her even more.

There's a queue stretching out from the venue. We tag onto the end and wait until it finally dwindles down to our little party when the bouncer utters those two tiny letters that chill every underage teen to the bones.

'ID.'

The others reach into their pockets, producing driving licences without a second thought. I stand there, quaking in my Birkenstocks.

'ID,' the bouncer says again, when the others have all filed through. I want to shout, 'Wait!' But I don't.

'I don't have any with me,' I reluctantly admit. 'But I *am* eighteen.'

'Sorry, love.'

He looks straight past me to the next person in the queue and I know that no amount of persuasion is going to change his mind so I step away from the door. My face burns as everyone stares at me. What the hell am I going to do now?

'Lily!' Josh calls to me from the door.

Phew!

'He won't let me in. I forgot my ID.' I give him a meaningful look.

Josh turns to the bouncer. 'Oh, come on, mate, she's just come all the way from England. You know what these Pommies are like.'

'I don't give a possum's arse if she's just come from Buckingham Palace. If she doesn't have ID, she's not coming in.'

Josh stares at him, frustrated, then he glances over his shoulder at his mates.

Bollocks to this. 'Just point me in the direction of the bus stop,' I snap.

'Are you sure?' he asks, looking guilty.

'Yep. I'll be fine.'

Of course, I realise as soon as I board the bus that I haven't got a clue how to find my way home from Crafers. I think it was a long bendy road . . . I should have borrowed Josh's phone again to call Mum. I rang her a few hours ago to let her know what I was up to. Maybe I should find a payphone. But when I step off the bus, there she is waiting.

'How did you know I'd be here?'

'Josh called Michael.' She leads me to her car. 'What on earth that boy is doing letting you catch a bus on your own at this hour . . . Michael had a few strong words to say to him,' Mum says, climbing into the car and slamming the door behind her.

My insides burn with shame. I hate the thought of Josh getting into trouble because of me. Although Lou will be making him feel better right about now . . .

'You're alive then,' Ben remarks when I turn up to work on Monday morning.

'Why wouldn't I be?'

'I hope you caught the bus home on Saturday night.'

'I did actually.' I don't want to tell him what happened. 'Why?'

'Josh usually drives when he's had a few.'

'Oh, right. Pass me the broom, would you?'

I was appalled when I woke up yesterday morning to see Josh's car parked in the driveway.

'Did you drive home?' I asked him. I'd assumed he'd be catching the bus himself.

'Yeah,' he replied defensively.

'When you were *pissed*?'

'I didn't have that much to drink.'

'You bloody did!'

'What are you – my mother?'

At that point I remembered that his mother was dead so decided to shut up about it, but he'd continued to justify himself. 'I drank a few beers, but it was over several hours, *and* I ate loads. I felt fine.'

I shook my head in disgust.

'Don't tell Dad,' he urged.

So here I am on Monday morning getting the third degree from Ben.

'That bloke is a menace behind the wheel,' he mutters, as he passes me the broom. We're mucking out the koala enclosures. 'Are we paying you for this yet?'

'I don't know,' I reply. 'I think Michael is speaking to Trudy today.' A little flutter of nerves passes through me. I *so* want a job here.

Good news comes at lunchtime, but my enthusiasm takes a nosedive when Michael presents me with my uniform.

'Did Trudy say yes?' I squeal, closely followed by, 'Do I really have to wear the shorts?'

'What's wrong with them?' Ben enquires, ploughing into his homemade cheese sandwich.

'I hate my legs,' I moan.

'There's nothing wrong with your legs,' Michael scoffs.

'How would you know?' I whine. 'You're practically elderly.'

Ben finds this very amusing.

'You can talk, you'll be thirty soon,' Michael jibes.

'Not for another two years,' Ben objects.

'The time will fly by, you mark my words,' Michael says knowingly. I just stare down at the shorts in despair.

The next morning my mum waits outside the door to my bedroom demanding a fashion show.

'Come on, Lily, they can't be that bad.'

'They're worse,' I cry.

The door handle turns. I leap to the door, holding it closed.

'Don't be ridiculous,' she snaps.

'Come on out!' Michael shouts.

'I look a right state,' I shout back. I catch a glimpse of myself in the mirror on the front of the wardrobe and want to cry. My mum turns the door handle again. I'm too slow to stop her and she bursts in.

'Go away!' I squawk, bending down to hide my legs.

'What are you going on about?' Mum says crossly. 'You look fine.'

'I do not!'

'You'll have a tan in a few days,' she tells me.

'Not if I keep applying Factor 30 like it's going out of fashion. I'm so bored of wearing suncream every day,' I whine.

'Well, you won't get any colour if you wear jeans all the time,' she says. I peek at myself in the mirror, warily, and she senses that my reluctance is waning. 'Think about what you'll be able to buy with the extra pocket money,' she adds.

I'm not getting paid much, but I'd work for free if they asked me to, so anything is a bonus. As it is, I'm doing five days a week until I start school at the end of January, which is about seven weeks away. I still can't believe how lucky I am – many people would kill to be in my position.

'Come on, darl. We'd better get to work,' Michael says.

Trying to buck myself up, I follow him out of my bedroom door and immediately spy a sleepy-looking Josh in the corridor. He notes my shorts and sniggers.

'Bugger off!' I shout.

'Language,' Mum says, annoyed.

Michael tries to jolly me up on the way to work. 'So, it's your birthday tomorrow. What time are you doing your theory test?'

Since Sunday I've been religiously studying the *Drivers' Handbook* – the Australian version of the *Highway Code*. The way it works here is I have to take a theory test before I can get behind the wheel, then I'll have to use Learner plates until I can take my proper driving test. If I pass, I'll switch to P – Provisional – plates for a year. I've wanted my licence for so long that I used to read the *Highway Code* just for fun, and the laws are not that different here.

'Eleven o'clock,' I reply to Michael's question. 'Will anyone mind me taking the day off?'

'Of course not. Especially not with all the work you've done up until now. We've been lucky!'

Ben doesn't even acknowledge my shorts when I see him, and I'm grateful. For him, it's business as usual.

'The vet's coming shortly for his weekly check-up and I want him to take a look at one of the koalas.'

'What's wrong with it?'

'He's been losing weight for a few days. Can you grab the record sheets from the office?'

'Yes, of course.'

When I get back, the vet has arrived. Ben introduces me. 'Lily, this is Dave. Dave's an old friend of mine from uni.'

'Hi.' I shake his hand. He's taller and lankier than Ben, with brown hair and a crooked smile.

'Ben told me you want to be a vet?' He speaks softly so as not to disturb the koala, but the question still catches me off-guard.

'She said her grades weren't good enough,' Ben chips in, adding, 'Lily's still at school. She's only fifteen.'

'Sixteen tomorrow,' I remind him.

'You've got time to turn them around,' Dave says.

I shift on my feet awkwardly.

'Birthday tomorrow?' Ben changes the subject as Dave lifts the koala onto a bench and starts to check him over. I notice his ears are back, one of the signs of ill health, as Ben informed me on my second day here.

'Yep.'

'Do you know what you're getting?'

I give him a cheeky look. 'Do *you* know what I'm getting?'

'No.' He quickly averts his gaze.

'You bloody do, don't you,' I whisper loudly. 'Does everybody know I'm getting a car except for me?'

Ben glances at me in shock and then stifles a laugh.

'Whoops,' I say under my breath as Dave looks up at us.

'Who told you?' Ben persists.

'Josh. But keep that quiet.'

'That dimwit,' he mutters, then speaks to Dave, who's making a note on the record sheet. 'Her mum's hooked up with Michael Fredrickson. She's living in the same house as Josh.'

'Sheesh.' Dave does a sharp intake of breath and bends down to zip up his black veterinary bag.

Will somebody *please* change the record?

I don't consider myself to be a particularly good actress, but I think I do a fine job the next morning of pretending to be surprised when Michael whooshes open the door to reveal a faded green Ford Fiesta sitting on the road in front of the house. My excitement, however, doesn't have to be faked.

'THANKYOUTHANKYOUTHANKYOU!' I scream at the top of my voice, running down the veranda steps and onto the path. I barely register the sharp stones digging into the soles of my bare feet as I race towards the car and tug on the door handle.

'WHEREARETHEKEYSWHEREARETHEKEYSWHERE-ARETHEKEYS?'

'Here, here.' Josh grins as he lopes down the path with a set of car keys dangling from a keyring. My mum and Michael beam at my reaction as they follow him. I hastily unlock the door and climb into the driver's seat, sticking the keys into the ignition.

'EEEEEEEEEEEEE!' I squeal. 'ILOVEITILOVEITILOVEIT!'

'Do you think she likes it?' Michael says to Mum and Josh.

'I think she does,' Mum replies, smiling.

'Who's going to take me for a test drive?' I ask Michael hopefully.

'Whoa,' he says, leaning in and swiftly extracting the keys. 'Not until you pass your theory test.'

'Oh,' I moan. 'What time do they open?'

Mum drives me into the city to take my test. It's easy. It's multiple choice, so even if I hadn't revised my bum off I would have stood a good chance of passing. Mum makes a snide comment about why I can't apply myself to my education in the same fashion, and I make one back about it being hard when your mother has dragged you from school to school all your life in pursuit of men. That shuts her up. But I don't want to have a go at my mum today. I have a funny feeling in the pit of my stomach that maybe, just maybe, it's going to be okay living in Australia.

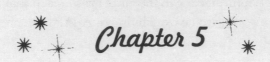

Chapter 5

'Fuck me, you've stalled *again*!'

'Piss off!'

'Hurry up, would you. This is embarrassing.'

'You are *such* a dickhead!'

Josh is teaching me how to drive. I know, I'm clearly not right in the head. Michael has been letting me get behind the wheel on the way to work over the last week and a half, but it's Saturday now and he's taken Mum on a weekend break to a town called Clare in the Barossa Valley to tour the wineries. I stupidly begged Josh to pick up where his dad had left off.

I wind down the window, but the hot air outside makes me feel like I'm in the direct airflow of a giant hairdryer so I put it back up again. Thankfully the car has air-conditioning, even if it's not very powerful. I flip down the sun visor and instantly flinch as I remember Michael's story about giant spiders hiding behind them. All clear.

Someone toots their horn behind me.

'Yep, I know how you feel, mate!' Josh calls out.

'Stop winding me up!' I snap, feeling the bite of the accelerator against the clutch. The car lurches forward and we fly through the traffic-lights.

'Whoa! Who do you think you are?' Josh says snidely. 'Michael Schumacher?'

I'm so angry by the time we get home that I refuse to speak to him for the rest of the day. He finally comes to make amends.

'Do you want to come to Stirling tonight?' he asks, after finding me sulking in front of the telly at seven o'clock.

'Not with you,' is my blunt response.

'Oh, don't be mad.'

I glare at the television screen in silence.

'It's Saturday night . . .' he carries on.

'Who's going?' I ask, thinking that if the answer involves Lou, I'll stay right where I am.

'Just Alex, Shane and a few of the guys from work.'

'No girls?' I check, because I'm not risking it.

'Nup. Not unless I get lucky later. I'm joking!' he exclaims when he sees my face. 'Come on,' he adds. 'You need a drink after all those near-crashes earlier.'

'Go to hell!'

'Hey, get a sense of humour. I'll even let you get me back by picking on *my* driving.'

'I'll pick on it on the way there. But we're catching a taxi home, geddit?'

'Whatever.'

Stirling is a pretty town. The streets are lined with long rows of single-storey shops, set back under a shady canopy of trees. Some colonial-style buildings are built out of cream stone and have intricate wrought-iron balconies.

The pub we go to is packed, smoky and full of drinkers. I know the only way I'll have a good time is if I join everyone else in their game, so when Josh goes off to play pool with one of his mates and Shane drags me to the bar to do a shot of tequila, I go gladly.

'Another?' he offers when I knock back the first.

'No.' I'm trying not to wince.

'Pommie lightweight,' he jokes.

'I bet I could drink *you* under the table.' As if!

'Is that a challenge?' He raises two dark eyebrows at me and flashes me a cheeky smile. He's actually not bad-looking. I don't think I've noticed before because it's hard to notice anyone else when Josh is standing in front of you.

'I wouldn't want to embarrass you,' I reply childishly and he laughs and pulls out a cigarette packet.

'Want one?'

'No, thanks. I didn't know you smoked,' I say as he lights up.

'Only sometimes.'

'Does Josh smoke?'

'Nah. Too much of a cheapskate,' Shane shrugs.

'Right . . .' Shane grins and I try not to smile. 'How long have you two known each other?' I ask.

He leans his elbow against the bar and manoeuvres himself closer to me. 'About six years. We were at high school together.'

I wonder if Shane knows how Josh's mum died. Before I can ask, Josh himself appears.

'You're not making my little sister drink shots, are you?' he asks, wrapping his arm around my waist and giving me a squeeze.

'Get off,' I grumble, pushing him away, but secretly craving the contact. I haven't been held like that for what feels like a very long time.

'Can we get some more shots, here?' Josh calls to the barman.

He hands one to me a minute later and I find I don't have the will to decline.

'Cheers.' The three of us chink glasses and knock back the booze, me trying hard not to cough.

'You alright, little sis?' Josh grins as he pats me on the back.

'Bugger off.'

Someone vacates their bar stool beside us. Josh props himself against it and wraps both of his arms around me from behind. I curse myself for blushing as I meet Shane's teasing eyes.

'Where's Lou tonight?' Shane asks Josh.

'Fuck knows,' Josh replies. Another stool becomes available behind Shane and he pulls it up so I find myself sandwiched between the pair of them. I try to stay cool.

'Oh man, you're not doing shots, are you?' Brian and Alex appear from out of nowhere. 'How many have we missed out on?' Alex whines.

'Only one,' Josh replies, not taking into account the shot that Shane and I did earlier.

'Can we get a few more?' Alex shouts to the barman.

Josh downs his shot left-handed and doesn't remove his right hand from around my waist. The next thing I know, it has slid under my top and his thumb is stroking the lower part of my stomach. I suddenly feel light-headed.

Brian nudges Josh. 'Karen's just walked in.'

Josh's hand whips out from under my top and my skin instantly feels cool from his lack of contact. I turn to see who this Karen person is and spy a slim, beautiful brunette wandering into the pool room.

'Fancy a game of pool?' Brian asks Josh mischievously.

'Let's go.'

Josh hops down from his stool and he and Brian stride purposefully after Karen, leaving me standing there with Shane and Alex.

'What are you drinking?' Alex asks me.

'Um, cider, please,' I reply, confused and disheartened by what has just happened.

'Is it Mount Barker High School you're starting at?' Shane asks.

'Er, yeah.' Like I really want to talk about this now.

'I'll have to introduce you to my sister,' he says.

'Really? Is that where she goes?'

'Yep. She's sixteen too, so you'll be in the same year.'

'That'd be good.' I mean it. I would love to walk into a new school and know someone. 'What's her name?'

'Tammy. She just broke up with her boyfriend so she's not too happy right now. You might be able to cheer her up.'

'A new year makes everything seem a bit better too, doesn't it?' I say.

'As long as the Millennium Bug doesn't wipe us all out,' Alex comments.

'Bloody Millennium bug,' I mutter. 'That's all anyone's talked about for years. I bet nothing actually happens.'

'I'll be stocking up on extra cans of baked beans just in case,' Shane comments, and I smirk at him.

'What are you doing for New Year?' I ask. I'm starting to forget the fact that Josh deserted me. At least these two aren't making me feel left out. To think I liked it when he touched me! My face prickles with embarrassment. I won't let him get away with that again.

'We're all going into the city to a club,' Alex replies. 'You should get your ticket soon if you want to join us – otherwise they'll sell out.'

My heart sinks. 'I'll probably get asked for ID again.'

'Oh, yeah,' Shane comments. 'That was a bit of a bummer.'

'Hmm. I suppose I'll think of something.'

At eleven thirty, Josh finally reappears – *sans* Karen.

'Shall we head off?' he asks me.

'Yeah, why not.' I slide off the stool and stumble slightly. Shane reaches in to grab me.

'It's alright, I've got her.'

Josh's steady arms take over from Shane, and as he grins down at me, I'm annoyed to find myself feeling flustered. Calling for a taxi doesn't even occur to me.

'No Mum and Dad tonight,' Josh comments a couple of minutes into the drive. TLC's 'No Scrubs' is playing on the radio. He glances across at me and says meaningfully. 'We've got the house all to ourselves . . .'

No, no, no, I tell myself sternly. He's not sexy. Not sexy at all. He's a wanker. And then I see the koala.

'Shit!' Josh exclaims as the weight of the animal thuds into our vehicle.

My senses violently kick into action. 'YOU'VE JUST HIT A KOALA!' I scream. 'PULL OVER! PULL OVER!'

He screeches to a halt and I stumble out of the car and run back in the direction we just came.

'Where are you going?' Josh calls after me.

'We've got to find it!'

'It'll be dead.'

'Shut up!' I don't want to hear that.

I arrive at the place where we had the collision. There's no sign of anything on the road so I squint down the slope into the darkness.

'Lily, come back!' Josh cries.

Just then, I hear a faint rustle in the undergrowth and, heart picking up pace, I carefully make my way down the steep incline, hoping and praying to find a living animal at the end of it. My feet hit something solid and I reach down to find my fingers sinking into thick, soft hair. It's still. Silent. Warm. Dead.

'No, please, no.' My eyes adjust to the darkness and I collapse on the ground in despair as tears prick my eyes.

'Where are you?' Josh hisses into the darkness.

'You idiot!' I wail up the incline.

Again, a rustling in the undergrowth.

'It wasn't my fault!' Josh whines back with the undertone of someone who knows, deep down, that it was exactly that.

More rustling . . .

'Shhh!' I say.

'I didn't see—'

'SHUT UP!' I stand up and follow the sound, stepping carefully through the dry leaves under my feet. And then I see it. The small furry bundle that was thrown off its mummy's back.

My heart lifts.

'Shhh,' I murmur, this time to the tiny koala at my feet. I bend down and gather it up. 'Shhh . . .'

'What are you doing?' Josh calls again.

I don't answer as I climb back up the incline, past the baby's dead mother.

'What are you going to do with it?' Guilt makes Josh's voice tremble as he follows me back to the car, and it strikes me that he'd probably rather not have this live evidence of his dangerous driving.

My answer comes easily. 'We've got to take him to Ben,' I say.

'Do you know where he lives?' I look directly into Josh's dark eyes and he knows not to mess with me.

'Yes,' he mumbles.

'Then let's go.'

Ben lives only a few miles away, but the journey seems to take forever because the last place I want to be is in a car with Josh behind the wheel. Finally he pulls up outside a single-storey stone house with an iron roof and a white picket fence out at the front. He makes no attempt to move as I get out of the car.

'You not coming in?' I ask him flatly.

'No. He'll give you a lift home, won't he?'

'I suppose so.'

'See you in the morning then, yeah?'

'Bye.'

I shut the car door firmly, wanting to slam it, but not enough to risk frightening the animal in my arms. It's only when Josh drives off that I feel a prickle of regret for not wishing him a safe journey. But he didn't screech away from the kerb so I can only hope that he's learned his lesson, for tonight at least.

The house is dark as I walk up the footpath and only now does it occur to me that Ben might not be in. Then I see a thin ray of light peeking out from behind the curtains and relief surges through me. It's close to midnight and he shouldn't be awake, but perhaps I'm lucky. I press the doorbell. A moment later, the door opens and Ben is standing before me.

'Sorry to bother you.' The words tumble out of my mouth. 'But I – we – I . . .'

A muffled squeak interrupts my speech and Ben's attention is diverted by the package I'm carrying.

'Come in, come in.' He ushers me through the door and closes it before turning back to the bundle of fur in my arms. 'Here,' he says gently as I hand over the baby koala.

'Shhh, it's okay,' he murmurs, as he quickly checks the animal over. I notice now in the light that it has a swollen eye and a couple of scratches. I feel so bad I could throw up. Ben looks up at me. 'What happened?'

I swallow the bile in my throat. 'Josh was driving . . .'

His stare hardens and I know I don't need to say any more.

'Come through to the living room.'

I follow him meekly, wishing I didn't feel so helpless. He's dressed in jeans and a black T-shirt so at least I know I didn't get him out of bed.

'I was scared you'd be asleep,' I say, as he switches off the main light to darken the room. Two lamps on side-tables cast a glow across the space.

'I'd just got off the phone,' he replies. I wonder who he was talking to at this hour? 'I need to get a heatpad and some blankets. Can you hold her?'

'Is it a she?' I take the bundle from his arms.

'Yes.'

He leaves the room and I look down at the tiny creature. She starts to squeak again and my heart splinters. Tears are rolling down my cheeks by the time Ben returns.

'Hey,' he says kindly, touching my arm. 'Do you want me to take her?'

'No.' My voice sounds small.

'Okay. She'll prefer the heat from your body to a heatpad, anyway. I'm going to prepare her some milk. Do you want a tea while I'm at it?' And when I nod: 'Milk, one sugar – right?'

'Yes, please.' Ben's made me tea before in the staffroom. He returns after a while with two mugs of tea plus a lactose-free formula mixed from powder for the koala. He explains that koalas are allergic to cow's milk as he attaches a teat to a syringe and passes it to me to feed her. She'll switch to using a bottle when she's a bit older.

'What's going to happen to her?' I ask when the syringe is empty and the koala has fallen into a sleepy slumber. I sip my tea.

'I'll take her to work in the morning, but she'll probably spend her nights with me for the first week before we relocate her to the hospital room.'

'Hospital room?'

'It's where the animals are quarantined and handreared.'

'Do you need to call Dave?'

'No. We're trained for this sort of stuff. Luckily she only has surface wounds. She won't need to be euthanised.'

'*Put down?*' My eyes widen and then fill with tears.

'She won't need to be euthanised,' he reiterates.

'Would Dave have done that?'

'No, that would have come down to me.'

'That's awful!'

'It's part of the job. But yes, it is pretty awful.'

'I feel terrible,' I murmur. 'I only saw the mother a split second before the car hit her. I went back for her in case she'd been injured, but I think she'd been killed on impact. I found her baby by accident.'

'Joey.'

'Joey?'

'It's the correct term for a baby koala – and other infant marsupials like kangaroos and wombats. Were you two out together?' He's referring to Josh and me.

'I went to Stirling with him and some of his mates.'

He sighs with disappointment. 'I can't believe you let him drive you home.'

'I wasn't thinking.'

'Where are Michael and Cindy?'

'They went to Clare for the weekend.'

'Do you want to call them?'

'No. Let's not bother them. It's not as if they can do anything, right? Anyway, Mum's used to leaving me on my own.'

'Did she do that a lot?'

The corners of my lips turn down. 'Now and again.'

'Sucks, doesn't it?'

I remember what he told me about his nan raising him because his mother was so hopeless. The expression on his face is raw. I look away.

'I suppose you learn to cope,' I reply.

He yawns and stretches his arms over his head and I take in my surroundings. Most of the furniture in the living room is made from dark wood and looks old enough to be antique. 'This was your nan's house, wasn't it?'

'Yeah. Still got all her old furniture.'

'It's nice. I like it,' I tell him. 'How many bedrooms?'

'Three.'

'That's pretty cool. It will do you when you have a couple of kids.'

He chuckles. 'Give me a break, I'm only twenty-eight.'

'I thought you *country folk* got married and sprouted out sprogs before your twenty-first birthdays.'

'Really? Is that what *you're* planning on doing?'

'Puh-*lease!*'

He laughs and glances down at the koala. I follow his gaze.

'She's fast asleep,' I comment.

'That's good. She's going to need her rest.'

'Especially when she wakes up and remembers we killed her mummy,' I add, a lump forming in my throat. 'I'm so sorry, little one,' I whisper as my eyes fill up.

'Hey, don't beat yourself up,' Ben says softly. 'Most people would have driven off. She was lucky you found her.'

I don't speak for a while.

'Do you want me to take you home?' he asks eventually.

'Can I stay a bit longer?'

'Of course you can.'

'It's not like Michael and Mum will be wondering where I am.' And Josh will be out cold with all the alcohol he's consumed. I don't say that part out loud, because I don't want to make Ben angry again. I feel surprisingly sober, considering how much I drank.

'Have you spoken to your dad recently?' Ben asks.

'Yeah. It was Olivia's birthday last week.'

'How's your stepmum getting on with her pregnancy?'

'Fine, I think. I didn't speak to her.'

'Do you get along with her? What's her name again?'

'Lorraine. She's okay. She's pretty nice, in fact.'

'Just not nice enough to live with.'

'What do you mean?'

'You didn't consider living with your dad and Lorraine instead of with your mum?'

'Absolutely,' I reply. 'I would have gone to live with them instead of coming here if they'd had enough room for me.'

'Are you serious?' He stares at me in surprise. I nod. 'Blimey,' he comments. 'Would you go back to the UK now if you could?'

I cock my head to one side and think about this for a moment. 'I don't know,' I answer eventually. 'You'll have to ask me again when I start school. I'm dreading it,' I admit.

'I don't want to sound unoriginal and tell you it will be okay,' he says, 'but it probably will.'

I roll my eyes at him.

'It will! Look at how quickly you settled into work. You're obviously good at meeting people and making friends.'

At that comment I can't help but let out a sharp laugh.

'You *did* settle into work well,' he says, perplexed at my reaction.

'It's not that,' I reply. 'It was the bit about making friends.'

'What? Don't you have mates back home?'

I stare down at my fingernails. 'Not any more.'

'Why?'

I let out a deep breath and shift the koala into a more comfortable position on my lap, because this is a long story and I finally feel brave enough to tell it.

I didn't have many friends back in the UK. Because we moved around a lot, the friendships I made growing up were never close. But after Bill in Brighton – that was one of my mum's many men – we moved back to London, and that's where we've been for the last four years: the longest time I've been anywhere.

I started secondary school along with everyone else, so for once I wasn't The New Girl. We were all new. And that was when I met Shannon. I still don't know why she latched onto me. She was the pretty, blonde, vivacious one whom all the boys fancied, and for some reason she picked me to be her little pet. Not that it felt like that at the time. I felt as if the sun was shining on me for the first time in my life. I adored her. And it seemed as if the feeling was reciprocated. We did everything together. We were inseparable at school, and in the evenings and weekends it was no different. No one else got a look-in. Until we became interested in boys, that is, but instead of that causing a rift between us, it just gave us one more thing to gossip about.

Shannon got her first serious boyfriend before me, but soon set about hooking me up with his best mate. I fancied Dan instantly. In fact, to this day I don't know why Shannon went for Eddie over him. Dan was the better-looking of the two: tall, dark and very, very handsome. Shannon lost her virginity to Eddie within three months and then encouraged me to do the same. I didn't take much persuading, if I'm being honest. I was in love. Plus I fancied him like mad. We were only fifteen.

That was five months ago. Two months ago I went to the bath-room at a house party and discovered Dan screwing Shannon over the toilet seat. I didn't wait to see if he'd been wearing a condom.

I don't go into all this detail when I relay the story to Ben, but he's still pretty horrified.

'What did they say when you confronted them?' he asks.

'I didn't. I felt too sick about it to go back to school on the Monday and by the time my mum made me return on Wednesday, everybody seemed to know what had happened. I don't know how, because I certainly didn't say anything.' I pause. 'Shannon never even apologised.'

'What a bitch!' he spits. 'What was she like around you? Did she seem guilty?'

'Yes, at first. She wouldn't look at me. Then she latched onto another group of girls and I was out in the cold.'

'What about your boyfriend?'

'Eddie punched him in the face so he had a black eye for most of that week. But he never said anything to me either. It just seemed to be common knowledge amongst everyone that our relationship was over.'

'Fuck me. What a little prick.'

I can't help but giggle at Ben's reaction. I'm not used to hearing him swear. He's still too pissed off to smile back at me though. I suddenly have an urge to reach over and smooth away his frown.

'Don't worry about it,' I say instead. 'It's all in the past now.'

'I can't believe you dragged your feet about coming to Australia. I would have wanted to be as far away as possible.'

'Don't get me wrong, I didn't want to be at school either. But I would rather have gone to live with Dad. It's all a bit of a blur how I managed to get through the last few weeks.'

'I bet.' He collapses his head back on the sofa and stares across at me. There's concern in his eyes and it makes me feel a bit funny all of a sudden.

'Can you hold her for a moment?' I ask abruptly, nodding down at the sleeping koala. 'I need to go to the loo.'

'Sure.' He leans in and gently takes the furry bundle, but as his warm arms press into mine, my stomach flutters. 'Second door on the right,' he calls after me as I hurry out of the room, my face inexplicably burning.

What the hell? I close the bathroom door and sit on the toilet, confused by the sensations I just felt. Maybe I'm not as sober as I thought.

When I return to the living room, Ben has slumped further into the worn brown leather sofa and the joey is snuggled up in his arms. I take my seat next to him; strangely, the sofa seems to have shrunk in size.

'Do you want her back?' he asks me.

'No, no, it's okay,' I mumble. 'She looks happy there.' I glance at him as he gazes down at the koala and again the butterflies sweep through my stomach. *What's got into me? It's Josh I fancy!*

'How's the driving going?' he asks.

'Well . . .' I cast my eyes heavenwards. 'Josh took me for a lesson.' Ben looks unimpressed. 'It didn't go very well,' I add.

'You don't say,' he comments sarcastically. He looks straight at me and I want to look away, but instead I force myself to keep eye contact and try to act normal.

His eyes are surprisingly dark blue. He's really quite good-looking, isn't he?

There goes my face again. I quickly avert my gaze. *LILY! What is wrong with you?*

'Do you want another tea?' he asks.

'Er, yeah, that'd be good,' I mutter.

'Here, can you take her again?' He indicates the koala. 'Or shall I put her in front of the heater?'

'No, give her to me.' I have an odd desire to feel his arms pressing into mine again, and once more when they do, my pulse picks up its pace. Oblivious, Ben hands over his charge and walks out of the living room.

I cuddle the joey and tell my heart to calm down.

'Actually,' Ben says, coming back into the room and startling me, 'do you want me to take you home? I've just seen the time. It's one-thirty. I've been getting carried away, talking to you.'

'Do *you* want me to go home?' I ask unhappily.

'No, but aren't you knackered?'

I shake my head. 'No.'

'I'll get on with the tea, then.' He chuckles and goes back into the kitchen.

Hang on. He's got work tomorrow. Does he really want a teenage girl taking up his precious sleeping time? I feel very awkward by the time he returns.

'I forgot you've got work tomorrow,' I say. 'I could call a taxi?'

'You'll struggle to get one at this hour. Don't worry, I'll drive you home. You could even crash in the spare room, if you like. Oh no,' he immediately dismisses that idea. 'Josh might worry about you in the morning.'

I snort. 'Are you kidding me? Josh won't even know I'm not there. He never gets up before midday on a Sunday.'

Ben shrugs and sits down again. 'If you want to stay, you can take the baby to bed with you.' He nods at the fluffy lump in my arms.

'Hey?' My brow furrows.

'It's what a lot of keepers do in this situation. Others prefer to leave them alone so they can go through the mourning process on their own.'

'That's awful!' I exclaim. 'Of course she can sleep with me.'

'I thought you'd say that.'

'Would you have put her in a box by the heater?' I know I won't be able to help feeling disappointed if the answer is yes.

'The last two times this happened to me, the joeys lasted in the box for all of ten minutes.' Ben grins. 'She would have ended up in bed with me for sure.'

I smile back at him and feel my stomach tingle.

'Are you going to let Josh take you on any more driving lessons?' he asks casually.

'No. It's such a bummer though. Michael has been letting me drive to work on the odd days, but he needs his truck most of the time. I don't know when I'm going to learn and I'm desperate to pass my test.'

'Won't your mum teach you?'

'I'm not *that* desperate.'

'I'll take you for the odd spin if you like?'

'Would you?'

'Sure. You can drive my car home in the morning.'

'Aw, Ben, you're the best!' *I could kiss you!* Ha ha, have another drink, Lily. I beam at him in a ridiculously OTT fashion and he starts to look uncomfortable, but that only makes me giggle. He drinks his tea and drums his fingers on his thigh. I suddenly find myself yawning.

'Come on,' he says, putting down his mug. 'You should get to bed.'

I'd rather stay up talking to him, but I do as he says.

I follow him out of the room and down the corridor. He opens up the first door on the left and switches on the light. A double bed on towering bedposts dominates the room. It's covered with a pretty floral bedspread and I wonder if that, too, belonged to his nan.

'I think I've got a spare toothbrush in the bathroom,' he says. 'I'll just go grab it.'

'Thanks,' I say when he returns.

'Wake me up if the crying gets too much for you,' he tells me.

'Do you think she'll cry?' I ask worriedly, and he nods his head. The solemn look on his face makes *me* want to cry.

'It's okay,' he says softly. 'She's going to be fine.'

'I hope so,' I reply. 'I really hope so.'

The joey keeps me awake on and off throughout the night. I don't rouse Ben. I can't bear to ask any more of him, but I'm shattered by the time the morning light seeps under the curtains. I lie in bed for a moment, the koala thankfully asleep.

I dreamed about Ben most of last night. It was the strangest thing. I dreamed about kissing him, about him holding me, about him listening to me and being protective of me. But in the cold light of day, do I still fancy him?

Yes, I definitely do. *For God's sake, Lily.* What's the big deal? It's only a crush. I have a crush on an older man! Whoopeedoo. It's not as if it's anything serious. It's not as if anything is actually going to happen, is it? I laugh out loud at the thought. He'd be embarrassed for me if he knew. I shiver with horror.

The shower turns on in the bathroom. Ooh, I really need a wee. I climb out of bed and grab my clothes, leaving the joey sleeping while I go off in search of a toilet. The door across the corridor is open and I can see into what I assume is Ben's room. The double bed is still unmade and there are a few clothes draped over a wooden chair next to the closet. I don't want to pry so I move on to the room next to mine. It's the second spare room: two single beds, neatly made. The kitchen is at the back of the house with a door that leads out to the garden. There's another door to the left and I open it, hoping to spy the toilet because I'm getting a bit desperate now, but it's just a larder. Bollocks. The door to the bathroom opens and Ben appears, along with a cloud of steam.

'Hey!' he says, surprised to see me.

'Don't you have a second loo?' I ask, trying not to look at his really bloody gorgeous chest which is still damp from the shower.

'Sorry.' He shakes his head, grinning. 'Bathroom's free now.'

He turns and heads back into his bedroom while I hurry to the bathroom, my eyes on his glistening back and my heart fiercely pounding.

A minute after I get back to my bedroom, Ben knocks on the door.

'How is she?'

He's wearing his work clothes. *I've never noticed how nice his legs are before. For Christ's sake!*

'Did she cry much?' he prompts when I don't immediately answer.

'No. Yes. No. Well, a little bit,' I stutter.

'You're tired,' he comments. 'You're not at work today, are you?'

'No, not until tomorrow.'

'You'll be able to catch some sleep when you get home. Do you still want to drive?'

I smile. 'You haven't forgotten?'

Twenty minutes later I'm attempting to reverse up the steep incline of Ben's driveway. The koala is safe in a holding cage on the back seat.

'Are you *sure* you don't want to do this part?' I ask as the car judders violently and stalls for the third time.

'No,' he says firmly. 'You *can* do it.' The emphasis is on the 'can'.

'Okay,' I sigh. I put the handbrake on, the gearstick into neutral and turn the key in the ignition. 'Your car is so much bigger than my Ford Fiesta.' He drives a white Holden Commodore station wagon.

'You'll be fine.'

The car judders again, but I eventually manage the manoeuvre.

'Good,' he says. 'Straight ahead, left at the T-junction.'

Michael lives less than ten minutes away so it's a short lesson, but I'm pleased that Ben makes a much better driving instructor than Josh.

'Thanks, Mr . . . Actually, what is your surname?' I ask, my joke about him being my new teacher falling flat.

'Whiting,' he replies. 'Like the fish.'

'Fish?'

'Yeah, whiting,' he says again.

'Never heard of it.'

'I will have to take you fishing sometime.'

'You *fish?*'

'Sure.'

'A man of many talents,' I say stupidly. He unclicks his seatbelt and climbs out of his seat. We meet each other in front of the bonnet.

'Thanks for being there for me last night.' I feel like a shy schoolgirl all over again.

'No worries,' he replies with an even more exaggerated Australian accent than usual. 'See you tomorrow.'

I can't wait, I think sadly as I walk towards the house and turn back to watch him climb into the driver's seat. He lifts his hand in a wave and then drives off as I experience a comedown that has nothing to do with how much I drank last night.

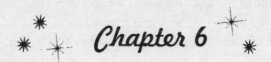

Chapter 6

As predicted, Josh is fast asleep when I get home. He emerges at five minutes to midday, looking hungover and strangely unattractive. He slumps down next to me on the sofa and instead of my usual flutterings at his close contact, I find myself feeling a bit annoyed that he didn't sit on the armchair. How very fickle of me.

'Can you not sit over there?' I grumble. 'I was about to lie down.'

'Tough shit,' he replies, reaching for my crisps packet.

'Get your own.' I snatch them back.

'Somebody's in a bad mood,' he taunts.

'That's probably because I've been up all night taking care of an orphaned koala!' I snap. *How did I ever fancy you?*

'Up all night?' he sniggers.

'Well, that's what it felt like,' I quickly tell him, not wanting him to cotton on to the fact that I stayed at Ben's. In the cold light of day I realise that he might find that slightly weird. I know it was perfectly innocent, but if he made a comment I might do something horrendous like blush.

'And the koala is going to be fine, thank you for asking,' I add sarcastically.

Josh gets up and goes to sit on the armchair. *Result.* Except now I feel a bit mean.

'Have some of these if you want.' I hand over the crisps.

'Thanks,' he mutters, and a tentative peace is restored.

Ooh, aren't his arms skinny compared to Ben's? Oh dear. I really must stop this.

My crush doesn't dissolve over the course of the day and by Monday when Michael and I set off for work, I feel irritatingly jittery. I hope Ben doesn't notice.

He's not in the staffroom when we arrive and that provokes my symptoms even more. I head off to the hospital room, wondering if he's with the joey. Quietly pushing open the door, I see him kneeling in front of the heater with our little orphan. My heart does a somersault.

'Hey,' he says, looking around at me.

'How is she?' There's a slight tremor to my voice.

'She's fine. I'm getting her settled for the day.'

'Did she keep you awake much last night?'

'Only a bit. She'll get better with time. What did you get up to yesterday?'

'Sat around watching telly.'

He gets to his feet and comes towards me. I have to stop myself from taking a step backwards. 'When do you want your next driving lesson?'

'Do you mean it?'

'I rarely say anything I don't mean.'

'When have you got the time?'

'When's your next day off?'

'Wednesday.'

'That's a stroke of luck.' He raises his eyebrows as he gazes down at me. 'It's mine too.'

Wednesday cannot come soon enough. The moments when I'm not with Ben at work drag by. The moments when I'm with him seem to fly by at high speed.

When Ben turns up on the doorstep on Wednesday morning, it's a hot and sunny day. After much deliberation, I've opted for a black skirt because I can just about cope with my legs being on view these days. I team it with a red top, and tie my dark hair up into a high ponytail. Ben is wearing white board shorts and a green T-shirt.

'All set?'

'Do you want to come in for a coffee, mate?' Michael calls from behind me. I moan internally at the distraction.

'Just had one,' Ben replies.

Phew.

Michael joins us at the front door and puts his hands on my shoulders. 'Take care of our girl.'

'You know I will.'

I step out of Michael's grasp and usher Ben down the footpath, keen to avoid further delays.

Ben turns around and jangles the car keys to his Holden station wagon in his hand. 'Your car or mine?'

'Mine, of course.'

He groans.

'Hey, remember I've got to take my driving test in it,' I add.

'Okay, okay,' he concedes, pocketing his keys.

'Where are we going?' I ask when we're both belted in.

'I thought we could go for a drive around the hills.'

'Sounds good.' I turn and wave at Michael, who's still standing in the doorway, then pull away from the kerb, stalling immediately.

'Sorry, sorry. I won't watch you,' Michael shouts, before going inside.

I wipe my forehead and attempt the manoeuvre again, this time with success.

'He's a good guy,' Ben says of Michael.

'I like him,' I reply. 'He's definitely one of my mum's nicer boyfriends.'

'Take a right here. Has your mum had a lot of boyfriends?' Ben asks casually.

'Oh, dozens.' I flick on the indicator.

'Don't forget to check your mirrors,' Ben reminds me.

'Whoops.' I do as he says and make the turn.

'Straight ahead through Crafers, then we'll take a right at the roundabout. Did you get along with all of them?'

'They were alright for the most part. I liked Bill, her last serious one.'

'He's the one who lived in Brighton, right?'

'That's right.' I mentioned him on Saturday night when I relayed the story about Shannon and Dan. 'She was with him for almost four years, which was practically a record. I was sad when she got bored of him and we had to go back to London.'

'That's a great little restaurant.' I glance left as we pass a place called Jimmies. 'A sexy blonde sometimes sings there on Thursday nights,' Ben adds.

I crunch the gears as my insides prickle with jealousy. I don't know why it hasn't occurred to me that of course Ben will have a sex life. For all I know, he could have a girlfriend. I immediately want to rule out that possibility, but the question won't slide off my tongue.

'Yeah, right here,' he directs as we approach the aforementioned roundabout. 'Mirrors,' he adds.

We start to climb up into the winding hills. Purple, pink and yellow wildflowers line the sides of the roads.

'How long was your mum with your dad?' Ben asks after a while.

'I think she was only with him for a few months before she got pregnant. They got married, but they didn't last long after I was born. After the divorce she moved on to Simon.'

We pass the gates to the conservation park.

'This is a different way to how Michael drives to work,' I comment.

'Yeah. I didn't want you to have to manoeuvre your way up a steep dirt track on your first lesson.'

'Thanks.'

'Straight ahead,' he says.

Out of the right-hand window I see the castle that I noticed from my bedroom window on my first day here.

'What's that?' I ask.

'Carminow Castle,' Ben replies. 'It burnt down in one of the bush fires and was left empty for years.'

'Spooky. And what are those?' On the other side of the road there are towering structures shooting upwards into the sky. I spy another burnt-out house to their right.

'Transmitter stations for television and telephone. Hey, look! Black cockatoos!' I nervously follow Ben's gaze to see two black birds flying over the roof of the car. 'Very rare,' he says.

93

'Cool,' I comment, looking hastily back at the road.

'So what was Simon like?' He reverts to our earlier discussion.

'I barely remember him,' I reply. 'But I've seen pictures of us all on a beach in Dorset when I was two. Then there was Desmond. We went to live with him, too. I have vague memories of collecting eggs on his farm in Yorkshire. Mum flitted from man to man for a few years after that. Most of the time we lived in a little flat in East London, until she met Bill and we were off again. I liked living by the sea.'

As if to illustrate my point, through a break in the pale-grey bark of the gum trees, we can see the city of Adelaide and beyond it, the ocean sparkling cool and blue.

'Wow. Do you mind if I stop and take a photo?'

'Course not.'

I manage to pull over on the side of the road near someone's driveway, and turn off the engine. While Ben waits patiently in the passenger seat, I remove my camera bag from the footwell and take a couple of shots.

I climb back into the car, commenting, 'The views up here must be amazing in the winter.'

'In the winter?'

'When the leaves fall off. You can barely see the coast at the moment for all the gum trees.'

'Oh.' I can hear the smile in his voice. 'The leaves don't fall off. They're evergreens.'

'Sorry. What an idiot.'

'You, Lily Neverley, are anything but.'

It's the first time he's said my full name. Warmth radiates through me as I check my mirrors, indicate, and pull out of the driveway and back onto the main road.

We continue to drive along winding roads and through tiny towns and barely-there communities. Occasionally I stop to take a photo of a broken-down car in the middle of someone's backyard, or horses the colour of rust grazing in a yellow paddock. Sometimes we run parallel to fields full of lime-green grapevines stretching out beside us, but we're almost always driving in the shadow of towering eucalyptus trees. At one point we pass a sign for a total fire ban.

'See how some of the gums are black?' Ben says. 'This whole area almost burnt to the ground back in 1983. They called it Ash Wednesday.'

'Do you remember it?' I try to work out how old he would have been.

'I was at primary school in Mount Barker. We were evacuated and I was taken to my nan's house because my mum was out of town on one of her many soirées. It probably would have been safer at school,' he says. 'I still recall Nan filling the bathtub with water and soaking towels in it to place in front of all the doors.'

'That must've been terrifying!'

'It was. A couple of my mates' houses burned down. Luckily I didn't know anyone who'd been killed.'

'How did Josh's mum die?' I ask out of the blue.

'Drink-driving accident.'

'No way?' I glance at him in horror. I thought it must have been cancer or a serious illness. Not an accident. That's one of the worst ways to go. 'What happened to the guy who did it?' I ask.

'She was the one who'd been drinking.'

There is a silence. I'm too shocked to respond.

'She ploughed the car head on into a tree,' he goes on.

'Shit.' My reaction sounds so feeble. 'Was she an alcoholic?'

'No. She'd been on a work day out to some of the wineries. None of her colleagues thought to make her take the bus home.'

'Bloody hell. I can't believe Josh still drinks and drives.'

Ben sighs. 'Neither can I. Take a left here.' I make the turn and then he says, 'Hey, do you fancy a coffee?'

'Sure.' Are you kidding me? That's practically a date!

'Have you been to Hahndorf yet?'

'No. I've barely been anywhere.'

'Come on, then. We have to jump back onto the highway.'

Hahndorf, I soon discover, is a small historic town situated not far from where we live. It was settled by Lutheran migrants and you can see the German influence in the architecture and cuisine of many of the old shops, cafés and restaurants.

'This is a great pub.' Ben nods ahead as we walk towards the Hahndorf Inn. People are seated at wooden bench tables on the pavement drinking beer.

'Would you rather go here?' I ask.

'Would *you*?' he bounces back, before immediately dismissing the idea. 'Actually, no, Michael wouldn't be too impressed if I dragged you to a pub.'

'I *do* drink alcohol, you know,' I say narkily.

'That was clear from the other night,' he replies meaningfully. I'm too annoyed to respond. I didn't want a bloody drink, anyway. I'm learning to drive, for crying out loud!

I've been forgetting it's Christmas in a few days, but the decorations adorning the street lamps and shop windows serve as a frequent reminder. Ben points to an old-fashioned sweet shop across the road.

'We'll have to go in there on the way back. I've been addicted to their sour peach hearts ever since I was a kid.'

Moments later we come to a stop outside the Hahndorf Kaffeehaus.

'Here we are,' he says. 'This place does the best Kitchener buns.'

'What's a Kitchener bun?'

'It's a bit like a doughnut with jam and cream. They do nice ham and cheese croissants, too. Are you hungry?'

'A little.'

'You're not a vegetarian, are you? Great pastries, if you are.'

'No, I'm not. Are *you* a vegetarian?' He strikes me more as a meat-and-two-veg kind of guy.

'Nah.' He shakes his head. 'Do you want to sit outside?'

'Okay.'

I take a seat on the green-picket-fence-enclosed terrace, and gaze down the busy main street. There are two horses pulling a cart filled with people. The horses' reins have been decorated with tinsel.

Ben returns a moment later from ordering our croissants inside and pulls up a chair. He reaches across and fiddles with the salt-shaker. He hasn't shaved this morning and there's sexy sandy-coloured stubble on his jaw. He looks up to catch me staring.

'Who's looking after the joey today?' I ask quickly.

'I dropped her into work on the way to you this morning,' Ben replies, still meeting my gaze with those dark-blue eyes of his. 'Janine'll feed her.'

'We really should give her a name.' I pick up the pepper-shaker and put it down again because I don't want to look like I'm copying him.

'Yeah, I was thinking that. What do you want to call her?'

'Me? Oh, I think you should do the honours.'

'No, no, you found her – *you* should.'

I think aloud. 'We could name her after one of my sisters?'

'Or you?' Ben suggests and my heart jumps.

'Lily?' I choke out.

He shrugs. 'Why not?'

'No, no, that would be too embarrassing.' Although if she were called Lily, he'd think of me every time he attended to her. Hmm . . .

'Kay or Olivia, then?' he continues. Damn. Too late. 'Or both?'

'Kalivia?' I suggest, deadpan.

He grins. 'Olikay?'

'Perhaps we'll flip a coin.'

He gets one out of his pocket as a waitress arrives with our drinks. He waits until she's unloaded them from her tray before continuing. 'Heads for Olivia, tails for Kay?'

'Go for it,' I say, and he neatly flips the coin and catches it, slamming it down on the back on his left hand. He lifts up his right hand so I can peer under it.

'Heads.'

'Olivia it is,' he confirms, putting the coin back into his pocket.

'That's good. So now we have a koala called Cindy and another called Olivia. Two more to go for Kay and me and then all of the Neverley girls are sorted.'

He chuckles as the waitress returns with our food. We both tuck in. The croissant has been gently warmed and the cheese is just starting to melt. Yum. After a while my eyes are drawn to the tinsel sparkling in the afternoon sun. I get out my camera and Ben leans out of the way so I can take a photo. I *so* want to tell him to get back into the picture, but I don't.

'I can't believe it's Christmas Day on Saturday.' I put my camera down on the table. 'It doesn't feel like Christmas here.'

'Doesn't it?'

'No. Christmas should be dark and frosty and full of fairy lights.'

'I guess it's just what you're used to. I'll have you know we do bloody good lights though. You should check out the lights at Lobethal. Maybe I'll take you there on your next driving lesson.'

A whole evening with him? I try not to let my excitement show. 'It's only three nights before Christmas.'

'What are you up to tomorrow night?'

I shrug, feigning nonchalance. 'Nothing much.'

'Tomorrow, then?'

YAY! 'Cool.'

'We could go straight after work.'

'In our *work clothes?*'

He rolls his eyes. 'You can get changed in the staffroom if you really can't bear the shorts.'

'Hey, I'm wearing a skirt today,' I point out.

'I noticed.' He smiles across at me and once again I have to look away so he can't see me blushing.

'I think I should drive so you can fully appreciate the wonder of the spectacle.'

'If you insist.' I sigh theatrically and reach for another one of the sour peach hearts we picked up at the Hahndorf sweet shop yesterday. *Seriously* addictive.

We've been driving around for an hour on my second proper lesson. It's the first time I've driven at night so I was nervous to begin with, but I think it's going pretty well. I've finally got a handle on the clutch so I don't think even Josh could take the mickey too much any more. We didn't go straight after work in the end, because Ben forgot that the lights wouldn't be switched on until later, but he came to the house after dinner and has been directing me on a tour around the hills. We've just been to see a giant rocking horse in a tiny town called Gumeracha where Ben informed me that South Australia also has a huge lobster and a massive galah (a pink and grey parrot – I had to ask). I am really starting to like this freaky part of the world.

'Jesus Christ!' I exclaim, twenty minutes later when we reach Lobethal.

'Using the Lord's name in vain at this time of year?' Ben tuts jokingly.

'Seriously, this is genius. Genius!'

When Mum and I lived with Desmond in East Yorkshire, I remember him taking me to see a house in a place called Driffield which was decorated with the most outrageously brilliant Christmas lights, spilling all the way down the garden. But this, I have to say, takes some beating. It seems as if *all* of the residents in this town have adorned their houses with festive displays, so street upon street is brightly lit by millions of multi-coloured bulbs.

'Look at that one!' I cry at the sight of a full-size Santa on a rooftop, equipped with sleigh and reindeer to boot.

'Take a photo, then.'

'Hold on, hold on.' I wind down the window and hold the camera as steadily as I can so the shot doesn't blur too much.

'Pretty specky, hey?' I assume he means spectacular.

'I bloody love it!'

'I told you we could do lights well here.'

'Say no more on the matter.' I wave my hand at him dramatically.

'Speaking of lights, have you seen the view from Mount Lofty yet?' he asks.

'Mount Lofty, up the hill from where Michael lives?'

'Yes. Up the hill from where *you* live.'

I laugh. 'Yeah, yeah, okay, where *I* live. No, I haven't seen the view from Mount Lofty yet.'

'Right, then, that's the next stop. Do you want to drive?'

'Too bloody right I do.'

'Now you're starting to sound like an Aussie.'

It's nine o'clock by the time we reach Mount Lofty summit. I carefully park the car and we climb out and walk towards the restaurant and gift shop. Ben leads me along the right-hand side of the building and turns back to point down the hill.

'That's Piccadilly Valley down there,' he says. There's a sign next to him and I skimread it to find that the name Piccadilly 'probably' came from the Aboriginal word *Piccodla*. Piccodla made up the eyebrows of Urebilla, the giant whose body formed the mountain ranges.

'That's interesting,' I say. 'And there's me thinking it was named after Piccadilly in London.'

Ben chuckles. 'It probably was. There's a sign outside a church in Piccadilly saying a Mrs Emma Young named it after Piccadilly in London back in 1853.'

'Oh. I think I prefer this explanation.'

'It's certainly more romantic. Can you see your house?'

I follow the line of his finger. 'Which one is it?'

'Here.' He puts his arm around me to draw me closer. It's a perfectly innocent gesture on his part, but it sets my insides on fire. 'There,' he says.

'Oh, yeah,' I reply, actually not seeing the house at all because my head is buzzing too loudly for me to be able to concentrate. He lets me go, but I'm a mess. I know I'll relive this moment over and over again later.

Around the front of the summit building there's a tall white obelisk. It would look striking against the blue sky – I'll have to come back in the daytime to photograph it. And then I see the view.

'Wow!' The city of Adelaide is lit up and sprawled out in front of us.

'Check out the moon!' Ben exclaims.

I turn around to see an *enormous* yellow disc rising above the dark hills in the east.

'That's incredible,' I breathe as Ben straddles a bench seat. I nervously sit opposite him.

'You can see it moving,' he murmurs.

'So you can,' I marvel. 'It's beautiful. I've never seen one like that in England.' I take out my camera and try to hold it steady as I click off a couple of shots. I know full well that I won't be able to do this sight justice.

'I love coming here at night,' Ben says quietly, glancing left towards the city lights, sparkling in the heat haze.

'Is it your second favourite place to go in the city?' I remember that his favourite place is the lily pond in Adelaide's Botanic Gardens.

'It's my *first* favourite place to go in the hills.' He smiles at me in the darkness.

'What, even better than the giant rocking horse?' I attempt to sound mocking.

'I think it even beats the Lobethal lights.'

'Now you're being ridiculous.'

He chuckles and brings his foot up onto the bench, wrapping his arms around his knee. 'So you're starting to like Australia.' It almost isn't a question, but I answer it anyway.

'I am.' Largely thanks to the present company, I manage to refrain from adding.

'I'm happy for you.'

It seems like a slightly strange thing to say.

'Do you reckon your mum is really into Michael?' he asks after a while.

'Definitely,' I reply. 'But she was into all the others, too, so who knows what's going to happen.' *And* I saw her flirting with the butcher the other day.

'I hope for your sake it works out.'

'I only have to get through two years and then I can do what I like anyway.'

'Two years?'

'Yeah. Then I'll be eighteen.'

He stares across at me, and even in the dark I can see the seriousness in his expression. 'You seem so much older than you are.'

'Everyone says that,' I reply nervously.

'It's true.' He sighs. 'You've got your whole life laid out in front of you.'

'So do you, Mr Melodramatic.' I'm trying to lighten him up because his sombre mood is freaking me out a bit. I want to ask him what's wrong, what's *really* wrong, because something is and I so want him to open up to me. 'Have you heard from your mum recently?' I prompt.

'Nope,' he replies sardonically. 'If I'm lucky I'll get a Christmas card in March.'

'Do you miss your nan?'

'All the time.'

'I expect you would, when you're living in her house. You must see her everywhere.' He scratches his head. I hope I'm not annoying him. 'You wouldn't ever think of selling it?' I add.

'Definitely not.' His tone is resolute and I'm almost sorry I asked.

I change the subject. 'Are you working on Saturday?'

'Just in the morning. You know I'm coming to your place for Christmas lunch?'

'*Are* you?' My voice rises an octave.

'Yeah. Michael asked me the other day.'

I suppose he doesn't have any family here. And then it hits me. He clearly doesn't have a girlfriend, either. I cast my eyes heavenward. Thank you, thank you, thank you!

He looks down at his watch. 'I'd better get you home before Michael thinks I've kidnapped you.'

I wish . . .

Michael himself opens the front door as I pull up. Ben's car is parked on the road outside the house, but he follows me up the footpath to chat to Michael.

'What time do you want me on Saturday?' Ben asks.

'One-thirty or thereabouts?' Michael suggests.

'Cool,' Ben replies.

'Your mum has saved you some dinner,' Michael says to me. 'It's in the oven. Go and say hi to her, won't you, love. She's in the living room.'

'Okay.' I drag my heels reluctantly. 'Thanks, Ben. See you tomorrow.'

'No worries,' he replies, as I turn and walk down the corridor in the direction of the kitchen.

'Thanks for doing that for her, mate,' I hear Michael say in a quiet voice.

'No problem,' Ben replies. 'She's a good student.'

Nausea sweeps through me. Are all these driving lessons just a favour for Michael?

'We'll have to pay you next time.' I hear Michael chuckle, but don't wait to hear Ben's reply before hurrying into the kitchen and closing the door.

Josh is getting himself a drink out of the fridge. 'Going out to Stirling tomorrow night. Christmas Eve. Usually pretty lively,' he remarks casually. 'Wanna come?'

'Why not,' I reply, feeling dead inside. I don't even bother to ask if Lou will be joining us.

Chapter 7

I'm still feeling like an idiot when I turn up for work the next morning. Ben isn't in the staffroom and I don't go looking for him in the hospital room. Instead I ask Michael if there's anything I can do to help out with the dingoes.

The dingo enclosure drops away down a steep hill and there's a pond at the bottom. Two high wire fences separate the animals from the public, but there's a locked gate which allows the keepers access. Michael leads me inside and the dingoes get up and stretch their legs before lazily approaching us. Michael pats them like they're pets. They have rusty red-coloured fur and look like small dogs, but they're actually a sub-species of wolf. They can't even bark.

Michael's walkie-talkie crackles and the sound of Ben's voice sends me into a flurry of nerves. He asks where I am.

'I've got her here with me. Do you need her?' Michael replies.

'Dave's coming in for his weekly check. I thought she'd want to be there when he takes a look at the joey.'

Michael glances at me, and I nod. 'She'll be with you in a sec.'

I head back up the hill and out of the enclosure.

106

'There you are!' Ben exclaims when I appear in the hospital room. 'Where were you?'

'I thought I'd see if Michael needed any help with the dingoes today.'

'Oh, right. Had enough of me, have you?' He sounds reasonably jovial, but do I detect a hint of hurt in his voice?

'I don't want to outstay my welcome,' I murmur.

'What's that supposed to mean?'

'Knock, knock, can I come in?'

We both jump as Dave, the vet, interrupts from the doorway. Ben immediately reverts to his normal self. 'Sure, sure, mate, come on in.'

'How's she going?' Dave asks. 'She looks like she's put on weight. That's good. Let's get the scales out.'

'Lily?' Ben points to the cupboard. I take out the scales and place them on the worktop, turning around to see Ben gently lifting Olivia. I can't help it; my heart melts. He glances up to meet my eyes and I find I can't look away.

'That's right, pop her in there,' Dave prompts, and our eyes dart away from each other simultaneously. I avoid looking at Ben again for the rest of the meeting.

I take my lunch outside that day, even though it's 36 degrees and the staffroom is beautifully cool. Wandering down the slope from the café, I sit on the grass under the shade of an enormous eucalyptus. I stare up at the sun through the leaves. The brightness pierces my eyes painfully and I have to look away. Grey, lifeless bark peels off the tree trunk in front of me in strips. It looks as if someone has taken a cheese grater to it and it's eerily beautiful, almost ghostly. I don't feel like eating; I haven't felt like eating for days. My stomach hasn't stopped churning. I hug my knees to my chest and try to find some comfort in the gesture.

He's too old for you.

He would never let himself fall in love with you.

Ever.

A pair of red and blue rosellas fly up and land in the branches of the tree. They distract me from the sound of Ben's footsteps.

'Are you avoiding me?' he asks, as I almost leap out of my skin at the sight of him. 'Sorry, didn't mean to scare you.' He smiles and collapses on the ground beside me. He leans back on the slope, the crispy, brown gum leaves crunching underneath his elbows as he props himself up.

'Well – are you?' He glances across at me, a twinkle in the depth of his blue eyes.

'Am I what?' I manage to ask; it feels as if the temperature has soared way past forty and is still climbing.

'Avoiding me,' he repeats.

'Why would I be avoiding you?'

'Now you're avoiding the question.'

'That's the only thing I'm avoiding.'

'Okay,' he replies bluntly. 'Glad we got that sorted.'

We both fall silent and he stares ahead, as do I.

'Where's your lunch?' I ask after a while, because the quietness is killing me.

'I ate it at eleven o'clock.' At least someone's still got their appetite. 'You should take a photo of that.' He gestures at the tree bark. 'It looks like something you'd take a photo of.'

'Maybe I already have,' I reply childishly.

'Have you?' He raises one eyebrow at me.

'No.'

'Do you want me to go and get your camera for you?'

My lips twitch at the corners. 'Would you? In this heat?'

'Sure.' He starts to get to his feet.

'No, no.' I instinctively reach for his wrist to pull him back down. 'I'm joking,' I add weakly. 'I'll take a photo another time.'

'Okay.' He leans back on his elbows again. I feel like the electrical charge between us has been turned up a notch, but I don't edge away. All of my nerve-endings are bolt upright.

'Why are you angry with me?' he asks gently.

'I'm not angry with you.' But there's no conviction to my voice.

'Yes, you are.' Pause. 'I can take it,' he adds.

I sigh loudly. 'Did Michael ask you to take me for some driving lessons?'

'No!' His reply is indignant.

'Did he ask you to show me around?'

'No! Is that what this is about?'

I shrug, feeling more and more foolish with every word that comes out of my mouth. 'I don't know,' I mutter.

He sits up and leans his elbows on his knees. 'Lily, I like you.' *What?* 'You're a mate.' Oh. 'I'm not being nice to you as some favour to a colleague.'

'Okay,' I reply lamely.

'What are you up to tonight?' He changes the subject.

'Going out with Josh.' I like being able to reply to this question for two reasons. One, I'm relieved I have plans for a change, and two, I know this answer will annoy Ben. I take a strange sense of pleasure from that.

'Oh, right.'

Yep, he's pissed off. Good.

'Where are you going?' he asks.

'Stirling.'

'Doesn't that guy ever go anywhere else?'

Of course he does, and Ben knows it as well as I do. But I don't want to push it any further.

'What about you?' I ask instead.

'Another night in front of the telly, I imagine.'

'Don't party too hard,' I say meanly, and regret it when he abruptly gets up. 'You off?'

'Lunchtime's over,' he says coolly, holding down his hand to me. I take it and he pulls me to my feet. I follow him up the slope, my face burning.

'Have fun with the dingoes. See you tomorrow,' he says with an air of finality as he breaks away to head towards the kangaroos. And quite bizarrely, I feel like I'm going to cry.

That night I find myself in the middle of some surreal game that Josh is playing with Lou. Her Army bloke ex that Shane mentioned to me a few weeks ago is back in town for Christmas, and Lou seems intent on making Josh jealous. He in turn, I suspect, is using me to get back at her. He's been trying to teach me to play pool, and even though my mind is stuck on Ben, it's still kind of nice to feel someone's arms around me as I'm shown how to hold a pool cue and bounce balls off the cushions into pockets.

By ten o'clock Josh has cornered me in a booth while I try to ignore Lou giving us evils from across the bar. Her attempts to flirt with her ex have backfired because he's currently chatting up a petite brunette by the toilets.

'It's weird how our parents hooked up, isn't it?' Josh says, his dark-brown eyes gazing intently into mine.

'Yeah, I suppose so,' I reply offhandedly, and I know that my indifference is driving him mad. He's so used to being the centre of every girl's attention. 'Have you shagged Lou yet?'

He looks taken aback at my direct question. 'No,' he replies, flustered. 'Why would I do that?'

'I thought you were into each other.'

'What gave you that idea?'

'Something Shane said on that night out in Adelaide.'

'What an arsehole,' Josh scoffs. 'She's been around way too much for me.'

'Oh, really?' I smirk. 'I thought *you* were the one who'd been around?'

'Did Shane tell you that, too?'

'No, it wasn't him, actually.'

'Who, then?'

'It doesn't matter. It's true though, isn't it?'

'Girls like guys who are experienced.'

'Do they, now?'

'Don't you?' he challenges me. 'Or haven't you got to third base yet?'

Now he's the one who's smirking and it pisses me off.

I put on a fake pout. 'No. Do you want to deflower me?' His eyes light up and I let out a sharp laugh. 'In your dreams, you sad git. Budge over, I need the loo.'

He doesn't move. He stares at me with defiance and a touch of anger, and I realise that Josh does not like being made a fool out of.

I don't give a toss.

'Move,' I hiss, snapping him out of his mood.

I come out of the toilets a few minutes later to see Josh at the bar, ordering whisky shots. I slip outside unnoticed and call a taxi with the mobile phone Mum lent me. I'll text him on the way home to let him know where I've gone.

'Ho, ho, ho, MERRY CHRISTMAS!'

This is the sound I wake up to on Saturday morning, Michael booming his way down the corridor and banging on every door he passes. I groan and fall out of bed.

My next thought is Josh. Did he make it home okay? There's no way I'm going into his bedroom to check so I pull on my dressing-gown and hurry down the corridor into the living room to look out of the front window. His car is on the driveway. Phew. I wouldn't want that on my conscience.

I've somehow managed to sleep in until ten, so I only have three and a half hours to get through before I see Ben again. Mum wants to do presents as soon as possible. We have to wait another half an hour though before Josh emerges, hungover and dishevelled. He ignores me and I don't particularly care.

Michael gives Mum a watch and she gives him a jumper, which he finds amusing considering it's the middle of summer. I get a bunch of little things like shower gel and body butter from the Body Shop, glitzy earrings that I'll probably never wear, and the new album from my favourite band, Fence.

Mum likes the candle and perfume I got for her, and Michael is excessively delighted with the socks I ended up buying for him. Josh didn't get me anything so he looks a little shamefaced when I hand over a gift-wrapped box of salted macadamia nuts.

I spend ages in the bathroom getting ready and take great care over my outfit, eventually deciding to wear my black skirt again, this time with a purple top. I leave my hair down, but go to the trouble of applying lipgloss, plus mascara to lift my light-brown eyes. Then I wait.

Michael cracks open the bubbly at one o'clock. At one-thirty, Mum tells us to take a seat at the table. I look at her in confusion.

'Aren't we waiting for Ben?'

'He's not coming,' she says, as though she thought I knew.

I feel as if she's kicked me in the stomach. 'Why not?' I glance from her to Michael in a panic. Michael answers.

'One of his koalas was taken ill in the night. Ben didn't want to leave it.'

'Was it Olivia?'

'I don't know.'

'But . . . but he can't miss Christmas!' I cry, utterly and irrationally distraught.

'He doesn't care, love.' Michael waves me away.

'But Mum's made a turkey for him!' Even to me, this sounds like a ludicrous thing to say.

'Maybe we can save him some.'

'Can we take it to him later? Today – after lunch?' I ask hopefully, my voice squeaking more and more with each question.

'Erm . . .'

'Please? Will you give me a lift?' I beg.

'Oh, Lily, would you stop going on?' Mum interjects with annoyance, but Michael concedes.

'No, it's fine.'

'I want to check that the koala is alright. It might be Olivia,' I add, ignoring Mum as she tuts and rolls her eyes. And of course, I *do* want to make sure Olivia is alright. She should have been my primary concern and I'm instantly ashamed at myself that she wasn't.

Lunch drags by. By the time Michael reaches for the bottle of bubbly to top up his glass for the third time, I can't stop myself from speaking out.

'Should you be drinking that if you're going to drive me to Ben's?'

Michael immediately looks sheepish and takes a sip of water instead.

'You know, you *could* catch a taxi,' Mum points out.

'I'll never get one on Christmas day!' I cry.

'Why the hell do you want to go over to his place?' Josh butts in.

'I want to check on the koala,' I reply, giving him a pointed stare. 'You know, the one whose mother you killed.'

'Lily . . .' Mum warns.

I turn to Michael. 'Do you want to take me now? Then you can have a drink. Ben will give me a lift home.'

'Well, if you're sure,' he says.

Mum stands up wearily and smoothes down her blonde hair. 'I'll get a plate together.'

Fifteen minutes later I'm in the front seat of the car nursing a plate of hot food covered over with aluminium foil.

'He'll really appreciate this,' I say to Michael.

'He sounded very pleased on the phone,' he agrees. 'It was nice of you to think of him.'

I don't say anything, but joy is bubbling over inside me at this turn of events. I glance out of the window as we pull up outside Ben's place. I was too busy concentrating on reversing out of his driveway when I last came here in daylight, but now I can see that his quaint colonial-style house is nestled in amongst the trees. Large round purple flowers have been planted around the front porch.

'He's been a bit lonely without Charlotte here,' Michael adds.

'Who? Oh, is that his nan?' It's not a very old lady-ish sounding name.

'No.' Michael laughs. 'Charlotte. His girlfriend – fiancée, rather.'

My heart stops. Literally – stops.

'I beg your pardon?' The blood drains from my face.

'Here's our man.' Michael nods past me and I turn to see a gorgeous, smiling Ben standing in the doorway. 'Have a good time, love. Hope the joey's okay.'

I'm frozen to my seat, staring out of the window in shock at the person who I now feel absolutely certain is the love of my life. His eyes meet mine and his smile wavers.

I come to life and open up the door, struggling to carry the plate as I step onto the steep incline of the driveway. Ben starts as though coming to my aid, but I find my footing and walk towards the door, my eyes on the pavement. I glance up to register the confusion on his face as he steps aside and waves to Michael. I look down again as I pass through the door. His feet are bare.

'Are you okay?' he asks, closing the door behind me.

'How's Olivia?' I blurt out.

'She's fine, don't worry. It was another koala at the park. I've given her an injection of antibiotics, so we should see an improvement in the morning.' Keepers rarely call the vet unless it's an emergency. They administer medications, take blood and complete all the medical recording. They even assist with operations at the park on occasion.

'I'm going back to check on her in a couple of hours,' Ben continues. 'It's okay,' he stresses, putting his hand on my arm. He obviously assumes this is the reason for my catatonic expression. 'Come through. Olivia's in the living room if you want to check her over for yourself.'

I lead the way then turn back to pass him the plate. 'I brought you this,' I mutter.

'Excellent, thanks. And I got you this.' He reaches behind himself to take a red-and-white striped parcel from the top of a cabinet. He hands it over, grinning. I didn't buy him anything in the end. I was worried it would make my feelings for him appear too obvious.

'What is it?' I ask. My heart is still in my throat. I feel like I could choke to death on it.

'Open it and see.' His smile falls from his face once more at my appearance. 'Are you okay?' he asks again.

I sit on the sofa in a daze and carefully open the present, not wanting to tear the wrapping paper for who-knows-what reason. Six rolls of film spill out. My eyes fill with tears and my face crumbles.

'Lily, what's wrong?' he asks in horror, taking a seat next to me and putting his warm hand on my arm. I shrug him off and immediately regret it. Burying my head in my hands I try so hard not to sob. I desperately want to know the truth about whoever this Charlotte person is, but I just don't know how to ask, especially not now that he's seen my reaction. I feel like such a stupid, silly little girl.

'Please tell me,' he urges quietly.

I shake my head violently from side to side, wanting him to disappear for a few minutes so I can get my act together. I so wish I had my licence so I could drive far, far away from here.

'Look, she's okay. She's over there.'

I glance up to follow his extended finger in the direction of Olivia, snuggled up and asleep in a box by the heater. It may be hot outside, but it's still cool within these thick stone walls. I nod.

'That's not it though, is it? Is it your dad? Kay? Olivia? Nothing's happened to the baby, has it?'

'No, no, no.' I avoid his gaze. 'Honestly, I don't want to talk about it.'

'I've never seen you like this. Is it Dan? Shannon?'

As if I give a shit about my ex-boyfriend and one-time best friend now. 'No.'

'Do you want a drink?' he asks hopefully.

Actually, all I really want is for him to take me home again so I can cry my heart out in the peace and quiet of my own bedroom. But that would be even more inexplicable, so I reply, 'Yes, please.'

'Good.' He stands up, looking relieved. 'Coke? Lemonade?'

'Lemonade, please.'

I cast my gaze around the room when he's gone, looking for anything that would give me a clue about this absent girlfriend. There are no photos of her that I can see, although I suppose there could be one lurking in his bedroom. I wonder what she looks like. Wait, could she be dead? My heart lifts and I know how awful it is to have that reaction, but maybe that's what Michael meant about him being, what did he say? 'A bit lonely.' Hmm. Not exactly the phrasing you'd use to describe someone who's lost his partner to the Other Side. I wonder what she looks like . . .

Ben returns, his expression grave. 'Nothing's happened with Josh, has it?' I take my drink from him and almost spill it.

'Hell, no!'

'Oh, okay. Good.' He laughs awkwardly.

'Oh, Ben.' I sigh and turn to put my glass on a side-table, feeling a bit more like my old self. 'Pass me a coaster, would you?' He takes one from the table at his side of the sofa and hands it over. I turn to face him. He's still looking confused and I don't know what comes over me, but I meet his eyes steadily and on impulse ask him outright.

'Who's Charlotte?'

'Charlotte?' He shifts uncomfortably. 'She's . . . er . . . she's my girlfriend.'

I don't know why he finds it so hard to say this out loud, but he's clearly ill at ease.

'Where is she?'

'England,' he answers, looking down at his mug and not meeting my eyes.

'England? Where in England?'

'London.'

I find myself laughing bitterly. 'You've got a girlfriend – or is it *fiancée* – who lives in the city I've just left, and you never thought to tell me?'

'I don't know, we haven't really talked about stuff like that.'

'Are you kidding me?' I cry. 'I told you how my boyfriend shagged my best friend right in front of me and you didn't even think to mention you have a *girlfriend*? Why not?'

I'm speaking to him as if I'm his equal. With confidence and as if I deserve these answers. The fact that I'm a sixteen-year-old schoolgirl has flown right out of my mind.

'Look at me!' I cry.

He raises two grave eyes to meet mine and we stare at each other for a long time. And then I crumble again and start to sob. He doesn't touch me, doesn't comfort me. Eventually I glance up to see him with his head in his hands at my side. He's a man, a grown man, but he looks lost. I put my hand on his back and it snaps him out of his reverie. I take my hand away as he looks at me, utter despair on his face.

'Say something,' I plead.

'I don't know what to say.' His voice is strained and it hits me that – *oh no!* – he's embarrassed for me. I've made a complete and utter fool out of myself.

'I want to go home.' I sound even younger than I am.

He gets to his feet. 'I'll give you a lift.'

We don't speak on the journey. I stare out of the window, mortified to my core. I don't know how I'll ever face him again. Back at the house, I open the car door before he's pulled to a complete stop. He reaches across to grab my hand and I snatch it away in shock.

'Lily, I'm sorry,' he says, anguish in his voice.

I don't say anything, just climb out, slam the door and run up the footpath as fast as my stupidly high-heel-clad feet can carry me.

Chapter 8

I feign a dodgy stomach and spend the rest of the afternoon in my room, trying to forget the day's events and musing about whether a large brick to the head would help me permanently erase my embarrassment. There is no way I'm going to work tomorrow. I'm actually toying with the idea of quitting altogether.

By early evening I drag myself out of my bedroom in need of distraction, hoping that there will be something good on TV. Mum, Michael and Josh are slumped on the sofas tucking into turkey leftovers.

'There you are, love!' Michael exclaims. He and Mum squash up closer together on the sofa so I can squeeze in. Josh turns up the TV. There's a Tom Cruise movie on the box.

'Are you feeling better?' Mum asks.

'Not really. I don't think I'll be going into work tomorrow,' I tell Michael, preparing the way for my absenteeism.

'See how you feel in the morning,' he annoyingly replies. 'How was Olivia?' he adds.

'She's fine. Another koala at the park was ill,' I reply, staring at Tom mixing cocktails in front of us.

'So this Olivia then, you called her after your half-sister?' Mum asks.

'Yes,' I reply bluntly. I don't need any of the usual grief I get from Mum about my dad's offspring.

'That's nice,' she says in a restrained voice, crossing her long, lean legs in front of her on the coffee table. I notice she has a tan. Probably spending her days in the garden, sunbathing. She continues, 'When you two talk about "the joey" I always picture a kangaroo in my head. I didn't know koala babies were called joeys, too.'

'Mmm.'

'How was Ben?' Michael asks me casually.

'Fine.' And then it occurs to me that I could get some answers here and now, if I play it right. 'I think you're spot on though. He misses Charlotte.'

'Who's Charlotte?'

Good work, Mum.

'His fiancée. She's a Pommie. Went back home a couple of months ago,' Michael explains.

'Oh, that must be hard,' Mum says. 'We know what it's like conducting a long-distant relationship, don't we, love?' She grins at Michael and I want to prod her to make sure she doesn't change the subject.

'He'll be with her soon enough,' Michael declares.

Bile rises up in my throat. I try to sound indifferent as I ask, 'When's he going over there again?' *Unless she's coming here instead.*

'Gosh, it's only a few weeks away now,' Michael replies.

So he is leaving. No, please, no.

'We'll miss him at work.'

121

'His fiancée will be pleased though,' Mum says, saving me from trying to formulate a response. 'When are they getting married?'

'As soon as possible, I think. Poor girl's had to make all the arrangements herself.'

'That's no good,' Mum says disapprovingly.

'It's not like they had a choice,' Michael goes on. 'Her visa ran out and she wanted to get married at home so she went back to the UK to wait for him to get his bits and pieces sorted.'

'Can you guys shut it?' Josh says rudely. 'Or go into the other room. I'm trying to watch telly here.'

'Sorry, son,' Michael booms, nodding towards the TV screen. 'What have we missed?'

I spend the next day in bed, and don't even have to pretend to be ill. When Michael gets home that night, I'm wondering how I can stay off another day. I'm not ready to face Ben again. I plan to skip work just like I skipped school when all that Shannon/Dan stuff hit the pan.

'I hope you're feeling better, darl, because we've got some understaffing issues at the moment.'

My heart sinks. 'Really?'

'Yep. Two of the team have come down with a weird summer flu strain, another is on annual leave and even Ben's got tomorrow off, so we could do with an extra pair of hands.'

I don't hear the last ten words because 'Ben's got tomorrow off' is all I need to know.

'I am feeling a bit better, thank you,' I say. 'I'm sure I'll make it in. I just hope I don't relapse,' I add, keeping all bases covered.

I'm on edge the next day at work, half-expecting to see Ben walk around the corner at any given moment. He doesn't, and as the day progresses, I start to relax. At lunchtime I wander down to visit Roy the roo, and as I approach I see a family standing in the shade near a group of kangaroos. I smile as a girl of about twelve excitedly points to a joey's foot poking out of the top of its mother's pouch. And then I watch, horrified, as the little girl's father creeps in and gives the foot a tug, trying to pull out the joey. The alarmed kangaroo mother jumps up and hops away, and the whole family bursts into laughter. I stare at them, disgusted. I hate people like this. They turn to go and spy me standing there.

'You shouldn't do that,' I say, as the smiles drop from their faces.

'Er, sorry.' The father looks suitably ashamed of himself. At least that's something.

'Come on, let's go and see the emus,' the mum says, and the family scurry away from me in embarrassment.

I sigh and scan the paddock for Roy. As soon as I sit by his side in the shade of a tree my spirits lift. I'm so lucky to have this job. I don't want to quit. I don't want to run away this time.

Unsurprisingly, my bravado doesn't last until the following morning when Michael and I set off for work. I'm trying to come up with ways to avoid Ben all day, but he's right there in the staffroom when we arrive.

'How was your day off?' Michael asks him, leaving me to attend to our teas in peace. I'm grateful to have something to do.

'Yeah, alright, thanks,' Ben replies.

'Do you want one?' I find myself asking Ben. *I will not be bowed by you!* And then I nearly crack up giggling at the sound of my own melodrama.

'Er, sure,' Ben replies, looking taken aback at the sight of me on the verge of hysteria.

That's right, buster, I say to myself. I will *not* be bowed by you!
I'm still fighting off the urge to laugh when I pass him his tea.

'Thanks.'

'Cheers!' I say chirpily and chink mugs with him and Michael.
They look at each other like they think I've gone mad.

'Might pop outside for some fresh air,' I tell them, swiftly
making an exit.

I take a deep breath and exhale loudly as I wander down the
path away from the staffroom, my mug of hot tea still in my hand.
I pause in front of some birdcages and stare through the wire at
a Bush Stone-curlew. Its huge, inquisitive-looking eyes stare back
at me. There's something almost childlike about these birds.

Approaching footsteps make me turn my head towards the
curve in the path and my hands begin to tremble as I see Ben
round the corner. I quickly force myself to take a sip of my tea to
give myself something to do.

'Hey,' he says.

'Hello.'

'How's it going?' To his credit, he's trying to sound upbeat.

'Fine.'

'Are you coming to help out with the koalas today?'

'Um, not sure.'

'Okay.' He presses his forehead with his thumb. 'I could do
with the help. Two of the koalas are on the Heinz diet at the
moment.'

That means they're underweight. We feed them pumpkin and
sweetcorn baby food – the one in a can – when their weight continues to fall.

'Oh, right.'

'Lily, I—'

'Yes, what the hell,' I interrupt. 'Count me in.'

He smiles with relief. 'Cool. Good. See you there in a minute, yeah?'

'As soon as I finish my tea.' Slurp.

'Cool,' he repeats.

And then he's gone. I sigh heavily.

As the day goes on, the awkwardness between us begins to fade. Humiliation had temporarily dulled my feelings for him, but as my embarrassment fades, the pain in my heart starts to return. I can't believe he's going to the other side of the world to get married to someone else. I must try harder not to think about it.

'What are you doing on New Year's Eve?' Ben asks as we wander back to the staffroom at five o'clock.

'I don't know yet. Josh and his mates are going to a club in Adelaide, but I don't want to risk getting asked for ID. They're a bit tighter on that down in the city.'

'Mmm, they are.'

I wonder how old his girlfriend is?

'What about you?' I ask.

'I don't know yet either, which is a bit crap considering this is the Millennium. My mates have all had their plans sorted for about a year, but I don't know . . . I hate clubs.'

'Do you?'

'Yeah. They're too smoky and crowded. Full of pricks,' he says, and I laugh. 'Sorry, I don't mean Josh,' he adds.

'Yeah, you do.'

He smirks. Then tells me: 'I'll probably just climb up to Mount Lofty and watch the fireworks from there.'

'On your own?' I ask in disbelief.

'Why not?'

'On New Year's Eve? To see in the year 2000? You can't do that!' I exclaim.

'Yes, I can.'

'Saddo.'

'Maybe I'll take Olivia with me.'

'That's even sadder.'

'Oh, well.' He shrugs.

We get through the next two days like this and before I know it, it's Friday night and New Year's Eve. I've reluctantly given up on the clubbing idea, and therefore I have to forgo seeing in the new millennium with people roughly my own age. The only option I have left is offered by Michael. He has some friends who live in the city, so the plan is to crash at theirs for the night so he and Mum can drink themselves silly, and then we'll all wander over to the park to watch the fireworks at midnight. I can't quite believe I'm going to spend the last night of 1999 with my mum, but I'm hardly going to climb up to Mount Lofty like some sad stalker in pursuit of Ben. However much I'd like to.

Michael's friends, Pete and Gwen, turn out to be great fun. They live in College Park, not far from the Botanic Gardens, and their house is party central. The front and back gardens are lit with thousands of fairy lights and Pete has the cocktails going from the get-go while Gwen dishes out a vast array of mouth-watering canapés. The time flies by as I chat to all manner of wacky and wonderful people, and pretty soon Pete's leading a gang of us out of the house and down the street and I'm being caught up in the moment as I sing along drunkenly with the rest of them.

The park is packed – there's barely space to put down a tissue, let alone a picnic blanket – so we stand where we can

126

and look up as multi-coloured explosions light up the sky above us. When it's over and everyone has given up hugging and kissing perfect strangers and has taken to dancing on the streets instead, I find myself in the middle of the throng, looking back up at the hills and thinking of Ben. I'd give anything to be with him right now. An ache starts up deep in the pit of my stomach and I look around for Pete to see if I can nab a swig of his vodka.

The next morning the whole house is dead to the world. These adults are unbelievable – they party harder than any teenager I've ever known. I make my way down the streamer-strewn corridor to the living room at the back of the house and turn on the television, keeping the sound down low so as not to bother the sleeping bodies of people who didn't quite manage to make it home last night. My head is pounding as I collapse on the sofa and dig into a bowl of leftover peanuts. It's almost midnight in England and I want to see what I missed out on. Fireworks burst off dozens of boats lined up along the River Thames, and the London Eye is lit up with explosion after glittering explosion. The banks of the river and bridges are absolutely heaving with hundreds of thousands of revellers.

It's bizarre – but strangely addictive – to see people celebrating when we did all of that last night. I'm glued to the television as more countries see in the year 2000 and eventually the sleeping bodies around me begin to stir.

Later that morning I leave the hungover crowd on the sofas and take a walk through the park with my camera. I snap away as attendants clear up the mess from the night and I take close-ups of foil confetti sparkling in the hot sun. Eventually I find myself in the Botanic Gardens at the lily pond.

I haven't allowed myself to properly dwell on Ben all week and I haven't cried for days. He's done the decent thing by me and has acted like business as usual so I'm hoping he's on his way to forgetting about my strange behaviour at his house. I've tried to think of ways to explain it, but can't come up with a decent enough lie so I know I have to leave it.

Now though, sitting here at his favourite place in the city, a wave of sadness and grief pulses through me. He's the only person in this whole country who I really want to spend time with. When he goes, it's all gone. I'm over Josh – that was just a fleeting attraction – and I have no friends of my own. Ben looked out for me, he listened to me, and now he's leaving.

Tears well up in my eyes and I surreptitiously brush them away, aware of strangers lazing in the sun nearby. In my peripheral vision I see a man with sandy blond hair and my heart stops, but I realise almost immediately that it's not Ben. What would I do if it were? If he sat down beside me now, would I be able to hide the pain I'm in? Would I tell him how I feel? I honestly don't think I'd be able to stop myself and oh . . . that would be so humiliating. I wouldn't have the strength of character to see out the rest of my summer at work – I'd have to quit immediately.

The thought of all this brings my tears to a halt and I suddenly feel full of determination to sort myself out. I can't ever let him see what he means to me. Maybe I need to find someone else to take my mind off him. Shane is nice, but no, I don't fancy him. I don't fancy any of Josh's friends. It would be good to meet Shane's sister though. What was her name again? Sammy, or something like that? Tammy, that's it. She's just broken up with her boyfriend; perhaps we could go out on the town together and take our minds off our heartbreak. Not that I plan on telling her about Ben. I'll never tell anyone about him.

I'm still full of resolve when Josh tells me he's popping into Hahndorf that night for a couple of drinks. Michael and Mum are nursing hangovers and can't quite believe we'd consider going out again, but it's Saturday night and quite frankly, I think I need to spend at least a few hours of 1 January 2000 with people my own age.

'Who else is going?' I ask when he mentions it.

'The usual gang,' he replies. 'Are you wondering about anyone in particular?'

'No, not really.'

'Good.'

My curiosity gets the better of me. 'Why?'

'Just checking,' he says.

'What are you checking about?' I'm a little irritated now.

'I'm making sure you're not wanting anyone in particular to go tonight.'

'Anyone in particular like whom?' I demand to know.

'Are you getting changed or what?' He gives me a pointed stare.

I glance down at my shirt with its tomato ketchup stain on the front. 'Er, yes.'

'Wear something nice for me,' he says with a look that would make most girls go weak at the knees. But it has no effect on me; I just ignore it and head down the corridor to my bedroom. I'm absentmindedly unbuttoning my shirt and removing a skirt from the cupboard when out of the corner of my eye I see Josh standing in the doorway.

'Josh!' I pull my shirt closed over my bra.

'What? It's not like I haven't seen girls naked before,' he says flippantly.

'But you haven't seen ME naked before! GET OUT!' I storm over and slam the door in his face.

Despite that little episode, I *do* make an effort to get dressed up that night, putting on make-up and high heels so I look older than my years. I'm steeling myself for a night out socialising. I don't really feel like it, but I need to get my head into making new friends and moving on.

We arrive in Hahndorf to find Shane, Brian and Alex sitting at a wooden bench table out the front.

'Hey guys!' I say brightly.

'Happy New Year,' Shane responds, patting the bench space next to him.

'Lily,' Josh snaps, grabbing hold of my arm. 'Are you going to go to the bar?'

'*You* go to the bar, mate!' Brian exclaims. 'Don't be a cheapskate.'

Josh grudgingly lets go of my arm and I slide in next to Shane, bemused.

'What's everyone having?' Josh asks.

Beer, beer, beer, cider.

He sets off to the bar with a foul look on his face. He doesn't think I fancy Shane, does he? So what if I do? Obviously I don't, but what's Josh's problem?

'Did you all have a good time last night?' I ask the three guys sitting around the table.

'Yeah, it was cool,' Alex replies.

'How many girls did you snog?'

Brian sniggers, but it is Alex who replies. 'Brian got his tongue down three.'

'I beat Josh for a change,' Brian comments.

'What was it, a competition?' I ask sarcastically.

'Yeah, it was actually,' Shane replies. 'They each bet a tenner.'

'Weren't you in on it?' I ask him.

'Nah,' he replies, giving me a meaningful look. 'I'm not into that sort of thing.'

Oh, shit. Don't fancy me. I'm not interested, I'm really not. Why do blokes have to complicate things?

Josh returns with our drinks and takes a seat next to me. He seems to have perked up from his earlier mood.

'I'm hearing about your snogging competition,' I tell him, raising my eyebrows.

He smirks. 'Brian won. I wasn't trying hard enough.'

'What did you get up to last night?' Shane asks me.

I fill them in and they can't quite believe it when I say I enjoyed myself.

'Don't worry, you can make up for it now,' Alex says, flashing a look at Shane.

Bollocks. How can I get out of this one?

Half an hour later of feeling Shane's thigh and arm pressing into me, I decide to extricate myself and take a trip to the ladies.

The pub is heaving, full of people in high spirits, delighted that the world didn't implode from the ludicrously over-hyped Millennium Bug. I almost feel a spring in my step as I weave through the crowds to the toilets at the back. It's impossible not to soak up the positive energy of those around me. Above the racket I hear my name being shouted and I glance over my shoulder towards the bar.

Who is that? It's Dave the vet! I beam and wave – and then his companion spins around to see me and I realise that it's Ben. My head goes fuzzy, my heart jumps, I almost trip over my own feet and then I'm turning in their direction, trying to keep the smile on my face and the confidence in my walk.

'Hello,' I beam.

'Hi!' Ben exclaims.

'I thought it was you,' Dave says.

'You thought right.' I keep my voice upbeat. 'What are you guys doing here?'

'Having a few drinks. Trying to make up for last night.' Dave grins.

'What happened last night?' I ask.

'Not a lot. This one spent it up at Mount Lofty all by himself.' He indicates Ben. 'And I spent it with the wifey in front of the telly.'

'What a couple of losers,' I joke.

'We know,' Dave replies. 'What about you?'

'I'm here with some friends,' I say.

'Josh?' Ben asks.

'Yep.'

'Josh,' he says tellingly to Dave.

'Yep, Josh,' I confirm. 'And some others.'

'Sit down.' Dave reaches for a recently-vacated stool. 'Have a drink with us.'

'I was on my way to the loo,' I reveal.

'We'll keep your seat warm for you until you get back.' He puts his hand on the stool.

'Okay.' I cast a hesitant look at Ben. His deep-blue eyes flicker towards mine and away again, but he doesn't say anything. 'Back in a tick.' I walk off, thoughts ricocheting around my head. Fuck, fuck, fuck, fuck, fuck!

Ben . . .

Oh, I fancy him.

No, you do not! I practically shout at myself. *Enough! Move on!* I sternly keep repeating this as I go to the toilet, but I reapply my lip-gloss before returning to the bar. I'm only human, right?

'Here you go, nice and warm,' Dave says, removing his large hand from the top of the padded stool.

'Thanks.' I sit down.

'Can I get you a drink?' he asks.

I check Ben's expression, wondering if he's going to make some wisecrack about underage drinking, but he's staring into his glass of – what is it?

'Thanks,' I tell Dave. 'I'm on the cider.'

He turns to get the barman's attention.

'What are you drinking?' I ask Ben.

'Whisky,' he replies, swirling the ice around in his glass.

'Straight?' I check.

'Yeah.' His eyes meet mine and he grins cheekily.

'Ooh, hardcore,' I tease, as a flutter goes through me.

'How was last night?' he asks, staring at me directly.

'It was strangely good fun. Much better than I thought it would be.'

'Why?'

'They were all oldies.'

He laughs and shakes his head.

'I went to the lily pond this morning,' I tell him. 'Well, afternoon.'

'Did you?'

'Yeah.'

Pause.

'Here you go,' Dave says, handing me my drink. 'Cheers.' He chinks my glass with his and Ben follows suit. 'Happy New Year,' Dave booms loudly, and it occurs to me he's been here drinking for quite some time.

'I didn't know you were married,' I say to him.

'Yep. Five years and counting.'

'Blimey. Five years. How old were you when you got married, then?' I flash a look at Ben.

'What was I?' Dave asks his mate. 'Twenty-three?'

'Something like that.' Ben looks amused. 'Lily thinks we *country folk* get married and have, what do you call them – sprogs? – before our twenty-first birthdays.'

Dave chortles and I giggle because I've been caught out.

'We haven't moved on to the sprogs stage yet,' he tells me.

'Give it time,' I say ominously.

'What about you, Lily? Have you got a boyfriend?'

'Nope!' I reply. 'Young, free and single, that's me.'

'Good. That's the way it should be,' Dave decides happily. 'Right – I'm off to the gents. Don't let anyone nick my seat,' he commands us.

An atmosphere settles over Ben and me the moment he leaves.

'Josh and the lads will be wondering where I am,' I comment.

'Don't get in the car with him tonight.' Ben's tone is insistent.

'Why?' I ask boldly. 'Are you offering to give me a lift home instead?'

'I'm catching a taxi.'

'Of course you are.' I don't know where my bitterness is coming from. 'Don't worry, *Dad*,' I add cruelly. 'I'll catch a taxi too if I have to.'

Just then, the barman materialises in front of us. 'Same again,' Ben says. 'You alright with that?' He nods to my half-full drink.

'I'm fine,' I reply sarkily. 'Wouldn't want to get you into trouble with Michael.'

'Don't be like that,' he says quietly, and I drag my reluctant eyes to meet his. The second they do, a shock zips through me. I know I should look away, but I can't. He's locked my gaze so intensely that we are like two magnets, drawn to each other.

I love you. You know it. And you feel something for me, too.

I'm overcome with a powerful urge to kiss him. He's still staring into my eyes and it feels as if whole minutes have passed, not mere seconds.

'What have I missed?'

Our eyes dart away from each other as Dave re-emerges.

'Where's my stool?' he asks accusingly. 'Did you let someone take my seat?'

'Aah, sorry, mate,' Ben apologises.

'Here, you can have mine.' I leap off my stool and push it towards him.

'You going already?' Dave asks, disappointed.

'I'd better get back to the others,' I murmur.

'Leave us oldies to it,' he says humorously. I glance at Ben and feel that force pulling me in again.

Then Dave clumps me on the back, knocking me out of myself. 'Happy New Year, Lily!' he shouts drunkenly. 'Good to see you again!'

'You too,' I reply, my smile wavering. 'Bye.' I glance at Ben and hurriedly drop my eyes to the ground. My feet take a step towards the door, but suddenly his fingers are touching mine.

'Don't let him drive you home,' he repeats with urgency.

I shake my head and reply quite seriously, 'I won't.'

And then I'm gone, my fingers tingling, my face burning, and every nerve-ending in my body standing on its end.

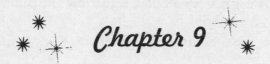

Chapter 9

Ben makes love to me that night, in my dreams. His warm, strong arms encircle me and it's hot, intense, our bodies moving together in a perfect dance. And then I wake up, shaking and feverish.

It's not just me; his eyes told me that last night. There is no moving on from this. I need to do something because I know he won't.

I have to get through a torturous Sunday on my own before I can go into work again, and on Monday the disappointment is crippling beyond belief as I realise it's his day off. There are no guarantees that he'll be in on Tuesday, and when there's no sign of him in the staffroom I head to the hospital room with a heavy heart. Olivia only spent her first week at home with Ben. Now she's been relocated here, but he's still her primary carer. I push open the door and come face to face with him.

'Hey,' he says, avoiding my eyes. 'Just getting her settled.'

'How is she?' I ask, shifting from foot to foot awkwardly.

He glances at the koala amongst the blankets. 'She's good.'

'Is she still crying at night, do you think?'

He shakes his head. 'I doubt it. Not much, anyway.' He turns back to me and nods towards the door I'm blocking. 'I'd better get on.'

I step to one side and he starts to walk past. 'Don't you want any help today?' I blurt after him.

He hesitates and turns around, registering the panic on my face.

'Of course.' He tries to sound enthusiastic. 'Let's do the koala check.'

I follow him out of the door feeling very unsure of myself, chasing after him like a small child as he walks two paces in front of me.

'I caught a taxi home on Saturday,' I call when I can bear the silence no longer.

'That's good,' he replies over his shoulder in a non-committal voice.

'What time did you stay until?' I prompt.

'Not long. I thought I'd better get home and phone Charlotte.'

There. He's said it. He's said her name. He's pushing me out and bringing her in. And I feel like he's knifed me through the heart.

Just then, Ben comes to an abrupt halt and puts his hand out to hold me back, saying, 'Watch out – here's a bilby.' A small animal hops out from the undergrowth. It looks a little like a mini-kangaroo crossed with a rat, with big ears and a long snout. I'm still in shock from the mention of The Name as we stand and watch the fluffy grey creature sniff at the paving stones.

A memory comes back to me of the night I turned up at his house with Olivia. He'd been on the phone. It must have been to *her*.

'When do you leave?' I ask solemnly, focusing my gaze on the bilby and trying not to think about the warmth of his body heat right beside me.

'Week after next.' I can barely hear him.

'Where will you work?'

He clears his throat and turns up the volume. 'London Zoo.'

'I can't imagine you working in a zoo.'

'Why not?'

'It doesn't seem, I don't know – *real* enough for you.'

'I worked at Sydney Zoo before coming here. It'll be a nice change.'

The bilby hops off into the undergrowth again, and Ben continues to walk along the winding asphalt footpath.

I take a deep breath and hurry after him. 'How did you meet her?'

He shrugs. 'She was travelling in Australia. She worked in the café here for a while.'

'How long is a while?'

'About three months.'

And she got his attention, just like that. *I bet she's beautiful.*

'Is your mum going over for the wedding?' I will the pain to dull.

He snorts and glances at me. 'What do *you* think?'

'Silly question. Dave?'

'Dave's coming,' he confirms with a curt nod. 'And Katherine, his wife.'

'When are you getting married?'

'March.'

'March? That's so soon!' I exclaim, feeling a little breathless now.

He looks at me sharply. 'Why do you think it's too soon?'

'You will have only just got there.' I'm reeling. I didn't think it was so . . . I don't know, definite. 'What if you don't like England? Don't you want to give yourself time to settle in?'

His footsteps seem to slow a little. 'I thought it would be fine.'

Thought? Strange wording. 'I didn't feel like I was rushing it when we decided,' he clarifies.

'And you feel like you're rushing it now?'

'That's not what I said.' *But it's what you meant.* His pace quickens once more. 'Anyway, it's all sorted now. Dave and Katherine have got their tickets booked.'

'Dave and Katherine can change their flights,' I say seriously.

'It'll be fine,' he insists, nodding towards the koala lofts we're approaching. 'I'll go and get started. Can you fetch the pad from the office?'

And that's the end of the discussion.

That night, Josh and I decide to go out for a bite to eat in Hahndorf. He'd come home and demanded to know what there was for dinner because Michael and my mum had gone out, and I'd grunted at him: 'I don't know, I'm not your mother.' Needless to say, I felt shit enough to want to make up for it.

It's a cooler evening than usual for this time of the year so we decide to sit inside at the Hahndorf Inn. Josh taps his tanned fingers on the table impatiently as I peruse the lengthy menu at leisure. Finally he slaps some money down in front of me.

'I'm going to the loo. Get me the chicken schnitzel, would you?'

We're sitting in the bar area because it has more atmosphere than the restaurant, but it has no waitress service, so once decided, I head up to place our order. Josh didn't specify a drink, so I opt for two lemon squashes because I refuse to deal with the drinking and driving issue tonight.

I've handed over the money to the landlord and I'm in the process of slipping the change back into my purse when something makes me look to my left, to the other side of the wraparound bar. Ben is sitting there, staring into his drink. I'm rooted to the spot and in that moment he looks up and his expression must mirror mine before his face breaks into a wavering smile. I walk around the bar to where he's sitting.

'Hello,' I say, hoping my voice doesn't shake.

'Hello.'

'What are you doing here?'

He lifts up his drink by way of explanation.

'Is Dave here?' I look around, but can't see him.

'No. Just me.'

'In a bar? On your own!' I exclaim. 'Ben, I didn't think you were the solo drinking type. You *are* drinking, aren't you?' I peer into his glass. It looks like whisky again.

He takes a swig, but doesn't reply to my question. Instead, he asks, 'Are Michael and Cindy here?'

'No, just Josh.'

'You're out alone with Josh?' He frowns at me.

'We're on the lemon squashes, don't worry.'

'That's not what I was worried about.'

'What were you worried about?' I give him a cheeky grin, but he doesn't smile back. I suddenly feel full of a strange confidence. I don't know what it is about him that makes me feel so up and down. 'Come on, Norman No Mates, come and join us.'

'I don't want to interrupt anything.'

'Don't be ridiculous,' I scoff, tugging him off his chair. 'Come on.'

Ben allows himself to be dragged reluctantly because he does-n't have much choice. I budge up the bench seat so there's room for Ben beside me, but he slides in opposite me instead. Josh returns to the table and I beam up at him.

'I brought Ben over to say hi.'

'Alright?' Josh offers a lame smile and sits down next to me. 'Hi.'

'Are you eating?' I ask Ben.

'No.'

'Go on, get something.' I pass over a menu.

'I'm not hungry,' he says.

'What?' I cry. 'Not hungry? That doesn't sound like you. What's going on?'

Ben shakes his head in slight bemusement and takes a sip of his drink.

'What's this?' Josh regards his lemon squash with disdain.

'Lemon squash. You're not drinking and driving me home,' I state with determination.

'Oh, for fuck's sake.'

And for the first time today, Ben gives me a genuine smile. I raise my eyebrows at him across the table. He looks down and then at Josh.

'How's work going?' he asks.

'Alright,' Josh replies. 'How's yours?'

'Fine.'

'Aren't you supposed to be moving to Pommieland soon?'

'Yeah, in about two weeks.'

'Nuts, mate, nuts. Who'd want to live in that grey old place?' Josh nudges me, trying to wind me up. On the contrary. 'When are you getting married to Kate Winslet?'

142

'Charlotte.'

'That's the one.'

She looks like Kate Winslet?

'March.'

'Good luck with that.' Josh turns to me with a beguiling smile on his face and I try to ignore the sick feeling in my stomach. So she *is* beautiful. 'Lils, you're not really going to make me drink this muck, are you?'

'Yes.' *Maybe she* sounds *like Kate Winslet.*

'Can't I have one beer?'

'No.' *Or it could just be that they're both English?*

He puts his hand on my shoulder and gives it a squeeze. 'Please?' His brown eyes look so appealing and expectant that for a moment I waver.

'No,' Ben interrupts angrily.

'Ben.' My brow furrows. As if I can't handle this.

'What's it to you, mate?' Josh removes his hand and glares across the table at Ben.

'Put your own life in danger, by all means. But don't put Lily at risk.' His dark-blue eyes glint with an unexpected menace and for a moment I forget that he's getting married to the star from *Titanic*. Josh snorts and backs down. 'Whatever.'

'Here comes our food.' I breathe a sigh of relief.

Ben abruptly gets up. 'I'll leave you both to it.'

I'd ask him to stay, but I can see that he won't. 'See you,' I call after him instead.

'What a wanker,' Josh mutters to his departing back.

'Don't be an arse,' I snap, getting up and going to sit opposite Josh because it feels too close for comfort beside him. The place where Ben was sitting is warm. I immediately realise my mistake.

143

Now I've got my back to Ben at the bar and I can't see him! I frown with annoyance at Josh, but then realise he's still fuming about Ben's comment so I change the subject.

'What are the others doing tonight? And no,' I add wearily, 'I don't want to get into Shane's pants.'

'He wants to get into yours.'

'Does he?' I can't keep the boredom from my voice.

'Yep, but he doesn't want to take away your virginity.'

I let out a burst of laughter. 'What? You've got to be kidding me.'

'I'm not,' he replies seriously.

'Well, I'm not a virgin, so—'

'*Aren't you?*' Josh interrupts, astounded.

'No. But there's no way in hell I'd sleep with him anyway.'

'When did you lose your virginity?' He's still focusing on that statement.

'None of your business. Eat up.'

I myself do as I've advised and tuck into my pasta, but it's hard to ignore the look on Josh's face as he considers me. I don't know what's going through his head and I'm not sure I want to know. I'm still kicking myself that I have my back to Ben. After a while I sneak a peek to the place where he was sitting earlier. I can't see him so I twist around further to search the entire bar area. Where is he? Did he go without saying goodbye? Maybe he's gone to the toilet.

'He left five minutes ago.' Josh interrupts my thoughts.

I spin around. 'What?'

'Ben. He just left.' He takes a gulp of his lemon squash, pulls a face and gets to his feet. 'Now I can get a proper drink without some know-it-all interfering.'

'Josh, don't,' I cry in dismay, but he's already at the bar. '*Don't!*' I hiss at him. By the time he returns, I am simmering.

'It's only one beer, for fuck's sake,' he says.

'I can't believe you've just gone and done that.'

'Chill the hell out! What's the big deal?'

'The big deal?' I practically screech. 'The big deal?' The diners at the next table turn to look at me. 'Bollocks to this!' I clatter my knife and fork on my plate and slide out from my bench seat, wishing there was a chair here instead because it's hard to look angry and bum-shuffle at the same time.

'Where are you going?' Josh asks in surprise.

'Home, you fuckwit, even if I have to walk.' I storm out of the restaurant and furiously dig out Mum's mobile phone from my bag. I'm sure I've got a taxi number in here somewhere. I wonder if Ben has gone far? No. I can't keep depending on him to rescue me, however much I'd like to.

'Lily, don't be ridiculous.' I turn to see Josh standing on the pavement.

'Piss off!'

'Come on, I'll drive.'

'Did you drink that beer?'

'Downed it in one.' Pause. 'I'm joking!'

'This is no laughing matter.' Again, people turn to stare.

'Come on,' he urges quietly. 'Everyone will think you're my bird and we're having a bust-up.'

'Fat bloody chance of that!' But I allow him to manoeuvre me around the corner to the car park.

I sit in silence for most of the journey home, still furious. Finally I decide I'm not ready to let it go. I know I've been in the car with him when he's drunk a hell of a lot more than one beer, but suddenly I've had it up to my eyeballs.

'Seriously, did you drink any of it?'

'Any of what?' he asks in frustration.

'That beer!'

'Are you *still* going on about that?'

'Did you?'

'I had a couple of swigs – so what? I'm not going to let a good beer go to waste.'

'I don't know why I ever got into a car with you,' I say darkly as we exit Crafers and pass a koala warning sign. 'You're clearly not bothered about who or what you kill.'

'Hey . . .' he cautions.

'Seriously, haven't you ever wondered what it would be like to run over a child?'

'Shut up!' he says nastily.

'You'd never forget it. You'd never get over it. It would ruin your life. All because you had one beer too many that impaired your reflexes.'

'I'm not kidding, Lily. Shut. Up.' We pull up outside his house.

'What do you think your mum would say?' My voice is deadly quiet, and he's too shocked at the mention of her name to speak. 'Do you think she'd be sad? Disappointed?'

'That's enough.'

'Do you think she'd be proud of her son?'

'GET THE FUCK OUT OF MY CAR!' he suddenly bellows, roughly reaching across me to open my door. He pushes me out and I go with the motion, stumbling onto the pavement.

'Josh!' I cry out.

But he's already crashed the door shut in my face. He then revs the engine hard and noisily screeches away from the kerb. I stare after him in horror. What have I done? Please don't let him kill himself! But as suddenly as he started, he stops again, slamming on the brakes so they glow red in the darkness. I run after him and open the door. I can't believe my eyes when I see him sobbing his heart out over the steering wheel. I quickly climb in and shut the door, reaching over to rub his back. He shrugs me off, but only half-heartedly, so I continue to stroke him soothingly.

'I'm sorry,' I whisper. 'I'm really so, so sorry.'

He cries harder. I don't think I've ever seen a boy cry before. Dan had a tear in his eye when I dragged him to see *Cruel Intentions* last summer, but that's hardly the same thing. I have no idea what to do in this situation.

'I'm sorry I said those things,' I try, when his sobs begin to quieten. 'I should have kept my mouth shut.'

He shakes his head tearfully. 'No, it's okay. She would have hated it.'

'Why do you do it, then?'

'I don't know.'

'Hasn't Michael told you to stop?'

'He's too caught up in your mum to notice what I get up to.'

'That's not true. He loves you. He adores you. Anyone can see that.'

Josh doesn't answer. He knows deep down that it's true.

'You can be careful from now on,' I say. 'You'll never have to live with a terrible mistake.'

'Or not live.' He manages a weak smile.

'Your dad would be devastated if he lost you, too. He'd never recover.'

Josh nods sadly. 'I know.'

'So. Taxis from now on?' I smile at him hopefully and he offers me a weak one back.

'Guess so.'

'She *would* be proud of you.'

'Don't say that,' he warns. 'I'll start crying again.' And right on cue his eyes fill with tears. He brushes them away angrily. 'Don't you ever tell Shane I did this.'

I laugh with indignation. 'As if I would!'

'Not even when you're snuggled up in bed with him.'

I lift my hand to whack him on the back with it, but he laughs and puts the car into gear. 'Joke. I'll tell him you're off-limits,' he says as he does a swift U-turn and drives along to pull up outside the house.

I breathe a sigh of relief. 'That'd be good. I don't need any more complications in my life right now.'

He exhales dramatically and gives me a teasing grin. 'Even *I'm* not going to be able to get you in the sack after you've seen me crying like a baby.'

'You wouldn't have been able to get me into the sack anyway, darling,' I say silkily. 'You're not my type.'

We both laugh and climb out of the car, peace restored.

Chapter 10

'You know, I *can* handle it myself,' is the first thing I say to Ben when I see him the following morning.

'You looked like you were about to give in,' he replies crossly, referring to the no-drinking argument I had with Josh at dinner last night.

'I wasn't,' I state with force, and tell my inner self to shut up. He doesn't need to know what went on after he left.

'Good,' is all he says before stalking out of the hospital room.

I don't see him again that morning because he's covering for one of Michael's colleagues on the dingoes and Tasmanian Devils. At lunchtime I wander down the slope past the café, trying not to think about how many lunch-breaks Ben must have spent getting to know Charlotte when she worked there. I sit alone on the grass and stare up at the big old gum with its grated tree bark. I'm strangely unsurprised when Ben sits on the grass beside me. He doesn't look at me, preferring instead to gaze ahead at the tree trunk while I study his profile. His jaw is clenched.

'I don't know why I feel . . . so protective of you,' he muses after a while.

I pick up a dead leaf and crackle it between my fingers, waiting for him to speak.

'I hate the idea of Josh taking advantage of you.'

'Are you referring to his drink-driving or something else?' I ask. He doesn't answer. 'I'm not interested in him,' I say. 'For the record. Although why it should bother you if I were is beyond me,' I add, glancing at him.

He steadfastly avoids my eyes. I sigh and lean back on my elbows, crossing my legs in front of me. He lays his head back on the grass and closes his eyes.

'I'll have to give you another driving lesson before I go.'

'That'd be good.' I take this opportunity to stare uninterrupted at his profile. It's so hot that a few strands of his hair are sticking to his forehead. I want to push them off his face.

'Tonight?' he murmurs.

'Great. I'd like to go home and change first though.'

He smiles, his eyes still closed. 'Still hate our shorts?'

'They look alright on you,' I find myself saying. He opens his eyes and turns his head, a sleepy grin on his face as he squints up at me. My heart flips.

'Have you been to the beach yet?' he asks out of the blue.

'No. That's terrible, isn't it? I've been in Australia for a month and haven't even managed to get to the seaside.'

'It's because you can't drive.'

'And because I don't have any friends to go with.'

'I'm your friend.'

'Yep, and you're buggering off to England. Thanks for that.' I try to sound glib and think I succeed.

'I'll take you tonight,' he says, closing his eyes again and turning his face up to the blue sky amid the gum leaves.

He arrives at Michael's house at six o'clock and soon we're heading down the winding road towards the city. My driving is definitely improving. I think these bends would have scared me a week ago. A jagged quarry juts out of the landscape, revealing naked stone instead of leafy tree cover. Chicken wire holds back the hills to stop stones from falling onto the road, but there's mesh over parts of the central concrete barrier, too.

'What's that for?' I ask.

'Koalas. So they can get across,' Ben replies.

'Oh, of course.' Pause. 'Do they have koalas at London Zoo?'

'No,' he replies bluntly.

'Kiss Me' by Sixpence None the Richer comes on the radio. I turn up the volume.

'How old is your girlfriend?' I ask suddenly. 'I mean fiancée,' I correct myself.

He stares out of the window, saying, 'I hate that word.'

'What word – fiancée?'

'Yeah.'

'Why?'

'It sounds so . . . I don't know – old.'

'Yet here you are, getting married.'

He sighs. 'Scary.'

'So how old is she?'

'Twenty-three.'

'Only twenty-three?' I'm surprised. She's not *that* much older than me! 'What's her name?'

He looks confused. 'Charlotte.'

'No, I mean her full name.'

'Oh. Charlotte Turner.'

'Does she really look like Kate Winslet?'

'Hey? *No.*' He brushes me off.

'What colour is her hair?'

'Er, brown. Or sort of dark-blonde.'

'Curly?'

'A bit. Come on now, eyes on the road, missy.' He points ahead and turns the volume down on the stereo. 'You need to concentrate.'

The sun is on its certain descent towards the horizon as we approach Henley Beach. Ben directs me into the car park, asking as he does so, 'Do you want some fish and chips?'

'Er, sure.'

'I'll get them,' he tells me as I climb out of the car. 'Meet you on the beach by the jetty.'

'Do you want some money?'

He waves me away. 'Of course not.'

I smile after him as he walks across the grass in the direction of some cafés, bars and restaurants. Ahead of me there's a long wooden jetty stretching out over the pale-blue stillness of the water. I head down the steps to the beach and take off my shoes. The soft white sand is cool between my toes, having lost its heat from the sun an hour ago. I sit down and stare out at the ocean. It's beautiful here. Ben joins me after a few minutes.

'Here you go.'

'Thanks.' I take my bundle and unwrap it. The battered fish pieces are long and thin, unlike the cod I'd have back home. 'What sort of fish is this?'

'Whiting,' he replies.

'Aha!' He smirks. 'You never did take me fishing,' I point out.

'I haven't gone yet,' he replies. 'When do you want to go fishing?'

'When are you next going?'

'We could go Sunday, if you're not at work?'

'I'm supposed to be, but I'll see if I can change my day off.'

'It's an early start.'

'How early?'

'We'd have to set off from the hills at four-thirty.'

'Are you taking the piss?'

He chuckles. 'Afraid not.'

'Why so early? Are they vampire fish or something? Do they only come out at night?'

He glances at me sideways. 'Want to give it a miss?'

'No way. You promised.'

'Okay, that's that settled then.'

We sit and eat in silence for a while, staring out at the sky as it turns from yellowy-blue to pinky-orange. A couple of sunset stragglers wander past us towards the steps, their feet kicking up sand as they go. Ben screws up our empty fish and chip paper into a bundle. A cool breeze blows across us and I shiver. Ben takes off his light-blue long-sleeved shirt and hands it to me. He's wearing a grey T-shirt underneath.

'Thanks,' I reply, accepting it gratefully. I slip it on, breathing in the scent of his musky deodorant. He doesn't wear aftershave. I glance down at his tanned, toned arms and absentmindedly edge closer to him.

'I hope you're not cold now.' I resist the urge to run my hand over his bicep.

'I'm alright.' He stares ahead at the ocean.

'Hey, you haven't seen any of my photos for a while.'

'Do you have any on you?' He looks at me with interest.

'As a matter of fact, I do.' I packed them all into my bag earlier. I've been meaning to show them to him for ages.

He slowly makes his way through the pack, commenting just like he did the first time. We come to the photo he took of me by the lily pond, way back in the beginning, before I fell for him.

He chuckles. 'I like this one.'

'It's okay,' I concede. My hair has fallen across my shoulders quite nicely and there's a slight smile on my face as I reluctantly pose for the camera.

'These are so good, Lily,' he says seriously. 'I really think you have a talent.' I wriggle with embarrassment. 'I do,' he says fervently. 'I hope you do something with it.'

'Maybe I will,' I reply.

'Promise me you'll keep up with the photography. And don't forget your passion for animals, either. It's not too late to train to be a vet, or even a keeper, if that's what you want to do.'

I smile, warmth filling me up. 'Maybe I'll be a wildlife photographer.' I flash him a cheeky grin.

He laughs. 'That'd work!'

'So which is your favourite?' I nod down at the pack.

He shuffles through it. 'I do like this.' He shows me one of the giant gum with its grated tree bark. 'But this is my favourite.' It's the photo of me by the lily pond.

'*You* took that one!' I exclaim with mock outrage.

'Does that mean it's mine to keep?' he asks cheekily.

'You can have it if you want it.' I shrug, feigning nonchalance. He wants a photo of me!

He peers closely at it. 'Your eyes . . .' He shakes his head.

'What?'

'They look almost – I don't know. Caramel-coloured.'

'Caramel?' I've never heard my boring eyes described like that before. He turns and looks at me, *really* looks at me, and the smile slips from my face.

'They are,' he says.

There's a strange intensity to his expression and my heart starts to hammer in my ears. 'Yours are the same colour as the water,' I say, not caring how clichéd it sounds because it's true.

The connection between us magnifies and then suddenly he starts and rises to his feet. 'We should be moving.'

'We don't have to.' I look up at him with disappointment.

'No, I'd better get home,' he states, turning away and pushing the photo of me into his back pocket. I follow in his footsteps as we cross the sand to the steps.

Later, I pull up outside Michael's house. 'Thanks for the lesson,' I say.

'Sure, no worries,' Ben replies, seemingly in a slight daze.

'See you at work?'

He nods. 'I'm going to be a bit late in. I've got a doctor's appointment.'

'Are you okay?' I ask with concern.

'Yeah, yeah, it's fine. A last-minute check-up before I leave.'

'Alright then.'

I climb out onto the pavement and meet him in front of his car.

'See you tomorrow,' I repeat, pulling his shirt closed across my chest and folding my arms to keep warm.

'Sure thing.' He stares at my arms and moves to pass me. I step to one side.

'Take care,' he says softly.

'You too.'

I stay rooted to the spot as I watch him climb into his car and start up the ignition, and he doesn't glance back as he pulls away from the kerb.

That night in bed, I hug his shirt to me tightly. He didn't ask for it back, and I'm not going to surrender it willingly.

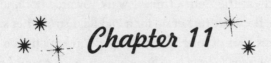

Chapter 11

The next morning passes by painfully slowly as I wait for Ben to get in. When he still hasn't turned up at lunchtime, I'm nearly pulling my hair out.

'Where's Ben?' I ask eventually when Janine appears in the hospital room to check on Olivia. I've been stalking the place in the hope I'll bump into him.

'He called in sick,' she tells me.

'Did he?' Did the doctor find something wrong with him?

'It's nothing serious,' Janine reassures me upon seeing my expression. 'He got some food poisoning from something he ate last night.'

But he ate the same thing as me and I feel fine.

The next day is Saturday and it's usually my day off, but as I'm going fishing with Ben on Sunday, I've arranged with Trudy to change my shift. My mum gives me a ride to work because Michael's having a lie-in.

I head straight to the koala lofts to see if Ben is there.

'Is Ben still sick?' I ask Janine.

'No, he's here,' she tells me. 'The vet's coming in to check up on one of the wombats so Ben's gone down to see him.'

I get on with clearing the lofts and after an hour, I take a break and go to see Olivia.

'Hey, you,' I say gently as I open the hospital-room door to see our rapidly growing joey snuggled up amongst the blankets. She squeaks softly at the sight of me. I walk towards her and kneel down on the floor, lifting her up for a cuddle. I stroke her soft ears and she wraps a set of long black claws around my finger.

How is Ben going to be able to bring himself to leave you? I silently ask. I notice there's a burr caught up in the grey-white hair of one of her ears and I gently tug at it with my fingers, trying to pull it loose. 'Wait here, little one, I'll go and get a brush,' I tell her soothingly as she looks at me with those warm brown eyes. I place her on her blankets and wander to the room next door, opening a cupboard in search of some grooming utensils. Suddenly I hear footsteps in the hospital room.

'Pull it closed,' Ben says to someone as I freeze on the spot.

'You look like crap, mate,' Dave replies as I hear the outside door to the hospital room shut.

'I know.' He sounds like crap, too. He's obviously still feeling off colour.

'Has anything happened with Charlotte?'

Has it? I creep towards the door with the purpose of hiding behind it.

Ben sighs wearily. 'No.'

Damn!

'What's up, then?' Dave continues and I hold my breath, waiting for Ben's explanation. It occurs to me that I probably should have revealed myself. Now I've got no choice but to eavesdrop.

'It's . . . kind of hard to talk about.'

'Mate, we've known each other for ten years. You can talk to me about anything.'

'I don't think you'd understand this.'

Hang on, hang on, what's going on?

'Try me.'

Ben doesn't say anything for a long time. Dave, thankfully, is patient as my mind races and I try to concentrate on breathing evenly so I don't make a noise.

'Have you ever . . . had feelings for . . .' Ben's words come with difficulty. And then he stops.

'Go on,' Dave urges.

Yes, go on!

'Forget it.'

No! Wide-eyed, I peek through the crack in the door to see Ben sitting on one of the tables. His mate takes a seat next to him. I hide behind the door again, my heart pounding.

'When I was getting married to Katherine,' Dave starts, 'I was terrified.'

'It's not that.'

'Have you met someone else?'

Silence.

Now my head is pounding, too. I ask again, *What's going on?*

'Do you love her?' Dave asks.

Who? Charlotte?

'I don't know,' Ben replies eventually. 'I've never been so fucking confused in my whole life.'

'Do I know her?'

Who? WHO?

'You've met her.'

Silence again.

'Who is she?'

White noise is rushing through my head. A tiny little voice inside asks, 'Is he talking about me?'

'I can't tell you,' Ben replies.

When Dave speaks again, he speaks quietly. 'I think I know who it is.'

'I doubt it.'

'Lily.'

I stifle a gasp of shock. I can't believe Dave has just said my name.

Ben doesn't confirm or deny it. His friend is the next person to speak and I wish I could stop the words that come out of his mouth.

'I saw the way you were looking at each other the other night. I just had a feeling. Mate, you have to stop it.'

'Nothing's started.'

'Well, it can't do. Ever. She's how old? Fifteen? Sixteen?'

'Sixteen.'

I feel faint.

'Ben! Come on! She's just a kid.'

'She seems older.'

'They all do at that age, but they're not!' *Please stop talking.* 'Listen, I know you're confused. Getting married is a big thing to do. But you and Charlotte are great together. It would break her heart if you called this thing off now.' Dave continues with his words of so-called wisdom. 'Lily is everything you feel you're not. You're getting older and doing grown-up things, she's still in the prime of her youth. No wonder you're attracted to that, but it's wrong, mate. You're going to have to stay as far away from her as possible until you get on that plane.'

Nooooo! I want to scream.

'I know,' Ben responds softly. And then, with an air of finality: 'I know.'

When they've gone, I don't know what to do with myself. He loves me! Didn't he say that? Or maybe he didn't go so far as to say that, but he has feelings for me! I knew it! I knew from that look in his eyes on New Year's Day. He's tried to overcome his emotions, but he can't. And I don't want him to – ever. Oh, I wish Dave hadn't told him to stay away from me. What if he does? No, he can't. I won't let him. He might not do anything about this, but there's no way I'm letting the love of my life get away. I'd never get over it.

I've been absent for ages and Janine will wonder where I am soon enough, so I come out of my hiding-place and return with trepidation to the koala lofts. There's a jackhammer inside my chest and even a pint of Prozac wouldn't calm me down as I pick up a broom and continue mucking out the lofts. When Ben rounds the corner with his head down, my heart skips a beat and the world around me starts to spin. He looks up and almost reels backwards.

'I thought you were off today,' he says.

I shake my head mutely before finding my voice. 'I changed my shift.'

'Oh, right.' He's not smiling at me. He has an odd expression on his face and it's making me feel uneasy. 'Well, I'm helping out with the wombats today so I'll see you later.'

'Okay,' I say apprehensively. And then he's gone.

I don't see him for the rest of the day. I'm always on the look-out, but he doesn't come near the koala lofts, or me.

At the end of the day I leave five minutes early to try and

catch him at the gates. I have a sick feeling in my stomach that he's going to cancel our fishing trip tomorrow. After a while I start to fear he's already left so I wander slowly to the car park to see if his car is still there. It is. I stick to it like a limpet, hoping my mum will be late like she usually is when she comes to pick me up. Thankfully, Ben appears before she does.

'Hi!' He looks taken aback. 'What are you still doing here?'

'I'm waiting for my mum,' I say. Then: 'Look, I wanted to check we're still on for fishing tomorrow.'

He shifts on his feet. 'I'm sorry, Lily, I'm not going to be able to make it after all.'

'Why?' I ask, panicked.

'I don't think I'm going to have the time.'

'Oh no,' I say quietly.

'I'm leaving in a week and I've got so much to do. Monday's my last day at work—'

'Monday's your last day at work?' I can't keep out the alarm. He nods. 'I thought . . . I thought you'd be working longer,' I stammer. But of course, why would he? He's leaving anyway. He must have a ton of stuff to do. Why would he carry on working up until the last minute?

'No.' He shakes his head regretfully. 'I've got to get my house packed up. Make it suitable for the next tenant.'

'You're not selling it? You said you'd never sell it.'

He gives me a small smile. 'No, I'm not selling it. I'm renting it out to some friends of friends.'

My mum pulls around the corner in my car. I look towards it, anxiously.

'Is that your mum?' Ben asks, and I remember he hasn't even met her yet.

'Yeah.'

She pulls up beside me and winds down the window. 'Sorry I'm late!' she shouts. 'I brought your car so you can drive home.'

'Thanks,' I reply, but there's no enthusiasm in my voice. She looks at Ben expectantly.

'Hi,' he says, stepping towards the car with an outstretched hand. 'I'm Ben Whiting.'

'Nice to meet you, Ben.' Mum smiles up at him through her lashes.

'I'd better get off,' he says to me. 'See you Monday. Nice to finally meet you, Cindy.'

'The pleasure's all mine.' She flicks her hair back.

I yank open the driver's door and Mum stares up at me in alarm.

'I'm driving – right?' I say tersely.

'Oh, yes.' She comes to her senses and climbs out of the car. Ben, meanwhile, gets into his car and pulls out of the car park.

'Who was *that*?' Mum asks the moment she's shut the door.

'Ben,' I reply firmly.

'The Ben who was going to have Christmas dinner with us?'

'That's the one.'

'He's a bit of alright, isn't he?'

'Mum!' I squawk.

'It's okay, I'm only teasing,' she says, but I can see she's not. The thought of my mum with Ben . . . I could throw up.

'So he's the one who's been giving you all these driving lessons?' she continues as we set off.

'Yes,' I say crossly. 'Speaking of driving lessons, do you think I can concentrate now?'

'No need to be so snappy, Lily,' she huffs. I try to ignore her so we can move on, but I know her mind is ticking over, wanting to interrogate me further about my beautiful Ben.

My stomach is churning terribly. And it has little to do with my mum's twisted interests. Ben has cancelled our day out tomorrow. He's only here for a few more days and then he'll be gone forever. I don't know what I'm going to do.

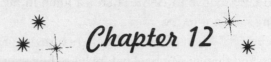

Chapter 12

I can't bring myself to speak to anyone on Monday, but even though I feel sick to my bones, I refuse to take time off. It's Ben's last day, and time is running out to confront him.

'Darl, you look awful,' Michael says to me at lunchtime. 'I hope you're not coming down with that weird flu virus.'

'I'm sure it's something I ate,' I murmur.

Ben doesn't appear for lunch so I couldn't talk to him even if I could muster the courage. It also seems that wherever he's working, one of his colleagues is always there, chatting to him about his forthcoming move. I can't get a moment alone with him. It breaks my heart that afternoon to stand there in the staffroom with a bunch of smiling faces as they sing 'For He's a Jolly Good Fellow' and Ben cuts his leaving cake. I shake my head to refuse a slice as yet another person tells me how unwell I look. It feels like Ben is the only person yet to comment on my lifeless appearance.

As he turns to leave the staffroom I reach out to get his attention in desperation, but at the last millisecond another of his colleagues spins him around to shake his hand. I stand there nervously waiting, but he moves in the other direction across the room saying his goodbyes.

'Come on then, love,' Michael says to me. 'We should get you home to bed.'

'I want to say goodbye to Ben.' There's a lump in my throat and I'm trying hard not to cry.

'Ben! We're off!' Michael shouts as Ben turns around. He glances at me and then at Michael before bounding over.

'See you soon, mate.' Ben shakes Michael's hand warmly.

'I hope not,' Michael jokes. 'All the best for the future. Stay in touch, won't you.'

'Of course.'

I stare up at him, willing him to convey something to me with his eyes. This can't be the last moment I spend with him.

'Bye, Lily,' he says, not holding my gaze for any length of time. 'Thanks for all your help with the koalas. Take care of Olivia for me.'

I nod, unable to speak for fear of breaking down.

'Good luck, Ben!' another colleague calls and Ben moves away to speak to them. Michael ushers me out of the door, while every single part of me is screaming out to stay.

I can't go into work the next day and no one is surprised. I lie in bed, red-eyed from crying myself to sleep. I can't make it into work the day after that. Or the next. It's only when my mum starts talking about taking me to see a doctor that I pretend to feel better. But inside I'm dying.

On Friday when I finally make it in, pale-faced and delirious from the pain of losing him, I can find no comfort in my work or the animals I tend to. I can't even bear to look at Olivia because she reminds me too much of Ben. It's only two weeks until term begins and then I could continue to work on weekends. But I can't see how I can stay here, even for another day. I go to see Trudy in the office and tell her I need a couple of weeks to get my head together about starting at a new school. She's taken aback that I'd want to leave, but she doesn't question it. I know they have a waiting list of teenagers as long as her arm who would work here for free. I don't tell Michael of my decision to leave. I don't tell anyone. I plan to go quietly, without a fuss. I couldn't bear to stand there and eat cake and say my goodbyes when the only person I've ever truly loved is leaving tomorrow.

I've been trying to think of ways to see him again, even though I know there's no point. Dave has convinced him to stay away from me, to marry Charlotte. I know in my heart of hearts there's not a thing I can say to change his mind.

Friday night. His last night. Mum and Michael are having dinner in the city and Josh invites me to Stirling. I would go if I thought there was any chance of bumping into Ben, but I know that's unlikely. I tell Josh I still feel ill and go to sit outside on the wrap-around veranda. I stare up at Mount Lofty as the sky darkens and tears silently roll down my cheeks.

I love him. So much. I'd never feel alone with Ben by my side. I'd never feel unhappy or unsafe. He'd protect me. He believes in me. I don't feel like I'll believe in myself ever again.

I wonder where he is, right now. Would he go up to Mount Lofty to say goodbye? What if he's up there, staring down at my house and asking himself if he's making the right decision?

I leap to my feet, full of determination. I have to go. I have to give it one last shot. What have I got to lose? Everything. I have to try. I could walk, but what if he leaves before I get there?

My mind races as I stumble into the house and search for my car keys on the hallstand. Then I run outside, slamming the front door behind me. I know what I'm doing is highly illegal, but I don't care. I pray no one sees me.

It takes everything in me not to put my foot down. I'm nervous, and I don't know if that's because I'm driving for the first time on my own or because I'm going to find Ben.

The car park is practically deserted so I pull into a space without too much trouble and walk towards the side of the building with my heart hammering. I'm hoping to see Ben looking down at Piccadilly and I'm shaken when he's not there. I continue around the corner and scan the darkness for people sitting on the benches overlooking the city lights, but again, nothing. In a panic I search every face, just to make sure, and one by one as the strangers stare up at me in surprise, my heart slows to a dull thud. He's not here. I was wrong. I thought I knew him better than this.

I collapse on a bench and stare down at the city of Adelaide glittering before me. Then I think: I could go to his house! It's further than Mount Lofty and even more risky, but I can't let him leave without telling him how I feel. I set off back around the side of the building, full of determination, but then my footsteps slow. This is crazy. I'll only embarrass myself all over again. I'll never recover from the shame. What's he going to do? Cancel his flight? Call off his engagement? No. He's not going to do any of that.

I stand and stare down at Piccadilly in despair. A lump forms in my throat and my eyes burn with the onset of tears. I need to get out of here.

'Lily?' His voice is quiet in the darkness, but it's unmistakably Ben.

'You're here,' I say, as he steps tentatively towards me from the direction of the car park.

'How did you know?' he asks.

'I didn't. I thought I'd got it wrong. I was about to leave.'

He reaches me and I stare up at him. Our eyes lock and connect and this time there's no looking away. Nothing can tear me away from him.

'I don't want you to go.' My voice is barely audible, even to my own ears.

'I know.' He breathes softly.

'I heard you.'

He cocks his head in confusion. 'You heard me?'

'I was there, in the room next to the hospital room. I heard you talking to Dave.'

Realisation dawns on his face. He looks horrified and it's enough to make him break eye-contact. I follow him to a bench as he sits down in silence and stares straight ahead.

'You can't leave,' I whisper. 'You can't leave me.'

'Lily . . .' He turns to look at me. 'I have to.'

'You don't.'

'You know I can't stay.'

'Yes, you can.'

'This . . .' he indicates the two of us '. . . would never work.'

'You're wrong.'

He leans forward and rests his elbows on his knees. 'I'm too old for you.'

'You're not.'

He's staring out at the blackness, but my eyes never leave his face.

'You're too young for me.'

169

'I'm not.'

'I can't believe we're having this conversation.' He glances at me sideways and I regard him seriously.

'I love you.' There. I've said it.

He doesn't speak for a while, then he reaches up and tugs at his hair. 'You don't. You don't know what you're saying. It's just a crush. You'll get over it.'

'I won't. It's not a crush, Ben. I love you. And I know you love me too.' I suddenly feel like I'm having another out-of-body experience. I can't quite believe I'm saying this to him. And then I'm back in the present again.

'I don't love you,' he says.

'You do.'

'I don't.'

'You do.' I'm not giving in.

He drags his eyes to meet mine and I know I've broken him. 'It couldn't work,' he whispers.

I reach over and take his hand. The butterflies go haywire in my stomach.

'No one would have to know.'

'No, no.' He abruptly pulls his hand away and stands up.

'You could wait for me!' I cry in sudden desperation. I thought I was getting somewhere.

'No.' He shakes his head resolutely. 'This is crazy. I don't know what's come over me. I'm not normally like this.'

'Please, Ben!'

'Lily, no. You need to stop this. *Now*. I have to go.'

I stand up and clutch onto his arm in anguish. 'No!'

'Lily, please,' he begs, shaking me free. I've never seen such pain on anyone's face and I hate knowing I've caused it, but I can't give up. A man and a woman appear around the corner, arm-in-arm. They momentarily halt when they see us. We force shaky smiles at them and say hello as they pass, and then we're alone again.

'How did you get here?' Ben asks suddenly.

'I drove.'

Shock mixed with anger appears on his face. 'You drove?'

'I know I shouldn't have.'

'Lily, what the hell did you think you were doing?'

'Ben, don't be angry!' I cry.

'Who do you think you are? *Josh*? You could have got yourself killed!'

'I know, I know. But I'm a good driver – I drove carefully!'

'You're not that good.'

'I'm sorry!'

His features soften as he regards me. 'That was really stupid,' he mutters.

'I couldn't let you leave without—'

'I'll drive you home,' he interrupts.

'How will you get your car?'

'I'll walk back up. Come on,' he snaps.

I obediently follow him to my car. He drives in silence, not offering to let me get behind the wheel. It's just as well cars get insured for anyone to drive here, otherwise he'd be angry at me for making him break the law, too.

He pulls up on Michael's driveway and turns off the ignition. He doesn't get out of the car. After a long moment of staring out of the window, he turns to look at me.

'You're going to be fine.' His eyes are filled with regret.

I begin to panic because I can sense that this is it. This is the end.

'You will. I know you'll be amazing whatever you decide to do.'

'No, Ben, please no.'

'I'll miss you,' he says tenderly.

'Please don't go,' I whisper. 'Come inside. There's no one home. We can talk about this some more.'

I want him to kiss me, to make love to me, even if it's the one and only time. I'll cope with that. I try to convey my emotions with my eyes, and very slowly, he reaches over and strokes the side of my face with the back of his hand. Tears start to roll down my cheeks. And then he climbs out of the car.

I sit there in shock as he vaults himself over the boundary fence belonging to the conservation park and starts to climb upwards in the direction of Carminow Castle and Mount Lofty. He's gone. I've lost him. It wasn't enough. *I* wasn't enough. My heart is broken beyond repair and I know I will never love anyone like this.

Ever again.

Now

Chapter 13

'Lily?' Richard laughs nervously. 'Are you going to answer my question?'

'Sorry,' I blurt out. 'I wasn't expecting this.'

'It can't be that surprising, surely? I mean, we have been together for almost two years. I love you. You love me. At least, I think you do.' Now he's looking hurt.

'No, I do!' I exclaim. 'Of course I do – you know I do. It's just that, well . . . we're at a wedding and I guess I wasn't expecting a proposal at somebody's else's wedding.'

'What, you want hearts and flowers, that sort of thing? I didn't think you were into all that stuff.'

'I'm not.'

'Then what is it?'

What should I do?

I look around at our friends. Richard's friends. We're on a green and cream ferry on our way from Manly in North Sydney to Circular Quay. Sam is holding up Mikey to look over the railings and the wind is blowing the little boy's blond hair back, making him laugh hysterically. Molly is nowhere to be seen. She'll be inside, knowing her. She hates it when the ferry messes up her hair and her bridesmaid barnet needs extra protection today.

'Forget it,' Richard says.

I turn back to him and am engulfed with regret. 'I'm so sorry. Of course I'll marry you.'

His eyes light up. 'You will?'

'Of course.'

He grabs my face and presses a long kiss onto my lips. I break away, giggling. 'But look, let's not tell anyone yet. It's Nathan and Lucy's day.'

'Okay.' He beams and I'm glad I've made him happy.

I've just said yes to getting married! What the hell am I thinking? My heart starts to pound and I feel dizzy. *Why did I do that? Why?*

Richard puts his arm around me and pulls me tighter. I feel like I'm suffocating. I flap my hand in front of my face.

'Are you alright?' he asks with concern.

'Feeling a little faint. I didn't eat enough for breakfast.'

'We'll be eating at the reception soon,' he says. 'Do you want me to get you anything?' He pats his pockets, as though expecting a packet of biscuits to appear miraculously.

'No, no, it's okay.' I manage a weak smile. 'I might stand up by the railings though, get some air.'

'Okay.' He rises to his feet to come with me. I wish he wouldn't. I want some time to myself right now, but I don't want to hurt his feelings. He leads the way and we go to join Sam.

'Alright, mate?' Richard says. 'Mikey looks like he's enjoying himself.'

'He loves boats,' Sam comments woefully. 'Always going on about them. "Boat! Boat! Boat!" It's all I ever hear.'

He tries to laugh it off, but there's fear in Sam's eyes. Mikey was named after Sam's dad. His parents died in a boating accident years ago and I imagine he's terrified of the same thing happening to his son.

I lean over the railings and hang out as we approach the Sydney Opera House. It's quite windy today and multicoloured sailboats are out in force. To my right, Sam and Richard continue to chat.

Are you happy, Ben?

I waited for him for two years. I was like a zombie when he left. I don't know how I managed to get through school. If it hadn't been for Shane's sister Tammy, I would have crumbled to dust. She picked me up. She introduced me to people. I made new friends. I settled in. I gradually started to move on.

But I never forgot him. And I never got over him. The day he got married was the day I felt like my life had ended. And a year later, when Michael revealed that Ben and Charlotte were trying for a baby, I found the willpower to stop asking about him.

My eighteenth birthday came and went. But there was no going back to England now. He had destroyed it for me. I never wanted to go home again.

The sad thing was, Michael asked Mum to marry him. I know, fancy saying that: 'the sad thing was . . .' It should have been a happy event, but it was the ultimate kiss of death for their relationship. Poor Michael. He should have known better. I still tell myself he had a lucky escape. Anyway, Mum decided to check out the men in Sydney. I didn't have to go with her, but I thought perhaps a fresh start would be a good idea. Adelaide was still too painful. Even after all that time, talk of the conservation park, glances up at Mount Lofty, going into the city or to the beach and – God forbid – any of my friends arranging to meet at the lily pond . . . It all hurt too much. And the pain never seemed to dull. No guy could have taken my mind off him. I was asked out on several occasions, but I always said no. I thought maybe I'd feel differently if I moved to another part of Australia. It took a while, but I finally started to date again.

I met Richard two years ago when he'd just returned from the UK, of all places. He went there with his builder buddy Nathan to travel and get some work experience in another country. Now the two of them own a small construction business together. It keeps them busy.

Cheering brings me back to the present. The ferry is pulling into Circular Quay and our wedding party is preparing to get off. Up ahead, Nathan has lifted Lucy into his arms. Everyone claps as he carries his bride off the boat.

Despite my own reservations about marriage, I can't help but smile. They make such a lovely couple. They always have. Lucy looks beautiful in a long, simple white dress. Nathan looks even more gorgeous than usual in a slim-fitting black suit and white shirt. No tie. I've never seen Nathan in a tie. He may be doing grown-up things like getting married, but he's still a messy dark-haired surfer boy at heart.

When I met Richard, it didn't take him long to introduce me to his friends: Nathan, Lucy, Sam and Molly. Sam is Nathan's older brother and is married to Molly, and Mikey is their eighteen-month-old son. They welcomed me into their group with open arms, and for that I'm thankful. I had made friends in Sydney through work, but I never stopped missing my old pals Tammy, Vickie and Jo from school in Adelaide. Richard and his friends finally made me feel like Sydney was my home.

At the moment I'm working as a receptionist in the city for a large publishing house called Tetlan. It publishes all sorts of magazines, from celebrity ones to women's glossies, teen titles and lads' mags. I sit with two other girls and it's our job to make a good first impression on the visitors coming to the building. My colleagues, Nicola and Mel, are grab-life-by-the-horns individuals who always make me laugh. It's a good job. I like it. Shame it's temporary. The girl I'm covering for is only on maternity leave for a few more months. I don't know what I'll do after that.

When Ben left, I couldn't take photos any more. I didn't have the heart. I thought my passion would return some day, but I try not to think about it too much. And now it all feels like I've left it too late. As for becoming a vet, well, that's almost laughable. I didn't go back to work at the conservation park. To this day I can't think of our little koala Olivia without a lump coming to my throat. I never saw her again. She was relocated to another conservation park in South Australia and I didn't even get to say goodbye.

I put all these things into a little box inside my heart and keep it locked tightly shut. They only come out to bother me in the darkness of the night sometimes when I can't sleep and when I allow myself to imagine what might have been if he hadn't left . . .

The wedding reception is being held at a trendy bar right on the harbour. Richard takes my hand and swings it enthusiastically as we follow the crowd.

'Are you feeling better now?' he asks, looking down at me.

My Richard has short brown hair and warm brown eyes. I thought he was quite fanciable when he started chatting to me at a bar on the night we met, but I swear he's become better-looking the more I've got to know him. At six foot two, he's taller than me by just the right amount, and he's tanned and toned from working outside on building sites all day. Even though he and Nathan own the company, the pair of them like to muck in and get their hands dirty, which is something I respect him for.

Holy mother of God, I'm engaged. What will my mother say?

I should go and see her. I haven't seen her for ages. Not since Jeremy, and that's saying something. She's moved from man to man since we came to Sydney, but hasn't settled into anything serious. Michael, on the other hand, is now happily married to Janine from the conservation park. She's quite a bit younger than him, but apparently they hooked up after Mum and I left and Michael has never looked back. I'm happy for him. My mum is less so. Whenever I mention him she tells me off. 'What are you going on about *him* for?' I know it's sour grapes on her part, but it's not like she didn't bring it all on herself. I can't imagine what my life would be like if she'd stayed with Michael and I'd remained in Adelaide. I guess I would have eventually met a nice local boy. Or not.

Josh and I are still good pals. We chat on the phone every so often. He's coming over to Sydney in a couple of weeks, actually, for Easter. He's doing really well for himself and I'm proud of him. He still works with cars, although now he restores classic cars that are worth bucketloads of money. He hasn't got married yet, but he's been with the same girl for almost a year. Tina. I've never met her, but she must be a catch to be able to pin Josh down for this long.

Tammy, Vickie and Jo get over to Sydney for a girls' weekend at least once a year. The rest of the time we spend catching up on the phone. Richard always tuts at me when the bill comes in. He doesn't mind really. He knows I miss my girlfriends.

I have met people through various temping jobs I've done – but I never seem to have the time to consolidate those friendships before having to move on to the next job. The work can be fun while it lasts, but I'd like to stay where I am for longer than my nine-month maternity cover.

'Lily!' I turn to see Molly at the bar. Molly is tall and slim with a mop of red hair. 'Get your arse over here!' She claps her hand over her mouth and casts a horrified look at Mikey who's in Sam's arms to my left. 'Mummy didn't mean to say, "arse", darling,' she coos. 'Don't you say "arse", my little love, it's a bad word.'

'Now you've said it three times, he'll have it imprinted on his brain,' Sam points out. 'Pissed as a newt and it's only one o'clock,' he says as an aside to me, tutting affectionately.

Nathan and Lucy got married on the beach in Manly, a short walk from their home. We all went for a drink at a beachside bar by the ferry before hopping on board to come to Circular Quay for the reception. I suspect Molly had a few drinks with Lucy before she tied the knot. Although saying that, Lucy doesn't look tipsy. She looks radiant.

'Lily!' Molly shouts again. 'Are you coming or what?' I squeeze Richard's hand and he grins down at me as I leave him to join Molly at the bar. 'Tequila slammers?' she asks hopefully.

'Molly,' I laugh. 'It's a wedding.'

'And?'

'We can't do shots at a wedding.'

'Of course we can! Lucy would expect nothing less from us.'

'But we haven't even had lunch yet,' I protest.

'I knew you'd let me down.' She shakes her finger at me. 'Can we get a couple of white wines, please?' she asks the barman. 'Wine okay?' she checks with me.

'Wine is fine.'

'Wine is fine! Wine is fine! Wine is fine!' she sings, wrapping her arms around me. 'Don't they look great together?'

We look over at Nathan and Lucy. The look in his eyes as he gazes down at her . . . I've never seen a love like theirs. That's a terrible thing to say, isn't it? Especially when I'm getting . . . I'm getting married! *Stop, stop, stop, don't think about it now.* But it's true about Nathan and Lucy. They're made for each other.

The funny thing with Richard is that there was never any build-up to us getting together. I was out at a bar with a couple of colleagues from a temping job I had at an insurance firm and Richard came along and offered to buy me a drink. I thought, why not? He seemed nice, we got chatting, and the evening culminated in a drunken snog on the steps outside. He took my number, I hardly even expected him to call, but when he did the very next day I thought, at least this guy isn't someone who plays games. What the hell, of course I'll go out with him.

We went to see a movie a few days later and our relationship progressed from there. But there were never any, 'please let him fancy me' moments. We just kind of fell into step with each other.

I do love him. There's never any doubt in my mind about that. And I adore his friends and our lifestyle. Lucy and Molly are probably my closest girlfriends here. They've never made me feel left out, even though they've known each other since they were kids.

'Cheers!' Molly brings me back to the present. 'Oh, it's nice to have a drink,' she says. 'I swear I was more nervous about this wedding than the bloody bride.'

'What were you nervous about?'

'The weather, my shoes, my hair, whether Mikey would have his nap on time . . .'

We glance over at the little boy. Sam is holding his hands as he climbs along the back of a white leather sofa. 'He seems pretty happy.'

'I hope no one minds him having his shoes on that. Sam! Can you get him down?' Molly calls.

'He's fine,' Sam calls back.

'I hate relinquishing control,' she admits to me. 'But Sam promised he'd take the reins today so I could be there for Lucy. *And* have a few drinks. Cheers,' she says again.

'What are you two talking about?' Lucy appears at our side. About my height, with long brown hair and hazel eyes, she's slim, curvy and pretty.

'Do you need anything?' Molly asks her. 'Top-up of lip-gloss? Want me to come to the loo with you and hold up your dress?'

'No, thanks.' Lucy laughs. 'Maybe if I was wearing a meringue. I could do with some lip-gloss, though.' She holds out her hand while Molly rummages around in her silver beaded clutch bag.

'Where the bleedin' heck is it?' Molly mutters. 'Honestly, you'd think I'd be able to find lip-gloss in a bag this small when I usually have a nappy bag the size of Tasmania to contend with. Ah, here it is.'

She produces a pale pink tube and a compact mirror. Lucy surreptitiously applies some and then hands it over to me.

'Thanks.' I do the same before passing it back to Molly for her turn. We're used to this routine.

'Have you had a drink yet?' Molly asks Lucy.

'No. I'm dying of thirst.'

'What do you want? Wine? Champagne? Tequila slammer?' Molly suggests hopefully.

'Ooh no, I'll have one of those.' Lucy points towards a tray of ruby-coloured drinks being carried past by a dashing young waiter. I reach over and swipe one for her just in the nick of time.

'Sorry,' the waiter apologises, looking back over his shoulder and spying me handing the drink to the bride. He immediately comes our way.

'What are they?' I ask, as he offers the tray to Molly and me.

'Singapore Slings,' he and Lucy say at the same time. 'Seriously, you should swap from wine. These are gorgeous,' she urges Molly and me.

'I'll take one for later,' I tell the waiter.

'Not for me,' Molly says. 'Wine is fine! Wine is fine!'

She says it so loudly that Lucy and I pull faces at each other. 'Is she pissed?' I mouth, and Lucy nods and grins.

'I saw that,' Molly growls. 'I am not pissed! I'm just a bit . . . off my face.'

We all laugh.

'How are you doing?' Richard asks me half an hour later when we go to take our seats for lunch.

'Good,' I reply, not meeting his eyes.

'Still feeling faint?'

'No, I'm okay now.'

'What's that?' He nods at my drink.

'Singapore Sling. Lucy's favourite.'

'Nice?'

'Really nice. Have a sip and see what you think. Are *you* having fun?'

'Yeah. Nathan was just saying we should plan a surfing trip for when he gets back from his honeymoon. Go up to Byron when the swell comes in.'

'That'd be cool,' I say.

'Do you want to come?'

'No, you know what I'm like.'

'Lucy will be there.'

'Yeah, well, Lucy can surf, unlike me.'

'You've never even tried!' he exclaims. 'Nathan taught Lucy, why don't you let me teach you?'

'No, thanks. When are you thinking of going?'

'Last weekend in April, if that's okay with you.'

'You know that's Anzac Day Bank Holiday, right?'

'That's the plan. Get an extra day in – maybe go camping.'

'That's when my dad and everyone arrives.'

'Oh, shit. No worries. I'll see if we can do it some other time.'

'Actually, do you know what? It would be nice to spend some time with my sisters and have a girls' weekend. You'll see them the rest of the time they're here.'

'Are you sure?' Richard asks.

'Definitely.'

I can't believe Kay has just turned fifteen. Olivia is eleven now and Isabel, my youngest sister, is nine. It's been two years since I've seen them. When Ben moved to England, it effectively crippled my own desire to ever want to return. My dad has been pretty good about bringing the family over here to visit me. I still feel like I'm missing out on so much though. But after all the fuss I made about leaving the UK, I do think of Australia as my home now.

Sam makes everyone laugh with his best man's speech and Lucy's stepdad Terry says some lovely things during his, but Nathan's words bring tears to everyone's eyes. It's astounding that all the guys here don't hate him because you'd better believe the girls are turning to their boyfriends right now and whining, 'You never say stuff like that to me.'

'I do so!' Richard exclaims. 'I promise I'll come up with something good for the big day.' He puts his hand in mine and gives it a squeeze. A shiver goes through me. *Holy hell.*

'Do you want a summer wedding?'

'Erm, I don't know,' I reply nervously. 'I haven't had time to think about it.'

'A summer wedding would be nice,' he decides. 'Maybe early January so we can take longer for our honeymoon after the Christmas break.'

'January 2012?' I ask distractedly as I tuck into my pavlova. Lucy may not have opted for meringue as a wedding dress, but I'm glad she didn't skimp on it for dessert.

'No, 2011,' Richard replies. 'Next year.'

'Next year?' I manage to choke out. 'What, January as in only nine months or so away?'

'Why not?'

I shake my head furiously. 'Too soon. I need time to organise everything.'

'You're the most organised person I know.' He laughs. 'Nine months is *ages.*'

'Nathan and Lucy were engaged for two years.'

'Yeah, but they got engaged almost as soon as they got together. Lucy's mum would have gone nuts if they'd tied the knot straight away. Anyway, Nathan wanted to save up so he could do it properly. We don't need to save up; business is great. And we could always do it mid-week like this and still get a great venue for lower rates.'

'Stop rushing me into it!' It comes out of my mouth before I have time to think it.

'*Nice.*' He pushes his plate away, disgruntled.

'Sorry.' I put my hand on his arm. 'I don't mean to be awkward. I'm still getting used to the idea.' I try to placate him. 'You know what I'm like about marriage.'

He turns and regards me with hooded eyes. 'No. I don't know what you're like about marriage. Why don't you enlighten me?'

I remove my hand from his arm. 'You don't understand. Your mum and dad have been happily married for thirty-odd years. Mine lasted a few months before they split up and my mum has been running for the hills every time the M word has been spoken ever since.'

Richard lets out a sharp laugh. 'Your mother is hardly the best role model though, is she?'

'Now you're starting to piss me off,' I say darkly.

'Sorry.' He reaches across the table to give my hand another squeeze. 'Let's talk about it later.'

'That's what I wanted to do in the first place,' I mutter.

'Well, you're getting your own way,' he replies pedantically, letting go of my hand.

I put down my fork on my plate a little too noisily and turn to the people sitting next to me, Lucy's stepbrothers Nick and Tom. I don't know if they were aware that Richard and I were having a barney, but they make a good show of hiding it.

Chapter 14

Nathan and Lucy got married on a Thursday, so the next day I have to go into work as usual. Tetlan's offices are only a short walk from Circular Quay. It's an amazing location. Definitely makes working here that little bit easier. Not that it's hard. But I think that's the point. It's not challenging. It's glamorous, sure, sitting here at this big, interior-designed, glossy front desk in a double-height ceiling, hi-tech lobby, but the most exciting thing I get up to is laminating passes for new employees. Either that or ordering sandwiches and setting up the boardrooms for executive meetings. Not really something you need a degree for.

Not that I have a degree. I didn't go to university. My grades weren't good enough. At one point Ben inspired me to work harder and really make something of myself, but then he went and left. Not that I'm blaming him. I'm not bitter. Not about that, at least.

I'm bombarded with questions from Nicola before I even sit down at our receptionists' front desk.

'How did it go? What did she look like? Have you got pictures?'

Nicola loves weddings. I once joked that she was like Muriel out of *Muriel's Wedding*, but she didn't find it very funny.

'It went beautifully, Lucy wore a gorgeous, long, simple dress, and no, I haven't got pictures.'

'Dammit!' Nicola says crossly. 'Why not?'

'What do you mean, *why not*?'

'Don't you have a digital camera?'

'No.'

She pulls a face. 'Seriously? Everyone's got a digital camera.'

'Not me,' I say firmly.

'Don't tell me you still use film.'

'I don't use anything.'

'You haven't got a camera?'

'I've got a camera on my phone. That's enough for me.'

'Why didn't you take any photos with that?' she screeches.

'I was too busy enjoying myself,' I snap jokily.

She huffs and turns her back on me while I switch on my computer. Then Mel's Gucci handbag plonks onto the stool next to me and I look up to see its owner standing there.

'Good morning,' she chirps brightly. 'How was the wedding?'

'She didn't even take photos,' Nicola cries from behind Mel. The three of us sit in a row, with Mel in the middle.

'Didn't you?' Mel asks with mild surprise. 'Did they have a professional photographer?'

'A friend of a friend was doing it,' I say. 'All the photos will be on the website and will be free to download next week.'

'Why didn't you say so?' Nicola beams.

Mel gives me a look and mouths 'Muriel' before clasping her hands together. 'Who's for tea?'

'Yes, please,' Nicola and I both chorus.

I feel mildly guilty. Mel always makes the tea when she

comes in, usually five or ten minutes after me. I've become lazy now and wait for her to appear rather than go to the kitchen myself.

'I've got Tim Tams,' Nicola proclaims, pulling out a packet from her bag.

'Oh, you shouldn't have,' I say, reaching for the chocolate-covered biscuits. 'I'm supposed to be going on a diet.'

'You don't need to diet,' she scoffs as I hand the packet back to her. 'Here, have another,' she urges, waving it in my direction again. I comply.

Isn't that what brides-to-be do? Go on diets? I open my mouth with a sudden impulse to tell Nicola I'm engaged, but shut it again. Maybe later.

Richard and I barely spoke to each other for the rest of the reception, but this morning when we woke up, he pulled me into his arms and tenderly kissed me on the forehead.

'I love you,' he said. 'We can get married whenever you want.'

'Thank you,' I breathed, full of relief. 'I love you too.'

I hope he doesn't want to tell Sam and Molly yet. Nathan and Lucy go to Bali tomorrow for two weeks. Maybe we can postpone the announcement until after they return and the glow from their honeymoon has dimmed? I don't want to take anything away from them.

At least, that's my excuse and I'm sticking with it.

'Here you go.' Mel returns and places mugs of hot tea in front of Nicola and me. She removes her designer handbag from her stool and sits down, just as the double doors to the building whoosh open and the Editor-in-Chief of *Marbles* magazine walks in.

'Good morning, Mr Laurence,' Mel says silkily.

The tall, olive-skinned man in the expensive suit chuckles as he approaches the desk. 'You know, you *can* call me Jonathan.'

'I know,' she replies, looking up at him through her dark lashes. 'But Mr Laurence sounds more powerful somehow.'

He flashes her a grin and nods at Nicola and me before walking to the staircase. It's five flights to his floor, but he never takes the lift. Nicola and I gawp open-mouthed at Mel as soon as he's gone.

'I can't believe you speak to him like that!' Nicola shakes her head in alarm, but Mel sighs dreamily.

'He's so sexy . . .'

'And married,' Nicola points out.

'Happily?' Mel asks, the picture of innocence.

'That's none of our business.' Nicola gives Mel a warning look, but Mel clearly won't be put off.

'I can fantasise, can't I?'

Nicola and Mel have worked together for four years. The girl I'm replacing on maternity leave, Debbie, has been here for five. They're all still firm friends, but whenever they get together for rare nights out – rare because Debbie has a baby now – I'm never invited. I suppose it would be a bit weird for Debbie to go drinking with her replacement. I wonder if they gossip about me to her? Probably. She must be interested to know what I'm like. I don't think they'd say anything nasty though. We've never had a tiff. I don't speak to Mel the way Nicola does. I'm not sure I could get away with it.

'Not many early risers today,' Nicola comments.

'Quiet morning?' I ask.

'Very.'

Nicola starts at eight o'clock, an hour earlier than us to accommodate people coming into work early. She leaves at five whereas we stay on until six. I'm usually a little early because of the time my ferry from Manly comes in. Nicola has blue eyes and long blonde hair with a slight curl to it. Mel is a green-eyed brunette, with longish, dead-straight hair. Both girls are slim and petite, slightly more so than me.

What would you think if you could see me now?

I think I look quite different. I had my dark hair cut shorter years ago and now wear it in a shiny, blunt bob with a fringe that falls just above my eyebrows. I've learned how to apply make-up properly and my eyes are still light brown, *obviously*. No one else has ever called them caramel. The temping jobs that I do require me to look the part, and the thought of my old self sitting here next to gorgeous girls like Nicola and Mel makes me shudder.

Nicola pulls out a nail file from under the desk and begins to file her already-perfect talons. The door whooshes open again and she quickly puts it down to flash her welcome smile at the latest employee to arrive this morning. It's funny working here. You get to see all kinds of people. The suits tend to get in early. The creatives: late. And you don't see a single lads' mag bloke arrive before ten o'clock, usually looking hungover and pasty.

Three tall teenage girls wander waiflike through the doors and approach the desk.

'We're here for a casting,' the one in the middle says.

'With which magazine?' I ask, reaching for the phone.

'*Blinker*.'

That's a glossy teen title.

'Take the lift to the third floor, turn right and go through the double doors. Good luck!'

192

'Thanks,' they mumble and wander off listlessly.

'I hate models,' Nicola comments when they've gone.

'Only because they're younger and more beautiful than you,' Mel teases.

'No, because they have the personalities of a dishcloth.'

'They're not all like that,' I chip in.

'The only reason I'd want to be a model is because of the photographers,' Nicola states.

We get a lot of male photographers through these doors, and most make Nicola go weak at the knees. Neither of my colleagues have boyfriends, but if they date they usually go for wealthy, well-dressed men (Mel) or sexy, dishevelled boys (Nicola). My Richard falls into neither category. At twenty-eight he's two years older than me and seems strangely unlike a man or a boy. I guess I'd call him a man if pushed, but . . .

Twenty-eight is how old you were when I met you.

I can't believe I've never thought of that before. Ben seemed older somehow. Or maybe he didn't. Maybe it was me. *I* seemed younger. I thought I was so mature at the time. Looking back, how wrong I was.

But I did love him. I still do.

That's the scary thing about unrequited relationships – there's no line you can draw underneath them. The love just keeps on living, bubbling away below the surface.

I wonder what you look like now? You'd be thirty-eight. Is that old? I don't know.

'What are you thinking about?' Mel breaks into my thoughts.

'Nothing,' I blurt out.

'You looked all mysterious there for a minute.'

I smile and raise one eyebrow, trying to act the part.

'Tell us,' she urges.

'I was thinking,' I start – she's all ears – 'about whether I should go for tomato and basil or carrot and coriander today.'

Mel's expectant smile slips into a look of irritation.

'Tomato and basil,' Nicola interjects. 'Although they did have leek and potato yesterday.'

'No way!' I say. 'I can't believe I missed out on a leek and potato day.'

The three of us have practically lived on soup all summer. This trendy soup kitchen opened up around the corner a few months ago and the concoctions are so tasty we've become addicted despite the heat. Summer's almost over now and the weatherman is predicting a wet and chilly autumn, so I hope we haven't out-souped ourselves because a hot lunch should go down a treat when the temperature dips.

'Nice little change of subject there, Lily.' Mel gives me a sly look and I flash her an innocent one.

I don't usually think about Ben during the day. I've learned quite a lot of self-restraint over the years and try not to think about him at all. Sometimes I wonder if I could have done things differently. I still cringe when I remember how I practically threw myself at him on his last night. As if he would have had sex with me! I shudder at the memory.

'Seriously, what *are* you thinking about?' Mel again.

'I'm cold,' I say. 'I hope I'm not coming down with something.'

'Swine flu,' Nicola states. 'Are you feeling achy all over?'

'No.'

'Shivery?'

'Not really,' I admit.

'Headache?'

'Yes. Actually I'm probably just hungover.'

'Have another Tim Tam,' Nicola offers.

'Thanks.'

I can't blame Mel for latching onto my expression. Gossip plays a big part of our lives. How could it not, when we're sitting here without a manager to oversee us every second of the day. Strictly speaking, Nicola is supposed to be in charge. She's the most senior of us. But that's almost laughable. She's the biggest gossip of the lot.

I have nothing to be ashamed about, I remind myself. *I know you loved me too. And now I must stop thinking about you.*

'Plans for the weekend?' Nicola asks towards the end of the day.

'I've got my friend coming over from Brisbane,' Mel says. 'Shopping tomorrow daytime, followed by dinner in the city, bar crawl then a club. We seriously need to pick up some men. You?'

'Going to see my mum,' Nicola says. 'And Sunday's supposed to be hot so a group of us are going to the beach for a picnic.'

'I should go and see my mum, actually,' I state.

'Has she got a new boyfriend yet?' Nicola asks.

'Not since she found out that Jeremy was banging his secretary.'

'Ouch,' Mel interjects.

'Your mum has been so unlucky in love,' Nicola comments.

'On the contrary. She's been incredibly lucky, but the good guys – like Michael – never stand a chance.'

'When's the gorgeous Josh coming over?' Nicola asks excitedly.

These two know everything about my life in Australia to date. Well, not *everything*. But like I said, gossip is practically in our job descriptions. Anyway, Josh emailed me a few weeks ago with a picture of himself standing next to a car he'd done up. Nicola almost fell off her stool when she saw him.

'Easter weekend.' I grin.

'What are you planning to do with him?' she asks.

'Big night out. You can come if you like.'

'Seriously?' Nicola is already reaching for her diary.

'Can I come too?' Mel asks.

'Sure!' I'm pleasantly surprised they'd both want to. We don't usually catch up on weekends, let alone holiday weekends. But a night out with a bunch of us would be fun. And I'd like to introduce Nicola and Mel to Molly and Lucy. Although saying that, Lucy will have just got back from her honeymoon. And Molly and Sam might not want to pay for a sitter so they can come out with me and my one-time-almost-stepbrother for the night. I'll ask Richard what he thinks later.

'I hope he looks as sexy in real life as he does in pictures,' Nicola says wistfully.

I give her a pointed look. 'Can I remind you that he has a girl-friend?'

'I can admire him from a distance, can't I? And anyway, his girlfriend isn't coming, is she?'

'Now you're sounding as bad as Mel,' I state and she looks suitably shame-faced while Mel raises her eyebrows smugly.

Chapter 15

The warm, late-summer air hits me as I step out of the cool, air-conditioned building. My heels clicking on the paving stones, I set off at a brisk pace towards Circular Quay. I'm hoping to catch the 6.10 JetCat to Manly if I get there on time and if it isn't crammed to the brim. The streets are buzzing with people leaving work in time for the weekend. I walk past bars and pavement tables packed with people from local businesses. Mel has dragged me for the occasional after-work drink at some of these places hoping to pick up a suit, but the vibe doesn't appeal to me – even with the presence of free olives.

The JetCat is pulling into the port as I arrive and I run to join the hordes. I think I might be lucky and get a seat as people clamber off, ready for Friday night on the town. Salty ocean air caresses my face as I step onto the boat and make my way to the benches at the front. I always sit above deck. I don't care about my hair in the way that Molly does. She curses me for being one of the only people she knows who doesn't suffer from damp-air frizz. I don't quite know how that happened, but looking back, when I was younger, my longer locks never went particularly frizzy either.

As men in uniform pull up the platform and prepare for departure, I have a sudden urge to travel standing up, despite my luck at getting a seat. I see the eyes light up of a frazzled woman standing across from me and am pleased for her as she hurries to engage my bench space. I squeeze past crowds of people and make my way down the side to the back of the JetCat, where I manage to find a small space at the railings. I wriggle between a young guy and a Japanese tourist and look down as the water below churns up a great storm and we pull away from the harbour. Tiny ant-like figures are climbing the enormous dark structure of the Sydney Harbour Bridge. I've been meaning to do that for years, but I've never made the most out of living here. Weekend tourists probably do more in Sydney than I've managed in years. I haven't even been to the Sydney Opera House. I should try to take Kay, Olivia and Isabel when they arrive.

The evening wind has picked up and the sailboats are out in force. I watch as they twist and turn and manoeuvre past each other. A boat with a red and orange sail almost collides with a blue and yellow-striped sailboat. The sun is hitting the waves between them at the very point that they pass each other, and a sparkle of light pierces my eyes. *I wish I had my camera.*

Where did that thought come from? You don't take pictures any more, remember?

Why not?

You just don't!

But *why?*

Because I knew you'd be disappointed. I think that's the reason I stopped – to punish you. How stupid is that? How would you ever know? I've cut off my nose to spite my face and now I'm living with this disfigured regret, so to speak.

I could have been a photographer, not a receptionist.

Don't be stupid, Lily. No, you couldn't have.

But Ben told me I could do anything.

Well, Ben was wrong.

My mum still has a box of my things from when we first moved here, before I got a job and a place of my own. My camera is buried deep inside. I should call her, see if she's free tomorrow. Richard might even fancy a trip to Bondi.

That's where my mum lives: Bondi Beach, in a small flat with a distant view of the ocean. She works in a restaurant as a wait-ress-cum-manager. The customers seem to like her because she usually gets tips even though that's not the done thing Down Under.

The JetCat chugs into Manly and people start making their way to the front. I wonder if Richard fancies takeaway tonight? I could do with chilling out in front of the box. I still haven't watched the last *So You Think You Can Dance*. I love that show. Richard loves it substantially less than me, but I might be able to persuade him to shoot some soldiers on one of his PlayStation games while I watch it.

I walk along the ocean front past the tall apartment blocks overlooking the water and turn left up a residential street. I start the trek up the steep hill, but finally have to admit defeat and pause on the footpath as I rummage around in my bag for my flip-flops. Yes, I still call them flip-flops, even though I've lived in Australia for ten years. I can't accept that thongs aren't some-thing that get stuck up the crack in your bum. I hop on one foot and undo the strap on my high heels, slide my left foot into my flip-flop and repeat the procedure with my right, breathing a sigh of welcome relief afterwards. Then I set off again up the hill, swinging my shoes from their straps. Fifteen minutes later I turn into our road.

We live in a small, two-bedroom bungalow which Richard did up as one of his first projects with Nathan. Nathan had completed work on several similar rundown houses prior to that, but he and Lucy loved the last one so much that he never sold it on. They still live there now. The same thing happened with Richard and me. We'd only been together for a couple of months, so even though I adored the house and wanted to move into it with him, it was too soon to buy anything together.

With his parents' help, Richard bought the place. He's already paid his mum and dad back. They didn't ask for or particularly need the money, but I'm glad he cleared his debts. I already feel beholden to Richard by living in his house; I didn't want to feel beholden to them too. Not that anyone makes me feel like that. His parents are very welcoming. But I've grown up to be fairly independent and I like it that way. I insist on paying the going rate for rent, even though it's well over half what Richard pays on the mortgage. He wishes I wouldn't, but I won't budge.

I push open the dusky green-painted wooden gate and flip-flop my way up the stone footpath, which is surrounded on both sides by leafy green ferns. Three wooden steps up and I'm at the matching green-painted front door. It's still double-locked, which means Richard isn't home yet. I push open the door and dump my heels in the tiny hall, then go into the kitchen. Being single-storey, our house has two bedrooms and a bathroom on the left, and an open-plan kitchen and living room on the right. The place was dark and gloomy when Richard and Nathan first started working on it, but they've opened it up and put skylights in so it feels light and airy despite its small size. There's a garden out the back which has been decked and is enclosed within a high bamboo fence, and all the plants are leafy and tropical. It's like a little oasis. I love it.

I open the fridge and pull out a bottle of rosé that has been sitting in there since the weekend, pour myself a glass then wander to one of the cosy sofas and slump down, grabbing the remote control for the telly from the coffee table. Richard comes in halfway through a contemporary dance routine. I press pause.

'Hello.' I look over my shoulder at him.

'Hey.' He bends down and gives me a peck on my lips.

'How was your day?'

'Good. I'm filthy though. Going to take a quick shower.'

'What do you want for dinner tonight?'

'What are you thinking?'

'I was wondering about a pizza takeaway.'

'You don't want to go out?'

'I'm knackered,' I say.

'Are you sure? I thought we should celebrate.'

'Celebrate what?'

He looks momentarily crestfallen, but I recover quickly.

'Oh! Of course we should! What a great idea.'

'Cool.' He smiles. 'Let's get dressed up and have a think about where to go.'

He leaves the room and my heart sinks. I barely even have the will to unpause *So You Think You Can Dance*, but I do it anyway. I really, *really* wanted a night in tonight. But I can't pour water on his bonfire. I realise I've missed half of the judges' verdicts, so I press the rewind button and try to concentrate.

Richard pops his head around the door a few minutes later, saying, 'Aren't you getting changed?'

'Hmm?' I turn to see he's emerged from the shower. His tall, slim body stands naked before me as he towel dries his short brown hair.

'You're still watching telly. Aren't you getting changed?'

'Oh, yeah.' I press pause again and reluctantly prise myself off the sofa. He stares down at me with dark eyes as I approach the doorway he's blocking. I look up at him expectantly. Is he going to move?

Richard raises the hand that's not holding the towel and gently strokes my cheek with his thumb. Then he bends down to kiss me. My lips part as our kiss deepens and I step towards him, feeling his growing hardness pressing into my stomach. He pulls away, desire in his eyes and suddenly we're scrambling onto the sofa and he's pushing up my skirt and I'm sliding out of my knickers and we're locked in a heated embrace as I claw at his chest and he nibbles my neck.

And then I think of you. And I'm crushed with an overwhelming desire to sob, sob so hard that I could choke on my tears.

Richard bucks and grunts and collapses on me, taking my breath away as I'm crushed beneath his not inconsequential weight. It's enough to distract me from my emotions. I wriggle underneath him.

'Sorry,' he says, propping himself up. I take a deep breath to fill up my lungs and he grins down at me. 'Where do you want me to take you?'

I look up at him with pleading eyes. 'You don't fancy just staying here?'

'Seriously?' He regards me with interest. 'Don't you want to crack open a bottle of bubbly?'

'We could get some from the offie,' I suggest, my voice full of hope.

He bends down to kiss me tenderly. 'And I guess I could see to you again later.'

I kiss him back and then laugh and prod his shoulders. 'Get off me, I need to breathe.'

He chuckles and disengages himself.

Later we're lying, legs entangled on the sofa watching TV, when he says something that makes my blood run cold.

'When do you want to tell our parents?'

I hesitate, then force myself to speak. 'When do *you* want to?'

'I was wondering about going to see mine tomorrow?'

'I wanted to see my mum tomorrow,' I quickly say.

'Oh, right.' He sounds less than thrilled. 'Didn't you see her recently?'

'I haven't seen her for a month.' I try not to sound cross.

'Okay, so we can tell *her* tomorrow.'

'Yes, we could do, but . . .'

'What?'

'Well, it's just that I haven't seen her since Jeremy did the dirty on her and I thought she might need some TLC.'

Actually, I *did* originally want Richard to come with me, but not if he plans to break the news. I'll postpone that as long as is humanly possible.

'Oh, right. Okay. I might see what Adam's up to.' Adam is one of Richard's many mates.

'Or you could go and see your parents.'

'What, and tell them?'

'Not tell them necessarily.'

'Good, because I'd want you there for that.'

'Sure, sure. No, I mean, maybe just go and see them, catch up –

you know.' And then there won't be as much pressure for me to visit them anytime soon.

'Or we could see them tomorrow night?'

'Yes, I guess we could.' Dammit!

'Are you going to tell your mum tomorrow?'

'I might see how it goes. I don't want to rub our happiness in her face.'

He gives me a look, but I ignore it. I'm sure he can see right through me.

'The other thing we need to do is find you an engagement ring,' he says.

Oh, no.

'Mmmhmm.'

'What, don't tell me you don't want one of those either?' Now he's looking annoyed.

'I . . . I'm not sure,' I admit.

'Lily!' he snaps.

'No, it's only that I quite like the idea of one ring. A wedding band with diamonds. Engagement rings can be so . . . fussy.'

'I thought you liked Lucy's ring.'

'I do like Lucy's ring. A diamond solitaire really suits her. But I wouldn't want one.'

He sighs. 'Fair enough. I guess you've put some thought into it.'

'Yes. I definitely have.' I stifle a sigh of relief when he leaves it at that.

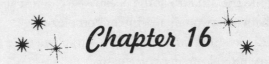

Chapter 16

'Where's Richard?' Mum asks the next day. We're sitting out on
her space-challenged balcony drinking ice-cold water.

'He's catching up with a mate.'

'I haven't seen him for ages.'

'No, I know. He did want to come.'

'Why didn't he then?'

Whoops, walked right into that one. 'I thought it'd be nice to
spend some time, just the two of us. How are you, by the way?'

'I'm fine,' she says breezily, shaking back her shoulder-length,
medium-blonde locks.

'Still cut up about Jeremy?'

She scoffs. 'Hell, no. His loss.'

'That's the spirit, Mum.'

She drags the plastic side-table over and props her feet up. Her
legs are still slim and tanned and I notice she's given herself a
pedicure.

'Any more men on the scene?'

'Not really.'

'You don't sound too sure.'

'You know what I'm like, Lils.'

'Yes, Mum, I definitely do. Tell me about him.'

'Nothing much has happened yet. I will when it does. Don't want to jinx it.'

I stare off into the distance at the ocean. We can just about see it, squeezed between two tall apartment complexes.

'Do you still have that box of my things from when we moved here?' I ask, trying to keep my voice casual.

'Yes, it's in the cupboard in your room.'

Bless her, she still calls it my room even though I haven't lived in it for four years.

The living room is intimate, but light, decorated in neutral cream tones. There are two bedrooms directly off it. I wander into the smaller of the two. It still looks like a spare bedroom; I never did make it my own. I slide open the mirrored door of the built-in wardrobes and peer up at the top shelf. Sure enough, there's my box. I pull over a chair, climb onto it and drag the box down onto the bed. Making myself comfortable, I peel back the packing tape.

This box hasn't been opened since we left Adelaide, and it's the strangest thing how it smells like our home in Piccadilly. I close my eyes for a moment as memories flood back. I still remember packing it after Mum had told Michael they were over. It was a horrible time. He was distraught and Mum just wanted to get out of there as quickly as possible. Josh came into my bedroom while I was putting my things away and I had to ask him to leave me alone because I was upset. He was twenty-one, almost twenty-two then, but he still lived with his dad. I remember feeling glad that Michael wouldn't be alone when we walked out of the door. And I still recall the look on his face when I kissed him goodbye. He was heartbroken. Mum could barely even look at him, let alone give him a hug. Oh, it was ghastly. Ghastly. I don't usually use that word, but it pretty much sums up the proceedings.

I pull out my school books and take a quick flick through, smirking at the teacher's comments – a reaction I've had to master because it's better than feeling disappointed in myself. I put down the books before regret hits and instantly spy a set of brown spidery legs poking out from under a folded-up poster. I leap off the bed, clutching my hand to my mouth. Were they moving? I don't think so. I take a tentative step towards the box and peer in. Definitely dead. Phew. The spider must have sneaked in when I packed the box all those years ago.

I grab a tissue and grimace as I reach in and retrieve the deceased squatter. I drop it in the wastepaper basket with a shudder and return to the job at hand. I pull out the poster and unfold it to see it's of Fence before they split up and their hot lead singer Johnny Jefferson went solo. There's another of Blur, plus some CDs, books, old pieces of costume jewellery and . . . Oh my God. It's his shirt. His shirt. The one I nicked and never gave back. I lift it up and breathe in deeply. Somewhere in its depths I can still smell him. Or is it my imagination? I slept with it under my pillow for a year, always living in fear that my mum would find it. I gingerly put it to one side and then – there it is, my camera. And underneath it are stacks and stacks of photographs. I'm not sure I have the strength for this.

For a moment I close my eyes and feel the weight of the camera in my hands. It's partly smooth and partly ridged, heavy between my fingers. And then I can see the shots that I took, one by one as though clicking through a projector in my head. New Year confetti sparkling in the hot Australian sun; a giant rocking horse; a kangaroo called Roy; Olivia the koala; the lily pond . . .

But no Ben. I remember I took no shots of Ben.

But you took one of me, didn't you? Do you ever look at it? Do you ever wonder what might have been?

'You didn't say what you wanted for lunch.'

I jump guiltily at the sound of my mum's voice.

'You scared me!'

'Sorry. What are you doing, sitting there with your eyes closed?' she asks.

'Resting.'

'Resting?' she scoffs. 'I thought you stayed in last night?'

'I did. What is there? For lunch,' I add, when she looks confused.

'Oh. A sandwich? Some soup?'

'A sandwich, please. I have soup every day at work. Do you want me to make it?'

'No, no, I think I can just about manage it myself,' she replies with amusement. 'Cheese? Chicken?'

'Cheese is good.'

'I'll get on with it.'

'Thanks,' I murmur, turning back to my camera. I gently place it down on the bed and reach into the box for the photographs. They're better than I remembered them, which surprises me. There's no holding back the regret now. Why did I stop taking pictures? Why?

I'm still sitting there, staring into space, when my mum returns.

'Lunch is ready.'

'Okay, cool.' I look down at the opened box. 'I'll be out in a minute.'

'Leave it there. I'll sort it later. Come and chat to me.'

I reluctantly get up and leave the room, knowing that I'll return in a while to pack up my things. I don't want my mum to touch anything, especially my photographs

We sit at the small round wooden dinner table to eat.

'Have you seen much of Jeremy since – you know?' I ask.

'Nope. Coward used his key to clear out his stuff when I was at work. I haven't seen him since.'

'You're well out of it,' I tell her.

She shrugs nonchalantly. 'I know.'

'Josh is coming over in a couple of weeks.'

'Is he?' She tries to sound disinterested.

'Would you like me to bring him over here to say hi?'

'What would I want you to do that for?'

'I don't know, I thought you might miss him.'

She laughs. 'No way. I'm surprised you two stayed in touch.'

'Why?'

'Well, he seemed so – and don't take this the wrong way – but out of your league.'

'Thanks very much!' She laughs, which does nothing to lessen my annoyance. 'Do you think Richard is out of my league too?' I continue indignantly.

'No, no, you're much more of a catch now.'

'What's that supposed to mean?'

'Oh, you know, Lily, you didn't make very much of yourself back in those days. I even thought at one stage that you were a lesbian.'

'Mum!' She laughs again, clearly enjoying herself. 'What about Dan? Did you think *he* was out of my league?'

'Absolutely. Darling, didn't you? I mean, look how that turned out.'

209

Now I'm properly stung.

'Oh honey, don't be upset. Look at you now – you're gorgeous. Richard is a very, very lucky young man.'

'He's asked me to marry him.'

'*What?*'

I cringe, inwardly *and* outwardly. I wasn't planning on telling her, but it just came out.

'What did you say?' she asks when I don't speak.

'I said yes,' I tell her.

'Did you?' She looks surprised, and not pleasantly so.

'Yes, I did.'

'Oh.' The corners of her mouth turn down and she picks up her sandwich.

'Is that all you're going to say?' Now I'm getting cross again.

'What do you want me to say?'

'Congratulations would be nice.'

'Congratulations, darling.'

'But you don't mean it!'

'You know what I'm like about tying the knot. I didn't think anybody did that these days.'

'Well, they do. And I'm going to. Okay?'

'Of course. It's your life.'

'Oh, you are really pissing me off now.' I throw my sandwich down on my plate in disgust.

'Don't be so sensitive,' she chides, which doesn't help. Neither of us speaks for a while. I sit there, refusing to eat because I'm fuming. 'Have you got an engagement ring?' she asks.

'Don't you think I'd be wearing it if I did?'

'Are you going to get one?' she goes on, ignoring me.

'No.'

'Really? I thought Richard could afford an engagement ring.'

'He can, Mum, but I don't want one.'

'Don't you? Free diamonds are the only good thing about getting married, as far as I'm concerned.'

'Well, why didn't you do it more often, then,' I say irritably. 'It's not like you didn't have the opportunity to. By the way, I hear Michael's very happy with Janine.'

'Good for them,' she says bluntly.

I set off soon after that, but not before I've gone into my bedroom to pack away my things. I take one last inhale of Ben's shirt and place the photos back in the box, feeling twinge after twinge of painful regret. I pick up the camera, but can't bring myself to put it down.

Why don't you take it? Why don't you take photos again?

It's too late, that's why.

It's never too late.

Stop it, Ben! Get out of my head!

But nothing can prise the camera out of my fingers. I can't even bear to put it down to pack away the box so I hang it from its strap around my neck and a strange sensation of elation passes through me as the weight of it thuds into my chest. I climb up onto the chair and slide the box back into the top of the cupboard, pausing for a moment as I think of the photos. I could take them too? No, they're too heavy to carry up the hill to home and I have to catch the bus back to the ferry terminal as it is.

'Have you still got that old thing?' My mum nods at the camera when I come out of the room.

'Yes, I thought I'd take it with me.'

'Take it to the charity shop, is what you should do. I can't believe your dad bought you such a clunky contraption.'

'It wasn't clunky when he got it for me,' I state. 'And anyway, I like it.'

'Like it so much it sat in a box for years.'

'It's seeing the light of day again now.'

'He should get you a new one, that's what he should do. It's not as if he doesn't have the money.'

'I don't need Dad to buy me a new camera, so don't go on about it, alright?'

'Okay, okay. When are they coming out here?'

'In a few weeks. I can't wait to see the girls again.'

'I take it Lorraine's coming?' My mum hates Lorraine. You can hear it in the tone of her voice.

'Of course.'

'I hope they're using contraception. I can't believe she had a third baby at her age.'

'She was only thirty-five!'

Mum pulls a face and I go over to give her a peck on the cheek. 'Bye, Mum. See you soon, okay?'

'If you can drag yourself all the way out here again.'

'You know, you *could* always come and see Richard and me sometime too.'

'No, you're too busy. I'm too busy as well. I'm working all manner of shifts at the moment.'

'Still getting good tips?'

'The best.' She smiles smugly and on that note I leave her.

'Where did you get that?' Richard asks when he sees my camera later.

'It's my old camera. My dad got it for me when I first moved to Australia. I used to take loads of photos.'

'Did you?'

'Yeah. I was kind of pretty good,' I admit.

'Kind of pretty good?' he teases. I blush instead of reply and he doesn't interrogate me further. 'How was your mum?'

'Okay, I think. She asked after you.'

'That's nice,' he says half-heartedly.

'I told her we were getting married.'

'Did you?' He looks up, surprised.

'Yes.'

'I thought we were going to tell our parents together?'

'Sorry, it just kind of slipped out.'

'What did she say?'

'She was happy for us. Sort of.'

He laughs wryly. 'I bet. I hope it gave you good practice because we're going over to Mum and Dad's for a late lunch tomorrow. Sally and Brenda are going to be there, too.'

Sally and Brenda are Richard's sisters. They're a bit full of themselves. Sally is younger than Richard by eighteen months; Brenda is older by three years. Neither has settled down yet, but I did hear through Nathan that Sally has set her sights on one of his employees.

'Oh, really?'

'No need to sound quite so excited,' he says jokily. He knows I'm not a big fan of his sisters and, quite frankly, it's going to be hard enough telling his parents without having Little and Large making snide comments in the background.

'Here you go, love.'

'Thanks.' I gratefully accept a glass of champagne from Richard's dad. I'm going to need this.

Anne and Joe's house is in Mosman, a short drive from Manly. I don't own a car because I commute to work by ferry quite happily, so we had to take Richard's truck. He keeps it reasonably tidy, but I always feel like it's dirty and I regretted my decision to wear a cream dress as soon as I stepped up into the cabin.

'You look lovely today, Lily,' Richard's mum Anne says.

'Thank you.' My natural impulse is to dust down my dress. 'I hope there are no marks on it,' I say.

'No, no.' She glances behind me as I look round at my bum. 'It's perfect.'

I do like his parents, but I don't feel at ease in their home. It's strange because they've never been anything but nice to me.

Anne is a plump woman of about five foot five with tightly-curled brown hair. Richard's grey-haired father Joe towers above her at six foot three. He's skinny as a beanpole and has a large nose, upon which sits a pair of horn-rimmed glasses. Brenda and Sally take after each of them in stature: Brenda is short and plump, and Sally is tall and willowy. As for Richard, he has his dad's height, but he's not lanky. I guess years of pulling his weight on building sites has built up muscles his maths teacher father otherwise lacks.

Anne doesn't work, but she does knit. A lot. Sally sells some of her hand-knitted children's rattles in a shop where she works in Manly. It's actually the shop where Molly used to work before she became Mikey's full-time mum. I say full-time, but Molly also beavers away at home as a fashion designer. Her offbeat, quirky clothes have become quite popular with Sydney's trendsetters.

'How are you?' Brenda interrupts my thoughts. 'How's the job?'

'I'm good, the job's fine,' I reply breezily. 'How about you?' Brenda works in finance for a large bank in the city.

'Fantastic. Business is booming! I can't believe they ever said we were in a recession; *we* haven't seen any cutbacks.'

'You're lucky,' I comment.

'Luck! Nothing to do with luck. Life is what you make of it, that's what I always say.'

'Tell that to the mates of mine who have lost their jobs,' Richard interrupts crossly and I'm pleased. I hate the way Brenda goes on sometimes.

'Top-up?' Joe tactfully produces champagne as we hear the front door open and slam.

'Where is everyone?' Sally calls.

'In here!' Joe shouts back.

'Sorry I'm late.' She bustles into the room, removing a heavy knitted black cardigan as she enters. 'This super-rich bloke came in at ten to six and bought out half the shop. He took some of your rattles, Mum.'

'Ooh, how lovely,' Anne comments agreeably.

'Do you get commission?' Brenda interjects.

'No,' Sally replies.

'You should sort that out with your boss,' Brenda tells her. 'No point working in a shop if you can't get commission.'

'Champagne, darling?' Good old Joe.

'So, we have some news,' Richard says when we're all sitting around the table tucking into Anne's home-baked chicken pie. Nerves swirl around my stomach as the attention falls on us both.

'You're pregnant!' Sally bursts out.

'No,' Brenda says decisively. 'They're getting married.'

I told you they were annoying.

'Let them tell us,' Anne chides gently.

'Well?' Joe prompts as Richard gives me a wry look. 'Which is it?'

'I've asked Lily to marry me and' – cue shriek from his mum – 'she said yes.'

Another shriek as Anne pushes out her chair and leaps to her feet. 'Oh, darling, that's wonderful news!'

'Congratulations, son.' Joe stands and shakes Richard's hand while he's in the midst of being smothered by Anne. His mum turns to me so I stand up, too.

'Such exciting news, Lily,' she says, pulling me in for a cuddly hug. I can't help but smile.

Joe leans over to peck my cheek, saying, 'Well done, dear, that's fabulous.'

'Congratulations!' Brenda booms from her sitting position.

'Yes, well done!' Sally also doesn't get up. We all take our seats again.

'When's the big day?' Brenda asks through mouthfuls of chicken pie.

Richard glances at me before tactfully replying, 'We haven't decided yet.'

'Oh, do make it soon,' she says. 'Long engagements are so tedious.'

'We'll let you know as soon as we know,' Richard assures her firmly.

'Don't get married in January,' Sally interjects. 'I'm going to Thailand then.'

'Are you?' Joe turns to her in surprise.

'Yeah. We haven't booked our flights yet, but that's the plan.'

'Who's we?' Anne asks, similarly taken aback.

'Me and Cathy from the shop.'

'But you've never travelled out of Australia!' Anne exclaims.

'About time she did, then,' Brenda says. 'When I went to Bali in my twenties' – she says this as if her twenties were decades ago, but she's only thirty-one – 'I swore I'd partake in international travel every year.'

'What happened?' Richard asks.

'Life took hold,' she says, trying to project an aura of mysterious wisdom. Then: 'Anyway, we should eat up before our dinner goes cold.'

And that's the end of the discussion for now.

'That went well,' Richard says later when we're in the truck on the way home. He rushed me out of there at four forty-five because the Australian Grand Prix is about to start and he's a bit of a sports nut.

I look at him and grin. He smirks back at me. 'At least they didn't subject you to the Spanish Inquisition,' he adds.

'True. That's probably on the cards next time.'

For want of something better to do I sit with him to watch the start of the race. I don't mind Formula 1. Some of the drivers are quite sexy, especially that Brazilian Luis Castro, who's starting from pole position.

'Do you really not want a ring?' Richard glances at me with a doleful expression on his face as the drivers set off on their warm-up lap.

'No. Honestly, no,' I assure him. 'A wedding band will be fine.'

'A wedding band with diamonds though – right?' He smiles at me hopefully.

'Yes.' I smile back. 'A wedding band with diamonds would be lovely.'

'And what about getting married in January next year?'

'The January that Sally's going to Thailand?'

'Or February, if we have to.'

I shake my head. 'It's too soon. Really, it's too soon.'

'We could have a winter wedding?'

'No. Summer would be better.'

'Spring?'

'Summer. Summer 2011.'

He sighs. 'Okay, then.'

'Brenda will just have to suck it up,' I add.

'Indeed she will.'

'Look, the race is about to start.'

And until sexy Luis Castro crosses the line in first place and snogs his annoyingly beautiful girlfriend, that – for the time being – is the end of the matter.

Chapter 17

Nathan and Lucy get back from their honeymoon on the same day that Josh arrives from Adelaide. He catches a taxi to our place.

'What's with the rain?' he humphs when I open the door. 'It was thirty degrees in Adelaide when I left.'

'It's supposed to clear up tomorrow for Easter Sunday,' I assure him. 'Anyway, you moody bugger, give me a hug.'

He grins and steps into the hall, dropping his bag to engulf me. 'Even after all these years you still sound like a Pommie.'

He's still unbelievably good-looking, but after my initial attraction, I only ever had eyes for Ben.

And now Richard, of course.

'Where's Richard?' He glances past me to the living room.

'He's gone to welcome his mate back from his honeymoon.'

'Three's company . . .' he says jokily.

'He won't stay long. He just wanted to drop in some supplies.'
Which I thought was very nice of him, *actually*.

'Can I get you something to drink?'

'What have you got?'

'Coke, Fanta, apple juice, wine, beer . . .' My voice trails off.

'Fanta, thanks.' He never did go back to drinking and driving. 'Hey, this is cool.' He looks around. 'I like the garden.'

We'd only just moved in when Josh last came to Sydney to visit. It's changed tenfold since then.

'Thanks. Do you want to chuck your bag in your room? It's that one there.' I point across the hall.

He comes back as I'm pouring our drinks into glasses. We take them to the sofa.

'How are Michael and Janine?'

'Really good. Busy at work, as ever. Janine's been caring for a baby koala at home for the last few days.' I wince as a memory of Ben gently holding a tiny Olivia comes back to me. 'I popped in to see them last night before I left,' Josh continues, oblivious to my pain.

'How's Tina?'

He shrugs. 'Yeah, she's good. Fine.'

'Have you two moved in together yet?' He lives in Mount Barker now, in a small house of his own.

'Hell, no. I'd never get her to move out,' he jokes.

I laugh. 'Some people would say that's the point of being in a relationship.'

'I'm not ready for that yet.'

'Fair enough.'

I hear a key turn in the front door lock and Richard appears a moment later. Josh gets up to shake his hand.

'Alright, Richard, how's it going?'

'Yeah, good thanks, mate.'

'How were the happy couple?' Josh asks.

'I had to wear sunnies to shield my eyes from their glow.'

220

'Really!' I grin. 'Good time, then?'

'The best.'

'What was the resort like?'

'I didn't stick around long enough to ask. Didn't want to out-stay my welcome. I did tell them about us though.'

'Richard!' I exclaim. 'It's supposed to still be all about them.'

'Sorry.' He holds up his hands to shield himself as though I'm going to rain down blows on him. 'I couldn't help it.'

'What's this?' Josh interjects, looking confused.

I turn to him and compose myself. 'We're getting married.'

'Are you?' He looks taken aback. 'Wow. Congratulations.'

'Thanks.' I can feel my face heating up.

Josh addresses Richard. 'I hope you know what you're letting yourself in for.'

'Hey!' I exclaim, mock indignantly, but Richard wraps his arm around my neck and pulls me in, saying, 'I've got the ball and chain ready.'

I whack him on his chest and free myself. 'What do you want to drink?' I ask my – I was going to say boyfriend, but it's fiancé now, isn't it? I cannot cope with this.

Richard glances down at the half-full glasses on the coffee table. 'Fanta would be cool.' He and Josh sit on the sofa.

Fiancé. *Fiancé!* It sounds so . . .

Old?

Yes, Ben, it sounds old. I know what you mean, now.

'So what are the plans for tonight?' Josh interrupts my internal conversation.

'We're meeting some friends of mine from work.' I turn to Richard. 'Are Molly and Sam coming?'

'No, they've got Molly's parents round,' Richard replies. 'The invite is still open for tomorrow's Easter barbecue though. I said I'd let them know because I wasn't sure what you two had planned.'

I glance at Josh and I'm unable to read his expression. 'Cool, thanks.' I don't know if he'd rather go sightseeing, but I'll check with him later.

Nicola and Mel are already at the bar when we arrive later that night. Even from the doorway I can see that Nicola is practically vibrating with excitement. We're meeting at one of the trendy bars at the International Passenger Terminal near Circular Quay. It doesn't sound glam, but it is. The girls have got there early enough to bag us a table with a view of the Opera House.

'Good work!' I beam as we approach. 'Nicola, Mel, this is Josh. Josh, Nicola, Mel.'

Both leap to their feet to shake his hand. Even in the low light I can see that Nicola has gone red.

'You remember Richard,' I add.

'Hi,' Richard says, leaning in to kiss them each on the cheek. 'I'll go to the bar. What are you two drinking?'

'We're on the cocktails,' Mel says, snatching the menu from the centre of the glossy orange table. The guys wait with remark-able patience as we fuss and coo over the different concoctions, then Josh sets off to the bar with my boyfriend.

Yes, *boyfriend*. I'm not using that other word, it sounds too ridiculous.

'Holy shit!' Nicola breathes as soon as their backs have turned. I look at her and grin at the wide-eyed astonishment on her face. 'He's even better-looking in real life!'

'I told you,' I warn her. 'He has a girlfriend, remember.'

'Yeah, whatever.' She waves me away. 'And you honestly expect me to believe you never shagged him?'

'I never shagged him,' I say firmly, rolling my eyes at Mel.

'What a wasted opportunity,' she says wistfully. 'Not even when your parents were out?'

'Not even when our parents were out. So what did you two get up to yesterday?' I turn the subject to Bank Holiday proceedings and am soon bombarded with details of Mel's conquest on Thursday night with a banker from the city.

'He stuck around for breakfast?' I ask. 'That sounds promising.'

'Yep,' Mel replies gleefully. 'We went for pancakes.'

'Woohoo! Are you seeing him again?'

'He's going to call.'

'Fingers crossed, then,' I say as Richard and Josh return with a variety of multi-coloured drinks.

'I can't remember which is which,' Josh says, plonking the drinks on the table.

'Well, *I* ordered an Orgasm,' Nicola says flirtatiously. 'And I want to have at least one of those tonight so you'd better deliver one way or another.'

I stifle an outraged cry as Josh grins down at her before slumping into a chair. Mel and I gawp at each other, then at Nicola, but she pretends not to notice.

'How was your flight?' Mel asks Josh. I look across at Richard, still reeling from the shock of Nicola's brazenness, but he shrugs and grins.

A few cocktails in and I've lightened up considerably.

'Where are we going from here?' Josh asks. He's been basking in the glow of Nicola's attention for the last two hours.

'A Mexican restaurant I know. It's got a good party atmosphere,' I say.

'Sounds great.'

'And then we'll hit a club if you haven't collapsed by then.'

'Collapsed?' Josh sniggers. 'Don't you remember, I'm a hardcore party animal.'

'That was years ago. You're an old man now.'

'Twenty-eight? Old? Please!'

Twenty-eight. Twenty-eight. That age again.

Clear as day I see Ben's dark-blue eyes staring into mine on the night we bumped into each other in Hahndorf. That was when I knew he felt something for me.

'She's got that far-off look in her eyes again.'

I come back to the present with a bump to see everyone staring at me. Mel is grinning mischievously.

'What *are* you thinking about?' she prods.

I shake my head, dumbly.

'She's been like this loads over the last couple of weeks, hasn't she, Nicola?'

'Yes,' Nicola says, smiling.

It's true. I've been thinking about Ben a lot recently. Much more than I ever used to. I can't get him out of my head, day *or* night. He's there. Like a permanent resident.

'She's probably wedding planning,' Richard chips in.

'Wedding? Whose wedding?' Nicola shrieks.

'Haven't you . . .' Richard's question trails off as he gives me a querying look. I shake my head briskly, but it's too late.

'You're NOT!' Nicola cries.

I shrug, embarrassed.

'*She is!* When? When did he ask you?'

I glance at Richard, who is staring at me with a strange expression on his face. 'Two weeks ago.'

'And you kept it from us?' Nicola all but hollers. 'Why? Why would you do such a thing?'

'Yes, Lily, why?' Richard asks as quietly as the loud music will allow.

I give him a hopeless look. 'I didn't want to take anything away from Nathan and Lucy.'

'Who the hell are Nathan and Lucy?' Mel chips in, very unhelpfully I might add.

'They don't even know Nathan and Lucy,' Richard says, and I shrug again. Even Nicola, who is halfway down the tipsy hill to drunk, starts to register the uncomfortable atmosphere.

'I'm starving!' Josh exclaims. 'Can we get out of here, or what?'

'I didn't want them to make a big fuss,' I tell Richard later as we lag behind the others on our way out of the restaurant. He's been avoiding my gaze throughout the entire meal and I need to say something now because I've been feeling a bit sick for the past two hours. 'I'm still getting used to the idea myself,' I continue to explain when he doesn't comment. 'Richard, please say something.'

'It's fine.'

'You don't sound fine.'

'I'm a little concerned,' he admits, glancing at me with his warm brown eyes and it does nothing to expel the bad feeling in my stomach. 'You've been acting strangely ever since I . . . I just don't know if there's something else going on. You're always off out with your camera, and I guess you seem different somehow.'

'I don't know what you mean. Yes, I've been taking photos,' I

225

say crossly, 'but how could you possibly have a problem with that? It makes me happy.'

'It never made you happy before.'

'It did! I used to love using my camera.'

'Why did you stop then?'

I can't find the words to answer.

'It seems to have come out of nowhere,' he explains. 'I feel like I don't know you.'

'I'm sorry if it makes you feel threatened,' I say coldly.

'It's not tha—'

'But I'm not going to stop.' I cruelly cut him off, even though I heard the softening in his voice.

'Suit yourself,' he says unhappily, as he stalks off down the pavement towards the others. Mel is trying to flag down a taxi while Nicola is gazing up at Josh through her heavily mascaraed lashes. He's grinning down at her with his hands in his pockets. The sight does nothing to quell my nausea, but I've had just about enough. If he wants to screw her, so be it. I don't know Tina, but I'll be disappointed in Josh if he lets her down.

A six-seater taxi pulls up and we all climb in. Richard and I get in the very back and sit apart from each other, staring out of the window at the city lights flashing past. Nicola has squeezed herself between Mel and Josh. The last place I feel like going right now is a club. I know Richard feels the same. I glance across at my boyfriend and have a sudden impulse to take his hand. But I don't.

We wind our way through the streets and pull up outside the venue in Kings Cross. Josh helps Nicola out of the taxi. I give Mel a rueful look as we walk up the steps to greet the bouncers.

'This is turning out to be couples central,' she murmurs. 'I'm starting to wish my horny banker could have come along.'

'Does your horny banker *do* clubs?' I ask.

'No, probably not,' she admits.

'Then let's go and dance our asses off while we can,' I say, full of determination. I drag her through the crowds towards the dance-floor as the beat of the drums reverberates through our bodies. It's not long before a couple of drunken idiots start gyrating against us. I grab Mel and move away so we can dance without interruption.

I hate clubs. Full of pricks.

Get out of my head, Ben.

A short while later, Nicola joins us. Soon afterwards, Josh does too.

'Where's Richard?' I shout into Josh's ear.

'At the bar. Didn't want to dance!' he shouts back.

No, he hates dancing. Out of the blue I'm wracked with guilt. I've been horrible to him! I excuse myself and go to find him. He's nursing a rum and coke and is people-watching. I sidle up to him and he looks down at me, a blank expression on his face.

'I'm sorry,' I say seriously. He nods and looks away. 'Please look at me.'

He tears his eyes away from a group of clubbers outrageously dressed in neon colours and meets my gaze.

'I really am.'

'It's okay,' he says quietly, his face softening. He pushes a strand of hair away from my face. 'You know, your dad and Lorraine have been married to each other for almost twenty years and their marriage works.' I nod. 'It's nothing to be scared of, Lily.'

I nod again as he leans behind himself to place his drink down on a ledge. He turns back and puts his hands on my waist, pulling me between his legs.

'I love you,' he tells me, stroking my cheek with his thumb.

'I love you, too.' I offer him a weak smile and he dips his face to touch his lips to mine. Our kiss turns into a full-on snog.

'Right, that's it. I'm off.'

We break away to see a disgruntled Mel standing there. 'I've had enough of feeling left out with you randy lot!'

I laugh and give her a hug, but we all decide to call it a night soon after that.

Chapter 18

'So did she manage to get her talons into you?' I ask Josh the next morning. Well, closer to afternoon, really. Some things never change.

'Who? Nicola?'

'Yes.' I give him a look.

'Fuck off,' he snorts as he chews on a mouthful of Easter egg. 'I wouldn't do that to Tina.'

'You looked pretty cosy there in the back of the taxi,' I say ominously. 'Are you sure she didn't slip you her tongue on the way out?'

'She didn't even slip me her phone number,' he says.

'Really?'

'Really.'

'Well, I *am* surprised. I'm sure she'll ask me for yours when we get back to work on Tuesday.'

'You'd better not give it to her.' He winks at me. 'Tina knows I'm a flirt, but she wouldn't take kindly to a girl actually calling me.'

I smile at him, full of relief. 'So what do you want to do today?'

'Suggestions?'

'We could go for an Easter barbecue at Richard's friends' house. Or we could go sightseeing, body boarding, check out a museum or aquarium or the zoo or something like that?'

'Would Richard be offended if we didn't go for lunch?'

'Of course not. You've hardly got any time here – he'll know you want to make the most of it.'

'I wouldn't mind going for a walk around the Rocks, play tourist for a day.'

'We can do that.'

In the end, Richard decides to drop in at Sam and Molly's and leave us to it, and I encourage him. We've got in some champagne and a lobster for tonight so we'll still spend some of Easter Sunday together. As I rarely get to see Josh, it's nice to be able to have quality time alone with him.

We walk down the hill into Manly and hop onto a green and cream ferry to the south side of the harbour. It's a clear, sunny day, but there's still a hefty breeze whipping my hair around my face.

'It really suits you like that.' Josh nods at my haircut.

'I had it done years ago!' I exclaim.

'I know,' he says. 'But I don't think I've ever said it out loud.'

'Well, thanks.'

'You're quite a babe these days.'

'Josh!'

He shrugs. 'You are.'

'Now you're winding me up.'

He laughs. 'I'm not.'

It's funny how we can be like this with each other, but there's absolutely no attraction there whatsoever. I love it. It's comfortable.

I notice a couple of girls staring at us enviously and instinctively want to mouth, 'I'm not with him!' but manage to restrain myself.

The sailboats are out in force again and the sun is hitting the waves with the same spark of light that made me first wish I had my camera back. On impulse I get out my clunky old contraption and aim it at a sailboat which is about to criss-cross with another. I click off a shot, but don't think it quite works.

'I recognise that camera,' Josh interrupts before I can line up another shot. 'You used to take loads of photos when you first moved to Australia, didn't you? Then you stopped. That dawned on me one day when you were at school, but I never remembered to ask you why.'

I pause for a moment and stare down at the object in my hands. 'I guess I got caught up with my new friends and forgot about my hobbies.' I put the camera away, feeling too self-conscious to continue now. 'Hey, do you ever bump into Tammy down the pub?'

'Now and again.'

'How's Shane?'

Josh grins. 'He's pretty good. I'll tell him you asked after him. His spirits will soar and then I'll reveal you're getting married and they'll crash and burn.'

'Meanie.' I slap him on his arm, good-naturedly. 'Has he got a girlfriend now?'

'No. Still pining for you,' he says sadly.

'Stop it! Shane never fancied me, really.'

'Yes, he did,' Josh says firmly. 'But then you became friends with his little sis and Tammy would have threatened to smash up all his computer games rather than see any friend of hers hook up with her brother.'

I laugh. 'She *was* a bit like that, wasn't she?'

'Demented,' Josh says fondly. He always did like Tammy. Not in that way, but she was feisty and never took any rubbish from him. I dare say he respected that.

'Do you think I'm crazy to get married?' I suddenly find myself asking him.

'Er, no – not if Richard's the right guy for you.'

'Do *you* think he's right for me?'

He laughs. 'What a question! I hardly know him, but you both seem pretty happy.'

'We are,' I murmur. 'Most of the time.'

'What was going on with you two last night?' he asks. It would have been impossible to miss the fact that we were having a row.

I sigh. 'Oh, he was annoyed with me for not telling my colleagues about our *impending nuptials*.' I say the last bit in a comedy fashion to make it sound less scary. It doesn't work.

'He's got a point,' Josh says thoughtfully. 'Why hadn't you told them? Most people wouldn't be able to keep something like that to themselves.'

I shrug. 'I don't know. I didn't want them to make a fuss.' Even to me I sound unconvincing. 'Are your dad and Janine happy?'

'Yeah.'

'That's good to hear.'

'You know, just because things haven't worked out for your mum, doesn't mean they won't work out for you,' he says directly.

I grin at him. 'That's very perceptive of you, Joshua. Richard says the exact same thing.'

'Oh well, if he's like me, why *wouldn't* you want to marry him?'

We laugh and turn away from each other, but I'm thinking that he's wrong. And Richard is wrong, too. It's not the concept of marriage that frightens me. It's Ben. It's always been Ben. I told

232

myself I'd lost him when he left, but deep down, I don't know if
I did. What if I met him again? What if his marriage didn't work
out? What would I do then? *That's* why I can't get married. I can't
take that risk. Should I try to find him again?

Lily, what the hell are you thinking? This is crazy talk. Ben is gone.
Richard is your here and now, and he's a good here and now. No,
better than that, he's a *great* here and now. Of course you have the
odd little argument, but so does everyone. I can't believe you're
even contemplating finding Ben.

I swivel to face Josh and open my mouth to speak, but quickly
close it again.

'What?' he asks.

Too late. Can't stop the words from coming out. 'Does Michael
ever hear from Ben?'

'Ben who?'

'Ben Whiting. You know – Ben who used to work at the conservation park.'

'Oh, him.' Recognition lights up Josh's face and my heart
jumps. 'No,' he replies, making it wither again. 'Not that I know
of. I didn't think you knew him that well.'

'I didn't.' I try to cover my tracks. 'But he looked after me
when I started work and I wondered what became of him after he
got married.'

Josh shrugs as the Opera House comes into view. He's soon distracted while I stand there, full of guilt and kicking myself for
taking steps towards a path that could potentially devastate my
relationship, my boyfriend – and of course, me.

As predicted, Nicola asks me for Josh's email address when I get
back to work on Tuesday. Josh left yesterday morning and he

admitted he was quite looking forward to getting back to his 'bird'.

'Sorry. No can do.'

'Come on!' Nicola cries.

'Don't shoot the messenger.' I shuffle some papers on my desk, trying not to meet her eyes.

'What do you mean, "messenger"?' she asks. 'Did he tell you not to give it to me?'

'Technically speaking, he said "phone number", but it amounts to the same thing.'

'It does not.'

'It does.'

'Not.'

'Does!'

'What are you two going on about?' Mel breaks us up as she arrives for work.

'Nothing,' Nicola mutters, a little flustered as she refocuses on her emails.

I could try to placate her, but I don't think there's anything I can say so I get on with checking my own emails instead.

Jonathan Laurence, the Editor-in-Chief of *Marbles* magazine, walks in.

'Good morning,' he says to Nicola and me. Mel has gone to make tea so he'll have no flirty chat today. 'Good weekend?'

'Great, thanks,' I answer pleasantly.

Nicola manages a small shrug, but that's it.

'Can I ask you girls a favour?' Mr Laurence says.

Mr Laurence? His name is *Jonathan*. Now I'm sounding like Mel!

'Sure,' I respond.

Nicola says nothing, so *Jonathan* directs his attention at me.

'Our editorial assistant is ill and our picture assistant is on holiday this week, and we've got a bunch of photographers coming in with their portfolios. Could you have them wait down here and call up to me when they arrive?'

'Of course,' I tell him. 'Do they have allocated time slots?'

'Yes.'

'Shall I make a note of them, and then I won't bother you if you're still with the one before?'

He looks relieved. 'That would be great.' He rummages around in his briefcase and pulls out a diary, flicking through to the correct week. 'Here they are.' He passes it across the reception desk to me and I glance down at the notations under today's date. I quickly scribble down the names and times on my pad and hand back his diary, but not before my curious eyes have unwittingly scanned the next couple of day's worth of entries.

Wednesday: Lisa flowers

Thursday: Anniversary/Pier Frank launch

Pier Frank . . . I know that name. That's right, he's a photographer. I remember seeing an article about him in . . . I think it might have been *Marbles* magazine, actually. Not that I read *Marbles* – it's a glossy men's title – but we try to keep up with what's happening in all our publications.

'Thanks so much for that – sorry, I don't know your name.' He looks apologetic.

'Lily.' I smile. 'And it's not a problem.'

'Are you English?' he asks as Mel returns with our tea. I see her momentarily falter and tea sloshes over the side of one of the cups. She winces as the heat scalds her hand, but skilfully manages to stay quiet.

'Yes, I grew up there.' I answer his question.

'Good morning, Mr Laurence,' Mel chirps.

'Good morning, Melissa,' he says back.

'Good weekend?'

'Lovely, thanks. Yourself?'

'Fab.'

'Great. Well, thanks for that, Lily.'

'You're welcome.'

He smiles at Mel and me and looks towards Nicola, but her head is still buried in her computer.

'Have a good day.' And then he's off up the stairs.

'What was all that about?' Mel asks excitedly, pulling out her stool.

'Are you alright?' I check the burn, concerned.

'Oh yeah, don't worry about that.' She waves her hand dismissively. 'Tell me,' she insists, so I fill her in. 'You held his diary,' she says dreamily.

'I also noticed that he's buying his wife flowers for their anniversary on Thursday.' I nudge her jokily.

'Talk about kicking her in the guts,' Nicola snaps spitefully.

Mel and I glance at her in shock, then Mel gives me a look that says, 'What the hell's got into *her*?'

I shrug and avert my gaze, not wanting to say anything. I hate confrontation and Nicola's nastiness instantly makes me feel quite nauseous.

'Sorry,' Nicola mutters, so I dare to look up again. She glances from Mel to me and back again. 'Josh didn't want me to have his number. Or email address,' she adds. 'I'm a bit mortified.'

'Well, he does have a girlfriend.' Mel states the obvious.

'I know.' Nicola looks away, embarrassed. 'It's just that I put so much time and energy into getting an Orgasm . . .' Her face breaks into a grin and we all crack up. 'Bastard,' Nicola says under her breath when our laughs subside. Then she grins again and relief washes over me. 'So, when are all these sexy photographers coming in?'

Mel has to organise a conference this morning so she has no choice but to leave me to liaise with Jonathan. It all goes swimmingly until the fourth photographer needs to use the toilet and then walks into the lift without his portfolio. I rush after him, but the doors close in my face.

'I'll bring it up!' I shout, not sure if he can hear me. I push the button to call another lift and step inside when the doors swish open. The black portfolio is heavy in my hands. I glance down at it and am on the verge of unzipping it to have a quick look when the lift stops at the third floor and someone gets in. We travel up to the fifth and I walk out, but there's no one waiting on the landing. I dither for a moment and watch the red light display above the lift the photographer took. It's now on the ninth floor. I glance at the door to *Marbles* magazine and go through, remembering that the editorial assistant is ill so there's no one to immediately ask. Jonathan's office is on the other side of the room and I feel self-conscious as I walk past all the trendy magazine people. Through the glass I can see Jonathan sitting at a desk along with the Picture Director, Guy Jenson. I knock on the door and push it open.

'Sorry,' I say as they stare at me questioningly. 'David Snide, your eleven-thirty, forgot this.' I place the portfolio on the table and let it go with a slight thump.

'Ah, thanks, Lily,' Jonathan says as we glance out of the glass divide to see a flustered Mr Snide enter the *Marbles* quarters. He looks around, panicked.

'I'll go get him,' I say, grinning.

Jonathan smiles back, a twinkle in his eye.

The next day when Jonathan appears for work he walks straight up to the reception desk, eyeing me with a look of determination.

'Good morning,' he says brightly.

'Good morning,' I chirp back, giving him an inquisitive look and wondering what this is about.

'Lily, our editorial assistant Bronte has appendicitis and she's going to be off all week and quite possibly next week too.'

I can feel Nicola's curious eyes on us. Mel, thankfully, is off making tea.

'You seem very capable,' Jonathan continues. 'Much more capable than the last two temps we've had in to cover for people. Would you be up for working at *Marbles* until Bronte's better?'

'Aah,' I start. 'I'd have to check with my boss.'

My *boss* boss, i.e. the person who employed me, is the Head of Human Resources, Darren Temper. He tends to leave us to it with Nicola at the helm.

'I hope you don't mind,' Jonathan continues. 'I know Darren well and asked him last night. He has no problem with it if you don't.'

The chance to work at a magazine – an actual magazine, with a whole team of people: photographers, picture editors . . .

He's standing there, waiting for an answer.

'In that case, I'd love to!' I beam. *Shit, is Mel going to kill me?*

As soon as he's gone, I turn to Nicola and hiss, 'Do you think Mel will mind?'

'Will I mind what?' Mel interrupts, returning with three mugs of tea on a small tray.

'Good idea.' I gesture at the tray, then feeling like a meek little lamb, manage to look her in the face. 'Jonathan asked me to cover for their sick editorial assistant.'

'You lucky bitch!' she cries.

'Do you mind?'

'Of course not. Get in there. Debbie's coming back in a few months, you've got to make all the contacts you can.'

'Is Debbie definitely returning?' My heart sinks a little and Mel looks sympathetic as she nods.

'It's pretty much a cert. She can't afford not to. So you go for it – don't you think, Nicola?'

'Absolutely. I totally agree,' Nicola responds.

'Okay.' I smile at them shyly and start to pack up my things.

Jonathan settles me at my temporary desk by the magazine entrance. Thankfully, most of his staff have yet to arrive, so it's not too mortifying standing there while he explains the bare basics. He tells me he'll fill me in on other stuff as and when I need to know, but for now I'm to answer calls and emails and help out with anything anyone asks of me.

The rest of the staff who make up *Marbles* magazine begin to filter in. Some ignore me, others nod and say hi. Only one girl with a cheerful-looking face asks if I'm filling in for Bronte, shortly afterwards commenting, 'Hey, aren't you one of the girls from reception?'

'Yes,' I tell her, fully aware of how invisible we receptionists can appear to people, even though they see us every day.

'I'm Xanthe,' she says. 'I work on the health desk.'

'Oh, cool. Do you get loads of free stuff?'

'Hell, yeah. It's why I took the job. *Marbles* may be a men's mag, but PRs still send me girlie beauty products to butter me up. Listen, let me know if you need any help with anything. I started off as work experience and covered for Bronte myself once or twice in the early days, so I pretty much know what the job entails.'

'Thanks very much.' I smile up at her. It's nice to find a friendly face at last.

As the day wears on, I find my feet and start to relax. At one o'clock I knock on Jonathan's door.

'I'm popping out to grab some lunch,' I say. 'Do you want me to get you anything?'

'No, thanks.' He brushes me off. 'I've got to nip out myself to get the missus some flowers. It's our anniversary tomorrow,' he reveals.

'How many years?' I dare to ask.

'Eight.'

'Congratulations. Are you sure you don't need anything? I mean, I could even get the flowers if you want me to.'

'She'd kill me if I didn't get them myself.' He grins. 'Anyway, I know what she likes.' He gets to his feet. 'I'll come out with you now.'

I feel a mild sense of panic at the idea of walking down the stairs with him and entering reception together. He grabs his suit jacket and shrugs it on while I wait at the door and follow him out.

'I always take the stairs. Can you handle them in those heels?' He nods at my feet.

'Sure, the walk will do me good.'

'How are you finding everything?'

'Good, thanks. Have you spoken to Bronte?'

'No, she's recovering from the operation.'

'Poor her. How did you get on with all those photographers yesterday?' I ask, trying to keep up with his pace. I just about manage.

'Really well. One or two stood out.'

'I thought you'd already have a set bunch of people you use.'

'We do, but it's good to keep things fresh. Introduce some new talent.'

'Are there many people working on the picture desk?'

'Three. But as I said, Kip, our picture assistant, is on holiday until next week. Are you interested in photography?'

'Er, well – yes, I am, kind of.' His question takes me by surprise.

'So reception is a stepping stone?'

I've never really thought about it, to be honest, but I don't want to admit to that. 'I guess so.' And then I feel stupid. 'Not that I think I have much hope.'

'Why not? Everyone has to start somewhere. Darryl James, the Deputy Ed at *Flipside*, used to work in the post room.'

'*Did* he?'

'Yes. Everyone has to work their way up.'

'What about you? Where did you start?'

'My path was dull in comparison. I came straight out of college and started as a junior writer on the newsdesk. But most people do work experience.'

'Like Xanthe.'

'Exactly.'

We round the corner and I realise we're on the ground floor.

'I might go and say hi to Nicola and Mel,' I tell him.

'See you later,' is what he replies with. And then we break away to go in opposite directions.

'How's it going?' Mel squeaks, nodding after Jonathan's departing back as he exits the building. Nicola, it seems, is already out to lunch.

'Really well,' I tell her honestly. 'A bit nervewracking at first, but it's kind of exciting.'

'I knew you'd be fine,' she says, smiling. 'What's Mr Laurence like?'

I grin. '*Jonathan* is being very welcoming.'

Mel suddenly looks conspiratorial. 'I shagged my horny banker again last night.'

'Did you?' I breathe a sigh of relief. No wonder she's being so cool about things. 'And?'

'He was horny.' She smirks.

'You haven't even told me his name.'

'Terence.'

'Terence?'

'Yeah. Terence Horn.'

'You have got to be kidding me.'

'I'm not.'

We both burst into hysterics. I back away from the desk, shaking my head with laughter as some visitors enter the building.

'I'm off out for lunch,' I manage to say through my giggles.

She surreptitiously wipes away her tears and smiles politely at the approaching people. 'Good afternoon. How can I help you?'

God, she cracks me up.

That night I can't wait to get home and tell Richard all about my day, but he seems distracted.

'Are you okay?' I ask, as soon as I see his face. He's sitting on the sofa with a beer, but the telly is off.

'Had a bit of a rubbish one today.' He sighs and rests his head back on the sofa. I sit down next to him.

'What happened?'

He looks at me and his features relax. 'Some bits and pieces have gone missing from a building site and Nathan suspects one of our apprentices.'

'That's awful,' I say. 'What are you going to do?'

'It's hard to know unless we catch him in the act. But the trust has gone – even if he's innocent. He's a hard worker, it's such a shame.'

'Why does Nathan suspect him?'

'It's a feeling he's got.'

'That's not very concrete.'

'No. But he also thought his backpack looked a bit bulky yesterday when some tools went walkabout.'

'I'm sorry. That sounds like a nightmare.'

'It's a bit of a shit. How are you?' he asks.

'I'm pretty good.'

'Cool. Shall we get a pizza in?'

'Sure.' I pull out my mobile phone, knowing that this task will fall to me because it always does. 'Ham and pineapple?'

'That's the one.'

I dial the number and place the order, then turn back to Richard, asking, 'What do you want to watch?' He chucks me the remote control. This is not the time or the place. My day can wait.

Chapter 19

Last night Richard got a text from Nathan asking us over for dinner tomorrow night. Apparently Lucy is desperate to show me her honeymoon pics. That's all well and good, except that at lunchtime, Jonathan walks past and plonks an invitation to Pier Frank's photography exhibition on my desk.

'I can't go,' he says. 'I'm having dinner with the missus.'

'Happy anniversary,' I chip in.

'Thanks. RSVP on behalf of yourself and a friend, if you like. Just tell them I passed the invite on.'

'Oh wow, that would be so cool!'

'Don't get too excited. These things are often as dull as ditch-water, but you can have a free glass of wine and check out the exhibition if you're interested in photography.'

'I am, I definitely am.'

I've already asked Nicola – Mel is out with her horny banker so that was easy – and have emailed to RSVP when I suddenly remember Lucy and Nathan's plans for dinner tonight.

'Shit!' I mutter under my breath, and nip out onto the landing to call Richard.

'Honey,' I start, when he answers his mobile.

'What's up?' He can hear from the tone of my voice that something is.

'I can't go tonight.'

'What? Why not?'

'I've been invited to a photography exhibition.'

'And? Do you have to go?'

'I've already said I would.'

'Lily . . .' He sounds disappointed.

'Sorry, but it's really important to me.' Silence. 'Nathan and Lucy won't mind, I can see them at the weekend.'

'Well, they might find it a bit rude,' he snaps. 'You didn't come to Sam and Molly's on Sunday either.'

'I see them all the time!' I exclaim. Now he's being unfair. I *know* they'd all understand.

'What is this exhibition, anyway? Who invited you?'

I haven't told him about my temporary position yet. I wanted him to be excited for me and I knew I wouldn't get that reaction with the mood he was in last night. I'm not going to get it now either, I realise with a heavy heart.

'It's Pier Frank's launch. He's an up-and-coming photographer,' I explain before he can ask. 'I didn't get a chance to tell you yesterday, but the Editor-in-Chief of *Marbles* magazine asked me to cover for their editorial assistant who's off sick this week. He gave me the invite.'

'Are you going with him?' Richard asks suspiciously.

'No, of course not. I'm going with Nicola.'

'It's all arranged, then.'

'I'm sorry.'

Pause. 'Well, okay, then. See you later.'

'I'll text you when I'm on my way home,' I say, but he's already hung up.

I feel guilty for all of ten minutes, but soon my guilt subsides and is replaced by annoyance, shortly followed by anger. Richard is being so unsupportive of my interests. He may be happy being a builder, but I'm not happy being a receptionist. I have goals! Dreams! Okay, so I haven't had these goals or dreams for very long, but I do now, and he should accept that. Not just accept it, but *encourage* it. That's what a good boyfriend – I mean fiancé – should do.

You would be happy for me, Ben. You would encourage me.

That's unfair. You can't compare Richard to a ghost. That's what Ben is, practically. And maybe Ben's not all he was cracked up to be. You were only sixteen, you know. You were probably looking at him through rose-tinted glasses. He's probably a grumpy old git in reality.

You know I'm not.

Yes, I know you're not. But shut up, would you? You're not here and Richard is. Stop interfering!

I am sounding more and more like a crazy woman every day.

Never mind. The upshot is I'm going to this super-cool launch, Nathan and Lucy won't mind, and Richard will get over it. There. It's done.

'Phwoar, sexy!' Nicola squeaks into my ear, later that evening.

I knew she'd fancy the pants off Pier Frank. He's in his mid-twenties, with scruffy dark hair, stubble that verges on a beard, and skinny jeans. He's not that tall at probably only five foot nine, but Nicola is my height at five foot six, so she doesn't care one iota.

'Don't tell me *he* has a girlfriend, because I don't want to hear it,' she jokes, dramatically flicking her long blonde hair away from her face.

'Nah. He's gay.'

'*Nooo!*' she practically squeals.

'Shhh!' I giggle. 'I'm joking. I don't know if he's tied up or not.'

'Phew.' She breathes a sigh of relief and ogles him once more. 'Shall we go and say hi?'

'Not yet.' I drag her back. 'Let's check out the exhibition first, hey?'

The gallery is situated in the Rocks area, so we walked here in about ten minutes. Nicola wanted to hail a taxi because she's a lazy little minx, but I wouldn't let her. She only stopped complaining about her sore feet when we arrived at the venue.

The ceilings are high and the lighting is low, but each of Pier Frank's black and white photographs has been lit with a startling spotlight. His work is dark and disturbing – a dead dog at the side of the road; a man stalking a woman – and the atmosphere suits them well.

'I don't like his stuff very much,' Nicola reveals after ten minutes of browsing.

'No, me neither,' I agree. 'Shall we get pissed in the corner by the kitchen and nab the canapés as they come out?'

'I like your thinking.'

'So what are you going to say to him if you get a chance later?' I ask through a mouthful of goat's cheese and caramelised onion mini-tartlet.

'I don't know. Do you reckon I should tell him I think his work is pants?'

'It's not pants,' I say. 'It's just a bit disturbing.'

'Disturbing, then.'

'Why not? That's clearly the angle he's going for.'

'Of course, you're right. So he'll be delighted with that reaction?'

'Probably.'

'I might nip to the loo,' she says. 'Do you wanna come?'

'No, I'll save our place by the canapés.'

'Back in a tick.'

Five minutes later I'm still standing there like a lemon and starting to wish I'd gone to the toilet after all. I could go now, but it's a big gallery and there are so many people crammed into it that I'd probably miss Nicola on her return and we'd struggle to find each other. She'll be back soon.

But she's not. Another couple of minutes pass. I sip my wine self-consciously and continue to people-watch. I'm not at all comfortable here. There's a middle-aged woman dressed like a prostitute standing next to me, braying like a horse and talking fifteen to the dozen to a man half her age. The gallery is filled with people similar to them. And I don't like it. I couldn't stand being a part of this sort of crowd.

What am I thinking, wanting to be a photographer?

On impulse I pull out my mobile and check my texts. There's nothing from Richard and I suddenly feel sad. I miss him. I wish I was at Nathan and Lucy's right now.

Where the hell is Nicola?

I look up, irritated, and scan the room once more. I take a few steps away from my safe place and scan the second gallery up the stairs, searching for long blonde hair. I catch a glimpse of it, but unsure if it's Nicola or not, don't know if I should go and see. I hesitate for a moment as a fat bloke in a suit stumbles into me and glares at me rather than apologises. I storm up the stairs, feeling furious. That had better not be Nicola up there. If it is . . .

It is! It bloody well is! And she's talking to Pier Frank. What a cow! I halt on the spot for a split-second, then she sees me and looks so elated as she motions me over that my irritation evaporates a little by the time I reach her.

'Sorry,' she whispers urgently in my ear. 'He grabbed me on my way out of the loo. I thought you'd come to find me!'

'I did,' I say through clenched teeth.

'Can I introduce you to my friend, Lily?' Nicola says smoothly and I plaster a smile on my face as Pier turns his attention to me.

'Hi,' he says wryly as he offers his hand. 'Are you having a nice time?'

'Yes, thanks.'

'It seems I've fucked up again, then.'

Several people around him laugh, but I'm failing to see what the joke is. I shift on my feet uncomfortably, but he is no longer paying any attention.

'I'm going home,' I say suddenly.

'What? Why?' Nicola looks horrified.

'I blew out my boyfriend and his friends for this. I should be there with them.'

'But we've only just met him!'

'He's a prick.'

'Shhh! He'll hear you.'

'I don't particularly care.'

'He wasn't really being mean, he just wants people to find his work disturbing.'

I give her a look.

'I know you're already said that,' she continues desperately. 'Please don't go yet.'

My heart sinks. 'Okay.'

So I stand there, like the yellow citrus fruit again, while Nicola and Pier's cronies hang onto his every word, until my drink runs dry and I excuse myself to get another. When I return unhappily after ten minutes of waiting for the staff to find fresh glasses, Nicola is beaming like a beacon.

'He's asked me to go for a few drinks.'

'Really?' I try to look excited for her. 'Just the two of you?'

'No, with this lot, too, but hey ho.' She looks delighted. 'Will you come?'

'No, thanks. I'd better head home.'

'Okay.'

Not that I was invited, I imagine. I take a swig of my drink and put it down on a ledge and follow them out. Pier gets accosted by the braying prostitute so I take my leave.

'See you tomorrow,' Nicola whispers.

'Use a condom,' I whisper back and she cracks up laughing. I was joking! I hope she steers well clear of the moron.

There are no speedy JetCats waiting when I arrive at the terminal, and the ferry seems to take forever, but I stand outside in the wind, staring at the city lights as we pull away from Circular Quay. It's a surprisingly chilly evening – autumn is definitely on the verge of assaulting us – and even when it starts to rain, I don't go inside. I wonder if it's too late to pop by Nathan and Lucy's? Will Richard have already left?

I pull out my mobile and curse under my breath when I see that the battery has gone flat. Nathan and Lucy live only a short walk from the beach in Manly so I'll go via their house on the off-chance.

It's raining heavily when I come out of the ferry terminal and I rummage around in my bag, hoping and praying I have my teeny-tiny super-light umbrella in there. Thank bollocks, I do! I set off at a brisk pace, not bothering to swap to flip-flops because there's nothing worse than sloshing around wet-footed in rubber in the rain.

Nathan and Lucy's lights are on when I walk up the footpath. They live in a little house much like ours, made out of wood and painted greeny-grey with a white picket fence out the front. I knock on the front door and listen as I hear Kings of Leon's 'Sex Is On Fire' coming from inside.

Lucy opens the door. 'Lily!' she cries, giving me a hug. 'I thought you couldn't come.'

'Hello,' I say warmly, as she pulls away. 'Am I too late? Is Richard still here?'

'Richard *is* still here and no, of course you're not too late. Come in.'

Richard rounds the corner and steps into the hall, a look of pleasure and surprise on his face.

'Hey!' he exclaims. 'What are you doing here?'

'I left the gallery early,' I tell him.

'Was it alright? Are you okay?' Now he looks concerned.

'I'll get you a drink,' Lucy says. 'Molly and I are on the rosé.'

'Perfect,' I reply and she hurries off, leaving Richard and me alone in the hall.

'Are you alright?' he asks again.

'I'm fine,' I say flatly. 'It was okay, but I didn't feel very comfortable.'

'Come inside and have a drink, we'll soon cheer you up.' He puts his arm around me and I'm filled up with warmth. This is where I belong. With *my* Richard. I smile at him gratefully as he leads me into the living room.

'Hello!' Molly and Sam shout.

'Hey.' Nathan gets to his feet and bounds over, engulfing me in a lovely hug. 'I hear congratulations are in order.'

'Oh my God!' Lucy screeches, rushing through from the kitchen. 'I forgot to say!'

'No worries,' I laugh as she drags Nathan away to give me a hug. 'And hey, welcome back to you guys,' I say, already feeling a million times better. 'Did you have a good time?'

'It was ace,' Nathan assures me.

'What was the exhibition like?' Molly asks from the comfort of her snuggly sofa.

'It was a bit shit,' I tell her honestly and she laughs. 'I missed you guys.'

'Aww.' Richard gives me a squeeze because he's still by my side.

'Here you are.' Lucy hands over my wine.

'Cheers!'

'Cheers indeed.' We all chink glasses. 'Are you hungry?' she adds. 'We've already eaten, but there's loads left over.'

'No, it's okay, I'm fine.'

'It's lasagne . . .' she coaxes.

'Go on, then.' I detach myself from Richard so I can follow Lucy into the kitchen. I've been stuffing my face full of canapés, but no way can I turn down Lucy's lasagne.

'Here you go,' she says a short while later, handing over a plate full of scrummy, warming, comfort food. I follow her back to the living room, kicking off my heels in the hall as I go. Lucy perches on the arm of Nathan's chair, and I take a seat on the sofa next to Richard. I balance the plate on my lap and tuck in, feeling totally at ease doing so in front of all these people who have already eaten.

'Richard said you've been asked to cover for someone on a magazine?' Molly says, impressed.

'That's right,' I mumble through a mouthful.

'Which magazine is it?' Sam jerks a thumb at Richard and tuts. 'Your man here couldn't remember.'

'*Marbles.*' I load up my fork. 'It's a glossy monthly men's magazine.'

'I know the one,' Sam says. 'That's so cool!'

Once again I'm filled with warmth.

'How did you end up doing that?' Lucy wants to know, so I quickly fill them in on the story.

'Well done,' Molly says in awe. 'You must have really made an impression on the Editor.'

'He's married,' I blurt out, and they all laugh.

'I bet that thought didn't cross any of our minds,' Nathan says, as Sam shakes his head in amusement. I smile, a little embarrassed.

'Where's Mikey tonight?'

'He's asleep in the spare room,' Molly tells me.

'You're so lucky he can do that,' Lucy says.

'He's a good little guy,' Sam says affectionately.

'So when are you two . . .' I start, as Nathan and Lucy look across at me and grin. 'What?' I ask at their reaction.

'When are we having kids?' Lucy checks.

'Yeah.'

'That seems to be the million-dollar question.' She beams. 'We're just happy being the two of us for now. No rush.'

Nathan pats his knee and she slides down from the armrest and into his lap. He wraps his arms around her and kisses her cheek as she leans back into him. It's hard not to smile at their obvious adoration of each other.

'So tell us about your engagement,' Lucy cries. 'Richard hasn't filled me in on any of the details.' She glances at my boyfriend mock accusingly, then grins at me. 'How did he propose?'

'Er, it was at your wedding, actually,' I reply. 'On the ferry.'

'No way!' Lucy says. 'And you kept it quiet?'

'She didn't want to take anything away from your big day,' Richard tells them.

'Are you kidding me? It would have added to the excitement.' I can't help but laugh at Lucy's enthusiasm.

'Have you set a date yet?' Molly wants to know.

'No. Maybe the year after next.'

'Another long engagement,' Sam tuts, rolling his eyes at Nathan.

I just shrug and smile innocently.

I catch an earlier ferry the next morning so I can get in to work in time to quiz Nicola about Pier Frank. She tries to keep a straight face as I walk up to the reception desk.

'How was it?' I ask.

'How was *he*, you mean.' She smirks.

'You didn't!' I gasp.

'I did.'

'You didn't!' I cry again.

'I couldn't help myself,' she sniggers.

'You shagged him?' I'm unable to contain my reaction.

'Shhh!' she whispers. I glance behind to check no one has entered the building. We're alone.

'What was he like?' I'm still taken aback, but curiosity gets the better of me.

Her lips turn down and she cocks her head to one side. 'Pretty good.'

That doesn't sound too convincing.

'No, he was alright,' she says again when she notices my reaction. 'Pretty good? *Alright?*'

'He'd had a few drinks. And he's not that big anyway.'

I can't help but guffaw at her honesty. She starts to file her nails, nonchalantly.

'Are you going to see him again?' I ask.

She shrugs. 'Maybe. He knows where to find me.' She quickly puts down her nail file as a petite brunette in her twenties walks through the door, carrying three cups from Starbucks. It's Cara, the girl who's covering for me while I'm upstairs.

'I'll catch you later,' I mouth and she grins and raises her eyebrows.

'Good morning,' Cara says brightly to Nicola as I push the button for the lift. 'I brought you a coffee.'

'Awesome,' Nicola says gratefully as the lift arrives and I step inside.

Coffees? Takeaway coffees? And not cheap ones at that. What a bloody cheek, attempting to muscle her way into the affections of my friends! Don't get too comfortable, missy, I think grimly. I'll be back in a week.

'How was it?' Jonathan asks me on his way past my desk a few minutes later.

'Good, thanks,' I lie politely.

'I told you,' he says in a sing-song voice. 'Dull as ditchwater, right?'

I laugh. 'Am I that transparent?'

'Totally. Did you speak to Pier at all?'

'Not much,' I reply honestly. 'I did meet him though.'

'Good, because he's coming in later.'

'Oh, right.'

'We're doing a profile on him,' Jonathan informs me. 'In fact, could you book a meeting room for Niles to do the interview?'

Niles is one of the junior writers.

'Sure. What time?'

'Check with Niles this morning, but I think it's at two o'clock.'

'Will do.'

'Thanks.'

As soon as he's gone, I email Nicola: *Pier is coming in! I think at 2pm but I'll double check.*

She immediately replies with: *ARGH!!! Where the hell is my lippy?*

I grin and get on with my work.

Pier is indeed scheduled to arrive at 2 p.m., so I take an early lunch-break to ensure I'm back on time. Nicola is looking glossed-up and glamorous when I enter the building with my soup.

'Good luck,' I say on my way past. She tries to keep a straight face.

Reception calls at five past two.

'The bastard blanked me,' Nicola says heatedly down the phone.

'No!' I cry. 'Where is he?'

'He's on his way up.'

'What happened?'

'He went straight up to Mel and didn't even look at me.'

'What an arsehole!' I squawk as loudly as I can get away with. I see through the glass panel on the door that Pier Frank has just stepped out onto the landing. 'He's here, better go.'

'Give him a kick for me,' she says menacingly.

'Or you could give him one on the way out,' I say, as he pushes through the door.

'Not bloody likely,' she mutters at my unintentional *double entendre*. I end the call.

'Can I help you?' I ask coolly. The twat is wearing dark sunglasses.

'I'm here to see Jonathan.'

'Your name?'

He frowns with irritation. 'Pier Frank.'

'Mr Laurence is out to lunch,' I say. 'Niles is doing the interview.'

'Who's Niles?'

'One of our junior writers,' I say smoothly.

'I know you, don't I?' he asks out of the blue. 'Don't you recognise me?' He removes his sunglasses. His eyes are bloodshot and his skin is pasty. He's nowhere near as attractive as he was last night.

'I was at your launch. With my friend, *Nicola*, from downstairs in *reception*.' Then I add pointedly, 'I think you might have met *her* too.'

'Oh, right. Yes. Well, where's Niles?'

'Follow me.' I get up and lead the way, revelling in his obvious discomfort. 'Good luck with the interview,' I say as I open the door. 'I'm sure we'll write some *super-nice* things about you.'

'Whatever did you say to him?' Nicola squeals an hour later when Pier has left the building.

'What do you mean?' I play innocent.

'He pretended to be all surprised to see me and asked if I'd been on reception earlier. I said, yes I had, and he said he couldn't believe he hadn't noticed me. It must've been his dark glasses.'

From the tone of her voice I can tell she's not buying it and I'm glad.

'What a wombat,' she adds, and I grin at the use of the word. 'He said he'd call me.'

'Did he?'

'Yep. I shrugged and said I didn't have access to a phone, but you know, "good luck with things and I'll see you around".'

'Seriously?' I giggle at the thought of Nicola sitting there in front of three telephones on reception desk and saying such a thing.

She laughs along with me. 'Oh, I wish I hadn't shagged him. Oops – gotta go,' she adds, hanging up before I can comment.

The editorial assistant Bronte has recovered from her operation and by the end of the following week I feel quite sad that I have to leave. Xanthe has continued to be nice to me – we've gone out for lunch a couple of times – and I also got the chance to help out on the picture desk and chat to Kip, the assistant who returned from holiday on Monday. When I leave on Friday, Xanthe gives me a goody bag filled with beauty treats and Kip promises that he'll consider me if they ever need holiday cover on the picture desk. I also hand Jonathan a copy of my CV.

'Please think of me if you hear of anything,' I implore.

'I absolutely will,' he assures me. 'Thanks for stepping in at such short notice, Lily.'

'It's been my pleasure,' I tell him sincerely, feeling a buzz of anticipation at what the future could hold for my career.

'I'm going to find it quite strange going back to reception after working on a magazine for almost two weeks,' I say to Richard later that night.

'You'll be okay,' he tells me. 'It's not like you don't enjoy your job.'

'Yes, I do like it. Well, I like Nicola and Mel,' I correct myself. 'But it's not very challenging.'

'What, and working as a secretary was?' he asks.

'I wasn't a secretary,' I reply, annoyed.

'Editorial assistant, then. Isn't it the same thing?'

'No, it's much more than that,' I say crossly, even though in actual fact it's not that different.

'Hey, I didn't mean to upset you.' He looks contrite. 'I think you're great at what you do.'

I stare at the TV in a huff. Great at what I *do*. What about what I *could* do?

'Can you pass me the remote?' he asks when an advert break comes on five minutes later.

'What don't you get it yourself?' I retort. The offending object is on the coffee table in front of us.

'Hey!' he exclaims. 'Are you still angry at me?'

'Can't you bloody tell?' I rant. I've been sitting here getting increasingly worked up while he's been happily watching some crap on the telly. He should *know* he's upset me!

'But Lily, I didn't even say anything.' He looks utterly confused and taken aback by my reaction.

'You said I was a secretary,' I practically shout.

'So what?' Richard cries. 'What's wrong with being a secretary? Or a receptionist? I don't know what's got into you. You were happy enough before.'

'I was never happy!' I shout angrily. 'The only thing I've ever been happy doing is looking after animals and taking photographs!'

'WHAT?' He's a bit beside himself. 'What are you going on about, looking after animals?' He's raising his voice too, now, and a sudden sense of calm washes over me. I haven't told him how I worked at a conservation park as a teenager. I've tried to blank it from my past because it's too painful to relive. Now I've gone and done it and I have to explain. 'Lily, what the *fuck?*'

I sigh and close my eyes. I really, *really* don't want to go into this.

'I used to work at the conservation park with Michael. When I first came to Australia,' I add, glancing at him. He's still frowning with exasperation.

'Right?' Add confusion to that look.

'I really loved it,' I say simply.

'What, when you were fifteen?' he checks.

'Fifteen, sixteen . . . I only worked there for the summer holidays, but I've always regretted leaving. I know it's too late to do anything about it, but it still makes me sad sometimes.'

He reaches over and rubs my arm. 'Don't be sad. Come here.'

'No, I don't feel like it,' I say sulkily and he takes his hand away. I know I'm being high maintenance, but I can't help it. I don't want to go to him, I want *him* to come to *me*.

I'd like him to ask me to explain myself more, to tell him how at least working in the field of photography seems more attainable all of a sudden, but he's annoyed at my snub. I turn my focus to the television, and a minute later remember that dinner's in the oven and leap to my feet. That's the end of our so-called heart-to-heart for now.

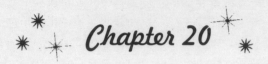

Chapter 20

On Sunday night, I get a call from my friend Vickie in Adelaide.

'I've got some bad news. Tammy's dad had a heart attack,' she tells me. 'He died overnight in hospital.'

'Oh no, poor Tammy! And Shane! How are they?'

'Devastated. The funeral's on Wednesday. Do you think you can come back for it?'

'Um . . .' I haven't been back to Adelaide since I left at the age of nineteen.

'I know she'd like you to be there.'

'I'll try,' I promise. 'I'll have to see if I can get the time off work.'

'You can stay with me and Jaegar, if you like. It'll be squashy, though.' They live in a studio flat.

'Thanks. I might even be able to get a cheap deal at one of the city hotels.'

'Please come,' she begs.

After I hang up the phone I turn to Richard.

'What's wrong?' he asks, having overheard my half of the conversation.

'Tammy's dad has had a heart attack. Vickie thinks I should go to the funeral. It's on Wednesday.'

He nods. 'Do you want me to come with you?'

I hesitate. On the one hand I would love his company. On the other, I wonder if I should go back to Adelaide alone.

'Don't worry,' I tell him. 'I know work's really busy at the moment. Have you had any luck replacing that guy?' I'm referring to the apprentice Nathan suspected had been nicking stuff. Nathan himself caught him in the act last week and fired him on the spot. They're now a man short with a build deadline approaching.

'Not yet,' Richard replies. 'I'm doing some interviews tomorrow. I'll come,' he decides.

'You don't have to,' I assure him.

'I will.'

It's a strange feeling returning to Adelaide after all these years. And with Richard with me, it almost doesn't seem real. So much has changed, the airport for one. Gone is the tiny old building, replaced with a brand new glass and steel structure, and when Vickie drives us along North Terrace, I barely recognise it. The trees have been taken down and the pavements widened, opening up the views to the old historical buildings belonging to the museum, university and churches. Blocks of flats and university housing have shot up everywhere.

Vickie works at a café in North Adelaide where she and her boyfriend Jaegar live, but she takes an hour out of her day to collect us at lunchtime and then hands over the keys to her silver Toyota Yaris.

'Are you sure?' I check. She said she'd lend us her wheels when I told her we'd booked our flight.

'Of course. I'll walk home after work and get ready. If you could pick Jaegar and me up at seven-ish, we'll go for dinner on Rundle Street if that's what you want?'

The funeral is tomorrow morning and our flight is at four o'clock in the afternoon, so tonight we're catching up with old friends. Jo and her boyfriend Ash are also meeting us later, but Tammy, understandably, is spending time with her mum and Shane.

'That would be great.' I smile warmly.

'Thanks, Vickie,' Richard adds.

'No worries.'

'Shall we go to the hotel to check in?' I ask when we're alone. We did manage to find a hotel doing a cheap last-minute deal, which is lucky because Vickie's studio flat would have been a squash enough with three people, let alone four.

'No point. We may as well check in later. Let's go up to the hills.'

I stifle a sigh. 'Really? We could check in and then go for an ice cream or something.'

'Lily . . .' Richard told me last night that he really wants to see where I spent my first few years in Australia.

'Why?' I'd asked.

'This place obviously made an impact on you. And I want to understand why.'

There's no hope of that without Ben here. But Richard was adamant about visiting Michael's house in Piccadilly at the very least. I reluctantly agreed.

'Okay, but I'm driving,' I insist now. If we're going into the hills, I have to be in control.

'Really?' he says, surprised. I don't think I've ever driven

Richard anywhere before. I used to occasionally use Mum's car when I lived with her in Bondi, but I could only afford public transport when I moved into a minuscule studio flat of my own. That was before I met Richard, of course, and then he had a car and I was happy to commute to work by ferry.

'Yes,' I say firmly. He's already in the driver's seat so we both climb out and swap places. I experience a strange little thrill about being behind the wheel again.

He grins across at me once we're all belted up. 'Let's go.'

Hardly anyone takes the long and winding road up into the hills any more. Soon after I arrived in Australia, they finished a tunnel which cuts right through the rock and shortens the journey considerably. Our ears pop as we pass through it. The grass is greener than it would have been in high summer, and I kind of miss the creamy-yellow colour of the dry stuff. I remember complaining about it when I first moved here, but I've learned to appreciate it.

I flick on the indicator and move left onto the slip-road to Crafers.

Piccadilly Valley is as familiar to me as it always was. We drive along Piccadilly Road, past houses nestled in amongst the gums, the paddock that's still filled with goats, and the small leafy-green vineyard. Eventually we round the corner and come across Michael's house. I slow to a stop and stare straight ahead at the boundary fence to the conservation park. Clear as day in my mind I remember Ben vaulting himself over it in the direction of Carminow Castle and Mount Lofty. I shake myself out of my flashback.

'That's Michael's house there,' I say quietly, looking left out of the window.

'Shall we see if he's in?' Richard asks.

I shake my head. 'His truck's not there. He must be at work.'

'You never know,' Richard says hopefully.

I decide to indulge him and unclick my seatbelt. He follows me up the gravel footpath to the front door. Instinctively I put my hand on the doorknob and turn it. When it opens I halt in surprise. Michael never used to lock it if he was in. I quickly and quietly close it again and then knock, nerves swirling around my stomach. I'm not prepared for this.

Moments later, the door opens and Michael stands there, his face registering puzzlement, recognition and finally, delight.

'Lily!' he booms. 'Is it really you?'

I nod, smiling. 'Yes, it's me.' Before I can speak the words he's got me in a bear hug.

'What are you doing here?' He clutches my arms and beams down at me.

'We came back for Kevin Stamford's funeral. You know, Tammy and Shane's dad?'

'Aah, yes. Such a shock,' he empathises, glancing at Richard.

'This is Richard,' I say, as he lets me go and shakes Richard's hand.

'Hello, there! I've heard all about you from my son. Did Josh know you were coming back?'

'I haven't had a chance to tell him yet. Is he going to the funeral?'

'I imagine so. Come in, come in! Can I get you a cuppa?'

'You certainly can.' How could I refuse? 'When I didn't see your truck, I thought you must be at work,' I say, once we're seated in the kitchen around the same old table, covered with the same green plastic tablecloth.

'No, Janine's got the ute today.'

'How is she?' I ask.

'She's great.' He smiles. 'She'll be sorry she missed you.'

'Please give her my best.'

'I will, darl.' I don't want to talk about the conservation park, so I'm horrified when he continues. 'She never did understand why you quit work like that.' I shift uncomfortably in my seat, ever aware of Richard's presence beside me. 'She always said you had a way with the koalas. I think she thought you'd return one day, but I guess you've moved on to bigger and better things. Josh says you work in publishing now?'

'I wouldn't say it's bigger or better,' I start to protest.

'Sounds pretty exciting to me,' Michael says.

'I'm just a receptionist,' I add lamely.

'Just a receptionist,' Richard scoffs, then to Michael, 'she's too modest.'

'She always was,' Michael agrees with a knowing look. 'What about you, Richard? What do you do?'

I would give anything to ask after Ben, but I can't.

'Why *did* you quit?' Richard asks when we're back in the car.

'I was starting school, it was no big deal.' I brush him off. 'What did you think of him? He's nice, isn't he?'

Richard nods. 'Yeah. Really nice.'

'I can't believe my mum dumped him.'

He raises his eyebrows. 'No comment.'

I grin, relieved I'm off the hook with the questioning. 'Where to, now?'

'Can we drive past the conservation park?'

'That's it there.' I point to the boundary fence.

'What's that?' he asks, looking up towards the top of the hills.

'Carminow Castle.'

'Can we go up there?'

'Okay.' I admit defeat. 'I'll take you up to Mount Lofty to see the view.' I cannot believe I'm doing this.

'Nice!' Richard breathes, gazing down at the city and the ocean beyond it. I brought him through the lobby, somehow finding the willpower to resist the side of the building that looks down on Piccadilly Valley. Even here though, I'm haunted by a vision of dark-blue eyes staring into mine in the darkness.

My phone starts to ring, rousing me from my reverie. I dig it out of my bag and peer at the caller ID.

'Hi, Josh.'

'Hey, you're back.'

Richard glances at me and I indicate that I'll take the call away from the crowds. He nods in understanding so I wander off slowly.

'Only for the funeral.'

'I know. Terrible, isn't it?'

'Awful. Kev always seemed so full of life. Is Shane okay?' I look over, and when I see that Richard is reading one of the information plaques, I continue walking.

'He's pretty cut up,' Josh answers. 'Have you spoken to Tammy?'

'Not yet. I'll try her later.'

'What are you up to this arvo?'

'I'm giving Richard a tour of the hills. We've just been to see your dad, actually.'

'I know – he called me.'

'Aah, so that's how you knew we were here.'

'That's right. Do you fancy meeting me in Stirling for a quick drink? Tina might be able to get off work.'

'Sure, but I thought your garage was in Mount Barker?'

'It is, but I need to take one of the cars for a spin. I can pop out for an hour.'

'What about Tina?'

'She works in the hairdresser's in Stirling. I'll give her a buzz now to see if she can take a break. See you at the pub in half an hour?'

'Perfect.' I end the call and stare down at the rolling hills of Piccadilly Valley, speckled with green and grey gums. This is where I told him I loved him. Did he ever tell me he loved me? No. Did he love me?

Did you?

His eyes stare back at me inside my mind, but he doesn't answer.

It's almost as though I expect some epiphany to come to me, standing here. Something to tell me what to do. But there's nothing. My heart says nothing. I turn and walk back to join Richard.

I don't mean to drive past Ben's house, really I don't, but some-how we end up taking a detour on the way to Stirling. As we approach I spy a red Suzuki parked on his drive and my whole body stiffens. I slow down and stare out of Richard's side of the car, painfully alert. And then the door opens and a woman walks out. She has curly dark hair and is wearing a long, tie-dyed maxi dress. I see the tiny hands of a small child wrap around her legs from behind and then we've passed them and I sit bolt upright in shock and stare out of the rearview mirror.

'Who was that?' Richard asks, glancing out of the back window and then at me with concern.

'I don't know,' I reply.

269

'You looked like you might know her.' He's confused at my reaction.

'I thought I did, but I don't,' I quickly tell him, my heart pounding.

Who was she? Who were they? He said he'd never sell it. Did he move back here? Did he bring his family with him?

Maybe it's a sign, a small voice inside my head says. Maybe it's time to let him go.

No. No. I'll never let him go.

Tina is gorgeous and personable and I urge Josh not to let her get away as he climbs back into the willow-green Jaguar convertible that he's supposedly test driving.

'I know.' He smiles contentedly. 'I'm beginning to come round to your way of thinking.'

'Really?' I squeak, so full of excitement that I momentarily block out the image of the curly-haired woman that has been plaguing me. 'Do you think you'll put a ring on her finger?'

'Maybe,' he says. 'I'll keep you posted.'

I give him a massive hug and let him climb into the car.

'Don't crash it,' I warn. 'I can't believe you're actually allowed to drive this thing out of the garage.'

'What they don't know won't hurt them.'

'Josh!'

He laughs. 'I'm joking. The owner is a friend of mine. He even trusts me to look after his children.'

'You *babysit* his children?' I'm astounded.

'Well, it's more Tina's thing, if I'm being honest.'

'That sounds more like it. See you tomorrow?'

'I'll be there.' He's a pallbearer at the funeral.

Richard and I climb back into the car. 'Where next?' he asks.

'Back to the hotel to check in,' I say firmly. 'I want to get ready for tonight.'

'Fair enough,' he concedes.

That night, after dinner with my friends, I walk out onto the small hotel balcony while Richard heads to the bathroom to get ready for bed. I stare up at the sky and see a full moon, yellow and enormous, like the one I saw years ago with Ben at Mount Lofty. Here the sky is lit from the lights of the city, but up in the hills I know it would be matt black and full of twinkling stars.

A single tear slides down my cheek and underneath my shirt.

'Hey,' Richard says quietly. I don't turn to look at him. 'Bathroom's free.'

'Thanks,' I choke out.

'Are you okay?'

I nod, unable to speak.

'I wish you'd tell me what's going through your mind,' he says.

'Nothing is,' I lie.

He tries again. 'You haven't been yourself here. At least, you haven't been the Lily I know.'

'Why do you keep saying that?' I suddenly snap, but when I turn to look at him, his expression immediately calms my mood. 'I'm sorry,' I sigh. 'It is strange to come back here.'

'I thought you loved Adelaide. You always defend it when anyone says anything negative about it.'

'Those people don't know what they're talking about,' I say crossly.

'See?' He smiles. 'I know you're fond of this place, so why does it make you so sad?'

'I don't know. Maybe I'm just freaked out about the funeral tomorrow. I've never been to one before, you know.'

'Oh, right,' he says.

I could leave it at that, but when I look in his eyes, I can't. I try to explain how I feel. 'I guess it was such an up and down time for me, being uprooted from the UK, starting at a new school. But I found my feet here and then Mum broke it off with Michael and we had to leave.'

'But you could have stayed?' he enquires.

I manage a wry smile. 'Do you wish I had?'

He chuckles and opens up his arms. I step into them and he kisses the top of my head. 'Of course I don't.'

I relax into his embrace and begin to feel safe again. Eventually I pull away and look up at him. 'Thank you for coming with me.'

'Do you mean that?' I nod as a lump forms in my throat. 'I wasn't sure if you'd prefer to come back on your own,' he adds.

'No,' I say honestly. 'I'm glad you're here.'

But in the morning, there's something I need to do alone.

As soon as the light starts to creep under the blinds I leave Richard dozing in bed and walk out of the hotel and down Rundle Street towards East Terrace. I take a left and I'm soon passing through the wrought-iron gates of the Botanic Gardens. On autopilot I head along the wide, straight path lined with freshly mown grass and turn right by the towering palm trees. The path curves left and then I'm passing under shady trees and sitting down on a bench. The place is empty. Deserted.

The reeds around the edge of the pond have grown so tall that I can barely see the large green lily pads from where I'm sitting. There are no pink flowers at this time of year, but Cupid sits still in the centre of the water, riding on the back of a grey swan. A dragonfly hovers above the reeds and I can see its wings shimmering in the sunshine. I'd forgotten how beautiful this place is.

I sit in silence for a long time until eventually I come to my senses to see hundreds and thousands of tiny black ants swarming around my feet. A man on an orange ride-on lawnmower appears at the edge of the pond, shattering my peace and quiet. It's time to move on.

Yes, it's time to move on. Really. In every sense. Ben left ten years ago.

Why are you still waiting for him?

I think of Richard sleeping soundly in bed this morning, his brown hair flat on one side from being squashed into the pillow, and I'm filled with an overwhelming sense of love for him. I suddenly want to be back in the hotel in his arms.

I hurry away from the pond with purpose, trying to pull my whole heart with it, but a piece of it tears off and remains. As I always knew it would.

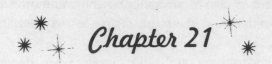

Chapter 21

Towards the end of April, my dad, Lorraine and my three half-sisters arrive for a two-week holiday. It's been a strange couple of weeks working back on reception after my time at *Marbles*, followed by the two days I had to take off to attend the funeral in Adelaide. It's been fine – in fact, it's been quite nice because most of the *Marbles* clan now smile and say hello to me on their way in. I feel like I'm a part of their little family somehow, even though of course I'm not. I have experienced a few insecurities, wondering if I should be buying coffees on my way in, but then I tell myself to get a grip. Plus Nicola and Mel were quick to reveal that Cara, my temporary replacement, had a really annoying laugh. She also hated soup and Tim Tams, so that didn't go down too well.

It's overcast and windy on the day my family touch down in Sydney. I go to meet them after work on Friday for an early-evening meal at their hotel. They only arrived this morning and are feeling worn out and jetlagged, so I don't drag Richard into the city for the sake of a couple of hours. He's off tomorrow on the surfing trip with Nathan and a bunch of people. Monday is Anzac Bank Holiday, so he won't be back until late Monday night.

My family are staying in a flat in the Rocks area. Dad called earlier to tell me the number of their flat, so I don't have to report to reception on my way in. My heels click over the polished floor of the spacious lobby and I press the button to call the gilded lift.

As a senior accountant, my dad is pretty well off. And Lorraine hasn't done badly for herself either, with her interior design business. My sisters don't want for much. I try not to think about the fact that they now live in a six-bedroom house in Sussex that would have had more than enough space to accommodate me ten years ago. Things were different back then.

'That's her!' I hear one of my sisters – Olivia, I think – scream from inside the flat. A stampede of footsteps races for the door and it bursts open, revealing Olivia and Isabel's beaming faces. A split-second later I'm being suffocated by their embraces. I can't stop laughing.

'Let Lily come in,' my dad gently berates them as he untangles his daughters' limbs from mine and pulls me in for a hug. 'How are you, my girl?' he says into my hair.

'I'm fine, thanks, Dad,' I reply, feeling the hot pricking of tears behind my tightly shut eyelids. It always hurts to see him after such a long time of being apart. He looks older, I realise with a pang. His grey hair has thinned out and his wrinkles seem more pronounced. 'Where's Kay?'

'Here,' Kay answers me, stepping into the hall. My eyes widen in surprise, but I quickly recover as I sweep her into my arms. She's grown so tall in the last two years! And so slim and beautiful! She's no longer a little girl.

She pulls away, slightly embarrassed.

'How was your flight?' I ask.

'Long,' Kay replies with a wry grin, and a memory comes back to me of that question being asked of me time and time again when I first moved to Australia.

'I watched five movies on the plane,' Isabel butts in.

'*Five?* Didn't you get any sleep?' I fake outrage.

'Nope,' she says happily.

'Hello, Lily.' It's Lorraine.

'Hey!' I say, going to give her a hug.

'I thought I'd better come out here as this is clearly where the action is.' She laughs and indicates the tiny hallway.

'Sorry, shall we come through?' I point towards the living room.

'Yes, come on in. What would you like to drink?'

'Or should we go straight down to dinner?' Dad interjects.

'Dinner, dinner!' Olivia cries. 'I'm starving.'

'Me, too,' Isabel pipes up. Kay merely shrugs.

'I'm easy,' I say. 'I'll fall in with you guys.'

'Listen to you, you're sounding all Australian these days,' Lorraine teases.

'Am I?'

'No,' Dad says. 'You still sound like Lily.' He wraps his arm around my waist. 'Go and get your shoes,' he tells his other daughters. 'Is it cold outside?' he asks me.

'A little. But aren't we eating in the downstairs restaurant?'

'Of course.' He laughs and gives me a squeeze. 'That's my girl, always thinking outside the box.'

I blush. He's still my doting dad and that, it seems, will never change.

*

The next morning, Richard and I rise early and say our goodbyes at the front door. He's leaving early to hitch a ride with Nathan and Lucy, and I'm going into the city to have breakfast with my family.

'Be careful,' I urge. 'Don't catch any waves that are taller than me.'

He laughs. 'I'll be sitting on the beach sunbathing, then.'

'That's what I'd prefer,' I say, trying not to think about him crashing into rocks or getting up close and personal with a shark.

'I'll be careful,' he promises, giving me a kiss on the tip of my nose. 'Love you.'

'Love you, too.'

'Have a good time with your family.'

'I will.'

I go straight up to my dad's flat when I arrive. Olivia answers the door to me.

'At last. I'm starving, as usual.' She drags me inside.

'What time did you get up?' I ask, surprised.

'Six o'clock. AGES ago!'

It's only seven o'clock now.

She leads me through to the living room, where Isabel is engrossed in some children's programme on the telly. Lorraine is washing up coffee mugs in the small kitchen. My dad is sitting in an armchair, reading the paper.

'Hello,' he chirps, getting to his feet with a little effort.

'Good morning,' Lorraine calls through.

'Can we go?' Olivia pleads.

'Where's your sister?' Lorraine asks.

'Still getting ready.'

'Retrieve her and we'll be off.' Lorraine nods towards what I assume is Kay's bedroom, and Olivia hurries away. Dad gives me a kiss and points to the sofa. I sit down next to Isabel.

'What are you watching?' I ask.

'I don't know what it's called,' she murmurs, not dragging her attention away from the kangaroos on the screen. Dad casts his eyes heavenwards for my benefit. I get up and go to peer out of the window. The view reveals the city's crystalline skyline, and the golden top of Sydney Tower is glinting in the sunshine.

'She's still not ready!' Olivia storms back into the living room and flops down between Isabel and me.

Out of my three sisters, Olivia, aged eleven, and Isabel, nine, look the most alike. Both have shoulder-length, wavy brown hair and slightly rounded features, and both have a little puppy fat. With Kay that's long gone. Tall and lissom, with long blonde hair, at fifteen, she takes more after Lorraine than my dark-haired dad. Lorraine is a natural blonde – unlike my mum, to her annoyance – and her hair swings around her shoulders with innate straightness. It's not the type of hair to go frizzy on the ferry either, but obviously I didn't get my good genes from her.

'How's your mum?' Dad asks me.

'She's good.'

'Anyone on the scene?'

'I think there might be someone, but she's not saying anything yet.'

My gaze is automatically drawn to Lorraine in the kitchen and I notice her purse her lips with disapproval. I find it irritating, even though it's not entirely uncalled-for, but I don't comment because I never do when it comes to my dad's wife. Moments later, Kay drags herself from her bedroom dressed in leggings and a purple T-shirt with a rock-style emblem on it. I notice she's started wearing make-up since I last saw her.

'Finally!' Olivia says bossily. 'Can we go now?' She jumps to her feet and the rest of us follow suit.

'What are your plans for today?' I ask later through a mouthful of French toast.

Dad shrugs. 'I don't know. What do you girls want to do?'

'I want to see some kangaroos,' Isabel cries.

'I wouldn't mind going into the city to look for a swimming costume,' Lorraine says, adding for my benefit, 'I left mine in the laundry after my last gym visit.'

'How annoying,' I empathise. 'Well, I could take the girls to the zoo if you like. It's not far from here.'

'Yes, yes, yes!' Isabel bleats.

Dad turns to Olivia and Kay expectantly.

'That'd be good,' Olivia agrees.

Kay shrugs. 'Alright.'

'In that case,' Dad decides, 'I'll take your mother shopping. I wouldn't mind having a look for a new watch, myself.'

It's been over four years since I last came to the zoo and that was also in aid of my sisters. I hadn't been to a conservation park or anything like it since working with Michael, but I finally conceded on the previous occasion when Isabel wanted to go.

I found that trip hard. Ben once told me he had worked in the zoo here in Sydney and I was on edge the whole time, almost as though I expected to bump into him. This time I need to stop being so ridiculous.

Easier said than done.

Nerves hit me as we walk up to the entrance gates. I pay for our tickets with the money my dad gave me and my hands are shaking as I take the change. This is crazy. He's not going to be here.

'Where are the kangaroos?' Isabel demands as she tries to make sense of the fold-out paper map in her hands.

'Here.' I take it from her and scan the diagram. 'This way.'

'Can we see the koalas, too?' Olivia asks worriedly.

'Of course. We can see everything,' I answer, willing my anxiety to dissipate.

Usually I walk with my head down, but today I'm on full alert, scanning every face, every person's profile from behind – just in case.

You're being stupid.

I know. I can't help it.

We buy a bag of pellets to feed to the kangaroos and I lead the way into their enclosure, waiting back to shut the gate carefully behind us. Isabel has already cornered an elderly male, sprawled out on his side. My two youngest sisters kneel down on the dirt and delightedly hold out palms full of pellets to feed to the now-interested roo. He reminds me a little of Roy, but Roy had darker ears. I wonder if he's still alive?

'Did you really name a koala after Olivia?' Kay interrupts my thoughts.

'Yes,' I reply, smiling. 'She could have just as easily been named after you, but we flipped a coin.'

We . . .

'I told you,' Kay says to her sister. Olivia glances up, but quickly returns her attention to the kangaroo.

'I'm surprised you remember,' I say to Kay. 'You were only four at the time.'

'I wanted you to name her after me, that's why.' She gives me a pointed look.

'I'm sorry. I thought there would be more orphaned koalas.'

'I suppose it's a good thing there weren't,' she concedes.

'That's true.' I touch her arm affectionately. 'So how are you? How are things?'

'What things?'

'Have you got a boyfriend?'

'Straight to the point!' she exclaims and I try to keep a straight face.

'Yes, and his name is Charlie,' Isabel chips in gleefully, alerted to our conversation.

'Shut up!' Kay snaps. 'I'm not going out with him,' she tells me and I nod encouragingly.

'But she wishes she was,' Olivia interjects.

'Shhh!' Kay frowns with annoyance. I take a few steps back from the girls and motion for Kay to do the same.

'Is he good-looking?' I ask conspiratorially, and her frown turns into a dreamy smile.

'Very.'

'Do you think he likes you?'

She shrugs. 'It's hard to tell.'

'What are the signs?'

'Well, he asked me if he could borrow my pen during maths.'

'Right.'

'He could just as easily have asked his best friend Lee, but he didn't.'

'That's a very good sign,' I agree.

'And I catch him looking at me sometimes.'

'He definitely likes you,' I decide.

'Do you think so?' she asks hopefully. It's the brightest I've seen her look since she got here.

'Absolutely. If you suspect it, you're right. A woman's intuition usually is,' I add, trying to sound wise.

'I hope so.' She beams and her whole face lights up.

I look away so she can't see me smiling to myself. Puppy love. How cute.

Wait, she's fifteen. *Fifteen!* How can she be fifteen already? I had sex with Dan at fifteen! I glance back at her, shocked. She's staring wistfully at the gum trees. She's far too young to be doing anything remotely like that. I must have been much more mature at her age. Surely? But a little trace of doubt is wheedling its way in.

Puppy love? A crush?

No. What I felt for Ben was real. It was. I'm sure of it.

Then suddenly, out of the corner of my eye, I see a male zookeeper with sandy blond hair come out of a hut by the kangaroo enclosure and go round the corner in the opposite direction. My heart lurches. *Ben!*

Of course it isn't!

It was him – I know it.

'Just going to nip to the loo,' I say to the girls, and hurry off before they decide to join me. 'Back in a tick!'

I rush through the gates and forget to close them so I have to turn around and swing them shut before looking wildly to left and right. Where did he go?

It's not him. It's not him. I chant this over and over to myself to prepare the way for my impending heartbreak.

There he is!

I halt on the spot. He has his back to me. He's wearing typical keepers' attire of beige shirt and khaki shorts.

It's not him. It's really not. He looks different. Broader. His hair is shorter. No. It's not him. My heart sinks and a lump forms in my throat, but still I can't walk away.

The sandy-haired keeper turns around, his head down, and then he looks up, straight at me, and my whole head spins and I feel like I'm going to faint.

Because it *is* him.

It's Ben. I've found him.

He stares at me, stunned. My head is tingling and the ripples spiral all the way down my body to my toes. I can't look away. I can't move. I can't do anything except stare back in total shock.

He's twenty feet away from me, and when his lips mouth my name I can't hear him, but I manage a slight nod of my head and then he's walking towards me and my heart is pounding and my stomach is cartwheeling over and over and over again, and then he reaches me and I'm gazing up into his deep-blue eyes, unable to say anything.

'Lily?' He speaks so quietly it's almost as though he's scared to say it out loud.

My voice has hidden out somewhere so all I can do is nod again, dumbstruck to my core. He looks almost the same as he did ten years ago, but more manly somehow – and I didn't think that was possible.

'I can't believe it,' he says, his eyes searching mine. 'What are you doing here?'

'My sisters . . .' My voice sounds husky. 'My sisters are here on holiday.'

'Do you live in Sydney?'

'Yes.' I have to clear my throat.

A male keeper with dark hair steps out from an office to Ben's right. 'Ready?' he asks.

Ben glances at him, startled by the disruption. 'Be there in a minute.'

His colleague disappears behind the building.

'I have the day off on Monday,' Ben says urgently. 'We could get a coffee – go for lunch?'

'Yes,' I manage to say.

He's still staring at me. Suddenly he seems to come to life. 'Do you have a card or something? Some way for me to contact you?'

'No. Do you?'

He produces a wry smile. 'Me? Business cards? No.' He digs into his pocket and pulls out a scrap of paper. 'Don't suppose you've got a pen?'

I rummage around in my bag and luckily can locate one. He leans the paper against his knee and scribbles on it before handing it over.

'Here's my number. Will you call me to arrange something?'

I nod and take it. The keeper comes out from behind the building again and stands there, waiting. Ben raises his hand in acknowledgement of him before turning to me.

'I've gotta go.' He sounds reluctant.

Again, all I can do is nod.

'Please call me. Please,' he implores, and then he turns away and walks off with his colleague.

Something happens to my stomach. Or is it my heart? It feels as though someone has cut me open and is ripping out my insides. I want to scream, 'No! Don't go! Don't leave me again!' Suddenly I feel like I can't breathe, and I'm gasping for air.

Then, deep inside my mind, the voice of reason speaks. *You have his number. You are going to see him again. You know where he works.*

Finally I remember my sisters.

It's this last thought that keeps me together and I manage to walk away, tightly clasping the piece of paper in my hand. When I reach the gates to the kangaroo enclosure I stand and look in, feeling a sense of relief as I see the girls feeding the kangaroo. Even Kay is kneeling on the ground. I glance down at the number in my hand and flip over the piece of paper. It's a supermarket receipt. I scan the contents of Ben's shop on . . . yes, there it is, 20 April. Bread, butter, milk, Vegemite, frozen pizza, beer . . .

Wait!

Was he wearing a wedding ring? I don't remember seeing one.

Wouldn't I have noticed that? Maybe not.

But this doesn't sound like a shop for two . . .

It could be, Lily. It absolutely could be a shop for two.

What if he's divorced?

'There you are!' Kay calls.

I look up and see my three sisters walking towards me. 'Sorry to be so long,' I tell them.

'I need the loo now, too,' Kay complains.

'And me,' Isabel pipes up.

'Where is it?' Kay asks.

I look around, thankfully spying a sign for the toilets. 'This way,' I say, and they all follow me.

How can I find out if he's married or not?

You can ask him when you see him on Monday.

Monday? Monday? I can't wait that long!

And that's what it's like for the rest of our outing. I can't concentrate, my sisters begin to get annoyed with my jitteriness, and all I can do is search everywhere we go for another sighting of Ben. He's nowhere to be found and it damn near kills me.

Eventually Isabel starts to whinge about her sore feet, and soon enough Olivia does too.

'We haven't seen the birds yet,' I tell them, panicked.

'I don't want to see the birds,' Isabel moans. 'I've had enough.'

I scan their faces for any sign of giving in. Resolute. I drag my feet all the way to the exit.

The zoo is in North Sydney so we have to catch the ferry back to their flat in the Rocks. The girls want to sit down so I find them a seat and slide away to sneak a look at Ben's number.

It's a mobile number. He hasn't given me his home number. Perhaps his wife would answer the phone. Or his kids . . .

God, it hurts.

A shiver goes through me. I don't know if it's anticipation or dread.

I've found him again.

What about Richard? I quickly crush that thought. I can't think about him now. I have to concentrate.

We make it back to the flat to discover that Dad and Lorraine are already there.

'Good day?' Dad asks.

'My feet are killing me,' Isabel whines.

'Mine are, too.' Olivia has to compete with her.

'But did you have a good day?' Dad tries again.

'Yeah.' Kay shrugs.

'We fed the kangaroos,' Isabel says proudly.

'*Did* you?'

'Yes!' Olivia exclaims.

'Wow! Were they big?' Dad's enthusiasm begins to get through to them and soon I can't hear myself think for all their chatter.

'Are you alright?' Lorraine asks quietly from beside me.

'Yes!' I overcompensate with my reply. 'Did you find another cozzie?'

She smiles. 'I did indeed. Want to see it?'

'Sure.' But I can't deal with this. I can't cope with all this noise. I need to be alone.

I find the strength to stay and play happy families, and after a while, the commotion around me calms down. Lorraine goes to make tea, Dad flops into the armchair and flips through a magazine, Kay disappears into her bedroom and the girls switch on the telly. I sit on the sofa to the left of them and allow my thoughts to take over. It soon becomes crystal clear that I cannot, I absolutely *cannot*, wait until Monday.

I get to my feet, full of determination. 'I'm just going to give Richard a call,' I tell Dad. Guilt courses through me in waves, but I walk towards the door, thinking of the hopefully-quiet corridor outside the flat.

'Use our bedroom,' Dad suggests. I swerve towards it. That makes more sense.

I pull out the receipt and panic hits me as I see how crumpled it's become, but thankfully I can still read the number. I dial it into my mobile phone, making two mistakes before I get it right. My hands are shaking intensely as it begins to ring.

'Hello?' Ben.

'It's Lily.'

'Hi!'

Warmth rushes through me at the obvious delight in his voice.

'I couldn't wait until Monday,' I tell him.

'Okay . . .'

'I know it's Saturday night and you've probably got other plans . . .'

'I'm free. Are you free?'

'Yes.' *What about your wife?* But the words won't come out. 'What time?' I ask instead.

'Seven?'

'Fine.'

'Where do you want to go?'

I wrack my brain. We can't go out in Manly, as I might see someone I know. The only thing that comes to mind is one of those terrible places full of suits that Mel likes to hang out in. I suggest a bar called Porters and describe its whereabouts.

'Cool,' he says. 'See you later.'

'Bye.' I try to press the button to end the call, but my fingers are made of stone. Eventually Ben ends the call for me.

I sit there on the bed, my heart pounding so loud I can hear it in my ears. Then I rise woodenly to my feet and return to the living room.

'How is he?' Dad asks.

'Who? Oh, Richard. Yes, he's fine,' I jabber, feeling that guilt prickling at me again.

'Good. He's back on Monday, right?'

'Yes.' I nod.

'Maybe we can come to you on Tuesday night?' Dad suggests. 'Save him having to come into the city to meet us?'

'Maybe, yes.' I return to my position on the sofa. Lorraine has put a cup of tea on a coaster in front of me. 'Thanks for the tea,' I say, reaching forward and finding the cup surprisingly heavy as I try to sip from it without spilling any.

'You're welcome,' she replies. 'So what are the plans for dinner tonight?'

'Um . . . I don't know,' I say. My heart is still thumping so loudly I fear it's going to burst my eardrums. 'I'm feeling quite tired,' I start. 'Would you guys mind if I bowed out and I'll see you in the morning?'

'Of course not,' Lorraine says.

My head was all over the place earlier and it didn't even occur to me what I must have looked like when I met Ben, but now I'm kicking myself for wearing such casual attire. Jeans and trainers and a boring black jumper. I'm not even wearing eye-shadow. Whoopie.

I don't have time to go home and change so I smooth down my hair in the mirror in the girls' bathroom and touch up my make-up with what little I do carry in my handbag: lip-gloss, mascara, compact powder. It'll have to do. It's sod's law that I see him on today of all days and not when I'm dressed in my high heels and swishy skirts.

I decide to set off early and take my time. My dad sees me out.

'Are you alright?' he asks as I reach for the door handle.

'Sure! Why wouldn't I be?'

'The girls said you seemed a little distracted today.'

'I wasn't distracted – I'm just tired,' I add, and give a little yawn when he doesn't look convinced. 'I'll see you tomorrow, okay, Dad?'

'Night, night, sweetheart – and thanks for looking after the girls today.'

A peck on the cheek and I'm out of there, wondering what exactly I have let myself in for, and feeling a mixture of excitement and sheer, utter terror.

Chapter 22

I arrive at Porters at six-forty – twenty minutes ahead of schedule – and buy a drink at the bar before hunting out a table. I perch uncomfortably on a low square stool, which has been upholstered in dark red velvet, and lean up against the wall. At least the suits aren't in the city on Saturday nights, but in some ways this is worse. The people here now appear to be mostly tourists or single girls dolled up to the nines, trying to pick up a rich man. The men seem old – like in their forties and fifties.

Ben's thirty-eight now. But that's not old, is it? No.

What if he doesn't turn up?

Nerves are rattling through me, but at least the pounding in my chest has settled down. A waiter comes along and puts a small bowl of marinated green olives on the table. I eye them, but remember the garlic and leave them where they are.

'Excuse me,' I call after the waiter, who is dressed in black trousers and a waistcoat with a pristine white shirt.

'Yes?'

'Could I get another of these, please?'

'I'll need to take your card, madam.'

'That's fine.' I get out a credit card from my bag and hand it over so he can start up a tab. The waiter looks pointedly at my drink, then at me. His greasy hair is slicked back and his nose is long and pointed.

'White wine,' I tell him.

'What sort, madam?'

'Any. I don't mind,' I add firmly.

He looks me up and down, giving my trainers a sniffy little glance, before mincing off. What a condescending twat.

'Do you come here often?'

I look up to see Ben standing there with a twinkle in his eye. He pulls up a stool.

'Hey!' I immediately sit up straighter.

'Are you alright?'

'The waiter is being a dickhead.' I indicate our surroundings. 'I couldn't think of anywhere else to suggest.'

He laughs and looks behind him. 'I might nip to the bar. You okay?'

'Yes, thanks. He's bringing me a wine.'

'Cool.' He gets up and walks off. I watch him go, feeling extremely surreal and disjointed from reality.

He looks gorgeous in faded grey trousers and a short-sleeved dark-grey T-shirt over a long-sleeved black one. It's the sort of thing Nathan could wear, and Nathan is twenty-five. Ben definitely, definitely doesn't look old, I decide once and for all. Thank bollocks for that.

Was he wearing a ring?

He returns a minute later with a beer. I can't see his left hand clearly from this position.

'This is weird,' Ben says, grinning.

'Mmm,' I murmur.

'So what have you been doing?' He leans towards me and rests his elbows on his knees. The waiter finally returns with my drink. I wait for him to leave before speaking. And then I see Ben's hand. No ring. My heart skips a beat. He's still waiting for my answer to his question.

'This and that.'

'What sort of this and that?' he persists. 'Tell me. We've got a lot of catching up to do.'

'Oh, I work as a receptionist in the city.' He nods. 'It's for a publishing firm. I covered for someone on a magazine recently,' I blurt out. 'That was good fun. I'm just temping . . .' My voice trails off.

'No photography?'

I shake my head. 'Sadly, no.' I feel like a massive failure. He expected so much of me and I've delivered nothing. My eyes return to the space on his finger where his wedding ring should be.

'Divorced,' he says suddenly.

'Pardon?'

He lifts up his wedding finger. 'Divorced.'

Someone is hoovering the inside of my head. My thoughts are befuddled with all the white noise.

'Five years ago,' he reveals.

'Five years?'

'Yep.'

'Have you been in Sydney for the last five years?' Out of the blue I feel like crying. If I'd met him five years ago I never would have met Richard. I never would have had to cause him any pain. But I'm getting ahead of myself . . .

'No,' Ben replies. 'I stayed in the UK for a while before moving back to Adelaide and then to Perth. I've only been in Sydney for a year.'

'A year. Okay.' I breathe a sigh of relief. 'Did you go to Perth because of your mum?'

He smiles. 'I can't believe you'd remember that.' I nod and he continues. 'I had to get away after a couple of years of it.' He looks at my left hand. 'What about you? No ring?'

'Ring? No,' I say hastily, unable to help misleading him.

He smiles, meeting my eyes so that my stomach does a somersault. I avert my gaze, guiltily.

'You look different,' he muses after a while.

'You look the same as I remember you.'

'I wasn't sure you'd remember me at all.'

'Of course I would,' I tell him. *I remember you every day.*

My nerves haven't dissipated yet, and every so often I experience a tingling sensation rippling over my face and down my arms. Unwittingly, I shiver.

'You're not cold, are you?' he asks.

'No.' I look around.

The waiter approaches our table. 'Can I get you anything else?' He enquires snootily.

'Do you want to move on?' Ben asks me.

'Yes,' I tell him. 'The bill,' I say to the waiter before turning back to Ben. 'Where do you want to go?'

'Are you hungry?'

I couldn't eat a thing. 'A bit,' I lie.

'I know a little bistro not far from here.'

'Sounds good.'

The waiter returns with the bill and I try not to baulk at the fact that he deliberately chose to give me one of the most expensive wines by the glass.

'Let me get this.' Ben reaches for his wallet, but I wave him away, slapping down some money. I follow him out of the venue.

'It's only a ten-minute walk,' Ben says. 'Do you want to catch a taxi?'

'No, no, I'm happy to walk.'

He sets off at a brisk pace, but I can easily keep up in my trainers. His hands are plunged deep into his pockets. I fold my arms across my chest.

'Are you sure you're not cold?' he checks again.

'I'm fine,' I assure him. A memory comes back to me and I can't help but giggle. 'Don't give me your shirt, you'll never get it back.'

He laughs out loud. 'I know, you little thief. That was one of my favourites, as well.'

'Was it? I'm sorry.'

He grins and nudges me. 'If it was anyone else . . .'

I blush unexpectedly at his tone. 'You can have it back now, if you like.'

'Have you still got it?' He regards me with interest.

'It's at my mum's.'

'No,' he decides. 'It wouldn't fit me now, anyway.' He indicates his chest. It's definitely broader than it used to be. 'How *is* your mum?' he asks.

'She's fine. You know we left Michael and Josh after Michael proposed to her?'

'I did hear something about that, yes.'

A pang goes through me. He knew about it? Wasn't he worried about me?

'Did you stay in contact with Michael?' I ask quietly.

'Not really,' he says. 'I'd only hear things through the grapevine. I tried not to ask.'

'Why?'

He shrugs and stares straight ahead. 'Fresh start,' he says bluntly. Then: 'Here we are, now.'

We come to a stop outside a tiny restaurant with red and white checked curtains at the windows. I peer inside and see candles lighting the tables. Cosy. Ben opens the door for me and I walk through.

'Benjamin!' A flamboyant middle-aged Italian man bustles towards us.

'Hello, Marco,' Ben says affectionately.

'So long since I have seen you!'

Ben shrugs. 'Sorry.'

'And now you have a new lady friend, no?' He glances at me.

New? I take it we're not talking about his ex-wife, here.

'An old friend,' Ben corrects him. 'Lily, this is Marco.'

'Hello,' I say, wondering about the existence of other women in Ben's life.

'Come, come.' Marco urges us towards a table at the back. 'No window,' he says regretfully. 'You should have booked.' He glares theatrically at Ben, who just shrugs.

'This is fine.'

'I bring you some menus. To drink?'

'Lily?'

'I might switch to red,' I say to Ben. 'A glass of house red, please.'

'A Peroni,' Ben answers, before turning to me.

'This is nice,' I say, looking around. 'Do you come here much?'

'Not really.'

I force a smile which I hope appears cheeky and unbothered. 'So what's this about your lady friends? You bring a lot of girls here?'

He looks down. 'No one special. Not for a long time.'

Relief floods my veins. A waitress returns with our drinks and a couple of menus. We turn our attention to food.

'Tell me what happened after I left,' Ben says when we've placed our order.

I was heartbroken. I was like the walking dead.

'I went to school. Made some new friends.'

'I told you you would.'

'So you did.' I manage a weak smile. 'Did you know Michael got married to The Map Bearer?'

'The what?' He looks confused.

I giggle. 'Janine. It's a nickname I gave her on my first day at the conservation park.'

He chuckles. 'Yes, I did know that. I go back to Adelaide occasionally to check in on Nan's house.'

'Who lives there now?' I ask curiously.

'It's being rented to friends of friends,' he explains. Aha! 'A family is in it at the moment.'

'Would you ever go back to Adelaide permanently?' I ask.

'Oh, I'll definitely end up there eventually. It's home.'

In a funny kind of way, it still feels like my home, too.

'What about you?' he asks. 'Would you ever move back?'

'I have some good friends there, but no, I don't think so. Mum's here, and I have other . . . *friends* here. And my career, you know?'

'Tell me about your job.'

'I'm only temping.'

'I know, you said that before. You're a receptionist?'

'Yes.' I feel small all of a sudden. 'It's good fun,' I say weakly.

'Cool.'

'I feel like I've let you down,' I blurt out.

'*What*? What do you mean?'

'You expected so much from me.'

'Lily! I haven't been around for the last decade – how can you possibly feel like you've let *me* down?'

'I just do.'

'Well, you haven't. I only ever wanted you to be happy.'

His eyes meet mine over the table and this time I can't look away. My head starts to prickle again and the room begins to spin. A waitress interrupts us with our mains.

'Thank you.' I lean back as she places a bowl of ravioli with sage butter in front of me. Ben has opted for a pepper steak.

'Tell me what happened after *you* left,' I find the courage to ask.

He glances up at me, then returns his attention to his food. 'I went to England and got married.'

'No kids?' *How can I have not asked this already?*

'No.'

I can breathe again.

'Charlotte couldn't,' he adds, and my heart plummets. So if they had been successful in that area, they never would have got divorced. 'But that's not why we broke up,' he continues.

'Why, then?' I'm relieved, but still I persist.

'Things weren't right. They were never right,' he adds.

'So why did you start trying for a family?'

'It's a good question.' He smiles wryly. 'I wanted it to be right.

I wanted to forge—' He cuts himself short mid-sentence. 'I was homesick, too.'

'You didn't like England?'

'I liked it, but I was homesick.'

That, I can understand. 'Did you have many friends?' I ask, remembering how that saved me once I started school.

'Of course, but they were mostly Charlotte's friends. I met a couple of decent guys through work, but one of them moved out to the country and the other had a family so he wasn't much up for socialising.'

'Where did you live? You worked at London Zoo, right?'

'London Zoo, yep, and we lived in North London in a suburb called Crouch End,' he replies. 'Do you know it?'

'I've heard of it, but have never been there. I was more of an East London girl.'

'You've never thought about going back to the UK?' he asks.

'No.' I don't add, 'Because you ruined it for me.'

'So your sisters and your dad are over here at the moment?'

'And Lorraine.'

'Of course.' He smiles knowingly. 'What did she have in the end?'

'Excuse me?'

'Girl or boy?'

'Oh! A girl. Isabel,' I tell him, smiling. 'She's a character. They all are.'

'Do you go back to England often to visit them?'

'No. Dad tries to bring the family over here every couple of years. It's good. It means I don't miss seeing my sisters grow up. Although saying that, Kay is frightening me!'

'What do you mean?'

'She's fifteen now. Like a little adult. It's a bit scary.'

He nods. 'And what about your mum? What's she up to these days?'

'She's okay. She lives in Bondi, works as a restaurant manager. Where do you live?'

'Cremorne, in North Sydney.'

'I know it.' In fact, it's not *that* far from Manly . . .

'Where do you live now?' he asks. I tell him. 'Nice,' he comments.

'I like it.' I pick at my ravioli.

'Not hungry?' he asks.

'Not as much as I thought.' I glance across the table, but he's had no problem tucking into his food – as was always the case. I smile to myself.

'What's it like, working at the zoo?' I ask.

'It's a zoo,' he says flippantly.

I lean back in my chair and stare at him. 'And London Zoo?'

He shrugs. 'Another zoo.'

'You prefer conservation parks?'

'You know I do.'

'I *know* you do?'

'"Zoos aren't real enough" for you, I think is how you described it.'

'You remember that?'

He seems to remember as many conversations as I do. He doesn't answer me. We're still staring across the table at each other. His eyes are even darker blue in this candlelight. My gaze wanders to his lips. Big mistake. I move on to his jaw and then his shoulders, followed by his arms. His T-shirt is tight enough that I can see the definition of his muscles. I blush and look away.

He's reduced me to a teenager again. I want him. I want him as much as I ever did. I shiver and lean forward, trying to focus on eating something. But my eyes are drawn to his lips and I want him to kiss me so much that it hurts.

Richard . . .

'How is everything?' Marco breaks the spell.

'Good, thanks.'

'You are not eating, *signora*.' He gawps at my almost-full dish in horror.

'I'm not that hungry,' I apologise.

'I get you something else?'

'No, no, this is lovely, really. I'm just not that hungry.'

'The steak was perfect, Marco.' Ben thankfully distracts him.

'Ah, I so pleased. You like another drink?'

'Sure.' Ben holds up his glass. There's only a little beer swilling around. Marco turns to me.

'I'm fine, thank you.' My glass is still half-full.

'Do you ever see Josh?' Ben asks.

'Actually, yes. I had to go back to Adelaide for a funeral a couple of weeks ago. My friend's dad,' I explain. 'And Josh also came over to visit at Easter.'

'Did he?' He gives me a look.

'He's a good mate,' I add, to clarify the situation. 'He's got a girlfriend, now. Tina.'

'Oh, right.'

'He stopped drinking and driving.'

'Really?'

'Yes. We had a massive barney about it.' I recall that night in Josh's car. 'I never got a chance to tell you.'

'What about you? Did you pass your driving test in the end?'

'First time.'

'Thought you might.'

Neither of us is referring to that night at Mount Lofty. I can't imagine how we could ever bring it up. It was such a strange, illicit situation – an almost-thirty-year-old falling for a sixteen-year-old girl. It would be like Josh falling for Kay! I put that thought out of my head.

'I never went back to the conservation park after you left,' I tell him.

'I know.'

'You know?' I glance up at him, surprised.

'Dave told me. I was sorry to hear it.'

I say nothing.

'You were so good with the koalas. It takes a certain sort of person to be able to deal with them. Not everyone has the right temperament.'

Janine had said the same thing. 'I missed it,' I admit sadly. 'I cried and cried when I heard they'd relocated Olivia to another conservation park and I never got to say goodbye.'

He nods sympathetically. 'It's tough when that happens.'

'I know it's part of the job . . .'

'. . . but that doesn't make it any easier.' He leans back in his chair and regards me. 'I am sad you gave up on photography. I really thought you had something.'

I shift in my seat. 'It's hard to get into that line of work.'

'That's not an excuse if you're still passionate about it. Are you?'

I meet his gaze. 'Maybe.' Pause. 'I actually went to a photography exhibition not that long ago.'

'Did you?'

'The guy was an arsehole.'

Ben chuckles.

'It's so odd to bump into you now, because I did get my camera back from Mum's recently. I have started taking pictures again.'

'Really?' He sits up with interest. 'Can I see them sometime?'

I smile. 'Sure. If they're not too horrendous. I haven't got any developed yet.'

'Are you still using film?'

'Yes. I know, digital cameras have improved like you said they would, but I've only just got back into it all.'

Ben grins and the waitress appears with some menus.

'Do you want dessert?' he asks me.

'No, I couldn't eat another thing.'

'Just the bill, thanks,' he tells the waitress. We fall silent. 'It's good to see you again,' he says after a while.

I look up at him. 'You, too.'

'Are you very busy while your family are here?'

'I can get away. Monday's your day off, right?'

'Yeah. You still want to catch up for lunch or something?'

'That'd be good.'

The bill arrives and Ben reaches into his pocket for his wallet while I take my purse from my handbag.

'I'll get this,' he tells me.

'We'll go halves.'

'Lily, put it away,' he says firmly.

I hesitate. 'Are you sure?'

'Of course.' He looks offended so I comply.

'Thanks.'

Marco sees us out. 'Come again, please!'

'We will,' Ben tells him.

302

We? A bubble of happiness swells up inside me.

Richard!

'Ferry back to Manly?' Ben checks.

'Yes. Do you go to Old Cremorne?'

'Cremorne Point.' That means we have to take separate ferries. 'We can walk together to the terminal.'

He sets off at a brisk pace and once more I hurry to keep up.

'Sorry, am I walking too fast?' He glances at me.

'No, it's okay. I've got my trainers on for a change.'

'You still call them trainers.'

'*Sneakers*, then,' I smirk. 'I'm pretty nifty in my heels, too. I don't usually look like this,' I add.

He gives me a quick once-over. 'What do you usually look like?'

'Skirts, heels, make-up . . .'

'You *are* wearing make-up,' he comments.

'I usually wear more.' It strikes me that maybe he wishes I looked the same as I did ten years ago. He told me I looked different when we saw each other at the zoo. Is that a good thing?

'I cut off all my hair,' I blurt out. Dur! *No shit, Sherlock.*

He smiles at me. 'I noticed.'

'Do you like it?' *Shut up, you moron!*

'Yeah.' He shrugs. 'I liked it long, too.'

Don't say anything else, I warn myself. Then: 'Did you prefer it longer?' *Argh!*

He glances at me sideways. 'You look as lovely as you ever did.'

My heart flips and my face heats up. And with that I'm rendered speechless. We arrive at the terminal and he looks up at the timetable. 'Quick, there's one leaving for Manly in three minutes!'

He rushes me to the barriers. Wait! This is all happening too fast.

'I don't have to catch this one,' I cry. I stare at him, panicked, and he freezes for a moment.

'Want me to come for the ride?' he asks.

'Yes!'

We rush to the ticket booth and board the green-and-white ferry seconds before they raise the planks. He follows me to the back of the boat and we stand there in silence, side by side, as Circular Quay and the Opera House grow smaller in the distance. Finally I can breathe again. He's still here. He's resting his elbows on the railings and I let go with my hands and do the same. Our arms knock together, but neither of us moves. I can feel the warmth of him radiating through my jumper. We should really go inside like everyone else around us, but my feet are stuck to the spot. Finally it's just Ben and me standing there in the wind.

'I want to ask you if you're cold,' he says, 'but it's at the risk of sounding boring.'

'I like it out here.'

He gestures at the empty bench behind us. 'It'll be more sheltered against the wall.'

'Okay.' I take a seat next to him. Instinctively he wraps his arm around me and rests his chin on the top of my head. I put my hand on his chest and snuggle up against him. It feels very comfortable, very natural.

The journey passes by quickly, even though neither of us speaks the rest of way. All too soon the ferry begins to slow. Ben relaxes his grip on me and I pull away and look up at him. Our eyes lock together. He's so close I could move my face two inches and my lips would be touching his.

A burst of laughter jolts me to my senses. A group of girls and guys in their twenties storm the railings, and shock slams into me as I recognise one of the girls. She's a friend of Nathan's. I quickly get to my feet as the ferry churns up a storm in the water. We're pulling into the terminal and the tipsy revellers start to make their way to the side of the boat. Ben stays seated.

'I'd better go,' I say shiftily. 'Are you going straight back to Circular Quay?' He nods. 'Sorry, what a trek.' He'll have to catch another ferry back to Cremorne Point.

'It's fine,' he brushes me off.

'I'll see you Monday?'

'Sure,' he replies. 'You want to give me a call and we'll make plans?'

'Yes, okay.' I back away from him, meeting his eyes for a final fleeting moment. I'm unable to read his expression. 'Bye,' I mutter. And then I turn and hurry off the boat.

What the fuck am I doing? That was one of Nathan's friends! Anyone could have seen me! Who else was on this ferry that I know?

The house is quiet when I get home. Quiet and dark. But my head is buzzing. I turn my key in the lock and push open the front door, flicking on the switch to light the hall. I drop my bag on the floor and walk into the living room, turning on lights as I go. I stand there for a moment, not knowing what to do with myself. I should go to bed.

I spin around and walk out of the room, switching off the lights again. In the bedroom I sit on the end of the bed. The wardrobe door is open and my eyes wander to Richard's clothes hanging there. I turn and look at his bedside table and guilt overcomes me as my gaze falls on the picture sitting there of the two of us.

You're engaged! You're engaged to be married! To Richard! *Richard!*

Nothing feels real. I'm detached from reality. I get up mechanically and go into the bathroom. The mirror greets me and I stare at my reflection for a while, not liking what I see. Reaching forward, I open the bathroom cabinet so the mirror swings away from me. I'm left staring at my toiletries on the shelves, and all of Richard's things – his toothbrush, his razor, his shaving foam. I lift up his aftershave bottle and put the nozzle to my nose, breathing in his scent.

And then reality hits. Sobs engulf me and I sink down onto the bathroom floor as grief pours out of my soul. I love my boyfriend. He's never done anything to hurt me. He's always been there for me. He's never left me.

But Ben – oh, Ben . . . I remember the warmth of his body and his arm around me. His lips so close to mine. My tears come to a standstill and I stare ahead in a daze.

This isn't fair. I love them both.

Somewhere deep inside me the chasm that cracked and broke open when Ben left splits even further apart. I can't lose Ben again. But I don't want to lose Richard, either.

Nathan, Lucy, Sam, Molly, Mikey . . . I would lose them all, too. I would even miss Richard's sisters, and what would his parents think of me? I can't bear it.

You don't have to decide anything right now.

It's true, I don't. Ben might not turn out to be the person I think he is. I've built him up so much over the years that he's almost not real to me.

I stand up, full of resolution. I need to see him again – of course I do. I can't decide now how I want to spend the rest of my life.

Ben's an uncertainty. This whole thing with him might fall flat on its face. Richard's here. He wants to marry me. He's not going anywhere. But Ben . . . I need to know him better before I can make any decisions about my future.

I get out a cotton pad from the bathroom cabinet, soak it with make-up remover and proceed to take off my make-up.

So that's what I'm going to have to do. Spend some time with Ben; see if he's all I cracked him up to be. It might be that my decision in the end is easy.

I throw the pad into the bin and cleanse the rest of my face before applying moisturiser.

Then again, I might be about to make things harder than I could ever imagine . . .

Don't think about that now. Put it out of your mind. It will all be okay. It will all work out for the best.

I close the bathroom cabinet, coming face to face with my reflection again. Suddenly I don't feel so sure.

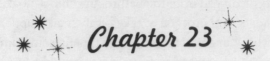

Chapter 23

I'm awake for hours that night. It's hardly surprising. If I manage to doze off, bad dreams soon drag me kicking and screaming to consciousness and then my thought process starts ticking over and I haven't a chance in hell of falling asleep again for a long, long time. When the phone rings, pulling me out of a long-desired slumber, I snatch it up and jolt awake as I spot the time.

'Dad?'

'No, it's me.' Richard.

'I thought it was my dad.'

'So I figured.' I can hear the smile in his voice.

'What's the time?'

'Ten o'clock. You sound croaky. Were you out late?'

'Not really.' I clear my throat. 'I didn't sleep well.'

'Missing me.'

'Huh. Guess so.' Silence. 'How are you?'

'Good. Thought I'd better give you a call, check up on you.'

'All's fine here.' I try to sound breezy. 'How's the surf?'

'Great. Already been out this morning.'

'Everyone having fun?'

'Yeah. But you're missed.'

'Am I?'

'Of course. So how's your dad and everyone?'

'Really good. We went to the zoo yesterday.' *Was it really only yesterday?*

'That's nice.'

'I'm glad you woke me up actually, as they'll be wondering where I am.' I was planning on going over to them for breakfast again this morning. Bollocks. 'I'd better go,' I say to Richard.

'Okay, honey,' he says sweetly. 'Have a good day with them and I'll see you Monday arvo.'

'What time will you be back?' *I can't miss lunch with Ben.*

'Late afternoon. I'll give you a call when we're on our way.'

'Alright.'

'Love you.'

'You too.' I wait for him to hang up before I put down the receiver. Oh, God . . .

As the day wears on, the night before seems more and more surreal. Sometimes I remember with a sharpness of clarity what it was like being in Ben's arms on the ferry, and then I shiver and I can't concentrate on what my dad or my sisters are saying to me. But mostly it's like a dream. I can't believe I saw him only hours ago.

That night when I get home I feel nervous. The thought of phoning Ben is hanging over me. I don't know if I should call him tonight or wait until the morning. I feel strangely uneasy with the thought of either.

Eventually it's ten p.m. and my decision is almost made. Won't it be too late to call him now? I remember turning up at his house the night Josh killed the koala. It was midnight and he'd been on the phone to Charlotte . . .

I reach for my mobile phone on the bedside table and find his number in my recent calls menu. I press the call button. It rings three times.

'Hello?'

'It's Lily.'

'Hi!'

'I'm sorry, is it too late?'

'No, no, I'm watching some telly.'

'What are you watching?'

'A wildlife doc.' He chuckles. 'You think I'm such a saddo, don't you?'

I laugh too and my nerves die away. 'Of course not.'

'Did you have a good day with your family?'

'Yes, thanks.'

'What did you do?'

'We went shopping and for a wander round the Rocks and the Opera House. The usual stuff. Botanic Gardens, as well. Did you get home alright last night?'

'Yeah, no trouble. I should be asking you that.'

'Why should you be asking me that?'

He yawns and I picture him stretching. 'It's the gentlemanly thing to do.'

I know he's grinning and I can't help but giggle. 'So what do you want to do tomorrow?' I ask.

'I'm easy. Are you sure your dad won't mind you ducking out of family commitments?'

'No, he won't mind.'

'Well, tell him I won't take his daughter away for too long.'

I'll be telling him no such thing. As if things aren't complicated enough without having to explain *your* existence.
Imagine if Dad mentioned Ben to Richard. I shudder at the
thought.

'They won't miss me for an hour or two,' I say without even
thinking. That's nowhere near enough time! 'Or longer,' I blurt
out, feeling panicky again. 'I can get away for the day if you like?'
But it's his day off. Why would he want to spend his whole day off
with me? 'Sorry, I bet you've got stuff to do.'

'No, not really. But I'll feel bad if I take you away from your
family. You haven't seen them for two years.'

'I haven't seen you for ten,' I can't help but say.

'I'm not going anywhere.'

'Are you sure about that?'

He repeats himself, but softly this time. 'I'm not going anywhere, Lily.' The sound of my name on his tongue fills me up with
contentment. I close my eyes. If I listen hard enough, I can make
out the sound of him breathing.

I can't lose you again.

Stop it.

'So what shall we do?' I ask. 'One of us is going to have to
make a decision.'

'Fishing?'

'Pardon?'

'Fishing.'

'You have a boat?'

'A yacht, yes.'

'Seriously?'

'Yep.'

'You're finally going to make good on your promise?'

He chuckles. 'It would seem so. If you're up for it.'
'Hell, yeah.'

He moors his yacht in Middle Harbour, which is less than a twenty-minute drive from Manly. He offers to collect me because he's got a car, but I don't want him coming to the house, so I insist on catching a bus. I call him when I'm ten minutes away so he's already waiting by the bus stop with the engine turned on as I climb off the bus. He's driving a dark-grey Audi Allroad, which is a bit of a change from the white Holden Commodore he used to drive back in Adelaide.

'Nice car,' I comment as I climb in.

'I got a good deal on a second-hand one,' he explains as he pulls out quickly into traffic.

'I don't remember you driving this fast ten years ago,' I say after a while.

He laughs. 'I guess I was more responsible back then.'

'Hmm.'

'What's that supposed to mean?'

I give him a meaningful look and he waves me away. 'Don't answer that. Anyway, I should be letting *you* drive – see if those lessons paid off.'

'I hardly ever drive these days. I miss driving, actually. R—' Shit! I almost said 'Richard drives a truck'!

'Sorry?' He glances across at me, suspecting I cut a sentence short.

'I just miss it.'

'You always were a natural at it.'

I shift in my seat at the compliment.

We arrive at the harbour where he moors his yacht and he parks the car and grabs his fishing equipment, a cool box – or Esky, as they call them here – and a small hamper from the boot. 'Lunch.'

'You packed a picnic?' I tease.

'What, you were thinking you'd indulge in some sushi?'

'Yeah, yeah, whatever.'

Our feet crunch across the gravel as we walk towards a fish tackle shop next to a boat ramp.

'I hope you're not expecting anything too impressive. I've had this yacht for fifteen years.'

'I didn't know you actually *owned* a boat in Adelaide?' I say, surprised.

'Yeah.'

'And you brought it here?'

'Sailed it over.'

'Wow! How long did that take?'

'About two weeks.'

'So that was another thing you didn't sell when you moved to England.'

'Mmm.'

'Ben, why the hell did you leave Australia if your heart wasn't in it?'

He shrugs, and for a split-second he looks like a lost little boy. I don't press him further.

He goes into the shop to buy some bait and then we head to his boat. It's a yacht of about ten metres long with a white deck and a dark-blue hull. Ben jumps on and dumps his gear before turning around to grab my bag and coat. He takes my hands to help me into the cockpit and it's like a flashback to ten years ago as a jolt of electricity shoots through me. I don't meet his eyes so hopefully he doesn't see my face heat up.

He starts up the engine and I grasp the ropes while he unmoors the yacht, then he jumps on again and pushes us away from the jetty. Ben sits on one side and quickly takes the helm at the stern. I sit opposite, facing him.

We move at a leisurely pace past numerous pretty bays and through The Spit, where hundreds of multi-coloured apartments and houses step down from the hillside and clamber for views of the water. The Spit Bridge is being raised as we approach and once we're through, Ben climbs onto the deck and goes to the mast to raise the sails. I watch, full of admiration and respect as two lime-green sails billow out. There's something very sexy about seeing him in this context. The wind picks up and I laugh as my hair whips around my face. Ben returns to the stern and cuts the engine. I look across at him, feeling jittery.

After a while we sail into the shallower waters of a secluded bay.

'You don't get seasick, do you?' he asks.

'No. At least, I don't think so.'

He climbs back onto the deck and drops the sails, followed by the anchor. 'You'll know once we rock here for a while. I'll nip below and make us a cuppa.' He returns to the cockpit, then jumps down into the cabin. 'You want one?' he calls up to me. I go to the cabin and peer inside.

'Sure, that'd be great. Aah, it's been so long since you've made me tea.'

It's only a small cabin but there's a sink, a tiny gas-fired stove and a toilet plus a bed at the back, which I assume forms a table and bench seats when it's not being slept on.

'Do you ever sleep in here?' I ask curiously.

'Sometimes,' he says, glancing at the bed. 'But not often. I couldn't be bothered to turn it back into a table again.'

'Typical man.'

He raises his eyebrows in amusement. 'Here you go.' He hands over a mug. Milk and one sugar, just like always.

'Impressive memory,' I comment.

'Do you remember how I take mine?' he asks.

'Milk, two sugars.' He grins, then I add: 'I just saw you do it.' I crack up laughing and step out of his way as he pretend-barges past me on his return to the cockpit.

I actually *do* remember. Of course I do. I even know that he likes two and a quarter sugars if he's drinking his tea and eating something sweet at the same time. And you have to stir it really well, otherwise he adds more sugar anyway. But I'm not going to tell him all that. I watch as he opens the hamper.

'Are you hungry?' he asks.

'A bit.'

'I'm starving.'

'You're always starving, Benjamin.' I laugh at his face and go to sit opposite him again. 'Is that your real name – Benjamin?'

'Only my mother calls me Benjamin.'

'And Marco.'

'Yes, and Marco.' He rolls his eyes good-naturedly. 'My nan could sometimes get away with Benji.'

'Cute!'

He chuckles and gets out sandwiches. 'We've got ham and mustard, cheese and pickle, tuna mayo . . . What do you feel like?'

'Cheese and pickle, please.' The boat is rocking, but I'm not feeling sick yet. I open up the aluminium foil to reveal a sandwich

315

made on thick-cut white bread which I'm pretty sure Ben sliced himself from a loaf.

'Did you make these yourself?' I ask.

'Yeah,' he replies, a touch defensively.

We chat between mouthfuls. 'Can you cook?' I want to know.

He shrugs. 'A bit – when I can be bothered. It's not much fun when you don't have anyone to cook for.'

'Did you used to cook for Charlotte?'

'Sometimes. Especially if she was late back from work or something like that.'

'What did she do? What *does* she do?'

'She's a financial analyst.'

'I can never understand what that means.'

'I won't bore you by trying to explain. I'd probably get it wrong anyway.'

'It sounds impressive. Is she successful?'

'She's good at what she does, yes.'

'Are you still in touch with her?'

'We speak now and again.'

I put my half-eaten sandwich to one side. 'Did you leave on bad terms?'

'Not really. But we weren't exactly the best of friends, either. No point in dragging it out.'

'Is she with anyone else?'

'She's had a couple of boyfriends, as far as I know. I don't think any of them have been serious. Don't you ever eat much?' He nods at my sandwich.

'Yeah. I do have an appetite, just not when I'm with you.'

'Do I put you off your food?'

I give him a look of pretend distaste. 'Yeah, you do a bit.'

'Huh!' he grumbles, and I laugh. 'Did you bring your camera today?'

'I did, actually.' I bend down and pull my bag up onto the seat, getting out my old friend.

He smiles. 'Have you thought about getting a smaller one?'

'I should switch to digital,' I concede. 'But I've only just got back into it. I wouldn't know where to start.'

'We should do some research on the internet. Go camera shopping.'

I love his use of the term 'we'.

'That's a good idea.'

'So what made you want to start taking pictures again?'

I don't answer immediately, then I shrug. 'Not sure.'

I'm not about to tell him it was because my boyfriend proposed and it made Ben seem even more lost to me than he already was. I had to do something to bring him back.

And now he's here. Literally – and not just metaphorically.

What if I hadn't gone to the zoo? It's inconceivable that I could have continued living in this city oblivious of his existence. Where would my life have taken me? At least I'm not already married. If I think being engaged is bad, marriage would have been much, much worse.

'What are you thinking?' Ben asks. I'm still staring down at the camera in my hands. I impulsively put the viewfinder to my eye and click off a shot of him.

'You could have warned me first!' he jokes irately.

'What would you have done – nipped below to check your hair?' I tease. I lean up against the side of the boat and rest the camera on my lap. 'You know, I never got a photo of you before.

It made me sad when you left,' I tell him honestly. 'Do you still have the photo of me?'

He nods. 'Yeah.'

'Did you take it to England with you?'

He gives me a sardonic look. 'No.'

'That would have been a bit shitty of you,' I agree.

'I put it in the loft at Nan's house with some other things,' he tells me. 'It's still there.'

I'm sort of disappointed he hasn't got it out again. He must be able to read this on my face because he says quietly, 'I had to try to forget you, Lily.'

'Even when you came back?'

'Even when I came back.'

'Why?'

'You would have moved on.'

'What if I hadn't?'

He doesn't answer, staring across at me with a grave expression on his features. His jaw is set into a hard line, day-old stubble making him look even sexier than usual. My mind flicks to the bed inside the cabin and the desire to have him make love to me there is suddenly overwhelming.

Richard, Richard, *Richard*! For fuck's sake, how many times do I have to remind you?

Oh, but maybe if we had sex I'd be able to put him out of my mind once and for all.

That is a crock of shit, and you know it.

Spoilsport.

I pull myself together and say, 'Did I spy some crisps in that hamper?'

Ben comes back to life, the atmosphere reverting to

normal. 'Yep. What do you want, salt and vinegar, chicken or plain?'

'Salt and vinegar, please. Who would ever opt for boring old plain, hey?'

'You're right. I should have known you'd have no interest in them whatsoever.'

'Why, because I'm a fussy cow?'

He laughs. 'No, because you're anything but boring.'

Stop saying things like that to me. It's making me think of the bed again.

'Are you going to catch me a fish, or what?' I say rather huskily.

'You can catch one yourself,' he replies with a smile.

Twenty minutes later, I feel a tug at the end of my line. We're using handlines, not fishing rods. I'm holding onto the line itself and I can actually feel when a fish takes the bait.

'Wind it in,' Ben insists excitedly.

A fish of about a foot long flaps and flutters as I drag it out of the water.

'You caught a whiting!' he exclaims, taking the wriggling fish off the line.

'Your namesake,' I laugh as he throws it in the Esky. 'That was easy. What was all this business about a four o'clock start?'

'Hey?' He baits up my hook with another wriggling worm.

'Back in Adelaide, you said I had to get up early. We're catching fish now, aren't we? What's the point in getting up before it's even light if you can catch fish in the middle of the day?'

'If we were sitting out here in the midday sun during a hot Australian summer, you'd know.'

'Fair enough.'

We catch one more whiting, a flathead and two 'shitties' as

Ben calls the inedible fish, before we set off back to Middle Harbour again. He throws the latter back, but promises to cook me a fry-up sometime. 'Maybe you could bring your family over to mine for dinner later this week?' he suggests. 'These won't go far, but I can come back out here and get some more before then.'

'Oh.' I feel jumpy, can't think what to say. 'I doubt that will be possible.'

'Oh, right. Sure.' He looks away.

'They're going to be very busy, you see. It might be too much to organise.' I try to convince him, but I'm guessing he thinks I'm embarrassed to introduce an older man to my dad. I feel awful, but there's nothing I can say to make him think otherwise – except to tell the truth and explain that I have a fiancé. But let's not go there, eh?

'I never felt seasick.' I try to project a tone of joviality into my voice to lighten things up as we pass through the Spit Bridge again.

'You didn't. Another thing you're a natural at.'

I suddenly feel aggravated and self-conscious. 'I'm not a natural at anything, Ben. I don't know why you keep saying things like that.'

He glances at me, taken aback by my reaction.

'I clearly see a different person from the one you see,' he says after a while.

'Yes, you clearly do, and I don't know why.'

'Hey,' he says gently.

'Just stop,' I snap. 'Stop saying these things to me.'

His jaw clenches and he falls silent. The mood doesn't shift even when we're back in the car and he's driving me to the bus stop.

'I'll take you to Manly,' he says.

'No, the bus is fine. Please – I mean it,' I add firmly.

He nods and pulls over on the side of the road. My stop is up ahead. He doesn't speak.

'Thanks for today,' I say.

'You're welcome,' he replies.

I sigh. 'Sorry, I—'

'It's okay,' he interrupts. 'Here's your bus coming now.'

I hesitate, feeling panicky as the bus whooshes past me.

'Quick,' he urges, leaning across me to open up my door. I stumble out onto the pavement. 'Call me,' he shouts, and I turn and run for the bus.

My heart is still in my mouth when I'm safely seated. What is wrong with me? Why do I get so anxious about leaving him every time? I'm going to see him again, aren't I? *Aren't I?*

I sit on the bus and stare out of the window. My phone beeps and I see that I've missed a call from Richard and now he's texted me. He's home and is wondering where I am. I feel sick. I don't want to see him. I want to run away.

But I stay on the bus. I walk all the way down the hill to our house. It's five o'clock and I should have been back hours ago. My mind has been ticking over fifteen to the dozen and I've decided to tell Richard about Ben. No, not everything. I'm not that . . . *decent.* But I'll tell him that I bumped into an old friend and hopefully I'm a good enough actress that he won't suspect there's any more to it.

'Hello?' I call as I walk into the hall, shutting the door behind me. If I wasn't seasick before, I certainly feel it now.

'Hey!'

I follow his voice into the living room. He's lying on the sofa.

'Have you been asleep?' I ask edgily.

'Yeah.' He yawns. 'Crashed out.'

'Busy weekend?'

'Full on.' He opens up his arms to me. I hesitate a moment before walking towards him. He shuffles up against the back of the sofa so there's enough room for me to squeeze along beside him. I lie down, feeling horribly deceitful as his arms encircle me. I rest my head on his chest. He feels different. Unfamiliar. He's leaner than Ben. Not yet a *man*, man. I think he's similar to how Ben was ten years ago, and I imagine Richard will become even broader in a few years, too. I wonder if I'll be around to see it.

'Mmm.' He presses his lips to my forehead and squeezes me. 'I missed you,' he murmurs.

I pull away from him. 'Everyone else have a good time?'

'Yeah, great.'

'Did Lucy do much surfing?'

'She did some. The waves were too big most of the time though.' He continues. 'She and Nathan are going back to England.'

'No way! When?'

'In a couple of months.'

'What about the business?'

'I'm going to carry on with it here – he's going to do a renovation down in Somerset where Lucy's family are from.'

'How long will they be away?'

'It's looking like six months.'

'Blimey. That's a bit sad.'

'You're telling me. But you know what they're like, they have to split their time between two countries, two families. That's the way it is with them.' He sniffs my coat. 'Where have you been today?'

'Well,' I force a smile which I hope looks relaxed, 'I didn't get a chance to tell you on the phone, but I bumped into an old pal on the weekend who used to work at the conservation park.' My heart is pounding.

'Really?' he asks with interest.

'Yeah. Anyway, we caught up today.'

'That's bizarre because I heard from an old friend, too, yesterday.'

Is that it? Am I off the hook? 'Who?'

'Do you recall me telling you about a girl called Ally who I met in England?'

'Of course I do.' My heart plummets. 'She was your girlfriend, wasn't she?'

'She was,' he admits. 'Only for a couple of months. We broke it off when I came back here. We hadn't been together long enough to put our lives on hold for two years.'

I only knew Ben for a few weeks and I've put my life on hold for a decade . . .

'I remember,' I say. 'She was staying on in the UK, but you only had a three-month work visa.'

'That's right. Don't worry about it,' he says quickly, touching my arm.

'Is she back?' I ask.

'Yeah.'

'Why is she calling you?'

'Lily, it's okay,' he insists, sincerity radiating from his warm brown eyes. 'She was only calling to say hi. I told her about you. About how we're engaged. She was really happy for me.'

'Oh.' My voice softens. 'Are you planning to see her?'

'Nah,' he says. 'I realise that would be a bit weird.'

How bad do I feel now? 'You can if you like,' I say begrudgingly.

'No!' He laughs and wraps his arms back around me. 'There's no point.'

I sigh and settle into his chest, guiltily.

'How are your family?' he asks.

'Good. I saw them this morning. Dad mentioned about coming here for dinner tonight, but I thought you might be too knackered.'

He yawns. 'I am a bit, but we can have dinner with them. I guess I'd better get showered.'

'Me too.'

'So where have you been today?' he asks as he gets up.

Dammit! 'Er, I went fishing, would you believe?' I turn away quickly and lead the way to the bedroom.

'Fishing!' he echoes. 'Is this friend male or female?'

'Um, male.' I try to sound casual.

'Right.' There's uncertainty to his tone.

'He's an old friend of Michael's. He's, like, forty or something. He used to look out for me when I worked at the park.'

'Sounds a bit dodgy if you ask me.'

'Richard!' I turn around and slap him, relieved to see he's joking. 'He was a good mate.'

'As long as he wasn't a cradle-snatcher.'

I laugh, long and hard. A bit too long and hard because he's looking at me in a funny way. 'Don't be a dick. Get in the shower.'

He grins and walks out of the bedroom to the bathroom.

Shit! I sit on the edge of the bed. That was horrible. Horrible! I cover my eyes in consternation, then immediately sit up straight again in case Richard returns. The shower turns on in the bathroom so I relax. But it's only a momentary respite. I know I'm going to feel on edge for some time to come.

'What did you get up to today?' Dad asks me when the seven of us are seated at a huge wooden oblong table in Manly's fancy new fish restaurant.

'I went fishing actually, with an old friend.'

'Did you catch anything?'

'I did indeed.'

'Did you?' Richard interrupts with surprise.

'Yep. I caught a whiting.'

'Where is it?'

'Oh, I left it with Ben.' His name is out of my mouth before I can think of how else to say that sentence.

'Bummer.' Richard laughs.

'He was going to fillet it.'

'I know how to fillet fish,' Richard says casually.

'Do you?'

'Yeah. I used to go fishing with my uncle all the time.'

'I didn't know that.'

'There are a lot of things you don't know about me,' he says jokingly, then puts on a comedy voice. 'At least we've got our whole lives together to find out.'

My dad looks across at us and smiles warmly.

Holy shit! I haven't told him I'm engaged! I cannot *believe* I forgot to tell my dad – my DAD! – that I'm supposed to be getting married. I've been waiting to tell him in person, but then it didn't even occur to me with everything else that was going on. How can I get out of this without Richard killing me?

I glance at Richard and smile serenely. 'I haven't told them yet,' I murmur.

He looks at me, dumbstruck. 'You haven't?'

'I wanted us to tell them together.'

'Oh.' The relief on his face is palpable.

'Go on,' I urge, plastering the smile even tighter to my face.

Richard looks momentarily panicked and then gazes across at my dad's expectant face. 'Er, I probably should have spoken to you first, sir, so sorry about that, but I've asked Lily to marry me.'

Squeal from Lorraine.

'And she said yes.'

'Aah, congratulations!' Dad gets up and comes around to shake Richard's hand while Lorraine leaps to her feet to give me a kiss and a hug.

'I can't believe you kept that quiet all weekend!'

'Neither can I,' I cry, aware of the irony that it's the absolute truth.

Kay, Olivia and Isabel, bless them, stay seated, as children usually do when adults are jumping around with excitement.

I sit down again and try to keep smiling.

'So when's the big day?' Lorraine asks with obvious delight.

'Probably the year after next,' I reply.

'That's good,' Dad says. 'That will give us plenty of time to save up again.'

'Great. We're thinking a summer wedding, too, so you'll be able to come over when it's nice and hot,' Richard tells him.

'That'd be great,' Kay pipes up.

'And is your dad going to give you away?' Lorraine pries happily.

'Of course,' I say.

Dad beams, Lorraine rubs him on his arm and underneath the table, Richard squeezes my hand – and I feel like the biggest bitch in the world.

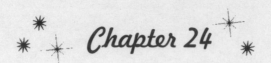

Chapter 24

This is what it must have been like for Ben, feeling like there was no way back once the wedding preparations got underway. The last week has been hell. Lorraine has insisted on taking me wedding-dress shopping. She's adamant that she and Dad will pay for the meringue, and her biggest desire is to get me fitted out and ready to go before they head back to the UK at the weekend.

I'm dragging my heels, telling her the wedding is so far away that I don't want to make a decision yet, but she persists with the endless shopping trips. She's met me for two lunches alone this week so we can exhaust more bridal shops. It's killing me.

Of course, at work, Nicola thinks it's marvellous. She's delighted I'm getting into the 'swing of things', as she puts it. And when Lorraine is off the scene, I know I'm in for even more torture.

I haven't seen Ben since the fishing trip. I texted him a few days ago to say things were manic with my family. When I'm at work the urge to be with him is overwhelming. But somehow, when I'm at home with Richard, I manage to put him out of my mind.

Mostly.

Yesterday I got my photos developed. I couldn't concentrate on the shots I'd taken over the last couple of weeks because I was so jittery about seeing the one of Ben on the boat. My heart stopped when I finally came to it in the pack. He looked so gorgeous. He had only a slight smile on his face because I hadn't given him time to pose, but his blue eyes stood out against the grey sea behind him. It was perfect.

In a half-wakeful state this morning, I dreamt that we were in the cabin of his boat together . . . Then Richard rolled up against me with a morning stiffie and I could *not* help it. I couldn't.

After I'd come down from a mindblowing orgasm, Richard chuckled. 'Is it your randy time of the month or something?' he asked.

'Must be,' I replied, getting out of bed and going to the bathroom with a red face. I sat on the toilet with my chin in my hands. I'd imagined it was Ben the entire time. I hated myself.

And now here I am at work, sitting alongside Mel and trying to concentrate.

'She's got that far-off look in her eyes again,' Mel says, grinning.

'More wedding-dress shopping this week?' Nicola enquires.

'Not if I can help it,' I shudder.

My family are going to the Snowy Mountains, which are about a five-hour drive from Sydney. They're staying there for a couple of days so I'm not seeing them again until Thursday. Which means that for the next couple of days, I have free lunchbreaks.

I need to see him.

I push my stool out from under the desk, saying, 'Anyone for tea?'

'Are you making it?' Mel asks dryly.

'I *do* make tea occasionally, you know.'

'No, thanks. I'm going to pop out for a coffee in a minute,' Nicola tells me.

'I'm alright, too,' Mel says. 'I've only just finished the last cup. What's up with you? Not pregnant, are you?'

'No!' I exclaim. 'Why would you say that?'

'Cravings?'

'Please, stop. There is no way I'm having a kid anytime soon.'

'Give it two years.' Nicola nudges Mel. 'Honeymoon baby, that's what I reckon.'

I roll my eyes and walk away, my fingers clutching the phone I surreptitiously pulled out of my bag. In the kitchen I start to text Ben, then I give up and call him instead. I don't want to wait for a text to come back. My stomach flutters with nerves as the phone rings and rings. I'm about to hang up because I don't want to leave a message and then he answers. He sounds breathless.

'What have you been doing?' I ask, smiling.

'I was wrestling with a joey.'

'Joey koala or joey kangaroo?'

'Kangaroo.'

'What are you doing with the kangaroos?'

'Just the usual check-ups. This one didn't want to co-operate.'

'Oh dear,' I sympathise. 'So you're at work today?'

'Yes, why?'

My heart sinks. 'I hoped you might have the day off. I wondered if you'd like to meet me for lunch.'

'That would have been great. Tomorrow?'

'Okay.' It'll have to do.

'Have you had your photos developed yet?' he asks.

'Yesterday.' They're still in my bag because I didn't want Richard to see the one of Ben.

'Can you bring them?'

'Sure.'

'Also, there's a camera shop around the corner from your work. We could pop in?'

I smile. 'That's a good idea.' We end the call and my mood slumps.

Tomorrow, Lily! You'll see him tomorrow! It's not long to wait.

But it feels like forever. And by the time I've got through another night full of the guilts with Richard, plus a morning of constantly checking my phone and willing the time to pass, Nicola has grown suspicious.

'What's up with you today?' she asks eventually. 'Who are you expecting to call?'

'No one – I'm just checking the time,' I reply defensively. Usually it's Mel who cottons onto anything out of the ordinary, but luckily she's busy making sure a conference this morning runs smoothly. I must really be overdoing it for Nicola to pick up on anything.

'Why are you checking the time so much, then?' she perseveres.

'I'm hungry. Waiting for lunch.'

'Soup today?' she enquires, and I'm not convinced I've got away with it.

'I might even go all out and get a sandwich.'

'Good for you.'

Nicola takes an early lunch at twelve and in the meantime, Mel returns. Finally it's one o'clock and I can hi-tail it out of there. I told Ben to meet me out the front because I didn't want him waltzing up to reception and piquing my colleagues' curiosity. After a quick dash to the ladies to top up my lippy, I hurry outside. I'm five minutes late so he's already standing there when I arrive, wearing the same grey trousers I've seen before and a black jacket. When his dark-blue eyes smile down at me, a memory slams into me of the sex I had yesterday morning. I inadvertently blush.

'Hi,' he says, looking at me with amusement.

'Hello. Sorry I'm late.'

'I'm early. Nice building.'

'Thanks. It's alright.'

'Pretty good place to work,' he comments.

'It's cool that it's central.'

'But you still want more from your job.'

'Shhh!' I look around. 'My boss might hear me and give me the sack.'

'Aw, sorry.' He wraps his arm around my neck and presses his lips to the top of my head. Then he lets me go again. It happens so quickly that I don't have time to react.

'The camera shop isn't far from here,' he says. 'I've been surfing the net, but it'll be good to pick the salesperson's brains, too.'

I fall silent. Suddenly I feel silly. What the hell am I thinking, going to buy a camera? Do I really believe I can become a professional photographer? I don't know anything about cameras! I haven't even attempted to research them. I come to a slow stop on the street.

'What's wrong?' Ben asks.

'I don't know.' I avert my eyes.

'Hey.' He reaches down and takes my hand. 'You can tell me.'

I look up at him, at the concern on his face. His hand is warm in mine. Yes, it makes me feel jittery, but it's also reassuring.

'I don't know what I'm doing,' I admit.

'What do you mean?'

'I know nothing about taking pictures.'

'But that's the point of getting a camera, so you can learn.'

I stare at him warily. 'I think I might be deluding myself.'

'No, you're not.' He shakes his head adamantly. 'Lily, you have something. It may be raw talent, but everyone has to start somewhere. Why don't you do a photography course?'

A spark of hope fills up my insides. Yes, I could do a course! But the spark just as quickly dims again.

'I still think I'm deluding myself.'

'You're *not*,' he insists, squeezing my hand. 'Trust me.'

I stare right back at him and take a large breath. 'Okay.'

'Good,' he says. 'Let's go.'

He drops my hand and I follow him, fighting the urge to grasp hold of it again.

I buy a camera on my credit card, and I'm practically bursting with excitement and delight as Ben walks me back to the office.

'I'm going to look into courses this afternoon,' I promise him. 'I can't wait to play with this tonight.' There's such a spring in my step, you'd think I'm wearing trainers, not high heels.

'I don't think I've ever seen you this happy.'

It's true. I haven't felt this happy for a long time. We reach the side of my building and I stop and beam up at him.

'Hey, I haven't seen your photos,' Ben remembers. 'Do you have time?'

'I can go back five minutes late,' I reply, getting the pack out of my bag and handing them over. He leans up against the building and comments on various shots as he goes. He agrees with me that I missed a trick with the sailboat photo.

'Josh distracted me,' I say, peering over his shoulder.

'Ah, was this the weekend he was here?'

'Yeah. Look, there he is.' I point at the next shot of Josh having a pint at a bar near the Opera House. 'He didn't bring his camera so you'll have to excuse the next few tourist shots. I promised I'd send them to him.'

Ben studies the photo of Josh. 'Still looks the same,' he murmurs, then he glances at me. 'Did anything ever happen between you?'

'Nope,' I reply, then before I can stop myself: 'Would it have bothered you if it had?'

He turns his attention back to the pack. 'You know it would have.'

There are photos of my family in there, but none, thankfully, of Richard. It hasn't occurred to me to take any of him, bizarrely.

Eventually Ben comes to the one of him on the boat. He gives me a playful look.

'You don't want this one, do you?'

'Give it here.' I reach for it, but he holds it away at arm's length.

'I might send it to my mum.'

'Oi. Give it back – *now*.'

'She'd really like it,' he teases.

I grab his arm and wrestle the photo from his grasp as he laughs. 'How rude.' I put on a prim and proper English accent. I meet his eyes and am greeted with a naughty look. For once, I don't go red.

'What are you doing tonight?' he asks.

I falter for a second before pulling a lie out of my cap. 'I . . . It's a friend's birthday. I'm having dinner in Manly.'

He nods and I swear he can see right through me. 'When's your next day off?' I ask shiftily.

'Monday,' he says.

'Do you . . . Would you fancy coming in to have lunch with me again?'

He smiles slightly. 'Yeah, sure. Same time and place?'

'Is that okay?'

'Of course.'

I force a smile and indicate the plastic bag holding my new purchase. 'Thanks,' I say. 'Thanks for persuading me.'

'Now you have to get onto that course,' he replies, backing away.

'Absolutely!' I practically shout, totally overcompensating for wavering a moment ago. He grins and turns away and I experience the usual horrible comedown. I walk around the corner of the building, feeling downhearted, and then I remember my new camera and the smile is back on my face in a flash.

I push through the doors to my building, all excited about showing Nicola and Mel what I've got, but as soon as I see them, I know something's not quite right.

'Who is he?' Nicola asks immediately as I approach the reception desk.

'Who's who?' I reply, but it's too late. She's seen my expression.

'I saw you on my way back in from lunch,' she reveals, smirking, as I walk around the desk to my seat.

My pulse races as I try to think what she could have seen. On her way back in from lunch . . . That was an hour ago. What? What did she see?

'What are you going on about?' I try to seem indifferent as I perch myself on my stool.

'That hot, sexy man?' Nicola persists. I can feel her and Mel watching me like a hawk for any sense of weakness.

'Who – *Ben*?' I pull a face.

'Is that his name? He's a bit of alright.'

'He's an old friend,' I say dismissively. 'He came camera shopping with me today.' I pull the camera box out of the plastic bag. 'Check it out.'

'Wow, that's a bit specky,' Mel says, leaning in for a look as I get out the camera from its box. 'How much was it?'

'Put it this way, it maxed out my credit card. Do you mind if I stick it on here to charge?' I indicate the power point underneath the reception desk.

'Sure.' Mel shrugs.

Nicola rests her elbow against the desk and grins across at me. I look away. 'So,' she says. 'Who's Ben?'

'I told you, an old friend.'

'I haven't heard you mention him before.'

'I only bumped into him again recently,' I explain. 'I used to know him in Adelaide.'

'Another sexy Adelaide boy.' She sighs.

'He's not exactly a boy.' I can't help but laugh. 'He used to work at the conservation park where I had a summer job.'

'What did he do there?' Mel's interested now.

'He was a keeper. He looked after the koalas,' I tell them.

'Phwoar. Sexy *and* good with animals,' Nicola says dreamily.

Out of the blue I see an image in my head of Nicola kissing Ben.

'What?' Nicola says.

'Sorry?' I ask.

'You looked like you were in pain.'

'No, no, it's nothing.' I brush her off.

I see Nicola throw Mel a look. 'Better crack on,' Mel says, and Nicola turns away as they both get on with their work.

I look down at the camera in my hands and feel dizzy. I try to take a couple of deep breaths, but the thought of Nicola with Ben is too much. The thought of *anyone* with Ben is too much. He's single now. I can't let him fall for anyone else, I can't!

Seeing more of him has not made it easier. There's no clear-cut decision. But I'm going to have to make a decision soon. I can't keep going on like this. It's wrong. Very, very wrong.

It strikes me that I've been carrying this weight on my shoulders for over ten years and I haven't had anyone to talk to about it. Not a single person. My friends in Adelaide wouldn't understand why I didn't tell them years ago, and they certainly wouldn't comprehend the gravity of it or the depth of my feelings for Ben because I always kept quiet. My closest friends here, Lucy and Molly . . . well, they'd be horrified at my betrayal of Richard. Could I confide in Nicola and Mel? I glance across at them, both diligently typing away on their keyboards.

I don't know them that well, and that could be a good thing. And they've only met Richard a couple of times so their loyalty would most certainly be with me.

Maybe it's time to talk to someone about this . . .

At that moment, the doors open and Jonathan Laurence strolls up to the receptionist desk. To my right, Mel flicks back her hair. Horny banker or no horny banker, she's still got the hots for him.

'Lily,' he says. 'Could I have a word with you?'

'Of course. Shall I come upstairs?'

'No, no, here is fine. Bronte has been given the opportunity to go abroad on a shoot next week and before she organises cover through the temping agency, I wanted to mention it to you. And your colleagues, of course.' He smiles at Mel and Nicola. 'Would you be interested – if Melissa and Nicola here are happy to arrange a temp for reception, of course?'

I glance at them and they both nod encouragingly. 'Thanks – I'd love to,' I beam.

'Great. I'll have Bronte email you the details this afternoon.'

'Thank you.'

'No problem.'

'That's so cool,' Mel gushes when he's out of earshot.

'Brilliant,' Nicola agrees.

'Are you sure you don't mind?' I check, but they both wave me away.

'Of course not,' Nicola says. 'You've got to do what you can.'

'Maybe you can get Cara back in,' I suggest.

'Maybe,' Mel says. 'Cara and her hooting laugh.'

'And her takeaway coffees.' Nicola stares off into the distance, wistfully.

'Is that a hint?' I ask.

'No, no, no,' she replies with a grin. 'But if you're passing Starbucks, make mine a skinny latte.'

The day goes by slowly because I'm desperate to get home and play with my new toy. I read the manual on the ferry journey to Manly, but I'm too nervous to actually take a shot in case I drop the damn thing.

Richard is already home when I get there. I'm disappointed because I'd like to practise in peace. It's an awful thought to have because we haven't spent any quality time together since he got back from his surfing trip. I don't know why. Or maybe I do. Maybe it's because I'm trying to prepare myself for the absence of him in my life. I push open the door and see him lying on the sofa watching television, and sadness washes over me. It's such a comforting sight. It's what I'm used to.

'Hey,' he says, reaching out for me.

I drop my bags and go around to him, suddenly wanting to be in his arms. I squeeze myself onto the sofa and lay my head on his chest. A split second later I'm fighting back tears. I shut my eyes tightly and force back the sensation.

'This is nice,' he murmurs into my hair. 'I feel like I haven't seen you properly for ages.'

'I know what you mean,' I reply. 'My family will be gone soon and you'll have me all to yourself again.'

He chuckles and pulls me up to face him. 'No disrespect to any of them, but that will be nice.' He leans forward to peck me on the lips. 'When are they back from the mountains?'

'Tomorrow.'

'Any plans yet for tomorrow night?'

'Probably dinner with them after work if you fancy traipsing into the city. But we'll need to see them Friday because it's their last night, so you could wait until then if you prefer.'

'I might do that.' I rest my head back down on his chest. He lightly runs his fingers over my back. 'What do you want to eat tonight?'

'I think there's some of that curry I made a few weeks ago in the freezer.'

'That'd be good.' He detaches himself from me and gets up from the sofa. I follow him into the open-plan kitchen area and get on with the process of defrosting our dinner in the microwave before hoisting myself up onto the countertop. Richard puts on the rice and comes over to me, standing between my legs and planting a kiss on my lips. 'What do you want to drink?'

'Cider?'

'Sure.' He gets to it, pouring cider into two glasses filled with ice and handing one over. My dad told me loads of people drink cider on ice in England now. And to think I thought it would never happen . . .

'Cheers,' I say, chinking his glass. 'Hey, the Editor of *Marbles* magazine asked me to cover for his editorial assistant next week.'

'That's cool,' he says, looking impressed. 'I keep meaning to ask if you get paid extra for it?'

'No, it's the same day rate. But speaking of money . . .' I jump down from the counter. 'I bought something today.'

'Did you? What?'

I retrieve the plastic bag from the hall. 'This.' I smile sheepishly as I pull out the camera box.

'A camera?' He's taken aback. 'How much did it cost?'

My smile flatlines. 'I put it on my credit card.'

He reaches into the bag and pulls out a receipt. 'Jesus, Lily!' he exclaims.

'What?' I'm starting to feel a little sick.

'Can we afford this?' he demands.

'It's not what *we* can afford, it's what *I* can afford.' I'm annoyed now.

'Oh, like that, is it? I thought we were supposed to be saving for a wedding.' He looks hurt and it immediately pacifies me.

'I put it on my credit card, like I said.' I actually was planning

on telling him Ben came with me to buy it, but now I'm thinking that's not such a good idea.

'But you still have to pay it back. Don't you already have a
camera?'

Now I'm annoyed again. 'Yes, but it's *really* old. It's hopeless. I
need something up-to-date if I'm going to be serious about this.'

'And *are* you going to be serious?' He looks confused.

'Yes,' I reply, calmly but firmly. 'I want to do a course in photography.'

He stares down at the floor. Then he briskly shakes his head
and goes to stir the rice.

'What? Aren't you going to say anything?'

'What is there to say? You've obviously made up your mind.'

'It's what I want to do.'

'Aren't you a bit old to have a sudden career change?' he snaps.

'I'm only twenty-six,' I counter, but inside, my usual doubts are
beginning to swirl around. I try to quash them. 'Why are you
being such an arse about this?'

'I'm not being an arse. I just. Don't. Get. It.'

'Then you don't get me.' I didn't mean to say that out loud. But
it's there now, between us.

'Fine, if that's how you feel.' He stalks out of the kitchen. I
stare in dismay as he puts on his coat in the hall.

'Where are you going? What about dinner?'

'I'm not hungry,' he replies bluntly, opening the door, walking
out and shutting it behind him.

I sit there in stunned silence. The microwave starts to beep and
I slide off the counter and open the door, turning off the gas cooking the rice on the stove. I'm not hungry now either.

My anger turns to sadness and then to regret. I sit on the sofa and wait for him, unable to bring myself to look at my new camera. My excitement is long gone. Eventually I start to see it from Richard's point of view. He thinks I'm changing, and he must believe it's to do with him. He's right, to an extent. I started to change when he proposed to me. But it's not his fault. It's mine. It's all because of Ben.

I hear his keys turn in the lock after fifteen minutes and he appears, looking downcast.

'I'm sorry,' he says, coming through to me without removing his coat.

'I'm sorry too,' I say. 'I should have asked you before buying it.'

'You don't have to ask me, of course you don't,' he says. 'I just wish you'd talked to me about it.'

'I know I should have. I'm sorry.'

He pulls me to him and we hug each other tightly.

'Are you still hungry?' I ask over his shoulder.

He glances through to the kitchen. 'Is the rice ruined?'

'Probably.'

'I could put some more on?'

I smile through the tears welling up in my eyes. 'Yeah. Let's do that.'

My camera stays on the floor where I left it. I don't have the will or inclination to play with it now.

Chapter 25

I'm sitting on a yellow swing in a park full of purple and pink wildflowers. A black and white magpie is singing in the background and I sense that it's early morning. I'm in a playground I recognise in the Adelaide hills, but it's different. Not quite the same. I hear my husband walking through the grass behind me and I smile and turn my face up to the sun. And then he's in front of me and I open my eyes to see Richard standing there, holding the hand of a little boy. My son. And he looks like Ben. I wake up with a start.

My family – minus Mum, of course – leave on Saturday afternoon. Richard and I see them off at the airport before heading to Nathan and Lucy's for a drink before dinner. I'm glad of the distraction because I always feel morose when Dad and the girls fly home.

'I'm so sad you're leaving,' I moan to Lucy. We're sitting on the decked terrace in the back garden. The boys are inside talking shop.

'Aah,' Lucy says. 'We'll be back before you know it.'

'Will this renovation really only take six months?'

'Hopefully,' she replies. 'We'll have to get cracking on it straight away. I can't wait. Obviously I'll miss you lot,' she adds. 'But it'll be good to spend some time with my mum.'

I take a sip of my rosé and dig into the salted macadamia nuts. 'Do you have many other friends over in the UK?' I haven't really spoken to Lucy much about her life on the other side of the world. I don't know why. I guess it's because I left it all behind.

'I have a few,' she says. 'They live in London mostly, but I'm hoping they'll come down occasionally to Somerset where we'll be staying with my mum, and Nathan and I will get up to see them, too.'

'Do you miss them?'

'Of course. But you can't have everything, can you? I chose Nathan, and everything else has a knock-on effect. We're lucky that we can spend time in two countries.'

I vaguely remember knowing that Lucy had a boyfriend when she met Nathan. Now I'm curious about him. 'Do you ever hear from your boyfriend before Nathan?'

'James? No, not any more. He harassed me for a while after we broke up, but he had to call it quits after I found out more about the lies he'd been telling me.'

'What do you mean?'

'Screwing around with women, taking drugs . . . Loads of things, but they were the ones that bothered me the most. That, and the fact that so many people knew the truth about him, yet I'd been with him for years and was completely clueless. I felt so stupid. And the worst thing was, I didn't find out everything at once. I used to hear dribs and drabs from people at his work and my work, since a friend of mine was going out with a colleague of his, and it was horrible – horrible! – not being able to get over him once and for all because some new shitty thing would always come along and make me feel like crap again. I know that no one likes to be the bearer of bad news, but I wish everyone had sat me down and told me everything they knew in one go.' Her hazel eyes are sparking as she remembers.

'That sucks,' I murmur, knowing my words can never fully sum up the extent of her ex-boyfriend's betrayal.

'It all worked out for the best in the end.'

I smile. 'It did. You and Nathan are perfect for each other.'

She laughs. 'I wish someone could have told me that two years ago. On paper it looked like we were anything but!'

I stare at her, bemused.

'James and I seemed like a match made in heaven, whereas Nathan's two years younger than me, and when I met him he was a bit of a surf bum,' she explains.

She glances inside and I follow her gaze to see Nathan and Richard huddled over some architectural plans around the coffee table.

We turn back and laugh at each other. 'Not any more.'

'I expect they're looking at the plans for Somerset,' Lucy muses, tucking her long chestnut hair behind her ears.

'Do you like working with Nathan?'

'I love it. Considering I thought my job in PR was the best job in the world, I should miss it more. Maybe if I didn't get to do the odd freelance job I'd find it harder.'

Lucy's old boss in London still gives her the occasional gig when she's over there and she also put her in touch with some PR friends of hers in Sydney.

She continues, 'The property developing and project

management are what keep me really busy, though. You know Nathan's parents ran a property development business together before they died?'

'I don't think I did know that.'

She smiles. 'Well, they did. And I know Nathan loves that we're doing the same thing.' She glances inside again. 'It's Saturday night, boys,' she calls.

'Just finishing up,' comes Nathan's reply.

Moments later they join us on the terrace. Richard squeezes my shoulder. 'Are you girls hungry?'

'Starving,' Lucy says. 'Shall we walk into town and see what we fancy?'

After a dinner spent laughing our heads off at Nathan and Lucy's crap jokes and getting increasingly tipsy, we zigzag our way to a bar on the waterfront. We manage to snag a table outside on the deck under large white umbrellas, and Richard and Nathan go inside to fetch the drinks. Lucy's eyes narrow as she studies a group of girls sitting at the next table.

'Do you know them?' I ask.

'I think I recognise that blonde one there, but I can't think where to place her.'

I take a surreptitious look over my shoulder to see a pretty girl with mid-length, tousled hair laughing at something one of her friends has said. Then she glances towards the inside entrance and her smile vanishes.

'Rich? *Rich?*' She recovers from her shocked expression.

I whip my head around to see Richard emerging from inside with two drinks. Nathan follows right behind him.

'Ally?' Richard asks, his brow furrowing.

Shit.

'It *is* you!' Ally beams and gets to her feet, rushing over to my distinctly uncomfortable-looking boyfriend.

'Hi!' he exclaims, throwing me an awkward smile before turning his attention back to Ally. He lifts up the drinks in his hands to indicate he can't give her a hug.

'I knew I recognised her,' Lucy murmurs.

'Hey, Ally!' Nathan appears from behind Richard. 'What are you doing here?'

'I've just rented a flat up the road.'

'You live in Manly?'

'Yeah!'

This is getting better and better.

'When did you get back from the UK?' Nathan asks.

'A couple of weeks ago. Settling in again, you know.'

'Hey, come and meet Lily,' Richard interrupts, indicating me with his beer glass.

Ally turns to look my way and somehow manages to keep a smile on her face. I try to show her the same courtesy.

'Cool.' She follows Richard.

'Lily, this is Ally.' I can tell Richard is trying to act normal, but it's obvious to me he finds this situation pretty excruciating.

'Hello.' I smile up at her.

'Hi.' She reaches down to shake my hand. 'So you guys are engaged?'

I nod.

'Wow, that's great! Congratulations.'

'Thanks.' My smile is starting to feel genuine.

'Hello, Ally.' Lucy gets up and gives her a hug.

'Lucy!'

'Look at you!' Lucy cries. 'Your hair's grown.'

'Aah, I could never afford to get it cut.' She laughs.

She's so warm and friendly that it's hard to feel jealous. 'Take a seat,' I urge, sliding up the bench. She glances over her shoulder at her friends.

'Sure, okay, I'll just grab my drink.'

Richard sits down next to me. 'Are you okay?' he asks in my ear.

'I'm fine,' I reply. 'She seems nice.'

Ally returns and takes a seat next to me.

'So you guys all knew each other in the UK?' I ask.

'Ally, Richard and Nathan shared a house in Archway,' Lucy explains.

'That place was a tip,' Nathan jokes.

'You can talk,' Ally responds. 'Your washing-up sat in the sink for days on end.'

'What did you do over there?' I ask her.

'Nursing.' She smiles at me. 'What about you?'

'I work for a publishing company,' I reply.

'That's so cool!' she exclaims.

'You're back at *Marbles* on Monday, aren't you?' Lucy chips in. I nod.

'*Marbles?*' Ally repeats. 'As in that trendy, glossy guys' mag?'

'That's the one,' Richard interjects.

'Wow – that's such an awesome job!'

'Aah, I'm only the secretary,' I say.

'Editorial assistant,' Richard corrects, smiling across me at Ally. 'She's too modest.'

'Sounds ultra-glam to me,' she says. 'What about you guys?' She looks at Nathan, Richard and Lucy. 'What are you up to these days?'

She stays and chats for another ten minutes before getting back to her friends. Richard puts his arm around me and kisses my temple.

'You okay?' he asks again.

'Yes.' I smile. Bizarrely, I am. I don't feel jealous or insecure. If Richard weren't the man he is, I'm sure I would feel both. Love fills me up and I kiss his cheek.

'Thank you for being so nice to her,' Richard says sincerely.

'It wasn't hard.'

He rubs my arm and gives me a squeeze. 'Shall we go home?'

I nod, happily.

That night, lying in the crook of my boyfriend's arm, I realise that I barely thought about Ben all evening. I almost felt as I did several weeks ago, when I didn't have this additional complication in my life. Maybe this is the way it's supposed to be. Maybe I *can* handle a future without Ben. But when I try to imagine it properly the pain is so intense I feel as if it could cripple me.

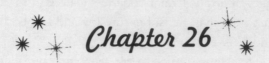

Chapter 26

It's my first day back at *Marbles* today and it should be fantastic, but I'm finding it hard to smile. Ben is coming to meet me at lunchtime, but even that brings little comfort. I haven't used my camera all weekend and I'm wondering if I should return it. I can't bear to confess this to him.

At one o'clock I walk down the five flights of stairs and attempt a cheery wave at Mel on reception. I'm hoping I'll miss Nicola this time. I leave the building and turn the corner, looking around for Ben, but he's not there. I stand and lean up against the wall and check the clock on my mobile phone.

'Am I late?' he calls, and I turn to see him walking briskly towards me.

'No, you're on time.'

He engulfs me in a quick embrace, then pulls away and looks down at me. 'What's wrong?'

'Nothing.'

'You look sad.'

'I'm okay.' But I can barely turn up the corners of my lips.

'Tell me.' He's still holding my arms as he searches my face.

'It's nothing,' I lie, looking away.

'No, it's not,' he insists, shaking me ever so slightly. 'I *know* you.'

'How can you say you know me when you've barely seen me?' I step out of his grasp.

'I just do.'

'Maybe I've changed.'

'You haven't.' He regards me so seriously that I can't tear my eyes away. Suddenly they're brimming with tears.

'Hey,' he says softly, putting his hand to my cheek.

I quickly take another step backwards. He drops his hand to his side.

'Shall we walk?'

I nod my head in agreement and set off. He hurries after me.

'Who needs sneakers when you can walk this fast in high heels, hey?' he jokes.

I glance at him sideways. 'Trainers,' I say.

'Trainers, sneakers . . . We can call them trainers if it makes you happy.'

I purse my lips to try to stop myself from smiling. 'I'm back at *Marbles* magazine this week,' I tell him.

'Are you really? That's excellent.' He knows all about how I covered for Bronte before. 'Is it just for a week?'

'Yeah. Apparently the editorial assistant is on a shoot.'

'A photo-shoot?'

'Yes. In Bali.'

'Cool. I didn't know editorial assistants got to do things like that.'

'Neither did I,' I admit. 'I think she's started helping out on the picture desk a bit more. I suspect that's where she'd like to work.'

'Pretty good stepping stone, then.'

'That's what I was thinking.'

'Would you like to work on the picture desk?' he asks.

'Yeah. Definitely more than what I'm doing now.'

'But it's still not photography, eh?'

I say nothing as my mood dips once more, then I tell him: 'I haven't used my camera at all.'

'Why not?' He's taken aback.

'I'm thinking it cost too much.'

He looks relieved. 'Well, if that's all it is, I can help you.'

'What do you mean?'

'Let me help you buy it.'

'No!' I say loudly, coming to my senses.

'Why not? Think of how many Christmases and birthdays I've missed out on over the years. I probably owe you a couple of grand by now,' he jokes, but I'm not laughing.

'No. Absolutely not.'

'Alright. In that case, I'll lend you the money and you can pay me back when you want to. Interest-free. How about that?'

'No, Ben.' I sigh.

'You can't return it,' he says adamantly. 'Have you looked into any courses?'

I shake my head because I can't bear to say it out loud.

'You've got plenty of time,' he says reassuringly. 'Stop doubting yourself. If you're worried you've left it too late now, think of how pissed off you'll be in five years' time when you're still regretting never doing anything about it.'

I sigh again. 'I know you're right. But enough about me. What have you been up to?'

'Well . . .' He hesitates outside a café. 'Do you want to go in here?'

'Sure. But Ben, what is it?'

'Come inside and I'll tell you.'

A feeling of dread starts to fill me up. I can't move.

'Lily?'

'No. I think you'd better tell me here.'

Concern washes over his face. 'It's okay,' he says. 'It's nothing bad.'

'Tell me.'

'It's just that I've been offered my old job back in Adelaide.'

The ground has opened up beneath me and I'm falling into darkness. Please God, not again . . .

'It's okay,' he repeats, putting his hands on my arms. 'I don't have to take it.'

Light returns. Light filling me up.

'I won't leave you.' He wraps his arms around me and I press my face into his chest, trying to breathe. 'If you're happy here, if things are working out for you and your career, then I won't go.'

He would do that for me?

'Do you want to go?' I mumble. I pull my face away from his chest so he can hear me. 'Do you *want* to go?'

'Well, you know I love Adelaide.' He glances down at me and shrugs. 'But it's okay. It'll still be there in a few years' time. Who knows what you'll be doing then.'

I open my mouth to speak, but nothing comes out.

'You might be a professional photographer,' he continues, smiling. 'A laidback Adelaide lifestyle might be right up your street.'

I can't do this. I can't go on like this. He's looking at me, waiting for me to say something.

'Or I might be married.' My voice is barely audible.

He chuckles, misunderstanding me. 'Oh yeah? To whom?'

'No one you know,' I say very, very quietly.

The smile leaves his face and he regards me gravely. 'Lily?' He's uncomprehending. 'What's going on?'

'I have a boyfriend,' I whisper. 'He's asked me to marry him.'

Ben drops my arms and steps away from me, his eyes never leaving my face.

'No.'

I nod. 'It's true.'

'You're engaged? No.' He rubs his head, disbelieving.

'He asked me a couple of months ago. Before I found you again.'

'And you never *told* me!' he exclaims, hurt written all over his face.

'I'm sorry.'

'You're not joking, are you? This isn't some sort of sick revenge you're getting on me for what I did years ago?'

He's still looking bemused, trying to work out what's happening, but I can see that he's slowly beginning to believe me.

'Ben, I'm so, so sorry. I wanted to tell y—'

'Then why didn't you?' he interrupts. 'How could you keep something like this quiet?'

'I was so confused when you came back into my life. I had no idea what was going to happen.'

'And now you're telling me this so I don't put my life on hold for you? So I go back to Adelaide?'

'No, that's not it at all. I don't want you to leave.'

'But if I do, then that makes your decision pretty damn tidy, doesn't it.'

'*Please*. I can't bear the thought of losing you again.'

'What about your boyfriend?'

'Richard.'

'I don't want to know his name!' he practically shouts, and I understand how he feels because I felt the same when I heard 'Charlotte' mentioned the first time – and every time since, if we're being truthful. 'What about him? Does he know about me?'

I feel ashamed. 'I haven't told him anything.'

'Were you planning on telling him?'

'I don't know. I've been so confused!' I cry. The sight of tears rolling down my cheeks seems to calm him. He takes my hand and leads me off the footpath into a quiet side street.

'It seems pretty clear-cut to me,' he says. 'You can never say anything to your . . .' He pauses, unable to even say the word 'boyfriend', let alone *fiancé*. 'And I'll go to Adelaide and you can get on with your life.'

'I don't want that.' I shake my head adamantly.

'Then it gets complicated.'

'I know.'

'Lily, I can't make this decision for you. It has to be yours.'

A bizarre thought suddenly strikes me. We haven't even kissed! He hasn't told me he loves me! Yet here we are, acting like I actually have a choice to make between two men. Isn't this conversation a little premature?

We meet each other's eyes. Mine are brimming with tears; his are filled with sadness.

'You've never even told me how you feel about me,' I say quietly.

'I thought it was obvious.'

'It's not.'

He looks even more pained. 'You know I think you're special.'

'My *dad* thinks I'm special. That doesn't count.'

355

'What do you want me to say?'

'I want you to say it out loud.'

'You want me to bare my soul to you.'

'Yes.'

'It's very difficult when I've just found out you're engaged to someone else.'

'I understand.' How could he love me when I've deceived him like this?

'I don't think you do,' he says. 'It was hard enough losing you last time. At least I didn't put my heart on the line, only to have it crushed to smithereens.'

'Unlike me. I told you how I felt.'

'I'm sorry,' he says softly. 'I hated walking away from you.'

'But you did. You didn't have to – and what you said to me back then was wrong. I wasn't okay, I wasn't *fine*, after you left. I was broken and no one has been able to fix me.'

'What else could I have done? You were sixteen, for Christ's sake!'

'You could have waited for me. I would have been eighteen in two years and then I could have done what I wanted.'

'That would have meant making *you* wait for *me*! I couldn't do that to you! I couldn't expect you to put your life on hold. For all I knew it was a teenage crush.'

'It wasn't a teenage crush.'

He steps towards me. 'I know.'

I stay where I am, rooted to the spot. He cups my face with his hands and I feel like I'm drowning in his ocean-coloured eyes.

'I love you,' he says. 'More now than ever. I've been talking to you inside my head for the last ten years.'

Me too . . .

356

'And the thought of losing you again kills me,' he continues. 'But you're right. I am the one who left. I hurt you back then and you have every reason to want to hurt me now.'

'I'm not doing tha—'

'Shhh. It's okay. I deserve it.' His hands drop from my face. 'But I've got to back off now. That's all I'm going to say. You have a decision to make and I can't interfere with that. I don't want to be responsible for ruining your life if this guy Richard is the right man for you.' He checks his watch. 'You'd better get back to work.'

'I can't go back to work now!' I wail.

'Yes, you can. You have to. You can't mess up this opportunity.'

I pull out another tissue and wipe away my tears.

'I'll walk you back,' he says.

'I'd rather you didn't.'

He nods, not looking at me.

'I need time to compose myself,' I sniffle.

'Okay,' he says.

'I'll call you.'

'I'll be waiting.' His eyes meet mine for a moment and the pain is intense. He nods brusquely. 'See you soon.' And then he walks away.

I stay down that narrow street for five minutes, trying to get myself together before I turn and walk hurriedly back to the office. My mind is racing, but all I want to do is find a quiet place to cry. Cry so hard that I'll have nothing left in me. Unfortunately though, I know there's no chance of using up my supply. I have many, many more tears to come.

I arrive back at the office fifteen minutes early and walk through reception, planning on keeping my head down. But the moment my eyes flick to Mel and Nicola behind the desk, they know that something is wrong.

'What's up?' Nicola mouths with concern. I glance at Cara to their right, and find my feet walking in their direction instead of towards the lifts. They both get up and hurry with me to the toilets behind the reception desk, Mel telling Cara to hold the fort because they'll be back in a minute. As soon as the door closes, I'm in floods of tears again.

'What's wrong?' Nicola asks out loud this time.

Mel puts her hand on my arm. 'Is it Richard?' she asks.

'No, no,' I manage to say, before qualifying that. 'Well, sort of.' I cover my face with my hands and sob so hard my body shakes. Nicola puts her arms around me and I vaguely hope I'm not snotting on her designer shirt as I cry into her shoulder. Mel rubs my arm comfortingly and eventually my sobs subside.

'Do you want to talk about it?' Mel asks.

I waver. Yes, in all honesty, I do. I really, really do.

'Is it someone else?' Nicola prompts.

I meet her eyes and she knows instantly that it is.

'Ben?' she checks.

I nod.

She and Mel glance at each other.

'Nothing's happened,' I say wearily. 'But I'm stuck. I don't know what to do.'

'How did you meet him?' Mel asks. 'Ben?'

'It's like I said. I knew him ten years ago when I worked at the conservation park. He was a keeper there.'

Her brow furrows. 'How old were you?'

'Sixteen. But it's not like that!' I insist. 'Nothing ever happened. But I fell head over heels in love with him and I knew he felt something for me too. But he would have never done anything about it.'

'How old was he?'

'Twenty-eight. He was engaged to someone in England, but there was this connection between us. I don't know how to describe it. He believed in me; I understood him. It wasn't tawdry,' I try to convince them. 'I've never loved anyone like I loved him.'

'Not even Richard?' Nicola asks hopefully.

'Not even Richard,' I tell her sadly.

'What happened?' Mel pries. 'Did Ben marry that other woman?'

'Yes. But not before I told him how I felt about him.'

'And did he tell you how he felt about you?' Nicola asks.

'I overheard him speaking to one of his friends about it. So I confronted him. It didn't make a difference. I was only sixteen. I thought he might wait for me, but he told me today that he would never have expected me to put my life on hold for him. His friend convinced him he was only scared of the commitment of marriage, and he shouldn't let his fiancée down. So he left. And I've never been able to forget him.'

'The one that got away . . .' Mel mutters.

'When Richard proposed,' I continue, 'I didn't want to say yes because I thought that would mean letting go of Ben forever, and then when I bumped into him a couple of weeks ago . . .'

'Is he still married?' Mel asks.

'Divorced. Five years ago. It was never right, he said.'

Nicola nods. 'What happened today?'

'I told Ben I was engaged.'

Mel's mouth drops open. 'You hadn't told him?'

'No. I know it's wrong, but I needed to spend some time with him again. I didn't want to risk losing everything with Richard if there was a chance I wouldn't feel the same way about Ben.'

'I get that,' Nicola agrees.

'But spending time with him has made everything worse,' I add miserably. 'I love them both.'

No one says anything. What can they say?

I don't know how I manage to get through the rest of the day at work, but my grief is replaced by melancholy on the way home. I sit there and stare into space as commuters and tourists hustle and bustle around me. It's time to come clean to Richard. I still don't know what I'm going to do, but I owe him the truth. And maybe Ben was right. Maybe I'm hoping someone else will make this decision for me. I'm aware that makes me weak as well as deceitful. I don't feel like I deserve either of them.

Richard knows something is wrong from the moment I walk into the living room.

'What is it?' he asks, starting to get to his feet.

'Stay there,' I say, and he hesitates before sinking back into the sofa with concern written all over his face. 'I have to tell you something.'

I feel sick to my core as I sit down on the armchair and face him. He's confused, not sure yet what's to come.

'What is it?' he asks.

I don't know where to start. I haven't rehearsed this. 'When I first came to Australia . . .' My voice falters.

'It's okay, you can tell me.'

He doesn't know what he's saying.

I take a deep breath. 'I fell in love with someone much older than me. I'd only just turned sixteen and he was twenty-eight.'

Richard frowns, but manages to keep it together.

'Nothing ever happened,' I say quickly, 'but I wanted it to. I've never been able to forget him.'

'Right . . .'

'He went to England and got married to someone else.'

'Wait,' he interrupts. 'Don't tell me this is the old guy you bumped into recently.'

I don't speak.

'Please don't tell me that,' he says again.

Tears well up in my eyes. I nod, ever so slightly.

'Oh, Lily,' he murmurs. 'What are you trying to say?'

I sorely wish I didn't have to say anything. 'I'm sorry,' is what I come out with.

'Sorry for *what*?' I don't know if it's anger or frustration or a mixture of both, but he pushes his hand through his dark hair and stares at me directly. 'Have you *fucked* him?'

'No!' I cry, and he visibly contracts with relief.

'Then what's happened?' he presses.

'Nothing's happened.'

'Does he know about me?'

'I told him today.'

'How many times have you seen him?'

'Only a few times.'

'A few times?' He regards me with disbelief. 'You only told me about the fishing trip!'

'I know, I'm sorry.'

'And you say nothing's happened?' He lets out a sharp laugh.

'No! Nothing has! He came to help me buy that camera . . .'

'Oh, now I get it,' he says bitterly. 'So he's the one who's been putting stupid ideas into your head.'

'Why are they stupid? See – this is why we have a problem. I feel like you stamp all over my dreams!'

'I'm not trying to crush your dreams, I'm just being realistic,' he says.

'But why is it so unrealistic to think I might be able to pursue a career in photography?'

'It just is!'

'You haven't even seen any of my photographs.'

'You haven't shown me!'

'Because you haven't demonstrated any interest whatsoever. I don't feel like showing you, just to have you shit all over them.'

'Nice.'

'It's true.'

'So show me now.'

'I'm not going to show you now.'

'Why not? Now's as good a time as any.'

'No.'

'Why not?'

'I don't have any with me.' Which is a lie. And he knows it. He gets to his feet and storms into the hall where I dropped my handbag when I came in. I rush after him.

'Richard!'

But it's too late. He's opened my bag and pulled out the pack. I stare at him in dismay as he starts to flick through them without paying them any attention, commenting sarcastically as he goes.

'Oh, super dooper. I really like your use of colour . . . *Fabulous* composition, darling.'

'You're being an arsehole,' I say angrily.

And then he comes to the picture of Ben.

'Is this him!' He's staring at me accusingly.

I don't confirm or deny it.

'This is him? This is the old fucker who's trying to get into my *fiancée's* knickers?'

'It's not like that,' I cry.

'What is it like then, Lily? What the fuck is it like? You'd better explain and quick because I've had just about enough of this.' Angry tears fill his eyes as he stares me down.

'Richard.' It hurts to say his name. It hurts to look at him, at the pain I've inflicted. But I have to go on. 'I love you.'

He says nothing.

'But I love him too.'

'You love him?' he bites back. 'You fucking *love* him?'

'Please stop swearing at me.'

'What the fuck am I supposed to say?'

'I don't know.'

'I fucking love you! I want to marry you! And you're telling me you're in love with someone else? This *fucking* arsehole?' He flaps the picture in my face. 'This fucking arsehole who's twice your age?'

'He's only thirty-eight.' It's out of my mouth before I realise I should have said nothing.

'Thirty-eight? Thirty-fucking-eight? What a fucking joke.' He starts to tear the photo into shreds.

'Richard, please stop,' I beg. 'I'm sorry.' Tears begin coursing down my cheeks – not about the photo, but because I know how much I'm hurting him.

He lets go of the pieces and regards me with fury as they flutter to the ground. I start to sob because I can't keep it in any longer. I clutch my hand to my chest because it aches so much.

I'm in too much of a state to look at him, but when I do, his anger has been replaced with sorrow. I hold out my hand to him and he takes it. I throw my arms around his stiff body and cry into his shoulder, but he's silent.

Eventually my sobs subside and I pull away to look up at him. His face is dead. He's staring ahead in a daze. We're still standing in the hall, the shredded pieces of my photo scattered at our feet.

'I'm sorry,' I say again.

'Are you leaving me?'

'I don't know.'

Emotion fills his eyes as he stares at me. 'You might leave me over this?' I can see now that he didn't quite understand that it was that serious. He tears his eyes away from mine and sighs deeply. 'I can't believe this is happening.'

'I never meant to hurt you.'

'You're going to *leave* me over this?' he asks again, looking at me with incredulity.

'I don't know. I don't know what I'm going to do.'

'Well, you'd better make up your fucking mind.' He's bitter again now, and I can hardly blame him. I try to take his hand, but he snatches it away. 'I can't be here with you.'

I watch as he takes the keys to his truck from the bowl on the kitchen counter and walks out of the door, slamming it behind him. I know he needs some space and I have no right to take that away from him, but it doesn't stop me from ringing his mobile time and time again. He lets it ring to start with, but answers on my fifth try.

'Where are you?' I ask.

'Nathan and Lucy's.'

'Have you told them everything?'

'Pretty much.'

They must think I'm such a bitch.

'Are you okay?' I ask.

'No.'

'Please come home.'

'I'm going to crash here tonight. I'll see you tomorrow.'

'I'm sorry,' I say again, but he ends the call.

I cry myself to sleep that night. In the morning my eyes are so red and puffy that I can barely open them. I want to call in sick, but Ben's words keep ringing in my head.

'You can't mess this up.'

I put on my make-up in a trance and go into work early. Nicola is on reception when I arrive.

'How are you?' she asks gently. I bite my lip at the concern on her face and say, 'I'll fill you in later. I need to get upstairs before I crumble again.'

'Alright,' she says, and I have to fight back tears at her expression. I hurry over to the lift and press the button, trying to think about something else.

Once in the office, I put my head down and try to act professional, but it damn near kills me. I call Richard at lunchtime, but he's at work and doesn't want to talk to me.

'Will you be home tonight?' I can't keep the pleading tone from my voice.

'I think so,' he replies.

'I'll see you later?'

'I have to go.' Again he ends the call.

I don't know how I get through the rest of the day, but at five o'clock Jonathan calls me into his office. I wonder nervously what it's about. I thought I'd managed to do a pretty good job of keeping my head above water.

'Take a seat.'

I do as he says.

'This is a bit premature because I haven't told the team yet, but Kip, our picture assistant, is leaving.'

Despite my predicament, my heart lifts ever so slightly.

'It's company policy to conduct interviews, but Bronte has already expressed her interest and I think she'd be the perfect candidate for the job.'

I nod.

'Which means we'll need a new editorial assistant.'

I hold my breath.

'Keep it under your hat for now, but I hope you'll apply. I know Debbie is coming back soon so you'll no doubt be keeping your eyes open for something, and I'd really like to see you back here with us. On a permanent basis.'

I can't help but smile.

'Would you like that?' he checks.

'Absolutely,' I reply.

'Good. But like I said, keep it under your hat for now.'

'I won't breathe a word.'

Two hours later, I'm back in the real world. Richard can barely look at me as he comes through the front door. I have a sudden overwhelming desire to have things revert to normal so I can share my news with him, but there's no going back now.

'I didn't know if you were going to come home,' I say feebly.

'Neither did I,' he mutters.

'Can we talk about this?'

'Have you got anything more to tell me?'

'No, I . . .'

'I can't deal with this, Lily. This whole situation is so far from anything I ever expected from you. Is this why you've been so funny about us getting engaged? Why you haven't wanted to tell people? Why you almost didn't even say yes?'

I nod, downcast.

He exhales deeply. 'So you've been hanging out for this guy for how long?'

'Ten years.'

'And what happened?'

'I bumped into him when I went to the zoo with my sisters.' I explain about Ben's divorce, how we worked together at the conservation park, how I discovered he had feelings for me back then. Richard, to his enormous credit, doesn't make any derogatory remarks this time, but I can tell by his face how hard it is to hear.

'I don't understand,' he says eventually. He's sitting on the sofa and I'm on the armchair across from him, as we were last night. 'How you could even consider throwing all this away.' He indicates the house around us. 'And you and me. We're so good together, Lils. At least, I thought we were.'

'We are,' I insist. 'We are. I love you, but—'

'Don't,' he says with anguish, so I cut my sentence short. 'Look, I'm not going to beg you. Either you love me enough or you don't. All I know is that I don't think I can be around you while you're making up your mind. And that doesn't mean I want you to be around him, either.'

He looks at me and says fiercely, 'I mean it. If you call him or see him again, it's over.'

Pain clutches my heart.

'Go and stay with your mum for a couple of days,' he suggests. 'Think it through. Then I hope we can move on from this. But I'm not going to fight him for you,' he adds bitterly. 'You can make up your own mind. And I hope to fuck you come to your senses and realise that the grass isn't always greener.'

Chapter 27

Richard goes back to Nathan and Lucy's house that night, because it hurts him too much to be with me. I'll go to Mum's flat straight after work tomorrow. Richard has asked me not to call him for a couple of days. I tell Mum I'll fill her in when I get there because I don't want to talk about it over the phone. I still don't know if I'll tell her the whole truth.

She's at work when I arrive the following evening. I have my old key from when I lived there so I let myself in. My bedroom is cold, damp and dark. I've barely eaten in days and I can't face making anything for myself now. That's even presuming there's anything in the fridge because, knowing my mum, it'll be as bare as Old Mother Hubbard's cupboard.

She comes home just after eleven to find me dozing, fully dressed, on my single bed. I wrestle my eyes open to see her looking down at me, still kitted-out in her restaurant manager's uniform of black trousers and a tight-fitting black shirt. She looks tired.

'Do you want me to get you anything?' she asks.

I shake my head blearily.

'A cup of tea?'

'No. Just sleep.'

'Will you get ready for bed?' she tries.

'No,' I murmur.

'Okay, honey.' She closes the door quietly behind her.

In the morning she's dead to the world. I don't feel like talking anyway, so I patch up my bloated face and red-rimmed eyes as best as I can and go into work. The journey takes longer than I thought it would, so even though I leave early, I end up arriving a few minutes late. I rush past reception, mouthing to Nicola and Mel that I'll talk to them later. I get an email soon after I sit at my desk.

Lunch? Mel writes. *I heard a rumour there was leek and potato on today.*

I manage a wry smile as I type back my assent.

Nicola has to man the desk so it's just Mel and me. We wander to the soup kitchen and pick up some takeaway before heading to a nearby square, where I fill Mel in on the latest.

'Have you seen Ben?' she asks.

'No. Richard doesn't want me to.'

'And you're going to abide by that?'

'Yes. It's the least I can do.'

'Blimey. You're a better woman than I am.'

'You've got to be joking, aren't you? I feel like the worst person in the world.'

'Why?'

'What do you mean why?' I laugh in outrage.

'You only fell in love, Lily. It's not like you could help it.'

I pause for a moment and think about this before realising that that philosophy comes nowhere near to letting me off the hook.

'Yes, but I should have told Richard about Ben from the beginning. And vice versa. I deceived them both.'

'I think you played it the only way you could have,' she says seriously. 'Like you said, what if you *had* built Ben up to be someone he wasn't? You would have been able to draw a line under the whole thing and move on to have a perfectly content life with Richard. And Richard would have been none the wiser, but a hell of a lot happier. Sometimes honesty isn't the best policy.'

'But the way things have turned out – it's all such a mess. Anyway, enough about me. Fill me in on the latest with Mr Horn.'

She puts her hand on my arm and gives me a sympathetic smile before she allows me to change the subject. 'It'll be okay,' she promises. 'It will all work out for the best.'

My mum is there when I get back to her place that evening and despite our often-volatile relationship, I'm glad not to be walking into a dark flat again.

'Hello,' she greets me, coming through from the kitchen.

'Hi,' I reply. 'I wasn't sure if you were working tonight.'

'I did the lunchtime shift,' she replies. 'And then rushed back here to cook you dinner.'

'Seriously? What are we having?'

She beams. 'Chicken in a cream and white wine sauce with new potatoes and veggies.'

'That sounds amazing.' It seems I have my appetite back.

'I thought you'd like it.'

'Thanks, Mum.' She checks her watch as I slump onto the sofa. 'What do you want to drink? I've opened up a bottle of white.'

I smile gratefully. 'That would be nice.'

'Back in a tick.'

I slip out of my heels and put my feet up on the coffee table, closing my eyes for a moment. They sting from stress and lack of sleep. Mum comes through a minute later with two wine glasses and passes one over.

'Feet on the table,' she tuts.

'Sorry.' I take them down again. She never used to mind.

'How was your dad's visit?' she asks, perching on the second, smaller sofa to my right.

'Fine. It was good. The girls have grown so much.'

'I bet they have. And Lorraine, how is she?' Her voice naturally becomes more forced when she asks after my dad's wife.

'She's fine. She's still the same.'

'Well, that's good,' she says abruptly. 'And what about you? Are you okay?'

I shake my head slightly. 'Not really, no, Mum.'

'Are you going to tell me what this is all about?'

I sigh and lean forward to put my glass on the table. I haven't taken a sip yet. 'I needed some time alone,' I reply eventually.

'From Richard? Why?'

'I'm not sure I want to get married to him,' I say with difficulty.

'Really?' she gasps, putting her hand over her mouth. 'Why not? Has he done something to hurt you?'

'No, of course not, Mum. It's me. I . . . have feelings for someone else.'

'Oh, Lily,' she replies with disappointment. 'How could you let that happen?'

'How could I let that happen?' I ask with incredulity. 'I didn't mean to fall in love with two men!'

'No, okay,' she placates me, 'of course you didn't. So who is he? How did you meet him?'

'I met him years ago.' I avoid the first question. 'Sorry, I don't really feel like talking about this now.'

She stares at me for a moment before checking her watch again and going back through to the kitchen. There's a knock at the door. Mum rushes through from the kitchen. 'He's early.'

'Who's early?' I sit up in my seat as she wavers between coming my way or going to the door.

'I wanted you to meet someone.' I recognise this look in her eye. Pleading . . .

'What?' I sit up straighter.

'Please, Lily, it's someone who's been on the cards for some time.'

'Tell me you're joking,' I say deadpan. 'I come here for some . . . *solace* . . . and you expect me to socialise with the latest shag in your life?'

The jaunty little knock comes again, albeit this time more insistently.

'He's important,' she hisses desperately as she turns towards the door.

'They're ALL important!' I get to my feet angrily. 'I can't believe you can be so selfish.'

'Please,' she begs. 'He'll hear you.'

She swings open the door to reveal a middle-aged, heavy-set, olive-skinned man beaming widely in the doorway.

'Come in, come in,' Mum urges, plastering her happy smile all over her face. 'This is my daughter, Lily.'

I don't know how, but I manage not to storm out of the room into my bedroom and slam the door like a teenager.

'Hello.' I don't manage a smile, however.

'Aah, this is your daughter.' He has an Italian accent, I notice, as he bursts into the room and gives me a huge smackeroonie on each cheek. My mum smiles nervously while I glare at her over his shoulder.

'And this is Antonio,' Mum says.

'I so glad to finally meet you,' he cries.

I wish I could express the same sentiment.

'Dinner's almost ready,' Mum says jollily. 'What can I get you to drink? White wine?'

'*Sí, sí, perfetto!*'

Mum emerges in record time with Antonio's glass of wine. She's clearly unsure about what trouble I might cause in her absence. 'Take a seat at the table, my love.' I realise she's talking to him, not me. Now I understand why I'm getting a home-cooked meal. And to think I thought she was looking out for me for a change.

'Lily works in publishing,' Mum tells Antonio, ushering me to the table.

No. I can't do this. I cannot do small talk tonight.

'Do you?' Antonio asks with interest as he sits down. Suddenly I feel as stubborn as a mule. My mum gives me a little push, but my feet are going nowhere.

'Lily, take a seat,' she urges brightly.

'No.'

'Lily,' she warns.

'I'm not hungry any more.'

Mum laughs a nervous laugh and looks at Antonio. 'She's not feeling very well.'

And with that, I'm out of there. I go into my bedroom and shut the door firmly, wishing with all my heart that it had a lock. I switch off the light and lie down on the bed, covering my face with my arms. I'm almost too tired to think.

It's a good twenty minutes before my mum comes to check on me.

'Please come out, darling.'

I don't bother to answer.

'Do you want me to bring you some food in here?'

Again, silence.

She leaves me to it after that.

I open my eyes and stare up at the ceiling in the darkness. The realisation hits me: Ben. I want to talk to Ben.

Richard knows my mum. He's met her on several occasions. Ben has met her just the once, but for some reason it's him I want to tell about her behaviour tonight. Out of the blue I remember the box in my cupboard. I leap onto the bed and pull it down, rifling through it like a madwoman as I feel, more than see, Ben's light-blue shirt at the bottom. I want to talk to him. I want to see him. I want him to hold me in his arms and tell me it will all be alright. I want to call him. Where's my mobile phone?

I look over the side of the bed for my bag. It's not there. I realise at once that I've left it in the living room, and the thought of going out there and interrupting my mum and Antonio's cosy little soirée makes me hesitate.

And then I think of Richard. Of our house. Of our friends. I'm not sure I'm ready to let go of all of that yet. I sink back on the bed and hug Ben's shirt tightly. My mum finds me like that an hour and a half later.

'Antonio's gone home,' she says curtly.

If she's expecting me to apologise, she's out of her frigging mind.

'He didn't want to stay with the *atmosphere*.'

'ARE YOU FUCKING CRAZY?' Is that *me* screaming? 'WHAT THE FUCK DO YOU THINK YOU'RE DOING? YOU'RE NOT MY MOTHER! GET OUT! GET OUT! GET OUT!'

White rage fills my head and I start to hyperventilate. I stare at my mum's shocked face, surreally aware of how demonic I must look. For once she's rendered completely and utterly speechless.

'GET OUT!' I scream again, and when she doesn't move, I leap off the bed and shove at her wildly. 'GET OUT!' I slam the door in her face and collapse back on the bed, pulling at my hair with my hands and letting out an almighty wail like a banshee. Eventually the pain brings tears to my eyes and my senses return. And then I'm filled with an overbearing sadness. My mother stays away, even though my sobs must ricochet through the whole flat.

When I eventually quieten down after a very long time, she tries again, and this time neither of us says anything. She sits on the bed and strokes my hair as tears slide down my cheeks and soak into my pillow.

'I'm sorry,' she whispers eventually. 'I'm so, so sorry.'

I don't let go of Ben's shirt and I see her look at it curiously, but she's smart enough to stick to her apology and leave it at that. I'm asleep before she leaves the room.

Chapter 28

It takes superhuman strength, but I somehow make it through the week at *Marbles*, and before I leave, Jonathan promises to keep me posted about the editorial assistant position. It's a relief to think I may get a permanent job at last – but it's hard to get excited about anything at the moment.

I haven't spoken to Richard since he left to stay at Nathan and Lucy's on Tuesday night and even though it was him who asked me not to call, I find I'm strangely unwilling to anyway. I think I at least need the weekend on my own to mull things over.

My mum always works on Friday and Saturday nights so I'm surprised to find her at home. The flat smells of spaghetti Bolognese and for a moment I'm suspicious.

'He's not coming over,' she quickly assures me. 'It's just you and me.'

I nod and go to the sofa, kicking off my shoes as I go. 'I thought you worked on Friday nights.'

'I changed my shift.' She disappears into the kitchen and comes back a minute later with a glass of white wine. 'I'm sorry,' she says, perching on the arm of my sofa. 'I was wrong to do that

377

to you last night. It had been arranged for a few days and I convinced myself I didn't need to cancel. But you're right. I was being selfish. As usual.' She hands over the glass and I accept her peace-offering. 'I hope you're hungry.' She gets up again. 'I'm doing garlic bread and everything!'

We sit outside on the small balcony because it's a surprisingly balmy night for May in Sydney. We balance our plates on our knees and eat in silence. I'm the one who breaks it.

'Who is he, this Antonio?'

'He owns the restaurant,' she replies. 'We don't have to talk about me,' she adds.

'No, I want to. So he owns the restaurant? You've known him for a while, then.'

'Yes, but it was six months before we discovered we had feelings for each other.'

'Last time I saw you . . .'

'We'd just got together,' she interrupts. 'I didn't know where it was going.'

'But it's going well now?'

'He's asked me to marry him.'

I stare at her in shock. She's smiling timidly. 'And you're not running for the hills?' I check.

She shakes her head. 'Not this time, no.'

'Are you serious?'

'I've said yes.'

I put down my fork on my plate and study her face. All her vital signs appear normal. She doesn't seem deranged. 'Blimey. I guess congratulations are in order.'

'Thank you,' she breathes.

'Where's your ring?' I'm being childish because she said this to me so I'm surprised when she places her plate on the tiny table and goes inside. She returns a moment later with an old ring box. She hands it over and I open it to see an antique gold ring inside with an intricate design surrounding a red ruby.

'What, no diamonds?' I can't help but say.

'It was his mother's,' my mum explains. 'I need to get it re-sized.'

I'm in shock. What's got into her? Antonio, clearly.

'I'm happy for you,' I say, and find that I mean it, even though I'm still very confused about what this Antonio has over all the men before him.

'I'm sorry,' she says. 'I didn't want to tell you like this when I know you're going through a tough time.'

'It's okay.'

'So fill me in on what's been happening.'

I sigh and look away. Oh, what the hell. 'Promise not to be judgemental?'

'I promise.'

'Do you remember Ben who worked at the conservation park? Michael's colleague – you met him once.'

'I remember,' she says immediately. 'In the car park. Tall, good-looking man with blond hair?'

'That's him.'

'Is *he* the one?'

I nod.

'But how old is he?'

'Twelve years older than me.'

'*What?*'

'Mum, you promised not to be judgemental.' She settles back into her seat and makes a conscious attempt to relax. I fill her in on the rest.

'Oh, darling.' She looks at me sadly when I've finished. 'We rarely get over unrequited love.'

'Tell me about it.'

She studies me sceptically, then opens her mouth to speak before shutting it again.

'What is it?' I ask.

She takes a deep breath and exhales loudly. 'I was in love with a married man before I met your father.' She pauses for a moment, her expression tense. 'Nothing ever happened between us, but I knew he felt something for me too. He had two children. He would never have left his family. I know it's wrong, but I slept with your father to make him jealous.' She pauses. 'I didn't mean to fall pregnant, but I did. Is this too hard for you to hear?'

I shake my head, willing her to go on.

'After that, I'd made my bed and had to lie on it, but I've never loved anyone like I loved him.'

'Did you ever see him again?'

'I bumped into him once in London. It was after we'd moved back from Brighton. He was still married. He told me where he worked and I've kept tabs on him on the internet ever since. He died last year.' I gasp. 'Heart attack,' she adds. 'So now I can finally get over him.'

A wave of understanding floods me. This is why she is the way she is. Why she's finally able to say yes to Antonio.

'Did you ever love my dad?' I find myself asking.

'Yes. In my own way. But he and I got together so quickly, and under such strange circumstances . . .'

'There was never any build-up? No sparks of electricity? No meaningful eye-contact? None of the things that send shivers of anticipation down your spine and make you long for someone you can't have?'

'Exactly.'

'Richard and I never had any of that either.'

'But Lily, that doesn't mean he's wrong for you.'

'I know. If it weren't for Ben, I'd be perfectly happy. But while there's a chance of him being in my life, I'll never be able to give Richard one hundred per cent. Is that fair?'

She looks thoughtful, then shrugs. 'That's a question you'll have to answer for yourself.'

The longer I'm away from Richard, the more my head starts to clear. The next day is Saturday and it's a cool, crisp day. I didn't bring many clothes with me because I wasn't sure how long I'd be away, but I did pack my new camera, still unopened in its box. I get it out now and study it.

I spend the morning down at Bondi Beach taking photographs of everything from the surfers to seaweed. I'm experimenting, and it's hugely liberating to be able to take as many photos as I like without worrying about the cost of developing. Most of my photos are average, but there are a few that I'm proud of, like the pile of brightly coloured beach towels with a small child running out-of-focus in the background, or the close-up of a half-destroyed sandcastle and the way the sun hits the shells that adorn it. Every time I review a shot I think of Ben and what he would say. My heart is becoming calmer.

I return to the flat to find an unexpected visitor waiting for me. It's Lucy.

'Hello,' I say warmly.

'Hi.' She looks uneasy as she stays seated on the sofa nursing a cup of tea. My mum switches off the telly that has obviously been entertaining them in my absence and makes herself scarce.

'What are you doing here?' I ask.

'Molly was bringing Mikey in for lunch with Sam.' Sam is a horticulturalist at the Botanic Gardens and he sometimes works weekends. 'I hitched a ride and then borrowed Molly's car to wing my way over here to see you.'

'You should have called.'

'I did. Your phone is switched off.'

I pull it out of my bag. 'Actually, it's run out of battery. I forgot to pack my charger.'

'I'm just going to pop down the shops,' Mum says as she comes out of her bedroom.

'Okay,' I call over my shoulder.

'Nice to meet you,' she says to Lucy.

'Now we can relax,' I say with a smile when she's gone, but Lucy still looks tense. 'How are you?' I vaguely wonder why she's not asking me that question under the circumstances.

'I'm fine,' she replies. 'Sorry, I know I probably shouldn't have turned up out of the blue like this, but I felt like I had to do something. Richard doesn't know I'm here.'

'Right . . .'

'Why haven't you called him?' she asks.

'He asked me not to.' I'm confused.

'He didn't mean it, Lily. He might've wanted you to take a day or so to think about it, but he never expected you to cut off contact like you have.'

Now I'm dumbfounded.

'He's a mess,' she continues. 'He hasn't been able to work. He's only just gone home after staying with us for days. He didn't want to be there without you. I don't understand how you could do this.'

Now I know why she looks so uncomfortable. She's not here as my friend; she's here as Richard's.

'What has he told you?' I manage to ask.

'That you had a childhood crush on an older man—'

'It wasn't a childhood *crush*,' I interrupt.

'Whatever it was, now he's rocked up in Sydney and you're thinking of running off with him.'

My face flushes. She makes it sound so trivial.

'Lucy, you don't know the whole story,' I respond firmly. 'I fell in love with Ben ten years ago and have never fallen out of love with him. On the contrary, I'm now in deeper than I ever have been.'

'But he's twelve years older than you!' she objects.

'So? It's not *that* ridiculous an age-gap. It felt like it when I was sixteen, but not now.'

'Have you really thought this through? I mean, you don't have a dad in your life . . .'

'I *do* have a dad!'

'Yes, but he hasn't been around much. And your mum has always moved from man to man. Maybe you unwittingly went looking for a father figure?'

'That is ridiculous,' I snap. Isn't it? I try to push the notion out of my head.

'I don't mean to interfere.' Yes, but you *are* interfering. And it's clear where your loyalties lie. 'But you and Richard are so good together,' she continues.

'I know,' I say, as sadness seeps through me. 'I love Richard. But I love Ben more. You yourself told me, that – on paper – you and your ex were perfect together and Nathan was no match for him. But you followed your heart. That's what I'm trying to do.'

'I didn't tell you that story to make you break things off with my husband's best friend,' she says miserably.

'I know you didn't. And it didn't take you telling me that to help me make a decision. In fact, I haven't made a decision yet. I'm still trying to.'

'Oh, Lily, please come back and see him,' she begs. 'Please give your relationship one last chance. You could come with me now?'

I politely thank her for coming to see me. But still I stay away.

On Monday, Jonathan makes the announcement that Kip is leaving. The advertisement for picture assistant goes up on the company website immediately with an end-of-week deadline. He obviously wants to get things moving quickly. Bronte emails me to say cheers for covering for her on such short notice. I reply with a good luck message for her forthcoming job interview and ask how the shoot went.

Brilliant location. The photographer was a dickhead though.

Who was the photographer? I ask.

Have you heard of Pier Frank? He's into all this weird arty shit. Jonathan thought it'd be fun to get him to experiment with an editorial shoot, but it was a bloody nightmare trying to reel him in. Hopefully we pulled it off.

For the first time I wonder how much I would enjoy working *with* photographers instead of *as* one. Is this what I really want to do? And let's not forget, Bronte slugged her way through three years as an editorial assistant before she got her break on the picture desk. She's only twenty-five. I'm twenty-six so if I work to her timelines I'll be lucky to score a job as *another* assistant before I'm thirty. Do I really want to go down that long and winding road when my heart isn't fully in it?

Richard would say I'm mad not to.

Ben would tell me to get onto those photography courses.

That night, I go back to Mum's and pull out all my old photos from ten years ago. I study the ones of Roy and Olivia and allow myself to dwell in the past for a while. I remember with a pang waking up on my second morning in Australia and begging Michael to take me to work with him. I never lost my enthusiasm for that job. I just couldn't go on once Ben had left. It was the same with photography. My feelings for him overrode my passion for anything else. Now he's back in my life I'm finding joy in the interests I abandoned years ago.

All the signs point towards a life with Ben. But before I see him again, I need to face Richard.

I go home after work the next day. I don't call ahead to warn him, but his truck is parked in front of the house and my heart is in my mouth as I walk up the front path to the house I adore, knowing I'm probably going to be leaving it forever. I unlock the door and step into the hallway to find the house in a state of disarray.

'Richard?' I call. I poke my head into the living room, but he's not in his normal place on the sofa, and then I see him outside on the deck, staring at the garden. I go to the door, trying not to notice my surroundings – the surroundings that I love and that I have made my own. 'Richard?' I say again more quietly so as not to startle him. I'm not successful because he jumps out of his skin and regards me with wide eyes.

'You're back!'

I smile sadly, but say nothing. It depends on his definition of 'back'. He gingerly gets to his feet, but I stay where I am inside the glass sliding door.

He looks a mess. He hasn't shaved in days and his face is pale and puffy.

'Lily?' He stands in front of me on the deck, his palms upright. I know he wants me to step outside into his arms, but I can't. I don't want to mislead him. His eyes fill with tears. 'You're leaving me.'

'Yes.'

His face creases with pain. 'No,' he moans.

'I'm sorry,' I whisper as he pushes past me and sinks onto the sofa. He buries his head in his hands, but suddenly looks up at me, his jaw working angrily as he demands, 'Have you seen him?'

'No.' I sit down on the armchair. 'I've done as you asked. I haven't called him or tried to see him. I've spent time away from both of you. I've never done so much thinking in my life.'

He stares ahead in a trance. 'What am I going to tell my parents?'

'I'm so sorry.' I hate that thought also. It's going to be horrible for him and they're going to be so disappointed in me.

'Is there nothing I can say or do to make you change your mind?'

I shake my head sorrowfully and wait a long time before he speaks again.

'I think you should go now.'

I nod. 'I'll pack some things.'

I get up quietly and leave him there on the sofa. In the bedroom I try not to think about everything I'm losing, but it's hard not to. My attention flicks to the picture of Richard and me on the bedside table as I miserably pack a small bag. I'll need to come back to clear out properly, but for now I just need a few more clothes to see me through this week. I plan to go back to Mum's tonight.

I want to call Ben, but I know it's a bad idea in the state I'm in. I don't think he should see me like this. I know I need time to recover before I go down that path. But that's my head talking. My heart thinks differently.

Richard appears in the hallway as I'm emerging from the bedroom.

'Don't go to him,' he begs urgently.

'Richard, I—'

'NO!' In a sudden, violent rage he punches the wall and I jump back in shock. 'PLEASE! I can't bear the thought of you with him!'

'Don't hurt yourself!' I cry, grabbing his hand. His knuckles are red and sore.

'Don't go. I don't want you to go,' he pleads, covering my hand with his. 'I love you.'

'I love you, too.'

'Then, *why?*'

'It's not enough. It would never have been enough. You never had *all* of me. You never *would* have had all of me. And you deserve to have the whole of someone.' I detach myself gently, but don't bother to brush away the tears that are running down my cheeks. 'I'm so sorry.'

'I can't believe you've chosen him over me.' His voice is dull.

'It wasn't a choice,' I tell my boyfriend of two years. My fiancé. The man I almost married. 'I've always been his.'

Chapter 29

It's a dark, windy night and I struggle with my bag all the way down the hill to the ferry terminal. The urge to ring Ben is overwhelming. At one point I pull out my mobile and curse loudly as I realise that yet again I've forgotten to pack my charger. I can't go back home for it now. What am I saying? It's not my home any more. I've never felt so miserable.

Yes, you have. You've felt a lot worse than this.

It's true. Of course it's true. This is nothing compared to the pain that crippled me when Ben left. Oh, God, I want to see him so much.

I make a right at the shorefront and am out of breath as I haul the bag over my other shoulder and fight against the wind. I pass the surf shop which closed hours ago, and peer at the ocean to see if I can spot any surfers in the enormous waves crashing against the shore. But it's dark now and they've all gone home for the night. I pass a restaurant lit warmly from the inside and spy a family of three eating a pizza. I halt in my tracks as I wonder if it's Sam and Molly with Mikey, but I realise it's not. A guy comes out of the shop with a takeaway pizza box and almost slams into me.

'Sorry!' he gasps. I look up to see Nathan. 'Lily!'

'Hi.'

His gaze falls on my bag before his bluey-grey eyes meet mine. 'Have you broken up with him?'

'Yes.' I can't bear the grave look on his face.

'How is he?'

'Not good,' I admit.

'I'll go and see him,' he decides. 'Where are you going now?'

'Back to Mum's.'

'Okay.' Sadness fills his features as he places his hand on my arm. 'Take care, alright?'

I nod hurriedly. 'When are you leaving, you and Lucy?'

'In a few weeks. We'll see him right before then.'

'Thank you,' I whisper and turn away.

I'll miss Nathan. I'll miss Sam, Molly and Mikey. And I'll miss Lucy. I'll miss them all. Am I doing the right thing? *Ben* . . . Thoughts and memories of him rush through my head, almost as though I'm watching a movie on fast-forward.

He's looking through my very first set of photos as we sit on the grass beside the lily pond.

He's gently taking the injured joey from me, pressing his warm arms against mine.

He's staring into my eyes across a table and I want to kiss him so much it hurts.

Enough. I want to be with him and I want to be with him now.

My heart lifts as I spot a public telephone box up ahead. Of course I know his number from memory. I committed it there along with everything else related to him.

He answers on the third ring.

'It's me,' I say.

'Lily!'

'Are you at home?'

'No, I'm on the yacht.'

'I'm coming to see you.'

'Do you need a lift?'

'No. There's a taxi right here.' I flag one down as it's passing.

'Do you remember where I'm moored?'

'Of course.'

It starts to pelt down with rain as I climb into the taxi. 'Jeez, you're a bit lucky,' the driver exclaims. 'Where are you going?'

I tell him and then settle back to stare out of the window.

The wind almost knocks me off my feet as I climb out of the taxi, dragging my bag with me. The rain soaks me through in an instant as I run towards Ben's yacht. There's a light on inside the cabin. I lean over and knock on one of the tiny windows and the cabin door bursts open, and then his arms are around my waist as he lifts me and my bag onto the boat. He hurries me down below and shuts the door against the storm.

'You're soaking!' he exclaims, his hands on my face and his fingers in my hair.

'So are you.' The rain is still running down his face and onto his T-shirt. His arms are wet.

'Are you okay? What's happened?' His eyes search mine for any clues and then he releases his grip on me and steps away to give me space. He glances down at my bag on the floor and suddenly we're staring at each other again and I know he understands.

I lift up my hand to touch his face. It's something I've always wanted to do, but have never been able to. The stubble under my fingers is rough. He stares back at me with blue, blue eyes as my thumb touches his lips. The rain pelts down hard from outside and the boat rocks to and fro in the harbour. I step forward and then I'm in his arms and tilting my head up and he's kissing me gently, as though he's afraid I might break or dissolve or disappear into dust.

Shivers travel all the way down my spine in waves, over and over again as his tongue touches mine and our kiss deepens. I slip my hands around his waist and try to get closer to him, never wanting to let him go. Not now, not ever, never ever again.

I lead him to the bed because it's still made up, and I drag his wet T-shirt up and over his head, feeling his hot, naked chest as I go. His eyes never leave mine as I unbutton my damp top and then he's kissing my jaw, kissing my neck and I'm pulling him on top of me, not wanting to wait any longer.

This is where I belong. This is where I want to be. We've lost ten years of our lives together and there is no way – *no way* – I'm going to lose any more.

Epilogue

'Will you marry me?'

I think of you, then. As I do sometimes. But not with sadness or regret. You're happy now and with someone who loves you with all her heart. You're no longer my Richard. You're Ally's. Lucy told me you two had found each other again, and every part of me believes you're meant to be together. I hope one day you'll see clear enough to forgive me.

Ben and I sailed back to Adelaide together. It took two weeks and the weather was touch and go, but I never got seasick. He took the job at the conservation park and I signed up to do a photography course in the city. Jonathan was sad I never went for the editorial assistant position at *Marbles*, but he's asked me to keep in touch. I hope one day to see my photographs in his magazine. I can but dream.

Two months ago, a junior position came up at the conservation park and the staff who were there ten years ago welcomed me back with open arms. It isn't well-paid, but I couldn't be happier, and I'm able to juggle my shifts around my course. It's lovely to work with Michael again; I was always fond of him. He got a bit of a shock when he found out about Ben and me, but it was nothing compared to the good-humoured stick I got from Josh. They've both accepted it now. How could they not when we're so happy together?

We live in Ben's nan's place and we've made it our own. I came home from work one day to find the picture that Ben took of me by the lily pond in a silver frame on the wall. He has an annoying little habit now of taking photos of me when I least expect it, and every so often I come home to find another picture on the wall. I protested at first, but he joked that it was his house and he'd do as he liked. I had the photo of him on the boat redeveloped and enlarged, and stuck that on the wall when he was out. Now I have to put up with his groans every time he walks past it. We've agreed to stick to joint photos from now on.

The garden needed some work when we first moved back here in the middle of winter and I've adored getting stuck in. I uncovered grape vines, an almond tree and an apricot tree. The latter made me smile because I remember Mum making apricot jam when we first came to Australia in her early attempts to impress Michael. I'll borrow her recipe when the fruit ripens. It won't be long now.

Tammy, Vickie and Jo are delighted to have me back on their turf, but I miss Mel and Nicola. Mel is still seeing Mr Horn, but Nicola is single. They're both coming out here to visit next month and I've promised to hook Nicola up with one of Josh's mates. I'm secretly thinking Shane might be a fun match. Josh is living with Tina now, but still no engagement. I'm sure their time will come.

Mum got married in a shotgun wedding to Antonio. I found out about it a week beforehand and had to fly back to Sydney at a moment's notice. I still find the whole thing slightly bizarre, but I've never seen her so content.

As for me, I feel complete for the first time in my life.

'Lily?' Ben asks again. 'Will you marry me?'

'Yes,' I reply as I look into his deep-blue eyes, our faces lit by the full moon as we stare down at Piccadilly Valley from Mount Lofty. And for the first time I can answer this question: 'With *all* my heart.'

Acknowledgements

Thank you, thank you, thank you to all my readers. Your overwhelmingly lovely Facebook messages and online reviews mean so much to me – please keep them coming!

Thank you to the whole team at Simon & Schuster for their limitless enthusiasm and professionalism, especially my amazing editor Suzanne Baboneau who I adore working with. And thank you always to the great Nigel Stoneman: I'm forever in your debt.

Huge gratitude to Donna Jensen from Cleland Conservation Park and Travis Messner from Monarto Conservation Park. I harassed them endlessly for information about Aussie wildlife and I don't know what I would have done without them. Although Lily's conservation park had to remain fictional, it was based on Cleland, which is one of my favourite places to visit in the Adelaide Hills.

A massive thank you to my brilliant second cousin Annika Beaty for all her help with the Hahndorf research. You're right, those sour peach hearts are addictive! Thanks also to her dad – my cousin – Grant Beaty for answering all my questions about yachts/fishing/Sydney etc, and thank you to Paddy Beaty and

Annie Lewis for allowing me to steal their father/husband away on New Year's Eve while I pestered him for help with the above, even as the clock counted down to zero.

Thank you also to my other cousin David Beaty and his sons Tom and Morgan for their help with the learner driver stuff.

A big cheers to Peter Brown – AKA The Unc – and Gwennie Philips for Lily's New Year's Eve inspiration. Your parties are legendary!

And thanks to my oldest friends, Bridie Tonkin, Naomi Dean and Jane Hampton. I love that we're still so close after all these years.

Thank you always to my mum, dad and brother, Jen, Vern and Kerrin Schuppan, for all their support and help with various things – especially Mum for driving me around the Adelaide Hills on memory lane trips. I had the best childhood growing up there and I still miss it.

Above all, thank you to my husband Greg and my children, Indy and Idha. Greg, because he's the most loving, talented, generous, honest person I know and he continues to make my books better with his seriously spot-on advice; and Indy and Idha, well, just because.

Simon & Schuster and Pocket Books proudly present

Paige Toon's sensational novel

Chasing Daisy ♡

Available to buy in bookshops now!

ISBN 978-1-84739-390-6

Turn the page to read a sample chapter of
Chasing Daisy . . .

Prologue

'YOU SON OF A . . . *Figlio di puttana!*' That jerk in a yellow Ferrari just cut me up! 'Yeah, that's right, you heard me, you *testa di cazzo!*' I shout at him as he pulls into the petrol station opposite me. His window slides down.

'What the hell are you saying to me, you crazy bitch?'

How dare he! He nearly squished my scooter and me to a pulp with his fancy car!

'You nearly ran into me, you *coglione!*'

He gets out of his car, looking cross. 'Cogli-*what?*'

'*Coglione!* Dickhead!' I shout at him from across the street.

'Why don't you speak in English?' he shouts back.

'Because we're in BRAZIL, *cretino!*'

'*I'm* Brazilian! And that's no language I know!' He throws his hands up in the air.

Well, okay, it's Italian, if he's going to be fussy about it. I always swear in Italian. But that's beside the point.

Oh no, he's coming over here.

'You almost ran over me, you arsehole!' I plaster my angry face back on.

'That's better,' he says sarcastically. 'At least I can understand what you're saying to me, now.'

It's then that I notice he's quite good-looking. Olive skin, black hair, dark-brown eyes . . . Don't get distracted, Daisy. Remember where you're at. And where I'm at is mightily annoyed.

'You almost killed me!'

'I didn't almost kill you,' he scoffs. 'Anyway, you didn't put your indicator on. How was I supposed to know you wanted to go over there?' He points to the petrol station.

'I did SO have it on! *Va fanculo!*'

'What?'

'*Va fanculo!*'

'Did you just tell me to fuck off?' He looks incredulous.

'Ah, so you *do* speak Italian?'

'Hardly any, but I know what that means. *Va se lixar!*'

'What?'

'Piss off!' he says, angrily, and starts to cross the road to get back to his car.

'Piss off? Is that the best you can do?'

He casts a look over his shoulder that implies he thinks I'm seriously deranged and then opens the door to his Ferrari.

'Hey! You!' I shout. 'I haven't finished!'

'I have,' he calls.

'Get back here and give me an apology!'

'An apology?' He laughs. 'You owe *me* an apology. You almost scratched my car.' He gets into his Ferrari and slams the door. 'Silly woman driver!' he shouts through the still-open window.

'How dare you! You, you, you, STRONSO!' Translation: bastard. 'I hope you run out of petrol and get car-jacked!' I scream after him, cleverly realising he didn't fill his Ferrari with juice. But he can't hear me. He's long gone.

Some people. Argh!

How dare he imply I can't drive! I'm still angry. Not angry enough to forgo my hotdog, mind. I pull out of the lay-by and cross the road to the petrol station, ignoring the stares from onlookers who witnessed our altercation.

Stupid five-star hotel . . . It doesn't *do* junk food, so I borrowed one of the team's scooters and sneaked out.

I shouldn't have to sneak out, but I work in hospitality and catering for a Formula 1 team, and we don't *do* junk food either. I'm supposed to be setting an example, but I'm American, for Christ's sake. How can I live without it?

Partly American, in any case. I was actually born in England. As for the rest of me, that's hot-blooded Italian. That's the side you just witnessed, there.

I arrive at the hotel fifteen minutes later and my friend and colleague Holly is waiting on the front steps. She hisses at me to hurry.

'Sorry!' I hiss back. 'Had to run an urgent errand!'

'Doesn't matter!' She beckons me towards her.

It's then that I catch a glimpse of yellow in the car park. Yellow Ferrari. Oh, no.

'Quick!' she urges, as my heart sinks.

I knew I recognised him from somewhere. He's a driver. A racing driver.

'The rumours must be true,' she says, gleefully pushing me into the lobby.

And at that moment, I see the Ferrari Fucker walking in the direction of the hotel bar with the team boss.

'Luis Castro is signing with the team!' Holly squeaks as I dive behind a potted palm tree.

Shit, damn, fuck, tits.

Not even Italian is going to cut it this time.

Chapter 1

'Don't you dare,' Holly warns, as I suppress an unbearable urge to crawl under the nearest table.

We're in Melbourne, Australia, for the start of the season, and Luis Castro has just walked into the hospitality area. I'm desperately hoping he will have forgotten all about me during the last five months, because until early November when we end up back in Brazil for his home-town race, we'll be seeing a LOT of each other.

There's no getting away from it – I'm going to have to face him sometime – but just not now. Please, not now.

'Daisy!' Frederick barks. 'I need you to run an errand.'

My boss! My saviour! Thank you, thank you, thank you!

'The look of relief on your face,' Holly comments with wry amusement as I scuttle away in the direction of the kitchen.

'Where are you going?' Frederick asks in bewilderment as I duck under the arm he was resting against the doorframe.

'Just in here!' I reply brightly, waving my hands around to denote the kitchen, which is excellently out of Luis's line of vision.

Frederick looks perplexed, but continues. 'Catalina wants some popcorn. And I don't have any goddamn popcorn. Go and get some from one of the stands.' He hands me some money.

'Yes, boss!' I beam.

He gives me an odd look as I hurry out of the kitchen and back through the hospitality area with my head down.

Catalina is Simon's wife. Simon Andrews is the big boss and he owns the team. But Frederick – Frederick Vogel – is my immediate boss. He's the head chef.

Frederick is German, by the way. And Catalina is Spanish. Simon is English and Holly, while we're at it, is Scottish. What a multi-national bunch we are.

The Australian Grand Prix takes place in Albert Park, and yesterday I spotted a popcorn stand being set up on the other side of the shimmering green lake. I grab one of the team scooters and start it up.

It's Friday, two days before race day, but the track is still packed with spectators, here to watch the practice sessions. I drive carefully, breathing in the fresh, sunny air. It's the end of March, and unlike Europe and America which are swinging into spring, Australia is well into autumn. We've been told to expect rain this weekend, but right now there's barely a cloud in the sky. Melbourne's city skyscrapers soar up in the distance ahead of me, and behind me, I picture the ocean sparkling cool and blue.

I can smell the popcorn stand before I see it, salt and butter wafting towards me on a light breeze. Mmm, junk food . . . I wonder if I could also squeeze some for myself in the scooter's storage box? I consider it while the guy behind the counter scoops the fluffy, white kernels into a bag, but eventually decide it's a no-go.

I pay for the popcorn and stuff Frederick's change into my pocket, then unlock the box under my seat. Hmm, this popcorn is going to spill out – the bag's full to the brim and I need to be able to fold the top over. I suppose I could ask for another bag to wrap over the top . . . Or . . . I could eat some! Yes, that's the only logical conclusion.

I lean up against the scooter and delve in. The guy at the popcorn stand is watching me with amusement. What the hell are you staring at, buster? My glare wards off his gaze, but he's still grinning. I stuff another handful into my mouth. It's so warm and so . . . perfectly popped. I've probably eaten enough, now. Maybe just a little more . . . Right, that's it. Stop, now. Now! Regretfully I close the bag and store it under my seat, then start up the scooter.

If there are this many people here now, it's going to be packed on race day, I think to myself as I swerve around a group of slow-walking pedestrians. All of a sudden I spot two men wearing our team's overalls up ahead, and just as I go to turn a corner in front of a set of grandstands, I realise they're racing drivers, one of whom is Luis.

My back wheel catches some grit and slides out from under me as I take the corner. Suddenly the whole scooter is skidding and I can hear the grandstand half-full of spectators gasp in unison as I shoot across the gravel in front of them.

'Whoa!' Will Trust – the team's other driver – jumps out of the way, but Luis stays put, frozen in a crouch as though expecting to catch me.

'JESUS CHRIST!' I hear an Australian woman cry as my bike comes to a stop right in front of him. 'She almost ran over Luis Castro!'

She pronounces the name, 'Lewis', not 'Lew-eesh', as she's supposed to. I may not like the jackass, but it still bugs me when people can't say his name properly.

'That'll make a nice change from him running over me, then,' I snap, getting to my feet.

I immediately realise my mistake. That woman's mispronunciation error distracted me and I've idiotically just reminded him about our altercation. Maybe he wasn't paying attention. I quickly brush myself off as I feel his eyes boring into me.

'You,' Luis says.

Darn.

'You. The girl on the scooter.'

'Er, not anymore,' I say sarcastically, indicating the fallen vehicle. I bend down to try to stand it up.

'Hang on, let me get it.' Will Trust appears by my side and lifts up the scooter. 'Are you alright?' he asks, clear blue eyes looking searchingly into mine.

I almost jump backwards. 'Yes, yes, I'm fine,' I reply, blushing furiously. Actually, I'm not fine. My right hand is stinging like crazy from where I put it down on the gravel, and my knee feels horribly tender beneath the black pants of my black, white and gold team uniform.

'Let me see that.' Will takes my hand in his, pressing down on my fingers with his thumb to straighten my palm. He leans in and studies the graze and I feel jittery as I, in turn, study him. His light blond hair is falling just across his eye-line. I have a strong compulsion to reach over and push it off his face . . .

'It *is* you,' Luis says again.

Is he still here? Bummer.

I look around to see that quite a crowd has gathered to watch me and revel in my embarrassment. At least they're more interested in the drivers than me. Speaking of which . . .

'The girl in Brazil. The petrol station,' Luis continues.

Will lets me go and looks at us, questioningly. 'You know each other?'

I flex my hand. The feel of him is still there.

'Yeah, she almost crashed into my Ferrari in São Paulo last year,' Luis says.

'*I* almost crashed into YOUR Ferrari?' I come back to my senses, outraged. 'You nearly killed me!'

'Ha!' He laughs in my face. 'You're ridiculous. *And* you can't drive. I said you were a silly woman driver at the time and now you've just proved me right.'

'You, you, you . . .' I glare at him, lost for words.

'You're not going to call me a *coglione* again, are you?'

'No, but you are a *testa di cazzo*,' I mutter under my breath. It means the same thing. Literally, 'head of dick'. I smirk.

'What did you say?' Luis demands. 'What did she say?' he asks Will.

Will shrugs in amusement and bends down to dust off the scooter. I suddenly remember what I've done.

'I haven't scratched it, have I?' I bend down beside him and scrutinise the bike.

'It's not too bad,' Will says.

'I hope Simon doesn't fire me . . .'

'Simon won't notice. He's got too much else on his mind.'

'Simon notices everything,' Luis helpfully interjects.

Will rolls his eyes at me and my heart flutters, despite my fear of being axed.

'Will, are you coming or what?' Luis butts in.

'Sure, yeah. Will you be okay, er . . .' He looks at the name embroidered in gold on the front of my white team shirt.

'Daisy,' I say before he does. 'Yes, don't worry about me, I'll be fine.'

'I've seen you around. You're a front-of-house girl, right?' he checks. 'You help out with the catering?'

'Jesus, that's all we need,' Luis grumbles.

Will and I look at him in confusion.

'She'll probably give me food poisoning,' he points out.

'Don't flatter yourself,' I can't help but say. 'I wouldn't go to the trouble of trying.'

I spot a so-tanned-he's-orange marshal running over to us. 'Are you okay, miss?' he asks in an Australian accent.

'We'll leave you to it,' Will says, winking at me. I feel my face heat up again so I quickly turn my attention to the marshal.

Orange Man eventually deems I'm not a danger to myself or others and lets me go on my way, so I carefully drive back to our hospitality area, resisting the urge to speed. I've been gone ages.

I park up and locate the, well, it's not really a bag *full* of popcorn anymore, and go inside to look for Catalina. I scan my eyes around the room. There are a fair few people here today, considering it's only Friday. The tables are peppered with guests: sponsors, wives or girlfriends and the occasional friend or family member of someone in the team. Bigger teams than ours often invite the odd celebrity, too, but Simon doesn't seem to know anyone famous.

Aah, there she is.

Catalina is sitting at a table next to a skinny, tanned brunette, with medium-length, wavy hair. They look alike and, as I approach, I realise they're speaking Spanish. I wonder if they're sisters. Holly will know. Holly knows everything.

'Hi, Catalina, Frederick said you wanted this?' I offer it to her.

'What is it?' Her tone is as horrible as the look she gives me. 'Oh, popcorn,' she says, spying the crumpled packaging. 'Where's the rest of it?' she demands to know.

'Um, I couldn't fit it in my—'

'Have you been *eating* it?'

'I couldn't fit it—'

'Put it there,' she huffily interrupts, pointing to the tabletop in front of her.

The catering here is excellent, so why she's demanding popcorn in the first place is beyond me. Actually, I take that back. Nothing beats popcorn. But unlike her, if the rumours are to be believed, I won't be throwing it up in the toilets later.

I finally return to the kitchen.

'Where the hell have you been?' Frederick shouts.

'I had a bit of an accident,' I explain.

'You smell like you've been eating . . .' He leans towards me and gives a single loud sniff through his extremely large nostrils. 'Popcorn!'

He looks like a cartoon gangster, Frederick. Big nose, greasy black hair. And he's very tall and extremely lanky. I glance back at him to see him eyeing me suspiciously.

'Um, do I?' I ask innocently. He has an annoyingly good sense of smell. I guess it's useful if you're a chef, but in situations like these . . .

'What sort of accident?' he snaps.

I anxiously lead him outside to the scooter.

'It could be worse,' he grumpily concludes after he's inspected the damage.

'What happened?' Holly appears around the corner, full of

concern when she sees us kneeling on the floor studying the scratches.

I fill her in, her eyes widening when I tell her who my audience was.

'Right, enough,' Frederick interrupts. 'Back to work. There are three bags of potatoes for you to peel, Daisy.'

I notice that Holly gets to decorate a cake. I always get the shittiest jobs.

'Hey,' Holly says later, when Frederick pops out of the kitchen. I've been watching her distractedly for the last ten minutes as she's cut a sponge cake into large cubes and plastered them with chocolate icing. 'A few of the lads have been talking about going out tonight. Fancy it?'

'Sure, where?'

'St Kilda,' she says, dipping one of the chocolate-covered cubes into desiccated coconut.

'What the hell are you doing?' Curiosity gets the better of me.

'What?'

'With that cake.' I nod at the furry-looking cube.

'Lamingtons,' she explains. 'They're Aussie cakes.'

We always try to cater according to the country we're in and it sometimes makes for an 'interesting' menu.

'Anyway, back to tonight . . .' She leans against the counter and wipes the coconut off her hands.

'Where's St Kilda?' I ask.

'It's a really cool suburb on the other side of the park.'

'Will we be able to get away in time?'

'Yeah, should be fine. We did the early shift and half the team is going to that sponsorship event anyway so we don't really need to be around after eight thirty. I'm gagging for a drink.' She puts her hands up to her head and tightens her high, bleached-blonde ponytail.

'I need a drink, too. Especially after earlier . . .'

'I still need to hear all about that,' she says. 'Not now, though,' she adds, as Frederick walks back in, so we both put our heads down and crack on.

'You called him a dickhead again? In front of Will?' Holly claps her hand over her mouth in wide-eyed shock, then starts laughing through her fingers.

The air is hot and humid and we're seated outside a pub in St Kilda. We walked here straight from the track, along Fitzroy Street's dozens of cafés, restaurants and bars, all spilling out onto the pavement with rowdy revellers.

'He deserved it,' I say flippantly.

'Who deserved what?' Pete, one of the mechanics, plonks himself down on a recently vacated chair next to us. A few of the 'lads', as Holly likes to call them, have joined us for a drink. It's ten o'clock at night and they've only just come from the track, although they swear they're heading back to the hotel by midnight. Last time they said this, we were in Shanghai towards the end of the season, and they were out on the town until three a.m. When Simon got wind of it, he was not happy.

'She crashed one of the team scooters in front of Will and Luis earlier,' Holly tells him.

'Holly!' I erupt. She's had a few too many beers.

'They're going to find out sooner or later,' she says to me, giggling at Pete.

'Oh, I've already heard about that,' he says dismissively.

'You've heard about it?' I ask, humiliated.

'Yeah, yeah, Luis was going on about it earlier. Said you could have broken his legs.'

'Broken his legs?' I explode, humiliation swiftly transforming into irritation. '*Figlio di puttana!*'

'Son of a bitch,' Holly casually explains to Pete. She knows as many Italian swear words as I do. One of the undeniable bonuses of working with me.

'Actually, it literally translates to "son of a whore",' I point out pedantically, before continuing with my rant. 'I can't believe that!'

Pete just laughs and raises his eyebrows, taking a swig from his beer bottle.

'Don't worry about it,' Holly soothes. 'No one will remember it by tomorrow.'

'*Eeeeeeeeeeeeee* . . . BOOM!' Another mechanic makes a loud crashing sound as he pulls up a chair and joins us at the table. 'Way to go, Daisy!' he laughs.

'Thanks, Dan. Appreciate your support,' I answer, glumly.

Dan is quite short compared to Pete, who's enormous at six foot four, but both are broad and muscular, unlike Luis and Will who are about six foot and slim-built. You have to be to fit in those Formula 1 cars.

Two more mechanics zoom past the table, pretending to screech to a stop.

'Haven't you guys got anything better to do?' I call after them.

I lean back in my seat and watch as a group of gorgeous girls in their late teens strut by. I feel old, and I'm only twenty-six. I know I look older. People tell me it's the way I carry myself. I think it's because of the size of my heels. I'm five foot nine, but I never go out in less than three inches. Well, that was back in America. I've started wearing flats since I got this job. I'm on my feet all the time and I'm not really a massive fan of torture. Plus, Holly is tiny at five foot one and I look enough like a giant next to her as it is.

'Wicked!' Dan interrupts my thoughts. He's looking down at his mobile phone. 'Luis is coming by for a drink. He's just left that event.'

Oh, for God's sake. I was enjoying myself. Now we'll have to find another venue to drink at and everywhere is so busy around here.

'Staying true to form, then,' Holly comments.

What she means by that is, Luis has a reputation for being a hard-partying ladies' man. This is his first year in Formula 1. Prior to that he raced in the American IRL – Indy Racing League – series and won the infamous Indy 500 three times in a row, which is why I vaguely recognised him – not that I've ever been that interested in racing before. Anyway, everyone speculated that he would have to calm down his wild ways and slot into the fold once he started working for Serious Simon, but he's clearly sticking his fingers up at that idea.

'I thought you guys were having an early night?' I say.

'He's a driver.' Dan shrugs. 'I can't blow him out. Another round?'

'Er . . .' I'm about to make our excuses about moving on, but Holly's response is too quick.

'Sure!' She lifts up her glass of beer dregs. 'Same again!'

'What did you go and do that for?' I complain as soon as Dan and Pete have left the table. 'I don't want to stay here if he's coming.'

'Aw, come on, Daisy, we're having fun. Maybe it'll do you good to get to know Luis socially.'

'I don't want to get to know him socially. He's a dick. I want to go somewhere else.'

'Just one drink? I wonder if Will might join him,' she muses.

A strange shiver goes through me at the sound of Will's name.

'I doubt it,' I answer, albeit slightly hesitantly. 'Isn't he a bit too committed to go out drinking the night before qualifying?'

'Maybe. But perhaps he'll take some time off for a change. Have a few beers with the lads, you know, good for team morale . . .'

A tiny glimmer of hope starts to flicker inside me. Dan returns with our drinks and then goes off to chat to Pete and the other mechanics standing on the pavement.

Unusually for a racing team, our previous drivers both retired at the end of last year, so we started this season with two newbies. Will, unlike Luis, has been in Formula 1 for a couple of years. The British have gone bananas over him, because he's young, good-looking *and* talented, so it was a quite a coup for Simon to scoop him up. I've seen him around the track a bit in the past, but have never been in close proximity to him. Until yesterday.

'Do you ever see him at team headquarters?' I turn back to Holly.

'Who?' she asks.

'Will.'

'Oh. Yeah, occasionally, yes. He's been in to use the simulator a few times.'

'Simulator?'

'It's like a car-sized PlayStation racing game. They use it to learn the different track layouts. It's wicked, actually. Pete let me have a go on it a few weeks ago.'

'Aah, right.'

'Why are you asking about Will?' She remembers my initial question.

'Um, no reason . . .'

'You fancy him, don't you?' She slams her hand down on the table.

'No!' I deny.

'You bloody do! You've gone all red!'

'I have not!'

'You have! I thought you were sworn off men?'

'I am,' I respond.

'Are you ever going to tell me why?'

I shake my head and take a sip of my drink.

'Why not?' she asks for about the zillionth time. At least, that's what it feels like to me.

'I can't,' I reply.

'Why? Are you worried your ex will hunt you down and kick your arse?'

I don't answer.

She looks stricken. 'That's not it, is it? Oh God, Daisy, I'm so sorry if it is. I would never make fun of—'

'I'm not a victim of domestic violence,' I wearily interject. 'I just don't want to discuss it.'

'Huh. Fine.' She looks put out, then she adds, 'Well, Will's got a girlfriend anyway, so he's off-limits.'

'Does he?' I try to keep my voice light, but the disappointment is immense.

'Of course he does. How can you not know that? They're always in the tabloids together.'

'I don't read the papers.'

'Still, how can you have missed them?'

'Why? What's their story?'

'Childhood sweethearts.'

My heart sinks.

Holly carries on, oblivious to my pain. 'They grew up in the same village together. The press back home love it how Will has stayed with her through thick and thin and has never been tempted by all the bimbos on the racing scene.'

This is getting worse.

'She works for a children's charity.'

'Are you making this up?' I look at Holly, incredulous.

She laughs. 'No, it's true. Sorry.'

'Well, like you say, I'm sworn off men.'

And yes, I am. I had my heart broken in America and felt like I had to leave the goddamn country because I couldn't go anywhere without bumping into the bastard.

Repeat: I am okay on my own. I am okay on my own. I am okay on my own.

And I am sure as hell not going to chase after someone who has a girlfriend. That's not my style.

I notice Holly wiping some of the lipgloss off her beer glass and smudging it back onto her lips.

'That is such a good look,' I say.

'You are really quite sarcastic for an American, aren't you?' she answers wryly, as Pete plonks himself back down at the table.

'I was born in England,' I remind her.

My mother is Italian and my father is British, but when I was six, he moved the whole family to America. I'd been there for almost twenty years when I relocated to the UK and secured a job working as a waitress for Frederick and his wife Ingrid's catering company in London. Then last October, Frederick asked me if I'd like to come along to the final three races as a front-of-house girl. That title means working in hospitality and making sure the team and its guests are looked after, but I also help out in the kitchen whenever it's required. Opportunities like this – to see the world and get paid for it – don't come along very often, so naturally I jumped at the chance.

Holly and I hit it off immediately. When we're not racing, she works in the canteen at the team's headquarters in Berkshire, England. I say canteen, but it's actually more like a Michelin-starred restaurant. We met for the first time in Japan last year where we got through several jugs of sake in the hotel bar one night. The jugs are only tiny, but boy is rice wine strong. We were shit-faced by ten p.m, and you don't even want to know what we consumed a week later in China.

After Brazil, Frederick asked me to stay on for another year to do a full season. I don't know what came over him, but yay!

Holly has been rummaging around in her bag for ages and now she finally emerges with a tube of pink lipgloss. She reapplies some, giving me an overtly smug look.

I could do with some of that, actually. Just in case Will does deign to join us. What am I thinking? No, no, NO!

Damn it. 'Can I have some?' I have very little willpower. I slick some over my lips, then tuck my long, dark hair behind my ears and wait.

A few minutes later, a taxi pulls up outside the pub and the high-heel-clad feet of a woman gracefully step out of it onto the pavement.

I recognise her. It's the woman Catalina was talking to in the grandstand . . . Her sister?

Then Luis climbs out of the car behind her. I crane my neck, but there's no Will. I feel momentarily crushed, but firmly tell myself it's for the best.

'Oi, oi, oi!' I hear a few of the lads behind us shout. Luis grins at them.

'Who's that he's with?' I ask Holly.

'Alberta. Catalina's cousin,' Holly answers.

Sister . . . Cousin . . . Close enough.

'Getting in with the boss's family, is he?' My tone is wry as I watch Luis put his hand on the woman's lower back to steer her through the crowd.

'Clearly,' Holly replies.

He reaches our gathering and is enthusiastically welcomed by the mechanics, most of whom are standing on the pavement behind our table. Holly and I remain seated, while Pete stands up and leans across us to clap Luis on the back. Holly smiles and lifts her hand in a half-wave of hello, but I can't bear to look at him so I busy myself pretending to pick a fly out of my wine glass.

'*Hello!*' I hear him pointedly say in my direction.

'Oh, hello!' I reply, as though becoming aware of his presence for the first time.

'Written off any scooters lately?'

The boys around him crack up laughing and a couple of them make loud crashing noises.

'Ha ha,' I reply sarcastically and turn back to the imaginary insect in my glass.

One of the lads lifts a chair over the heads of the people drinking at the table next to us and plonks it down beside me, waving his hand with a flourish to Alberta. Pete immediately offers his chair to Luis.

'No, it's okay,' Luis says. 'I'm happy to stand.'

'It's alright, I'm going back to the bar,' Pete says. 'What are you having?'

Luis produces a wad of notes. 'My round,' he says.

'That's too much, mate!' Pete waves Luis's money away.

'No, no, take it!' Luis insists. 'Put it in the, what do you call it? Kitty?'

Pete eyes it sceptically.

'Take it!' Luis forces it into his hand.

'Do you want a bottle of champers?' Pete asks Luis.

'No, no, a beer for me.'

'Saving the champagne for race day . . .' Alberta comments in a husky voice.

Luis just laughs. 'Will you have some?' he asks her.

'I wouldn't mind,' she replies, sexily.

'Go on then, Pete, get a bottle. Do you need some more?' He reaches for his wallet.

'No, mate, no!' Pete practically shouts, holding up the wad in his hand. 'I've got enough here to buy a house! Girls? Same again?'

'I'm fine, thank y ——'

'We'll help out with the champers!' Holly shouts. 'Daisy, stop being such a lame-arse,' she whispers to me when Pete has departed.

'So Frederick let you come out to play?' Luis looks straight at me.

I nod. 'Uh-huh.'

I feel Alberta's chocolate-brown eyes fall on me and am taken aback by how cool her gaze is, considering her eye colour is so warm. It's the same with her sister. Cousin, I mean. Whatever. The silly Bs are related, that's all I need to know.

'I heard he's a ball-breaker . . .' Luis continues.

I don't answer.

'I'm Holly!' Holly puts a stop to the awkwardness and offers her hand to Alberta, followed by Luis.

'Do you work with this one?' Luis asks Holly, nodding my way.

'As a front-of-house girl, yes.' She smiles warmly, cutting short whatever sarcastic comment I'm certain Luis was about to make. 'How was the sponsorship event?' she asks, her tone bubbling over with friendliness. I don't know how she does it.

'Boring,' Luis answers.

'Oh, thank you very much.' Alberta pretends to be upset.

'With the exception of the present company, of course.'

I'm about to put my fingers down my throat and make gagging noises when I notice her hand on his leg and am rendered speechless.

Pete returns with a tray full of drinks for the lads, plus glasses, champagne and an ice bucket. Holly and I help him unload it before he heads back to the bar to return the tray.

I hear a cork pop as Luis deftly pours champagne into three glasses, handing one to each of us girls.

'No, thank you,' I say, fingering the stem of my wine glass. I still have a few sips of Shiraz in there somewhere.

'Don't waste it,' Luis states.

'I'll drink yours, Daisy,' Holly offers, so I push it across the table to her.

'There's plenty to go around.' Luis pushes the glass back in my direction and turns to Alberta.

I give him a look of such distaste that he must surely feel my eyes branding the back of his skull, then I inadvertently glance down and am greeted with the sight of Alberta sliding her hand in the direction of Luis's crotch. Dirty cow! I look at Holly in shock. A split second later I hear the sound of a chair scraping on the pavement and turn back to see Luis standing up.

'Where are you going?' Alberta asks, her brow furrowed with annoyance.

'The men's room,' Luis tells her.

'I wouldn't mind going, too,' she says silkily, making me feel as invisible as that fly in my drink.

'I need a *piss*,' Luis says firmly, putting to a halt whatever naughty things Alberta had planned for their cubicle excursion. She slumps back in her seat and watches his departing backside.

'Have you been to a Grand Prix before?' Holly tactfully changes the subject.

'Of course,' Alberta answers dismissively.

'Do you enjoy the racing?'

'That's not what I'm here for.'

'Oh. What are you here for?'

'The fun! The glamour!' She casts her arms around her in an extravagant manner.

Glamour? I decide against pointing out the wasted youth who has just vomited on the kerb.

She takes a huge mouthful of champagne and reaches for the bottle.

'Let me do that for you,' Holly offers, making use of her hospitality skills. Alberta takes the refilled glass without so much as a thank you and sits back in her seat, crossing her legs so her mini skirt rides even further up her thighs.

I look away, bored and unable to play the game like my friend, and see Luis emerge from the pub doors. Alberta sits back up in her seat, but is visibly deflated when Luis stops to chat to the lads.

I know how she feels. I'd give anything to be able to gossip freely with Holly instead of watching my words in front of this beacon of bitchiness.

'Have you been Catalina's cousin for long?' Holly asks, in all innocence.

I look at her and crack up with laughter. She realises what she's said and joins me in hysterics.

'I've had too much to drink!' she squeals, lifting up her champagne glass in one hand and her beer glass in the other.

Alberta glares at us both before standing up, plucking the champagne bottle out of the ice bucket and going to join Luis.

'Come on, Holly, please can we go somewhere else, now?'

'Yeah, okay,' she agrees, knocking back first her beer, followed by her champagne and then rising to her feet.

We wind our way out towards the pavement, squeezing past the revellers already swarming to occupy our recently vacated chairs.

'We're off! See ya, lads!' Holly calls to the group of mechanics.

'Lightweights!' Pete shouts.

'We're not going back to the hotel, we're going partying, you pussy!' Holly shouts, and I pull on her arm, laughingly trying to ignore Luis's dark-eyed stare as we back away from the crowd.